WATCHING

ALSO BY TINA DAY

The Watching Trilogy
Watching
Wanting
Willing

WATCHING

THE WATCHING TRILOGY- BOOK 1

TINA DAY

Day and Knight
Romance
Publications

For my husband

CHAPTER

ONE

Charlottesville, Virginia. September, 2011...

A séance. An actual séance.

Abby couldn't believe her life had come to this. She forced herself to stare into Madam Rosemurtha's dark eyes. "Um...how much?"

"Hmm." Rosemurtha's candy-apple-red lips pursed. "Séance very hard. Difficult emotion, must leave body. Normally charge more, but for pretty young girl like you, I give half price. Thirty-nine ninety-five. Cash."

Abby glanced at the purple beaded curtain glittering behind the psychic's head. With a steep inhale, she dug inside her backpack and pulled out two twenties. She tucked the money into the woman's outstretched hand.

Madam Rosemurtha smiled as she shoved the bills into the orange sequined bodice of her billowy dress. "I keep change. You follow." She turned, sweeping through the curtain, the beads jingling in waves behind her.

Abby's eyes darted to the store's windowfront, brightened by artificial light against the backdrop of the night sky. The antique gold words *Psychic Readings and Palmistry* stared backwards at her. The hand-painted crystal ball beneath them did nothing to settle her stomach. Her head hung as she followed Rosemurtha through the beaded curtain into the back room.

Rosemurtha's inner parlor was exactly as Abby feared. The pungent odor of musk incense induced a coughing fit, making her swipe tears from her eyes while she struggled to absorb her surroundings. Everything was purple and gold and silver, all available surfaces draped in silks dyed with nebulous patterns, the floor littered with pillows large enough to sleep grizzly bears. She collapsed down on one as the woman said, "You sit." Abby coughed again, wondering if it was possible to develop spontaneous asthma.

Madam Rosemurtha bustled around in the far corner of the large room, pulling unseen items from dusty shelves. Abby tucked her backpack tighter against her body as she glanced at the woven tapestries covering the paneled walls. Several doors on the walls sat ajar, leading who-knows-where. "Is that how the spirits make their entrance?" she mumbled.

"You say something, child?"

"It's nothing," Abby answered, cringing as the woman approached. She knew the aged soothsayer saw her as a child, even though she was seventeen and nearly an adult. Her pale skin and straight blond hair always made her look more like a porcelain doll than a grown woman.

Rosemurtha reached to a dimmer switch on the wall, easing the lighting down several notches. She struck a match between her fingers, enflaming an enormous four-wick candle, holding it deftly under her chin to cast the planes of her hollow face in eerie shadows. The only sound in the room was the creaking of old kneecaps as Rosemurtha settled down on the facing floor pillow. She fit the candle between them before reaching out her hands. "We make circle now – our bodies."

Abby stared at the woman's weathered face while she placed their palms together. Rosemurtha pinched her eyelids shut. She held fast to Abby's fingers and began humming. "Madam Rosemurtha sees you have lost someone dear to you."

"Yes," Abby admitted, gluing her eyes to the wall, trying to decide if she could go through with this.

"Who is it we contact, child?"

She watched the candlelight glinting off the curtain beads and pillow sequins. She felt the psychic's thin skin against her fingers, skin much more worn than her mother's would ever get the chance to be. "I – I would like to talk to my mother. Her name was Crystal."

"Your mother. Of course. I call her now." Rosemurtha grinned in an all-knowing way, skewing the candlelit contours of her face. "Come to this place," her hoarse voice sang. "Crystal, come to us now..."

Abby's gut clenched. Bile crept into her throat. She stared at a tapestry of a unicorn and tried not to think.

Time passed while the medium's swelling chorus buzzed in her ears. Abby struggled to contain the pain in her heart – the deep, unrelenting grief she'd known since the day her mother died. She fought back tears as she watched the moaning-and-groaning spectacle in front of her.

Just when Abby decided to slam her eyelids shut, the candle flame flickered between them. She focused on that shifting light while a cold rush of air swept through the room, pricking up the hairs on the back of her neck. As the flame danced violently before her eyes, she caught sight of something moving in the far corner of the room. Holding tight to Rosemurtha's hands, Abby squinted to see better in the darkness.

A young man now stood against the back wall of the parlor, looming and silent in the shadows. He was her age, perhaps a little older. His thick body was rigid, his face a stone carving. Another chill of arctic air sent goosebumps flitting across her arms.

Where did he come from? she wondered. *He must have snuck in through one of the secret doors. But why is he here?*

Abby stared across the room, eager to read his intentions. His face was blank except for his eyes. They were a bright, clear blue – as clear as the sky on a cloudless summer day. His eyes were so clear that they captured the candle flame entirely in the dim room, giving them the odd appearance of glowing. She zeroed in on that brilliant blue, now only faintly aware of the increasing cadence of the psychic's chanting.

The shadowed guy stared back at her, remaining statue-still despite the striking display of soothsaying occurring between them. Eventually, he straightened from the wall and parted his lips. Abby leaned forward, straining to hear whatever he might have to say. But instead of speaking, he scrunched his brow, looking as perplexed as a puppy confronted by a new toy.

Madam Rosemurtha's arms trembled, pulling Abby's attentions to the woman's face. The medium snorted while her shoulders quaked up and down. Abby shook her head before turning back to the other person in the room.

She watched in wonder when he started walking, stalking the outer perimeter of the inner sanctum, his footsteps entirely silent. Her curiosity demanded that she follow his every move. She didn't look away and neither did he, not even when he started to pace. They ogled each other while he shuffled back and forth behind the old woman's back. Abby got the feeling that he was giving her some sort of eye exam – can you follow the moving object around the room?

It's really not that dark in here, she considered. *And this store is supposed to be for palmistry, not optometry.*

Her thoughts made her smile. Her smile made him stop. His baffled expression grew as he froze in place and gawked at her.

Rosemurtha's crescendo swelled. "Aye, aye, *aye*...the spirits, they *come*...."

Abby's brow rose while the psychic's head flopped back and forth on her spindly shoulders. Rosemurtha's ruby lips twitched out odd, guttural sounds. Abby winced with the bizarre display, finally forced to acknowledge just how silly all of this was.

"The Crystal-mother, may you come, oh shiny one," Rosemurtha sang.

That verse was the last straw. Abby cracked. She laughed – hard.

The baffled man watched her while giggles bubbled up from her throat.

"Are you supposed to be a spirit?" Abby asked him.

The V in his brow deepened.

Rosemurtha's eyes shot open. "What is that, child?"

Abby shrugged. "I really don't mean to question all this, but he doesn't look anything like my mother."

He finally smiled. Brief, but beautiful.

"Who?" the psychic questioned.

Abby worked her hand free of the woman's grasp in order to point. "Him," she said, gesturing to Mr. Mysterious just before he retreated through one of the paneled doors. She craned her neck to see where he'd gone, still searching even after he'd disappeared entirely from her view. "Oh. Do you think I upset him? I didn't mean to."

Rosemurtha's head whipped around to look behind her. "Upset who?"

"The guy who just went through that door."

"What guy?" Rosemurtha demanded, her tone much less mystical than it had been a moment ago. The woman jumped up from her cushion, rather spryly for an ancient oracle. She peered into several of the paneled doors before scurrying out to the parlor's front room, only to return a few minutes later. "There is no one else here, child," she announced. "The circle, it is broken. No spirits will come to us now."

Abby dropped her shoulders, painfully certain she would get no answers tonight. "Okay. Thank you anyway," she offered, sighing as she stood. "I really do appreciate you trying."

The psychic nodded before Abby strode across the floor and out of the room. She passed through the glittering curtain, wincing when a strand of her thin blond hair snagged on a cluster of beads. Wrenching herself free, she lunged for the front door.

The handle was already inside Abby's grasp when she felt the unnatural chill again – the frosty sweep of air that had come from nowhere during Rosemurtha's show. Maybe this place had air conditioning problems. Or maybe it was something else entirely.

Abby chewed on her lower lip as she turned back toward the room.

There he stood: Mr. Mysterious. He watched her from only a few feet away, his body a stiff column against the shimmering beaded backdrop. Adrenaline shot through her veins, dampening her palms. *Wasn't Rosemurtha just out here? Didn't she say the parlor was empty?*

More goosebumps flitted across Abby's skin. She attempted to steady her breaths, assuring herself that he must work here. Yet her heart continued to flip-flop while he studied her, especially since his eyes still glowed, reflecting candlelight that no longer existed.

But that's not possible. Eyes don't glow. His are just very clear, that's all. And you're weird about eyes, anyway.

Abby forced a smile onto her lips. "Hi," she said.

Confusion again – Mr. Mysterious seemed to be in a constant state of bewilderment. She wasn't sure if he would respond to her. Maybe he was mad that she got him in trouble with his boss. Maybe he didn't speak English.

"Um, hello," he replied. His voice was deeper than she expected.

She shifted from one leg to the other. "You work here?"

He shook his head. "I...kind of."

Now, it was Abby's turn to be confused. Maybe he spoke English, but not very well. She fidgeted with her backpack, unable to stop staring. She could see him much better here in the front parlor, without the technical effects of dimmed lighting and candles. Only one word could really describe him: magnificent.

His dark blond hair was trimmed "high and tight" as her ex-military father would say. He had a ruggedly handsome dude-in-a-Western-movie face, with a jawline so sharply angled that he could probably crack a walnut on his neck. And his body was so thick that she could pick out every muscle, even beneath his unusual fashion choices: a plain white T-shirt, brown cargo pants, and black combat boots.

Abby wondered why someone who obviously worked out all day while drinking nothing but protein shakes wasn't strutting around in muscle shirts and shorts, slathered in baby oil and striking body-building poses at random intervals. However, his clothing did trigger her memory. "Hey, I've seen you before," she realized.

If she thought he looked confused earlier, it was nothing compared to now. "You...you've *seen* me?"

She wasn't sure why he sounded so skeptical. People must notice him constantly. Especially female people. "Yeah, in the hallway at school." She'd caught a glimpse of his outfit a few days earlier. But she couldn't have seen his face, because she would have remembered. Especially the eyes. "You go to my school, right? Jefferson High?"

Mr. Magnificent nodded. "Yes."

"Did you just move here to Charlottesville?"

"Yes."

"Hmm." *He's not a big talker.* "Well, I guess I should go…"

"Tell me, please," he entreated, his confusion lifting for the first time. "Why did you come to this psychic parlor tonight?"

It was a perfectly logical question, yet Abby wasn't sure how to respond. *Because it's on the way home? Because it seemed like a good way to pass the time on a random Monday night? Because nothing else makes sense so why should this have to?*

"Just stupid, I guess," she answered, glancing down to her shoes.

He took a step toward her, redrawing her focus. "You're very sad."

His fierce blue eyes looked straight inside her, way too close for comfort.

"Yeah, well. It's late. I'd better go." Abby turned, throwing herself against the front door. She tumbled outside into the cool night air. Her feet didn't stop moving as she fumbled for keys in the pocket of her jeans.

Halfway to her car, his voice returned. "Can I walk you home?"

She jumped sideways. He stood close enough to touch. "Damn, you scared me," she muttered, clutching her backpack to her stomach.

"I'm sorry." He took a few steps back. "It's just – it's dark out."

"Yes, which makes it a little disturbing when someone shows up out of nowhere."

He pointed back to Rosemurtha's. "I came from the psychic store."

Abby couldn't help but laugh at his reply, especially since his eyes didn't glow anymore. Maybe the dull street lamps couldn't catch his clear blue the way the lights in the parlor had. Or maybe his eyes never glowed at all, and she was just crazy. "I know where you came from. I didn't really think you came out of nowhere. You just got here fast."

"Oh. Well, I wanted to make sure you'd get home okay. Will you be safe?"

"I will. I mean, I appreciate the chivalry, but I'm a big girl."

His forehead crinkled. "You're rather small, actually."

"I – I didn't mean that literally. I'll be fine. I promise."

"Okay," he said, his fingers fidgeting at his sides. "Only if you're sure."

"I'm sure."

Abby crossed her arms over her chest and stepped closer to her car. She knew she should leave now. Good girls shouldn't talk to strangers, especially ones who show up in the shadows of psychic parlors. But then again, good girls probably shouldn't visit psychics, either.

She dismissed her thoughts, since none of them changed the fact that he was wildly intriguing. Abby currently despised the darkness of the night. She wanted to look much deeper into his fascinating eyes.

In her gawking silence, he cleared his throat and asked, "Are you all right?"

That was a loaded question. She figured she should be ecstatic that such a beautiful creature even deigned to speak to her. However, her amazement over his attentions wouldn't change her new predicament. She wasn't sure when she'd entered the parlor tonight that she would get any answers, but she was certain her visit would be anonymous. Now that was a loss, too.

Abby scuffed her shoe on the sidewalk. "I'm fine, but can I ask you something?"

"Sure."

"Will I see you at school tomorrow?"

Mr. Magnificent considered her question. He considered for an absurdly long time. Just as she was about to assure him that she wasn't a stalker, he answered her with grave earnestness. "I honestly don't know."

"Oh. Okay. Well, if you are there, will you do me favor?"

"What favor?"

"Please don't tell anyone that you saw me here."

His head tilted. "You are really unusual. Aren't you?"

Abby's eyes widened to the point of pain.

"I'm sorry," he amended. "I guess that came out wrong. I assure you, I meant it as a compliment."

A compliment? Well, he could have called me awkward, bizarre, or nuttier-than-squirrel-poo. Maybe unusual is a compliment. "Thanks," she replied.

"You're welcome." He grinned – lopsided – frickin' adorable.

Grateful that her sneakers hid her involuntary toe-curling, Abby responded with grace. "I, uh, I really should, um, get going."

He nodded. "Yeah, of course. I understand."

They stood still, a few feet apart, staring at each other.

"Okay, then," she said.

"Okay, then."

Abby took a hesitant step back, bumping into her car door.

"I guess I'll go this way," he offered, pointing to the opposite direction.

"All right." She watched as he turned and walked away. He glanced back several times, as if making sure she still existed, until he disappeared into the blackness at the end of the street.

DRIVING HOME FROM THE PARLOR, the road seemed darker. Thankfully, the seat of Abby's well-worn Honda felt as soft as an old blanket, giving her an ounce of comfort while she acknowledged the fact that she would be alone again tonight. It didn't usually bother her. Her father, Mark, pulled the night shift at an auto shop a few doors down from Rosemurtha's parlor. Mechanics didn't usually work nights, but he preferred the solitude.

Abby often visited the little shopping center where he worked in order to check up on him. The four months since her mother's death had been horrible for both of them, but she worried about her dad on a more heightened level than she worried about herself. At least, until now.

"What on earth were you thinking?" she questioned herself as she drove. "A psychic? Really?"

Tonight's parlor visit was the most desperate thing she'd ever done. And she did understand that desperate people did desperate things, but not her. She liked order and predictability. They made her feel sane. She just wished that storefront window with its painted crystal ball hadn't taunted her so many times since her mother's funeral.

Because when you need answers from someone who isn't alive anymore, a psychic parlor seems like the most logical place to get them.

The familiar, terrible sadness pulled at Abby's stomach again. She struggled to form a mental picture of her mother, alive and well. She breathed a little easier when a slow but happy image of Crystal's face evolved. Abby held onto that image as she veered into the driveway of their small, one-story brick home. She hopped out of her car, wandered up the sidewalk, and stepped onto the porch. She entered through the front door before closing it securely behind her. The click of the lock echoed in the emptiness.

Moving from room to room, she flipped on every light until no dim corner remained. She'd had enough darkness for one night. Rosemurtha's sanctum was too unnerving, even despite the gorgeous guy in the shadows.

Abby walked into the kitchen and pulled open the fridge. When the cold, kempt air rushed against her skin, Mr. Magnificent's face pushed into her mind. She could still see his piercing eyes and hear his deep, rumbling voice.

She grabbed a soda and shut the refrigerator. She had to admit, the moment she saw him standing stiff as a statue in that corner, she'd thought he was a ghost – a ghost with glowing eyes and a chilling air. It was a totally rash idea, although not as rash as going to a psychic parlor in the first place.

Abby had known the séance probably wouldn't work, even though she did believe in the possibility of spirits. After all, a thousand movies and TV shows couldn't all be wrong. In truth, she needed ghosts to exist. Or, at least, one specific ghost. If she could just speak with her mom's spirit, then she could finally know what happened on the night Crystal died.

Popping the tab of her soda, Abby leaned against the door of the fridge and took a few gulps. She just needed to find a real psychic, since Madam Rosemurtha was a loss. Abby wondered whether or not Mr. Magnificent could help her. If he worked in a psychic parlor, would he know enough to direct her to someone with actual clairvoyance?

"Oh, who am I kidding?" she questioned her empty kitchen. "I doubt he'll ever speak to me again. He called me unusual, which I'm pretty sure means crazy. And if I stumble up to him at school and ask where to find a real psychic, I'll prove that theory beyond a doubt."

Abby finished her drink as she walked down the hall. Thankful she'd done her homework earlier, she washed her face, brushed her teeth, and fell into bed. She closed her eyes and sighed.

"The entire night was a loss," she grumbled, pulling her covers to her chin.

Well, except for him. He was interesting. And ridiculously good-looking, even if he dressed a bit strangely. If she did get to see him at school, she'd have to keep her mouth shut about the psychic thing. Deep down, she knew she should give up this dead-end search for answers anyway – even though a part of her honestly believed that the answers might save her life.

TUESDAY MORNING, Abby sat at her bedroom vanity and stared into the mirror. Her eyes were a little bloodshot, which was fairly normal lately. However, this morning it was because of fitful sleep as opposed to the typical tears. Perhaps this was progress.

She glanced at the picture of her mother tucked into her mirror frame, wishing for the millionth time that she looked like Crystal, with her dark hair and eyes, instead of like Mark. Her father's blue eyes and fair hair looked handsome on him, but made Abby look twelve instead of seventeen. She brushed through her wispy blond strands before grabbing her backpack. "I love you, Mom," she whispered to the photo as she headed into the hallway.

Abby could hear her dad in the kitchen, making his before-bed morning snack. He slept while she was at school and worked while she slept. The only time they really saw each other was in the afternoon, a little on the weekends, and a few moments on mornings like this.

She padded to the kitchen doorway, observing her father as he fixed himself a sandwich. Abby wondered what kind of day it would be. His shoulders looked relaxed. He leaned easily against the counter. His hands appeared steady. So far, so good. But the real test would be the eyes. "Hey, Dad."

"Hey, honey."

He raised his gaze slowly to hers. She froze in place, concentrating all of her efforts on looking deep inside his eyes. They were even. Still. Clear.

Abby allowed herself to breathe. "How was work?"

"Good. School?"

"Fine."

"You watch a scary movie last night?"

"No. Why?"

"You left all the lights on in the house."

"Oh. Sorry," she said, moving toward the sink. Abby's eyes drifted over the peculiar sight of the empty countertop beside the refrigerator. She was used to the counter being full of bottles – the never-ending supply of alcohol her mother used as an antidote – and still couldn't quite accept how empty it looked now. "I'll try to be better about the lights."

"It's okay. But if you'd rather I was home at night..."

"Don't worry about it, Dad," Abby shut down the familiar conversation. "Things work out fine this way. Really." She offered him a reassuring smile as she reached to the cabinet next to the sink and grabbed his prescription bottles. She examined each label before pulling pills from three different containers and handing them to him. She filled a glass of water and held it out.

Mark popped the pills in, took the glass, and swallowed.

"Under the tongue?" she asked.

He opened his mouth wide, showing her the empty space.

"Thanks," she said, grabbing a granola bar and a bottle of water. "Does spaghetti sound good for dinner?"

"Yeah. Sounds great."

She nodded as she turned to leave. "See you when I get home. Sleep well."

"Have a good day, honey."

ABBY PAID MORE attention to her surroundings this morning. Maneuvering the hallways of school, side-stepping kissing couples and fumbling freshmen, she kept her eyes up for once instead of focusing on her shoes. Would she see

Mr. Magnificent again? Would he suddenly appear beside her like he had in the parking lot last night?

Tiny bubbles of excitement filled her stomach as she glanced around. But after a few minutes of fruitless searching, she decided it would be more fun to have a full-body waxing than continue this quest. First, because she couldn't find him anywhere. Second, because it reminded her of how different she felt.

The people shuffling past her were her age, lived in her town, and sat in her classes. But Abby wasn't one of them. She watched as they laughed and talked and texted about clothes and dates and dances – awesome nonsense that sounded like a dream come true. Abby couldn't think about those things. Not because she didn't want to, but because she didn't have enough room inside her brain. It was all she could do to think about how her mom died. And fear her dad's illness. And wonder when it would be her turn to go insane.

But she wanted to be normal. She'd wished for it every day of the last five years. Abby figured a normal teenager would search the halls for the fascinating guy she'd met the night before, obsessing over his insane cuteness. Thinking about him meant she wasn't thinking about the laundry, or the bills, or what to make for dinner, or if Dad really swallowed his meds.

Still, even if an oddly-dressed psychic man could be her holy grail of normalcy, it was absurd to think he would wait for her in the hallway like they'd forged some instantaneous connection. He probably thought she was a maniac. For all she knew, he'd spent this morning signing all the necessary paperwork to transfer to a school as far away from her as possible.

Abby hung her head again while she stepped into her math class. She squashed her unfounded excitement, forcing herself to quietly endure the ninety minutes of pre-calculus before marching to her English class. Once she made her way to the back of Ms. Pennington's room, she took her seat and attempted to chameleon-blend with her surroundings.

"Open to page thirty in your text and begin reading," Ms. Pennington's bird-high voice chirped, her bony fingers raising the book high into the air as if it was the first time anyone had seen it. Abby tried hard to concentrate on the words in the pages. She failed miserably when images of purple beads and crystal balls floated through her brain.

Relief eventually arrived in the form of the lunch bell. Tossing her book into her backpack, disgruntled that she would have to reread everything tonight, Abby eased into the herding crowd in the hallway before turning in the opposite direction. She forged a path away from the cafeteria, shoved open the school's thick brown exit door, and stepped outside.

Still-warm September air hugged her as she walked through the school's back courtyard. She maneuvered past the few kids lounging in the grass and kept a wide berth between her and the students kicking a ball on the soccer field. Unnoticed by anyone, she moved farther away toward the weather-beaten picnic tables scattered behind the empty basketball courts. Satisfied only when she was far enough from school to make the other people look like ants, or at least meaty beetles, she flopped down on a splintered bench and tossed her backpack on the tabletop. She stared into the woods beside her. The trees appeared sparsely spaced at first, yet their thick trunks grew closer and closer into the distance, all the way up to the mountains of the Blue Ridge.

When they'd moved to Virginia last year, Abby had been upset about staying here when her father retired from the military. They'd certainly lived in a lot of other places she would have preferred to call home, but she had to admit this little suburb of Charlottesville had grown on her. Being close to the University of Virginia gave her a sense of hope for the future, and this high school was large enough that she could be ignored.

Anonymity, after all, had its perks. It meant no one had to know about her family. It meant she could move forward with her life without anyone prying. It meant she could be here, alone at lunch, enjoying a small sense of sanity.

Abby closed her eyes and sighed. The warm rays of sunshine swept across her skin. The soft chirping of birds echoed in her ears. The cool breeze fanned her hair across her shoulders.

"Why are your eyes closed?"

She jumped with the unexpected question, bumping her knee beneath the picnic tabletop. Her eyelids flew open. Mr. Magnificent stood in front of the next table over, like he'd been there for hours.

"God, you scared me!" she yelped. "Where did you even come from?"

He motioned toward the tree line. "I came from the woods."

"What were you doing in the woods?"

"Walking. I like walking. Don't you?"

Abby told herself she was okay. Her heartbeat had slowed back down to a life-sustaining pace, which meant Mr. Magnificent hadn't actually scared her *to death*. Now, she needed to focus on the fact that he was actually here. "Sure, I like walking. I guess I just thought I'd see you sooner today. I mean, in the halls, or something. Did you go to your classes this morning?"

"Yeah, I go to classes – except for when I take walks in the woods. I saw you sitting here alone and thought you might like some company."

Abby stared at him in utter fascination. For someone who possessed enough stealth and speed to rival a top-secret spy plane, he was incredibly nonchalant about it. "You know, that's the third time you've done that."

"Done what?"

"Scared the mess out of me by showing up out of nowhere."

"Hmm," he considered. "I remember you jumping when I showed up last night by your car. And just now, of course. But what's the third time?"

"When you first showed up in the back corner of the parlor."

"I scared you then?"

"Well, yeah. I mean, I knew you must have used one of those secret doors in the wall to come in, but you did it so quietly, I thought you were a..."

Abby sealed her lips shut.

His brow rose. "A what?"

"Never mind," she dismissed. After all, she couldn't exactly say she'd thought he was a ghost with glowing eyes – not when she was just getting used to the idea of having him around. She didn't want to give him a reason to think she was crazy right off the bat. Not *another* reason, anyway, in addition to her psychic parlor visits. Although, in her defense, he'd also been there. And she swore his eyes had glowed.

His eyes. Abby almost forgot how strange they'd been, like they were lit from the inside. But she must have been hallucinating, because looking at them now, she could see that they were just blue. A beautiful, bright, ocean blue, but definitely not glowing. Rosemurtha's chilling sanctum must have warped her senses beyond the usual.

In Abby's silence, he glanced around them, looking out to the beetle-students in the distance. "Do you spend your lunch break out here every day?"

"Yes," she admitted, playing her fingers on the empty tabletop.

"Then where's your lunch?"

"Not hungry."

"Well, you really should eat."

"Thanks for the tip." She hadn't eaten well since her mother's funeral, but he didn't need to know that. "How about you? Where's your lunch?"

He shrugged. "Not hungry."

"Well, you really should eat."

He chuckled, the sound warm and joyful. His eyes focused on hers and Abby swore he pulled her to him. She gripped the edge of the table to make sure she wasn't actually moving.

Good Lord, what is this feeling? She figured it must be the overreaction of her seldom-used teenage hormones in response to a ridiculously drool-worthy guy. She decided to tempt fate by motioning to the bench in front of her. "Do you want to join me?"

He nodded without hesitation, but didn't come any closer. He sat down at the picnic table behind him instead, facing her and yet still several feet away. The old wood groaned beneath his large body as he settled in.

Wildly amused by the distance he'd kept between them, Abby wondered what he was afraid of. Did he think, if he sat at her table, that she would crawl across the top in order to grope him? Sure, he was breathtaking, but they'd only just met. He didn't have to fear her imminent attack. At least, not today.

She bit her tongue to keep from giggling. "You know, I never caught your name last night."

"Oh. Right," he acknowledged. "I'm Nathaniel. And you are?"

"Abigail. But I go by Abby."

"So, why were you at Rosemurtha's last night, Abby?"

She coughed and choked simultaneously. "Wow. You don't pull any punches, do you?"

Nathaniel shifted on his bench. "I'm sorry. Was that too forward?"

Abby stared at him in stunned silence. A minute ago, she would have bet all-in that she was the social invalid in this scenario. Now, she wasn't so sure. "Well, most people get to know each other a little, and do the small talk thing, before diving in to something so personal."

"Yeah? What kind of small talk do you mean?"

"Small talk, you know. Hi, how are you, where are you from?"

"Hello, I'm fine, Oklahoma."

Abby grinned wildly, loving the fact that she'd officially discovered an anomaly of mankind: a stunning guy who had no idea how to talk to girls. He may as well be Bigfoot. "You're really not from around here, are you?"

"No. I just said I'm from Oklahoma."

"I didn't mean that literally, Nathaniel. I mean you don't..." Abby stopped herself. She was going to say *fit in*, but that sounded harsh. She didn't fit in either, and right now it suited her just fine. But Nathaniel seemed even worse off than she was. Her gaze drifted to his clothes – to the same white T-shirt, brown pants, and black boots he'd worn last night. The word *misfits* popped into her head.

"I don't what?" he prodded.

"You don't...seem at ease."

"Maybe not. But neither do you."

Abby cringed. That was too close to the truth. Part of her wanted to leap off this bench and run far, far away. Part of her wanted to leap on him. She settled for fidgeting with her backpack.

He shook his head. "I'm sorry. Again. I keep saying the wrong thing."

The worried look on his face calmed her. She shrugged, pretending his observation hadn't stung. "It's okay."

Nathaniel fell silent then. Abby figured she should look down at the bench, shriveling away from the awkward pause. But she didn't want to. She wanted to search his eyes.

What would she find when she looked inside him? Anger? Confusion? Pain? Why was such a marvelous specimen of handsomeness out here with her, sitting on her splintery cluster of benches? Why wasn't he strutting around the lunchroom, being happily overtaken by a hoard of pretty girls?

Just as she worked up the courage to focus in on his eyes, primed to dig her way fully inside him, he broke her concentration with a question. "So, will you please tell me now why you went to Rosemurtha's?"

Abby shook her head immediately. "Sorry, but no."

"A little too personal?"

"A tad."

Nathaniel laughed, as if getting a joke she hadn't heard.

"What?" she asked.

"Nothing. It's just..."

"What?"

"Well, you're just..." he said, eyeing her up and down, "you're not shy."

"Am I supposed to be?" Abby retorted. Maybe he was a thawed-out caveman who didn't think girls deserved opinions. That, at least, would explain why Bigfoot was alone.

He held his hands up in front of him. "No, no. You're not supposed to be shy. I just thought maybe you were. Because you're kind of, you know..."

"Kind of what?"

"Um, secluded? I guess?"

"Hey! I have friends!"

"Of course, you do. I didn't mean..." Nathaniel stopped talking and glanced down at his boots. "God, I'm really sorry. Did I mention that I have foot-in-mouth disease?"

She smiled with his apology, relaxing her tight shoulders. "Well, to be perfectly honest, I only have one friend. Her name is Julie."

Nathaniel looked back up again. "Why just one?"

Abby's smile fell. She didn't like this topic. It made her sound like someone nobody wanted to be around. It made her feel like a leper defending her good health while limbs actively fell off her body. "My family has always moved around a lot, and I only came here last year. I tried blending in at first, but everyone already had their friends. Then I met Julie. She was also new, because her dad travels for work. Now, she's my best friend."

"Then why isn't she sitting here with you?"

"Because they've already moved again, just across town. She goes to a different high school, but I still get to see her every weekend, so that's cool."

Nathaniel leaned forward on his bench. "And will you move away again?"

"No, no more moving for us."

"Why not?"

Abby eyed him, wondering how many more questions he planned to fire at her. "My dad used to be in the Army. That's why we moved a lot."

"He's not in the Army anymore?"

"No. He retired."

"And what does he do now?"

"He works as an auto mechanic." She cleared her throat, eager to change the subject. "You know, you actually remind me of Julie."

"Why? Is she awkwardly large and blunt?"

"No," Abby giggled. "She wants to be a reporter. She likes grilling people."

Nathaniel smiled. "Is that your way of telling me I'm too nosy?"

"Maybe. A little."

"So, you're really not going to tell me why you went to Rosemurtha's?"

"Wow. You're like a dog with a bone, aren't you?"

"Aw, come on. You know you want to tell me."

"I truly don't."

"Sure, you do," he insisted, attempting to convince her to go against every barely-formed grain of common sense in her body. "I won't tell anyone else, Abby. I only know one other person at this school, and I don't even like him. Your secrets are perfectly safe with me."

She shuddered. "Wh-what makes you think they're secrets?"

"Because I saw you last night. I could tell how scared you were. Scared and sad. I just want to know why."

His earnest plea cracked a tiny hole in her shell. For a freak moment, Abby considered answering him. But then she regained her wits and embraced reality, fully aware that his bizarre interest in her life didn't make any sense at all.

"Not to be rude, Nathaniel, but why do you care? Are you doing some sort of television scouting? Like: 'Next up on Dr. Phil, idiots who go to psychic parlors.'"

"Who is Dr. Phil?"

"Seriously?"

"And who is supposed to be an idiot?"

"Um, me."

"You're not an idiot, Abby. You just want answers. I understand that."

"Yeah, but I'm going to some crazy extremes to get them, aren't I?"

Nathaniel crossed his thick arms over his thicker chest. "I guess that depends on the kind of answers you're after."

"The incredibly-difficult-to-get ones, apparently."

"Well, maybe I could help."

"I don't think so," Abby said, even though her mind swam in the opposite direction. "I mean, unless you know of any *real* psychics."

His eyebrow ticked up. "Are you saying Rosemurtha's performance wasn't interesting enough for you?"

"Oh, it was interesting. Just not very informative."

"Then why don't you tell me what information you want, and I'll see what I can do about it."

Abby straightened in her seat. "Really? Do you think you can find a psychic who can actually help me?"

Nathaniel studied her for a minute before shaking his head. "No, I don't know any other psychics. But I still want to know why you went there."

"Oh," she sighed. "You know, you still haven't told me why you care."

"Would it make you feel better if I said I was doing a survey for Dr. Bill?"

"Dr. Phil."

"That's what I meant."

Abby smiled.

Nathaniel's answering grin was blissfully easy. And soft. And made her head feel fuzzy. "Talk to me, Abby. Please. I promise you'll feel better."

She almost believed him. There was something about his eyes, and the sincerity of his voice, that lulled her into a trance-like peace. For a few blissful moments, she felt like they were the only two people in the world. That is, until more people showed up.

Abby startled, bumping her knee on the picnic table again as her eyes darted to the woods. Two boys from her English class emerged from the trees – Jason Rathburn and Randy Thorpe. She held entirely still when they glared at her before walking back toward school. A chill swept over her skin, eerily reminiscent of the gusts she'd felt in the psychic parlor.

She refocused on Nathaniel, searching out his eyes. Unfortunately, he'd pivoted fully away from her. He'd practically transformed into stone, sitting stiffly on his bench, glued to the two boys' movements. The set of his body was so tense, his breathing so shallow, that Abby wasn't sure if he even remembered her existence.

"Do you know Jason and Randy?" she questioned, wondering if they were the reason Nathaniel was in the woods earlier.

He continued to study the two boys all the way across the schoolyard, until they disappeared through the distant door. "No, I don't know them," Nathaniel answered when he finally turned back to her. The warmth of his voice settled over her skin, dispersing the recent chill as quickly as it came.

Abby stared into his eyes. They were blue. Just blue. She didn't want to admit that she wondered if they'd been glowing again. Obviously, they'd never glowed in the first place.

Nathaniel opened his mouth to speak and Abby braced herself for what she knew was coming: more luring promises that her secrets would be safe with him. She sighed in relief when a distant ringing announced the end of their lunch break. "Well, that's the bell," she mused. "I guess it's time to head back to paradise."

He huffed out a laugh. "Yeah. I guess so."

She stood to leave, but he remained motionless. "Are you coming with?"

"No," he dismissed. "You go ahead. I'm going to wait here for a bit."

"Oh. Okay." Abby shifted away, pulling her bag in tow, until curiosity made her glance back. "But, seriously, aren't you going to your next class?"

Nathaniel shrugged. "Study period."

"So, you're just not going?"

"I don't think they'll miss me, and I'd rather go for a walk. I like walking."

"Yeah, you mentioned that." She turned again, taking a few steps away. "Um, Abby?"

Stopping short, she pivoted back to him. "Yeah?"

"I just, I wanted to, uh..."

"You wanted to what?"

Nathaniel exhaled. "I wanted to tell you I'm sorry. About your mom."

"My – my mom? What do you mean?"

"I heard you talking about her at the parlor last night."

Abby's feet turned to lead.

He searched her eyes. "Your mom's name was Crystal?"

Abby nodded mechanically, her heart sputtering inside her chest.

"I'm sorry," Nathaniel repeated, his voice so low that she could barely hear him. "I don't mean to overwhelm you. I just wanted you to know that I know, in case you need to talk."

The words floated mid-air while she shook her head over and over again.

"That's okay," he said, offering her the gentlest smile. "I understand. You should do whatever makes you happy."

This was definitely the point where Abby was supposed to take off running. She was supposed to sprint as fast as her little feet would go, tail tucked firmly between her legs. She was supposed to shove him out, to maintain the intactness of her cocoon by any means necessary.

Instead, she took a step forward. She held his eyes, determined to see what she could find. Nathaniel sat on his bench, motionless. He held so still, openly allowing her scrutiny, that she wondered if he was equally curious about what she might discover.

Abby focused on him with all her might, searching deep inside, knowing she could find some sort of answer if she tried hard enough. After all, she'd been only twelve years old when she realized she had a certain kind of ability. She realized that if she took her time – and really, truly concentrated – then she could read a person's emotions through their eyes.

It wasn't just the simple emotions, either. Things like happiness and sadness were obvious to most people. But Abby could see much deeper things. Hidden things. Scary things. The first eyes she ever read were her father's. That was the moment she knew something was terribly wrong with him. That was the moment she knew her life would never be the same.

She drew on her hard-won talent now. She allowed herself to fall into Nathaniel's ocean of blue, probing and grasping for the truth. She held her breath, her entire being honed in on his. To her surprise, it only took seconds to find what she sought.

Pain.

Dear God, Nathaniel was in so much pain. His eyes overflowed with it, distinct and powerful, so strong that her knees nearly buckled. She saw him flailing in the deepest, darkest waters, sinking under a brutal riptide, kicking and screaming as he drowned.

Sharp, aching seconds passed before Abby could breathe again. She stiffened her spine, unsure of what to do with her stolen knowledge. She couldn't stay, yet she didn't want to leave. She just continued standing in front of him and staring into his beautiful, pained eyes.

"I have to get to class," she finally told herself, compelling her feet to move.

Nathaniel stood from his bench. "Abby?"

"Yeah?"

"Can I not-eat lunch with you again tomorrow?"

Her heart thumped weirdly in her chest. "Sure. If you want to."

"I do. I want to."

She nodded and turned, trudging back toward school.

CHAPTER

TWO

Warped moments later, Abby sat in history class. She attempted to listen while her teacher, Mr. Puryear, droned on and on as usual about one horrible human event after another. She truly detested hearing about history. It was the tale of people doing wretched things to each other, over and over again, with no end in sight.

Abby didn't need the horrors of the world pounded into her. She just wanted to sit on her little picnic bench, stare into the woods, and pretend that everything was going to be fine. Normally, she wanted to sit there alone. But now...

Holy hell. What was she going to do now? The way she saw it, she had two choices. She could push Nathaniel away and go back to her solitary existence, dreaming about happiness and normalcy and other magical objects. Or, she could let him in and risk the triumvirate: exposure, ridicule, rejection.

Could she do it? Could she let him get that close to her? She could already hear tomorrow's question falling from his perfect lips: *So, Abby, it's been a whole day...are you ready to tell me why you went to the psychic parlor?*

Nathaniel probably wouldn't stick around if she didn't give him a plausible explanation. And since he already knew about her mom's death, Abby couldn't pretend that her parlor trip was just for fun. She would have to admit her real purpose, and that would open one giant can of slimy, wriggly worms.

How would she even begin to tell him the truth? Would she stay general, with a quick, "By the way, did I mention my dad's crazy?" Or would she plow right in with, "I wanted to talk to Mom so I could ask if Dad might have, you know, killed her, or whatever."

Abby's eyes glazed over. She couldn't do this. She didn't even talk to her best friend about her sick fears, and Julie already knew about Mark's lengthy history of mental illness. Julie had heard Abby say the words bipolar disorder, schizophrenic tendencies, and paranoid delusions. Julie knew about Mark's suicide attempts. She knew that Crystal drank herself into oblivion every night in order to cope. She knew that Abby wondered every day when it would be her turn to lose her mind.

Telling Julie all of those things had been awful, so how was Abby supposed to tell a total stranger? There was just no way. She needed to avoid it at all costs and never talk about the psychic parlor again. If Nathaniel actually came back for lunch tomorrow, she would have to insist that the topic was off limits. If he left, he left. If he stayed, he stayed.

She tried not to think about how much she wanted him to stay.

"Miss Forrest?"

Her classroom fell utterly silent.

"Abigail Forrest?" Mr. Puryear reemphasized.

"Yes?" she answered.

"Do you know what year the Invasion of Normandy took place?"

Oh, crap. "No."

"Um-hmm." Mr. Puryear looked down his bulbous nose at her.

Eric Nichols, the boy who sat in the seat behind her, snickered. Abby forced herself to sit still, even though she wanted to spin around to give Eric her most evil glare. Not that her glare would ever scare anyone, but it might make her feel better right at the moment.

Mr. Puryear moved on to his next victim as she sank lower in her seat.

AFTER SCHOOL, Abby went home, did laundry, and cooked dinner. She watched her father throughout the evening, gauging his emotions. He wasn't high; he wasn't low. He existed, as he had for several months, on a flat, even plane. They were okay here, the two of them. They moved around each other like tumbleweeds lolling across a desert, propelled by a peculiar breeze. It wasn't this dry calm that bothered her. It was the question of when it would end.

If their family history had taught her anything, it was that the calm would always end. Something would happen. Something remarkable. Or unremarkable. Then, her father would change. Morph. Transform.

What would it be next time? Maybe he would spend all of their savings in one day. Or fling himself from the roof of the tallest building he could find. Or tell her there were snipers under the floorboards of their house, waiting until they went to sleep to shoot them into pieces.

Abby couldn't know, and she really didn't want to find out. Especially not by herself. Not all alone, without her mother to guide her through.

But it would come. In some horrifying shape, in some twisted form, it would come. Would Nathaniel want to be with her when that happened? Did he even want to be with her now? Or was she just an oddity to investigate – a bizarre little girl who piqued his curiosity because she held hands with psychics? Abby couldn't know that, either.

Feeling more confused than ever, she packed her dad's bag full of food for the night and waved goodbye to him as he left for work. She locked the door, did her homework, and got in bed. She tossed and turned until morning.

***

ABBY MADE it through her first two classes on Wednesday as best she could, anxious and impatient for the lunch bell to ring. She wanted nothing more than to see Nathaniel again, yet she was also petrified of what would happen when she did. She'd thought about it all night – him interrogating her about why she went to the parlor, her refusing to discuss the topic, and him deciding whether or not he still wanted to hang around – and she'd come to one simple conclusion. She really, really wanted him to stay with her.

When the bell finally rang, no earthly force could stop her from getting to those picnic tables. Abby practically ran through the back courtyard and out toward the woods, avoiding everyone else along the way. She had trouble breathing when she finally plopped down on her favorite old picnic bench, and not just because she was winded from exertion. She was also worried that Nathaniel might scare the pants off of her when he showed up again, since he tended to appear out of nowhere.

Does he even know how strange that is? she wondered while scanning the trees. *Does he do it on purpose? Or is he really not aware of his spy-stealth?*

"Are you looking for someone?"

His voice came from behind her this time. Abby squealed in a freaked-out girly way, spinning around on her bench to see him. He stood only a few steps away. A huge smile filled his face.

"My God, Nathaniel! You actually enjoy doing that, don't you?"

"Doing what?" he asked with angelic innocence.

"Being super-sneaky."

"Sneaky? Am I really?"

"Oh, come on," she said, trying to maintain her bravado against the warmth in his eyes. "You must know that you're sneaky."

"No, I can't say I was aware of that."

"Well, you are. Please just let me know when you're going to show up next time. Be louder, or something."

"Okay," he offered with the smile. "I'll try."

Abby tried not to get too excited about his lopsided grin. Or about the assumption that a next-time existed. She turned back to her table and clasped her hands together on the top, working to keep her fingers from fidgeting.

Nathaniel walked to the table in front of hers and folded his large frame onto the inadequate bench. He still wore the exact same outfit she'd seen for the past two days. She wanted to ask why, but it seemed rude. What if he was too poor to buy other clothes? That would be awful.

He settled down and looked to her, his chest puffed out, his gaze determined. "So, how are you today, Abby? Are your classes going well?"

She couldn't help laughing.

"What?" he asked.

"It's...it's nothing."

"I really stink at the small talk thing, don't I?"

"No, no, you're doing great," Abby assured. "It's just, you're actually trying small talk. Which means you listened to me."

"Of course. I like listening to you."

Heat crept into her cheeks. She wanted to splash around in the compliment he'd sprinkled on her, but she feared ulterior motives. She could already hear his next words: *I'd like listening about why you went to the psychic parlor.*

"Mmm," Nathaniel hummed. "You have something on your mind."

"Why do you think that?"

"I can see the wheels in your head turning."

"Wow. Am I that transparent?"

"Trust me, it's a good thing."

"Why is it good?"

"Because I hope it means you'll tell me all about it."

His easy smile calmed her for a mere second before she refocused. The time for her Rosemurtha-ultimatum had arrived. Abby breathed in deeply, fortifying her will by thinking about brave people: knights in shining armor, astronauts, girls who wear thong underwear.

"Yeah," she admitted. "I do have something on my mind."

"What is it?"

"Well, um, yesterday you said some stuff about my mom…"

Nathaniel shifted on his bench. "Look, Abby. Before you go any further, let me say that I'm sorry. It's none of my business, and I shouldn't have said anything. I just thought I was being helpful, I guess."

Her jaw fell open.

"Are you angry with me?" he asked.

Abby pressed her lips together as she watched him. His eyes were so kind, his words so gentle. She didn't think anyone could ever be angry with him.

"No, Nathaniel, I'm not angry. But I can't talk about the psychic parlor. I'm sorry." It wasn't the heaviest gauntlet ever thrown down, yet she still thought she got her point across.

He stared at her for several year-long seconds. Abby's stomach churned while she awaited his verdict. Just when she thought he might get up from his bench and walk away from her entirely, he said, "Okay, then. But I need you to tell me what we *can* talk about."

She stared, dumbfounded. That was far too easy. Was he for real? Or was this some elaborate prank for a strange TV show? "We can talk about almost anything," she told him, resisting the urge to search for cameras in the trees.

"Almost anything," he echoed. "Can you please specify what's off limits?"

"Just nothing too heavy. Nothing that sounds like spilling your guts."

"But why don't you want to spill your guts to me?"

Abby huffed out a laugh. "Because people don't normally go around spilling their guts to people they just met. I don't want my goofy parts hanging out all over the place."

Nathaniel's head tilted. "Explain *goofy parts*, please."

"Goofy parts. You know. They're the things that make you weird. The things you don't want anyone else to find out about you." Abby stopped talking long enough to inspect him, from the top of his lovely blond head, down every solid muscle of his chest and legs, to the tips of what were sure to be adorable toes hidden inside his hideous boots. "But you might not have any goofy parts," she considered, "so you'd have no idea what I'm talking about."

"Wait a minute," Nathaniel countered, grinning even as he pinned her eyes. "You don't think I'm capable of having goofy parts?"

"I don't know. Are you?"

"Absolutely."

Really? What could such a splendid being find awkward about himself?

Nathaniel leaned forward. "I can see the wheels in your head turning again. You want to ask me about my goofy parts, don't you?"

"No!" Abby protested too much. "Well, I mean, I...kinda, yeah."

"Why don't you, then?"

"Because I told you not to ask about mine, so how would that be fair?"

"Well, the way I see it, I had stolen knowledge about you because I'd overheard about your mother. Therefore, if you want to ask me something, I think that would be fair enough."

Abby didn't hesitate. "I want to know why you're in pain," she blurted.

Nathaniel's grin fell. She immediately regretted her words.

"What makes you think I'm in pain?" he asked, his voice low and raw.

Her eyes remained steady even if her breathing wasn't. "I can just tell."

Nathaniel held her gaze, quietly examining her with a fine-toothed comb. He stayed silent forever. She heard each beat of her heart as she waited.

Finally, he spoke. "My mother and father are both gone. They died."

Abby stopped breathing altogether. How was that possible? How could anyone lose two parents and still be walking and talking? She'd only lost one and she felt like an invalid. "How...how do you do it?"

"I get by," he answered. "One day at a time."

She had a sudden urge to buy him new clothes. "I'm so sorry, Nathaniel."

"I'm sorry, too. About your mom." He looked away, into the surrounding trees. "You know, I think you and I have a lot in common."

Abby wanted to ask what happened to his parents. She wanted to ask how much time had passed. She wanted to know when the pain would stop. But he wouldn't have the answer, because his pain obviously hadn't stopped yet.

He turned back to her, the grin slowly reforming on his lips. "So, do you think we're even now? About the goofy parts, I mean?"

She nodded. "Yeah."

"Good. Then we can talk about other things."

"Other things?"

"Sure. Anything you like."

Abby stiffened her spine. "But no more goofy parts?"

"Yes, yes, I know," he sighed. "I can't ask anything personal. What is it I'm allowed to talk about again?"

"Anything at all, as long as it can be categorized as benign and superficial."

Nathaniel laughed. "Wow. I hope you don't take this the wrong way, but you don't exactly talk like a teenager. How old are you?"

Abby didn't know how to take that. "I'm seventeen. I'm a junior. And you don't exactly talk like a teenager yourself. Are you a senior?"

"Yes, I'm definitely a senior."

"How old are you?"

"Pushing ninety."

She grinned, fully understanding feeling like an older person trapped in a teenager's body. "I think you mean pushing nine*teen*, right?"

"Right," he said, running his fingers through his cropped hair. "Let's see... benign, superficial questions. How about, what's your favorite color? Is that too probing?"

"Hmm. I suppose I can make it through that one. I like purple."

Nathaniel chuckled.

"What?" she probed.

"Oh, nothing."

"Okay, then. What's your favorite color?"

"Um, I'll go with green."

"You sound uncertain."

"Well, blue is nice, too. And I've recently discovered the merits of purple."

"Are you an art student or something?"

"Nope. Forget drawing a straight line. I can't even make a crooked one."

Abby laughed, a sound so foreign that it nearly startled her. How long had it been since she'd heard real laughter come out of her body? Nathaniel made everything feel right. He made her life fuzzy and free. He made all the crazy moments stream together smoothly and easily. Minutes. Hours. Days.

She barely recalled the concept of time while the next week flew by.

On Thursday's lunch date, when Nathaniel showed up in the woods again, he flailed his arms around like a wild man until she waved at him. Abby truly appreciated him not scaring her to death, although his awkward gyrations looked ridiculous. But that was okay, because he made her smile so hard it hurt. She loved how he sat with her through lunch, and worked on small talk the entire time, and kept her smiling right up until the bell rang.

On Friday's lunch date, after flailing his arms in the woods again, Nathaniel actually walked up to her picnic table instead of his own. He settled down on the bench directly across from her and rested his hands on the table-top. His fingers were so close to hers that she could have touched them if she wanted to – which she very much did – although she didn't go through with it. She merely sat and listened to every word that left his mouth, fascinated by the fact that he liked English class but not math, and that he didn't own any electronics starting with a little *i*, and that he preferred racoons to rabbits because apparently rabbits have beadier eyes.

Abby wasn't sure why Nathaniel chose to sit with her every day, but she missed him when he was gone. For the first time ever, she didn't want the weekend to come. Over the treacherously long Saturday and Sunday, she thought about him incessantly. Which was wonderful, because it meant she didn't have time to worry about all the things she normally worried about.

She didn't even mind that he always wore the same clothes. She wanted to ask why he never changed his outfit, but feared embarrassing or offending him. Instead, she was left to contemplate whether he was poor, or just utterly unconcerned with fashion, or one of those people like Einstein who bought twenty of the same outfit so he didn't waste time deciding what to wear.

On Monday's lunch date, Nathaniel sat at her table again. He'd practically perfected the art of small talk, and could speak lengthily and brilliantly about the most superficial things. When Abby listened to him discuss the difference between oak and maple leaves, she vowed to never let another Arbor Day go by unnoticed. When he explained in all seriousness why he thought frogs were better singers than elephants, she reconsidered the value of karaoke.

On Tuesday's lunch date, she could barely contain her excitement when she spotted him flailing around in the woods. Sheer giddiness overtook her as their picnic bench slanted to one side once he situated his large body down across from her. She stared at him constantly, absorbing his easy grin, trying her damnedest to figure out why he kept coming back to her.

By Wednesday, Abby had reached the end of her rope. Nathaniel had spent an entire week not-eating lunch with her, which probably meant that he liked being here. And yet, despite all that time, he'd never touched her once.

Did he not want to touch her? Abby hoped and prayed that wasn't true, because she desperately wanted to touch him. Even as they sat together now, studying each other across the wood tabletop, their hands rested mere inches apart. She could barely hold herself still while listening to him enumerate the pros and cons of jellyfish.

To be blatantly honest, her desire to feel Nathaniel's skin beneath her fingers had reached a biblical hellfire-and-damnation level, and that fact made her ecstatic. He'd given her a lot of gifts over these past days, but the best by far was the realization that she truly was a normal teenager. She was normal because she wanted him. He was an overstuffed, boot-wearing teddy bear, and she wanted to talk with him, laugh with him, and just be with him.

But even though Abby liked to think of their lunch meetings as dates, she had no idea if Nathaniel wanted anything more than her friendship. She never saw him in the hallways, or anywhere other than this picnic table. He'd never asked to meet up with her outside of school, nor walked back to class with her when the bell rang.

His deep voice continued ringing in her ears as she ran her fingers across the tabletop. Feeling this cool picnic bench made her recall the chilled air in the psychic parlor the first time she saw him. Was Nathaniel afraid to touch her because he had some skin-temperature disorder that made him freakishly cold? Or was he just not attracted to her? Or was she an insane person who'd thought he was a ghost and was now ridiculously overanalyzing everything?

Abby figured it was probably a very sad combination of the last two.

"Don't you agree?" Nathaniel's voice derailed her crazy-train of thought.

She tried to remember what he'd just said.

Amusement sparkled in his totally normal, non-glowing eyes. "You're not listening to me at all, are you, Abby?"

"I am listening to you. I'm paying rapt attention."

"Sure, you are."

"No, really. You were saying something awesome about jellyfish."

His lopsided smile melted her. She would have to peel herself off of the bench when lunch ended. "I said I figure they must have a purpose," Nathaniel repeated, "even though they sting people and are generally disgusting. Everything is here for a reason, right?"

"Yeah, of course. We all have a purpose. Maybe they're here to brighten up the world. I mean, they do have really pretty tentacles."

"Hmm," he considered. "Yeah, I like that. Especially since only you would think a jellyfish can brighten the world."

Abby couldn't stand it anymore. The tender way he looked at her with those ocean eyes made her insides squishier than jellyfish tentacles. When the end-of-lunch bell rang, she practically jumped out of her skin. The shrill sound shot panic through her veins, since she had to do something fast. She had to touch him, just once, before she lost him for another day.

But how should she do it? She couldn't simply grab onto him for a spontaneous hug. And pretend-falling into his lap would be too embarrassing for words. Whatever she did, it had to appear accidental.

Abby glanced at her backpack, which sat on the bench beside her. Looking to Nathaniel's face, she plastered on an innocent smile. She scooted sideways until her bag casually tumbled off the edge. Once it plopped onto the ground beside them, he leaned over to pick it up.

The second he reached down, Abby dove in. Her hand landed on top of his at the same time he grabbed hold of the bag. Everything in her world stopped while she stared at the sight of their overlapping fingers. She grasped onto him, mesmerized by the feel of his skin beneath hers. Nathaniel was not freakishly cold. Not at all. He was warm – so amazingly warm – and the broad width of his hand made hers look small and pale in comparison.

Abby sighed out loud. She couldn't help it. He was incredibly gentle yet remarkably strong. In all honestly, she could sit here on her little bench, clinging to him, for the rest of eternity. That is, until his tentative words yanked her back to reality.

"Do you, um...do you want your bag?"

Now, his skin was nowhere near as warm as hers. She couldn't believe how long she'd lingered with her fingers clamped onto his, restraining his movements. If her cheeks weren't lit up like a fire engine, it would be a miracle.

"Yeah, thanks," she mumbled, snatching her backpack from under his hand. She jumped up from the bench and started toward school, assuring herself she couldn't actually die of embarrassment.

"Abby?"

His voice came from behind her. For the first time in a week, she was unhappy to hear it. She stilled her feet, pivoted slowly around, and forced herself to meet his eyes. "Yes?"

"I was thinking, um..." Nathaniel glanced to the ground.

"What is it?" she asked, fully prepared to apologize for manhandling him.

He looked to her face. "Would you like to go to dinner with me tonight?"

Her eyes grew two sizes bigger.

"I'm sorry," he backpedaled. "It's too much, isn't it?"

"Is what too much?"

"Me, being around all the time. I just really like talking to you. But I'm probably overdoing it, aren't I? Just forget I said anything."

"No! God, no. You're not overdoing it. Not at all."

Nathaniel's face brightened. "Really? That's...that's great. So, dinner?"

"Yes. Definitely."

"Wonderful. I don't know of many restaurants here. Where's good?"

"Well, there's a pizza place around the corner from Rosemurtha's."

"Pizza? Okay. Let's go have pizza."

"Pizza," Abby agreed, staring at him in utter amazement. "Would you like me to pick you up? I mean, you've never mentioned having a car, and I don't mind driving, so..."

"Actually, I thought we could meet in front of Rosemurtha's. At eight?"

"Um, yeah. That'll be good."

Nathaniel smiled up at her from their bench. "It will be good."

Abby continued gawking at him as she fiddled with her backpack.

He motioned toward school. "You should probably get to class."

"Oh. Right," she said, encouraging her wobbly legs to move.

"I'll see you at eight," he called from behind her.

She waved but didn't turn around, not wanting him to witness the neon glow of her cheeks.

THAT EVENING, Abby packed her father's meal for work with great care. She wanted to do every single thing right today, no matter how small. She'd never experienced anything like this – no luminous boy had ever fallen from the sky and landed in her lap – and she wanted so much to deserve this moment.

"Don't you look pretty," Mark said, rounding the corner to the kitchen.

Abby zeroed in on her dad's eyes. Part of her expected to see dark clouds of insanity staring back at her – a payment she owed in order to be with someone as perfect as Nathaniel. But Mark's eyes were calm and well.

"Thanks," she answered.

"Are you doing something special tonight?"

She shrugged as she handed him his food. "Just going out for a bit."

"Okay. Be careful, please."

"Yeah, Dad. I always am."

He smiled before turning to leave for work. Once the door shut behind him, Abby pondered how to make the next two hours go away. She busied herself with dishes and laundry. She inspected her straight hair and minimal makeup repeatedly. She stared at the clock in the living room, witnessing at least a hundred hours tick by, before she finally hurried out to her car.

The trip to the familiar row of stores where she would meet Nathaniel was quick. She knew the roads by heart, so it didn't matter how dark it was or which streetlights weren't working. She parked her little Honda in front of the nail salon, halfway between Madam Rosemurtha's parlor and Auto Pro's mechanic shop. Exiting the driver's side, Abby tucked her keys into the pocket of her jeans and stepped onto the sidewalk.

She looked up and down the deserted path in front of the store windows. Nathaniel was nowhere in sight – unless he lay in wait, plotting to scare her senseless. Abby glanced at the time on her phone, not surprised by the fact that she'd arrived a few minutes early. She tucked the phone into her pocket before wandering over to the mechanic shop to take a look at her father.

Using Nathaniel-like stealth, she plastered her back to the face of the brick building and side-stepped toward the window. Checking in on Mark like this was something she'd done quite often in the past few months, yet she still held her breath until she saw him. Abby peered into Auto Pro's window unnoticed, spying her father's legs sticking out from under a shiny red Mercedes. She watched his feet tap in tune to a song playing on the radio beside him.

With that reassuring sight, Abby released the air from her lungs and eased backwards. She didn't even have the chance to turn before she heard footsteps coming from behind her. However, they weren't exactly footsteps. They were more like foot*stomps*. She smiled as she pivoted toward the sound.

Nathaniel walked to her from the direction of the nail salon, dressed in his usual white T-shirt and brown cargo pants, slamming his heavy combat boots deliberately on the cement path with each step he took. Abby rushed forward with her heart skipping inside her chest. "Hi," she said when she skidded to a stop in front of him.

He planted his feet firmly on the sidewalk. "Hi. Was I noisy enough?"

"Oh, yes. Awesomely noisy. Not sneaky at all."

"Good, because I really tried."

Abby smiled even wider. "Where did you come from?"

Nathaniel pointed to the salon door. "I was just getting my nails done."

"Really?"

"No," he laughed. "I was looking for you. Are we still going to dinner?"

"Yeah," she said, staring into his soft eyes, certain he was a dream she hadn't woken up from yet.

"We should go, then."

"Yeah," she repeated, nodding her head but unable to make her legs move.

Nathaniel took a step forward, closing the slight distance between them. He reached out to place his hand on the small of her back. She knew he only touched her because she was too astounded to move and he had no choice but to physically uproot her from the sidewalk, yet the warmth of his fingers only mesmerized her further. "Ladies first," he offered.

Abby floated beside him. At least, she was pretty sure she floated, since she couldn't feel her feet. *Calm down, damn it. If you don't get these fantastical feelings under control, you're going to make a complete fool out of yourself tonight. And if you screw this up, you are going to need all kinds of therapy.*

"We can take the shortcut behind this next row of shops," she suggested while familiarizing herself with the feel of his body beside hers.

"Sure, let's take the shortcut," Nathaniel agreed, his hand dropping to his side when they strolled together into the dimly lit, brick-walled back alley.

Abby looked up to him, focusing on his face as her eyes adapted to the scarcer lighting. She wished his fingers were still pressed against her back, guiding her forward. She wondered if he would touch her again tonight, although she knew better than to dwell on those thoughts, since she still wanted to appear calm and collected.

Taking several deep breaths, she attempted to soothe her unruly mind. Eventually, she managed to calm herself beside him. The moment her thoughts settled, she heard several voices rumbling down the alleyway.

Abby could tell that the muffled sounds came from unseen people around the corner up ahead, creating a distant but distinct commotion. At this moment, she couldn't have cared less. She moved forward in utter happiness, content to walk beside Nathaniel forever.

She barely noticed him slowing his pace when the noises increased. She heard laughter and shouting, which all sounded like the unseen people were having fun. That is, until a woman screamed. Abby startled with the unnerving yell, unsure if it was playful or fearful.

The woman screamed again – shrill and piercing – her alarming shrieks echoing off the brick walls. A familiar chill crawled up Abby's spine. She craned her neck, trying fruitlessly to see around the corner ahead, scared to imagine what she and Nathaniel would find when they finally reached the end of their path.

Doing her best to not freak out, she reached for his hand. She struggled to touch him while her eyes sought his, wanting to take comfort in his calming blue. Nathaniel didn't meet her anxious gaze. He didn't attempt to comfort her in the slightest. Instead, he stopped moving and stood as stone, focused entirely on the ominous noises up ahead.

Abby couldn't see his eyes at all, so she reached for his hand again. She tried over and over to grasp onto his fingers, but she still wasn't able to feel them, no matter how hard she struggled. Her eyes darted to his arm. She huffed as she looked down, wildly frustrated that she couldn't find the strong hand she desperately needed to hold. Except that she *had* found his hand – she just couldn't hold on.

She stared blankly, watching as her fingers moved through his. Certain she must be hallucinating, she tried again to grab his hand. But she could only observe with bizarre detachment while her own hand disappeared into his skin before emerging unscathed on the other side. Cold air rushed over her body, turning her heated breath white before her eyes.

It was Abby's turn to scream.

CHAPTER

THREE

Abby stood in the dark alleyway, staring at Nathaniel. She heard some nutjob screaming absurdly loud somewhere off in the distance. Nathaniel turned back to her, his deep blue eyes searching out her pale ones. The expression now etched on his face was one of actual horror. Honestly, he looked downright terrified – which made Abby realize that *she* was the screaming nutjob.

She pressed her lips shut to make the screeching stop. Then it was quiet. Except for Nathaniel's voice.

"Oh, God. I'm sorry, Abby. That was stupid of me. I wasn't thinking."

She didn't want to listen. She wanted to scream again. But she couldn't make herself – not once the reality of the situation finally dawned on her. This was it. This was the moment she'd been waiting for since the first day she'd seen the insanity in her father's eyes. This was *her* moment.

"Abby," Nathaniel repeated, reaching out to grasp her hand.

"No!" she yelped, shaking her head on purpose while her body shook beyond control. "No, no, no, no."

He forced his arm back to his side. "I'm sorry. I won't touch you again."

She looked up to his eyes. *Why is he talking to me? He isn't real. I made him up. He's just a giant, Hulk-sized fantasy I created in my rotted mind.*

Abby laughed – rather maniacally, if she did say so herself. "Crazy," she muttered. "Deranged. Unglued. Completely insane."

Nathaniel's brow arched. "You're not referring to yourself, are you?"

She cackled again. "Headcase. Lunatic. Cuckoo for Cocoa Puffs."

He cocked his head to the side while keeping his eyes glued to hers. "Abby, listen to me very carefully. You are not crazy. I swear you're not."

She ogled her ultimate hallucination, who stood close enough to touch.

Damn it. There's no way he's real. But if not, then why does he feel so warm? Is my imagination that good, or am I just that nuts? Am I even here, or am I in a loony bin? Have the doctors shot me up with so many drugs that I don't realize I'm in a padded cell? And did they at least let me accessorize my straitjacket?

"I am crazy," Abby declared. "Are you really talking to me right now?"

Nathaniel straightened to his full height. "Yes, I am. I'm standing right in front of you. I'm right here."

"N-no. You're not here. You don't exist. I made you up. I'm just..."

"Don't say you're crazy. Don't even think it. I *am* here."

But he wasn't, of course. She knew that, because she'd put her hand right through his. And she could prove it. She actually needed to prove it.

"Then let me touch you," she insisted.

Nathaniel didn't hesitate. He held out his arm.

Abby's bravery faltered as she stared at his skin. She observed with weary detachment while her trembling fingers moved to his steady ones. With great care, she rested their hands together, palm to palm.

Holy hell. He's so warm and strong.

She yanked her arm away. A choked sob escaped her throat.

Looking back to his eyes, she witnessed the pain inside him like never before. But she couldn't focus on that now. "No, Nathaniel. I don't mean when you're *this* way. Let me touch you when you're the *other* way."

He stared straight into her. Moments passed, strange and slurred. Eventually, his shoulders deflated. He closed his eyes and stilled his body.

Abby studied his stoic face until a cool rush of air swept over her body. When the frigid chill embraced her, she knew Nathaniel had changed. He'd transformed into whatever bizarre thing he was. And yet, with his eyes closed, he looked exactly the same.

God, what is he? A hallucination? A figment of my imagination? A ghost?

She waited forever for Nathaniel's eyes to open. When they did, her breath caught. "Ah-ha!" Abby shouted, pointing to the bright, glowing blue she'd seen in the psychic parlor. "I knew it! I knew your eyes glowed!"

She'd talked herself out of it, but here they were – glowing. Like a candle flame. Like a street lamp. Like the frickin' Olympic torch.

Nathaniel looked at her like she was crazy. But that was okay. Because she was. "Let me touch you *now*," she demanded, although it came out as more of a whisper.

He hesitated only briefly before his hand inched toward hers. Abby had to tear her focus away from his unbelievable eyes to concentrate on his bared forearm. Oddly enough, his skin looked the same. It didn't glow. She couldn't see through it. But she knew this outline in front of her wasn't real, because she could still feel the cold rush of air washing over her body.

"You've got to do this," she told herself as she reached for him.

In slow motion, Abby's fingers moved to Nathaniel's skin. And then *through* his skin, disappearing from her sight until they came out on the other side. Another sob choked its way out of her throat.

She raised her hand and repeated her attempt to touch him, only harder this time, trying with all her might to grab onto something she could see but not feel. She struggled again and again, whooshing through the air that was his arm. She struggled until she became frantic, until her hand shook to the point of spasming, until she hit his solid flesh so hard that the stinging sound reverberated through the alleyway.

Abby looked back to his eyes. They didn't glow anymore. His skin felt warm beneath her fingers. And his beautiful face drew up in pain – terrible, wrenching pain – that obviously had nothing to do with her hitting him.

She cackled again. Then she started pacing in front of him. "I knew it. I just knew it. Crazy. Runs in the family. No escaping."

Laughter continued erupting from her chest while her feet shuffled against the concrete floor. This really was funny. This whole situation was absolutely hysterical. After all, she always knew her mind would leave her one day. She just hadn't thought she'd actually be able to *watch* it go. But here she was, and there it went.

"Abby, I'm not exactly sure what you're talking about, but I swear that you are not crazy."

Nathaniel's determined voice stopped her pacing. She'd almost forgotten that he was here. Of course, he wasn't really here. And yet, for some odd reason, he seemed to think he was.

She turned to pin his seismically stunning eyes with her peculiarly twitching ones. "So, you're a figment of my imagination, then?" she asked, hating the fact that she couldn't have him. She hated herself for making up something so wonderful and then getting her hopes up that she could keep it.

"I'm not," he assured, the words soft and sincere. "I'm real. I'm here."

"Good Lord," she huffed. "I have completely lost it. Haven't I?"

"Abby, you are not crazy."

"Stop saying that."

"You are not crazy."

"I am, damn it! I am crazy!"

Nathaniel took a deep breath. "You and I have been together almost every day for over a week. You can see me. You've touched me. I am real. I don't understand why you think you're going crazy."

"Well, since you insist on talking to me, Hallucination Man, let me count the ways. Your eyes glow. You generate cold air. Oh, and I can put my hand through yours. That all sounds pretty nuts to me."

He smiled softly. "But you're one of the most emotionally stable people I've ever met."

Her jaw dropped open. "Emotionally stable? Are you kidding me right now? I don't know what kind of weirdos you've been hanging out with, but I do know that I was destined to lose it, one way or another."

His gaze narrowed. "What do you mean?"

Abby chewed on her lip. She'd said too much, even to a figment of her imagination. This was the one thing she'd never wanted to tell him. But really, what did it matter now? Her worst nightmare had already come true – she'd gone entirely insane – so it wasn't like she had anything left to lose.

She pushed her shoulders back and raised her chin. "Okay, Nathaniel. Here it is. My dad's crazy. I mean certifiable. In fact, it's actually been certified. By numerous doctors. He's been in and out of so many mental hospitals, I can't even keep track of them all." She stopped talking when her heart pounded in her throat.

Nathaniel's eyes pierced into hers, his thick body way too close.

Abby backed up, numb legs stumbling away. "And now I'm crazy, too."

She hit a wall. Literally. Cold, unforgiving bricks met her spine. Her body slumped back against the solid surface of the alley wall. She wanted to stay upright, but her knees gave out. She sank down onto the frigid cement floor, a heap of gangly legs and mad thoughts.

Abby looked up from the ground at the unearthly being still standing in front of her. For long, curious moments, Nathaniel didn't move. He watched her, inspected her, read her. Eventually, he changed again. He transformed back into the thing he was – the thing she couldn't touch. She knew he'd changed because his eyes glowed for a brief instant before he closed them.

Nathaniel kept his eyes closed as he stiffened his spine. He gasped in air, steep inhales and exhales that grew more and more labored by the second. Abby didn't know what would happen next. Maybe he would catch fire. Or explode. Or evaporate into nothing. She wanted to run away screaming, but none of her muscles would cooperate.

A bare minute later, he changed back. When he reopened his eyes, they were normal again. Well, if she could call that amount of pain *normal*. The level of emotion radiating from inside him would have overwhelmed her, if she had any current capacity to feel. She'd never been so happy to be numb.

Through a telescope, Abby watched him step forward. Nathaniel eased down onto the pavement to sit directly in front of her. He folded his long legs over each other, making his body look a bit smaller. He sat so close now that she could easily touch him. She didn't.

After several moments of baited silence, he glanced to her face. "I must admit, this night didn't work out the way I'd hoped," he said, his voice moving through her skin in the most calming way. "Therefore, I'm just going to try to salvage what I can. I'm pretty sure you're in shock right now, so I'll keep talking until you're better. But you can feel free to chime in anytime, okay?"

Abby couldn't form any words.

Nathaniel offered her a tender smile. "Hmm. Where do I even start? I guess with the fact that you're the only living person who has ever been able to see me. I mean, when I'm not like this. Anyone can see me when I'm like this. But you're the only one who can see me when I'm in my...my other world. I think that's pretty amazing. Don't you?"

He paused for her to respond. She remained involuntarily silent.

"The amazing part is you seeing me, of course. Not the *other world* part. That isn't amazing at all. That is just..." his voice trailed as he looked to the brick wall behind her.

Abby wanted to hear the end of that sentence. Now, neither of them talked. They sat in silence, two mutes. Mutant mutes.

Nathaniel shook his head. "I suppose this is as good a time as any to tell you how sorry I am. I have so much to apologize for, I hardly know how. Please believe I never meant to hurt you. I just didn't know about your dad."

His eyes found hers again. "I wouldn't have tried to tell you about my circumstances if I'd known that, Abby. Honestly, I've spent this whole week trying to figure you out. I knew you were hiding something from me – and I knew it was painful – but, damn. It makes sense to think you're going crazy after what you've seen tonight. Had I known about your father, I definitely wouldn't have done that to you. I wouldn't have done any of this."

Nathaniel leaned closer. "But you just seemed so strong. Hell, you *are* strong. I felt certain that I could tell you everything. I knew you'd be shocked, but I also knew you could handle it."

Abby wanted to laugh. A lot. Instead, she just kept listening.

"I was going to tell you the truth tonight, after dinner. I was going to explain everything as best I can, although I hadn't yet worked out how or where. I definitely wasn't going to do it in a back alleyway, though. But then, I heard that woman scream and I..."

He glanced over his shoulder, down the empty alley to the distant corner where the initial commotion originated. His voice dropped in the now-eerie silence. "The woman is fine. She was with her boyfriend and they were playing around. I'm pretty sure he tickled her, which is why she screamed. It was such a silly thing, but I still overreacted, as usual. And now here we are, sitting on the cold ground, and I can't even get you to talk to me."

He held her fixed gaze. "And I really love it when you talk to me."

Abby cursed in her mind. Why did he have to be an illusion? It wasn't fair.

Nathaniel sighed. "I can sense emotions, by the way. It's a gift of mine – or maybe a curse – I don't know which. I'd love to get your take on it, because I think you can do it, too. You did it the other day, when you asked me why I was in pain."

He stopped talking to watch her, as if the answers he wanted would pop out of her head if he stared hard enough. "That was incredible, you know, when you read me like that. I've never seen a living being who could do it. But then again, everything about you has been incredible, right from that first moment at Rosemurtha's. You defy everything I know."

Abby's eyes nearly popped out of their sockets, since she'd just witnessed the ultimate pot-calling-the-kettle-black.

Nathaniel glanced down at her hands – those floppy things lying against her thighs. He peered back up to her face. "You're so quiet," he said. "I'm worried you might be too cold. People in shock can get really cold. I'd like to touch you now, to make sure you're warm enough. Is that okay?"

She thought about nodding, but nothing actually happened.

He smiled softly. "Okay, then. How about this? If you don't want me to touch you, blink twice."

Her eyelids stayed right where they were.

Nathaniel reached out tentatively, hand suspended mid-air. His fingers descended, slow and steady, until they found hers. He traced the lines of her skin, wrist to fingertips.

Abby gawked at the sight. Her fingers trembled, although she didn't really feel it. She felt him, though. The warmth of his touch was both foreign and fantastical. She watched his smooth, even movements until her fingers finally stopped shaking.

Nathaniel rested their palms together. Everything about him right now felt strong and perfect, which she couldn't understand at all. She didn't know what to believe, what to think, or what to feel.

"You…" she mumbled, the tiny word coming from a million miles away.

Nathaniel focused in on her face. "Yes?"

Abby worked to find her voice. "Y-you really are a hallucination."

He shook his head. "I'm not. I promise."

"But you are. Don't you see? You're too good to be true. You're sweet and caring and beautiful and you listened to me talk for days on end. You even wanted to take me to dinner."

His hand closed around hers. "I swear that I'm here, Abby. I'm just not here exactly the same way you are. And I do still want to take you to dinner."

"Can you eat?" she asked, unsure if a figment should do such a thing.

"Yes, I can eat. When I'm this way."

Abby stared down at his fingers wrapped over hers. "What way is this?"

"I – I don't know what to call it. *Human* seems wrong, since I still like to consider myself human. *Solid* is a better word, I guess."

"You guess? You mean you don't know?"

"No, I don't know. I don't have a manual for this. I'm just doing my best."

"Your best to what?"

"To live, I suppose. If that's what you call this."

Abby's heart filled with hope. "So, you're alive?"

"Well, not like you are."

Her heart sank into her feet. "What do you mean?"

"I mean I haven't been alive like you are for some time."

"Then are you…are you dead?"

Nathaniel squeezed her fingers. "I did die," he answered. "I remember that distinctly. But I never left. I can still walk and talk and breathe, if I want to. So, I don't know if you can say I'm dead. But I'm not entirely alive, either."

Abby struggled to grasp what she could. *His hand is holding mine. He feels warm and solid. His eyes are filled with honesty. Good God, is any of this possible?*

Nathaniel reached to her face, slipping a loose strand of hair over the curve of her ear. "Are you doing okay, Abby?"

"I'm…I'm…"

He exhaled. "You're still in shock. I know you are. Damn, I have screwed this up so royally. I need to do the right thing here, which means I can't stay with you now, no matter how much I want to. You need to go home."

Confusion swamped her battered brain. "Go home? But I thought…"

"I do still want to take you to dinner," he said as he detangled their hands.

"Believe me, I do. But we can't do that tonight, for a number of reasons. One of them being that the waiter might think I drugged you."

Abby frowned, just now realizing how shell-shocked she must look. "But I still want to ask you more questions."

"Do you?" Nathaniel countered, pinning her eyes. "Do you really?"

She stopped talking to chew on her lip. She knew what he was asking her. And she wasn't entirely sure how far down this rabbit hole she wanted to go.

He plastered on a smile. "It's okay. You don't have to decide right now."

Abby held her breath as he stood. He offered his hand to help her up and she took it without hesitation. Once she managed to lift her body from the alley floor, she locked her knees to stand in front of him.

Nathaniel reached to her face, trailing his finger down the side of her cheek. "I've been far too selfish with you, Abby. I haven't given you a choice in any of this, which wasn't fair at all. But I'm going to fix that now. I'm going to leave this up to you."

"H-how?"

He glanced down to the end of the alleyway. "The restaurant is just around that corner, right?"

"Yes."

Nathaniel looked back to her eyes. "Okay. I need you to go home and think about this, please. Take a day to really consider your options. If you decide you still want to ask me questions, then meet me by the front entrance of the restaurant tomorrow night at eight. I won't come to school, or see you at all, before then. I promise I will give you that time to yourself. Also, I don't want you to worry about anything that's happened before now. If you decide you don't want me in your life, I will leave. It'll be like I never existed. You can just go back to the way it was before."

Abby's stomach twisted into knots.

"However," he amended, "if you decide to come back to me, then I promise I'll work to earn your trust. Because I'm truly sorry for the way I forced myself into your life, but I'm not sorry at all that I'm here now."

Abby listened to him with her whole being. She desperately wanted to say something in reply. She just had no idea what that something was.

"Let me get you back to your car," Nathaniel offered, placing his hand on the small of her back. His gentle touch propelled her legs forward, yet she barely felt anything until they emerged from the alleyway onto the front sidewalk. In the light of the street lamps, Abby could finally ingest her unremarkable surroundings. Everything around her looked the same as when she'd arrived for a date with her dream man, although the night had turned out a bit differently than she'd hoped.

When they reached her car, Nathaniel waited patiently while she fumbled to extract her keys from the pocket of her jeans. He opened the door for her, standing guard until she slid down into the driver's side. She glanced up at him from the little cocoon of her seat.

"Can you drive?" he asked.

Abby nodded.

"Are you absolutely certain you can make it home safely?"

She didn't miss the concern in his bright blue eyes. She wondered if this would be the last time she'd ever see them. "Yes, Nathaniel. I'll be fine."

"Please. Please be okay." He closed her door and stood back.

Abby kept her gaze fixed on him for as long as she could, staring into her rearview mirror while his thick body faded into the darkness.

It had only been a few hours since she'd seen him. Only a day had passed since they'd last sat at this table during lunch. Yet her picnic bench now felt lonelier, harder, splinter-ier.

Abby adjusted herself against the cold, unforgiving wood as she stared out into the forest. Each moment since she'd driven away from Nathaniel last night felt dim and out of focus. At least, until now. Sitting here, alone once again, everything began to clear.

"You need to think this through," she whispered as her fingers slipped slowly across the uneven tabletop. "You're running out of time. You have to make a decision."

Abby sucked in a breath, wondering if her mind could even comprehend everything she'd been through in the past day. She wasn't sure of much, but if the knowledge she'd gained from watching countless TV talk shows was indeed reliable, then she knew that every process had steps. Whether someone wanted to lose weight, quit smoking, or grieve, there were steps they must take. Consequently, there must be steps to going insane, too.

She figured the road to insanity would involve a talking-to-yourself stage and a crouching-in-fetal-position stage. However, she wasn't sure where the making-up-gorgeous-guys-in-your-head stage came in. But it had to be there. After all, if that step didn't exist, then she was a mostly sane person who could see ghosts. And that wasn't possible, right?

This was the question repeating on a continuous loop in her mind since the moment Nathaniel tucked her into the seat of her car last night. Abby didn't actually remember getting to her house, although she did remember receiving an obscene finger gesture from a passing driver around the time she realized she was going twenty miles under the speed limit. Thank goodness her little car knew the way home.

She also didn't remember getting into bed. But she did remember lying there all night, thinking about Nathaniel. Not about how she'd put her hand through his – or how his eyes glowed – but about how wonderful he'd been to her all week and how much she'd wanted him in her life. She'd thought and thought and thought, far into the night and throughout her classes this morning, and she always returned to the same question.

"Am I crazy, or just able to see ghosts?" she asked as the breeze coursing through the Blue Ridge shifted the trees beside her, ruffling her hair.

She laughed at the sound of her voice echoing in the cool mountain air. "Okay, so I am talking to myself. But I'm not sucking my thumb, pulling out my hair, or rocking back and forth. Therefore, if I am crazy, it seems I'm being very rational about it. I suppose that means there's a chance I haven't lost her mind utterly and without hope."

Abby grimaced. "But ghosts? Really?" she huffed, forcing her windblown hair back behind her ears. "Of course, seeing a ghost was my entire purpose for going to the psychic parlor in the first place."

The granola bar she'd forced down hours ago threatened to show itself again. Abby swallowed hard. She was pretty sure that spontaneously vomiting while sitting alone at a picnic table constituted a stage of insanity, so she preferred to keep those tenacious oats down.

She glanced at the time on her phone. If Nathaniel did exist, then in eight hours he would show up at the restaurant. He would stand out front and wait for her to come to him, which meant she now had two choices.

On the one hand, she could take him up on his offer. That choice, simply put, would be a travesty of epic proportions. If she invited a ghost – or whatever he was – into her world, then she would destroy any chance she ever had at a normal life. And normal sounded so wonderful.

On the other hand, she could go back to the life she'd led a week ago. Yet she couldn't imagine purposefully choosing that state of being. Depressed, fearful, and empty: her sorry little trilogy. Nathaniel took all of that away. He gave her something to look forward to. He made her feel free and happy. He made her laugh.

How could she possibly give him up?

Abby barely heard the end-of-lunch bell ring in the distance. She dragged herself off of her picnic bench and hauled her backpack onto her shoulder. She stared at the grass as she plodded toward school.

After she forced her way through the thick brown metal door and into the bustling hallway, she did her best to blend in with the unruly hoard of students rushing to their classes. She wound her way into history class and flopped down in her chair, immediately looking out of the window to the world beyond. Her teacher cleared his throat mere seconds later, redirecting her attentions.

Abby pulled out her notebook and pen and jotted several words in the pages, pretending to be engrossed in Mr. Puryear's nasally lecture. It wasn't all that difficult. She certainly knew how to act normal. She knew exactly how to smile, sit at attention, and nod assuredly, so that no one could see inside. She'd had years of experience pretending everything was fine while her father inadvertently destroyed their lives.

Normalcy had always been her ultimate, seemingly unattainable goal. Yet sitting in this classroom now – maintaining poise through the unemotional recounting of strategic massacres – didn't give Abby any happiness at all. Pretending life was perfect didn't make it so. Striving for normalcy wouldn't help her find the joy that Nathaniel already provided.

God, Nathaniel gave her that joy so willingly. She couldn't fathom abandoning the bliss she felt whenever he stood beside her. She couldn't bear to lose the sound of her own laughter whenever it matched his. She couldn't simply forget how her heart skipped whenever he smiled. Whether he was a ghost, a hallucination, or something otherwise inexplicable, she just couldn't give him up.

Abby gripped onto her pen with all her might, wishing the answer wasn't so simple. She wished she had a fighting chance at normal. But in truth, she'd already known her answer last night in the alleyway. When Nathaniel assured her that she would never have to see him again, her entire body rejected the thought. She couldn't retreat into solitude anymore. She simply refused.

So, this is it. Crazy or not, ghost or not, I will invite Nathaniel into my life.

Abby exhaled as she released her death-grip on her pen. Her body eased down into her chair, overcome by a calming peace that made no sense at all. Maybe this was another step toward lunacy, but at least she'd made the decision herself. Now, she just had to make it through the next eight hours.

ABBY CONTINUED to act as normal as possible for the remainder of her classes. She held herself quite confidently as she drove slowly home from school at the end of the school day. She could have won an Oscar for her smile alone during the afternoon with her father, cooking dinner and packing his meal and saying goodbye before he left for work. No outside observer could have known how her mind and heart reeled as the sun sank beneath the horizon. No one could have possibly realized how uncertain and ecstatic and terrified she felt when she collapsed into the driver's seat of her car. She held it all together beautifully, right up until she parked in front of Madam Rosemurtha's parlor and killed the engine.

"Come on, you can do this," Abby encouraged her trembling fingers while they struggled to push her keys into the pocket of her jeans. After three fumbling attempts, she leapt outside, slammed the car door shut, and tried again. This time, she succeeded.

"Yes," she whispered, glancing into her sideview mirror to make sure she didn't appear too freaked out. She practiced smiling at what she could see of her reflection in the darkness. "Okay. Normal enough, I think."

Abby looked up to see the gold crystal ball painted on the parlor window before she turned around, crossed the lamplit street, and ventured into the dimmer back alley. She probably should have parked by the restaurant and simply walked to the front door, but something made her come back here. Perhaps she wanted to return to the scene of the crime and think about what had happened last night, in order to decide if it was real.

Glancing up and down the alleyway as she moved forward, Abby took note of the fire escape ladders and brick walls. Eventually, she found the spot where she'd collapsed onto the ground the night before. Her stomach did a somersault.

Had that actually happened? Had Nathaniel sat with her, talked to her, and held her hand? Or was he nothing more than a striking delusion? Was she going to look like an idiot tonight, speaking out loud to no one in particular? Or would other people see him, too? Was there any chance on earth that she would look like a normal teenage girl on a date with a beautiful boy?

Dragging her gaze from the empty spot on the ground, Abby forced herself farther down the alley. She turned the corner at the end, taking a few more steps before her feet halted in their tracks. From her shrouded position in the dark space between two stores, she could see the restaurant across the street. Her breath caught as she searched for Nathaniel.

She found him in no time at all. He stood by the restaurant entrance, entirely motionless. Abby reached to the wall at her side, using the cool bricks for support. She'd actually forgotten just how stunning he was. Breathtaking, in every sense. If he was her hallucination, she was a frickin' genius. Well, except for the white T-shirt, brown pants, and combat boots.

Am I not creative enough to have an imaginary friend who changes clothes?

Abby surrendered to nervous giggles, relieving a fraction of the tension in her body. But then, she saw him move. She quieted, even though he couldn't have heard her from this distance. He started pacing a five-foot section of sidewalk as his eyes scanned the street, and his restless actions made her realize the strangest thing: *Nathaniel is nervous.*

"My God," she mumbled as a rush of shame swept through her. "I've been so selfish." After all, she hadn't once stopped to consider what this must be like for him. She'd been too wrapped up in her own thoughts and fears. She'd been too consumed by her possible descent into madness to consider his own dilemmas.

"What if he is real?" Abby wondered. "How is he here? Why is he here? Why am I the only one who can see him? And is it possible that he's even lonelier than I am?"

Right at this moment, she didn't care if she was crazy. She only cared about Nathaniel. She started trembling. Anticipation, perhaps. Or excitement. But not fear.

Abby stepped out into the light. She moved forward, focused entirely on his anxiously pacing form. She slowed when she reached the intersection, aware that she still needed to look both ways before crossing the street.

Nathaniel saw her then. His eyes zeroed in on her as she teetered at the edge of the curb. The tension in his face eased in an instant. He smiled, igniting a bright spark in his ocean blue. Abby felt it across every inch of skin she owned.

She forgot to look both ways. Thankfully, nothing plowed her over while she drifted across the road. She didn't stop moving until she stood directly in front of him. Gazing up into his flawlessly clear eyes, she saw no pain inside them. All she saw was happiness.

"You came," Nathaniel breathed.

Abby managed to nod her head.

"That's wonderful. I mean, thank you. Really. Thank you. Do you...do you still want to go to dinner?"

"Yes." Her voice came out strong and certain. "I'd love to."

Nathaniel's grin widened. He didn't need to uproot her feet from the sidewalk this time. She matched his pace without any missteps, her eagerness to explore this new world growing by leaps and bounds. She felt absolutely giddy. That is, until they reached the door and the hostess appeared.

Abby's heart ground to a halt. Would this very pretty restaurant employee be able to see her imaginary friend? Or would her single-passenger fantasy ship crash and burn right now?

Abby fixed her sights solely on the other young woman who turned toward Nathaniel. The hostess smiled rather flirtatiously the instant she saw his face. A second later, she glanced down at his clothes and pursed her lips.

Good Lord, woman! Who cares how he dresses! You can actually see him!

"Yes, um, sir. How may I help you tonight?"

Nathaniel cleared his throat. "Table for two, please."

"Certainly. Just give me a moment."

The hostess glared at his boots before sauntering away, but Abby didn't pay the woman any further mind. She preferred to occupy herself by staring at Nathaniel. At the height of his shoulders, the curve of his jaw, and the intensity in his eyes as he scanned the crowded restaurant.

Her gaze drifted down his arm to the hand hanging lazily by his side. *He is real, right? That woman talked to him, so he must be real. But can I touch him?*

Abby reached out very slowly, with just one finger, and poked him on the wrist. His hand jostled a bit. She stared at the movement in utter fascination.

Still not quite sure of this reality, she poked him again. And again. And then again, amazed by the way his solid arm moved in response. The fifth time she poked him, he grabbed hold of her hand. He wound their fingers together, securing her to his side.

Her eyes rose to his face as heat rose in her cheeks.

Nathaniel shook his head and chuckled.

The hostess returned. "Right this way, please."

He pulled Abby alongside him as they followed the woman into the room.

FOUR

"Have I thanked you yet for coming?" Nathaniel asked.

Abby sat in her slatted wood chair, staring across the red-and-white checkered tablecloth at the huge slice of pizza sitting on Nathaniel's plate. It was piled with every imaginable topping. Double everything, just as he'd ordered. She watched while he examined it, turning the plate side to side, plotting his attack.

When they'd first sat down at their table, she was too amazed by Nathaniel's interactions with other people – the hostess who gave him a generous smile despite her obvious disapproval of his outfit, the waiter who arrived shortly after to take their order, the group of teenage girls sitting in the corner of the room who blatantly ogled him – to form conscious thought. But now, Abby's mile-high list of questions grew taller by the minute. "Yes, you already thanked me," she assured, wondering how to begin her inquisition.

"Well, I want to make sure you heard it. You had plenty of reasons not to come tonight. To be honest, I wasn't sure you would. So, thank you. Again."

"You're welcome," she replied, still staring. She'd been staring at Nathaniel constantly, to the point of rudeness, yet she couldn't stop. He was the North Pole to her internal compass and now she knew why. It's because he wasn't normal. Apparently, she and normal just didn't get along. Although, as she watched him prepare to pounce on his pizza, she honestly didn't mind.

Nathaniel finally picked up the gooey, gargantuan slice and shoved it in his mouth. Abby took a bite of her own pizza as he chewed and swallowed with a look of sheer curiosity on his face. He set the partially-devoured slice back down and looked to her. "Mmm. I can see why people like this so much."

She shifted in her seat. "I take it you've never had pizza before?"

"No, I didn't get pizza back in my day. I've heard people say so much about it through the years. Some people get very emotional over pizza. I've been quite curious." He picked up the slice again, his eyes rolling back in his head as he ingested another colossal mouthful.

Abby grinned at his giddiness. She figured his current existence was kind of like being a kid in a candy store, seeing all the goodies but never tasting them. *A ghost's life must really suck*, she considered, cringing at the words in her head. *Ghost. Ugh.*

Lost in his own little world of pizza-pies, Nathaniel shivered in delight.

"Hey, can I, uh..." she fumbled. "Can I ask you some questions now?"

"Um-hmm," he mumbled mid-chew.

"You said you didn't get pizza back in your day. When exactly was that?"

He returned the remaining crust to his plate. "I was born in 1926."

Abby coughed. "Oh. Okay." She took in a shaky breath in. "What, um, what did you die of? I mean, if it's not too hard to talk about."

Nathaniel took a sip of his soda, watching in fascination while the bubbles tickled the ice cubes. "That's really fizzy," he noted. "I died in World War II."

She stared harder. How could he be enraptured by soda fizz, yet entirely unconcerned about his own death? "World War II? Were you a soldier?"

"Yes, I was at Normandy. It's still a pretty well-known battle, I think."

"Normandy? What year was that?"

"1944."

Abby laughed. That information would have been handy to have last week in history. Then maybe her teacher wouldn't have given her the evil eye.

Nathaniel's head tilted. "What's so funny?"

"Nothing, really. Just more odd thoughts from my misfiring brain."

He wiped his hands on a napkin before matching her blatant stare. "Your brain is not misfiring, you know. Still in shock, perhaps, but that is completely my fault. I'm truly sorry about what happened last night."

"Which particular part are you referring to?"

"The part where I...I sort of left you alone for a minute."

Abby shivered. "Oh. Right. Why did that happen, again?"

"It was because I heard that woman's screams coming down the alleyway. I got worried and needed to know if she was safe."

"And did you fly over there, or something?"

"No, no. I can't fly. I was actually there with you the entire time. I just reverted back to my other world, in order to feel her emotions. I wanted to see if she needed my help."

"Then you're some kind of emotional – spiritual – policeman?"

"Policeman? Hmm," Nathaniel considered. "I've never thought of it that way. I'm just used to always knowing how people feel. I've been surrounded by emotions for so long that it's difficult when I can't immediately sense them. But that's no excuse for what I did. I should never have left you physically, not even for a moment. My actions were stupid and sloppy. I just hope you'll understand that I was trying to help, and that I don't have much practice being around people. I hope you can forgive me for not being more careful with you."

Abby's heart brimmed over with guilt. He'd been trying to help someone last night and all she did was whine about the bats invading her belfry. "Please don't apologize anymore. Coming to terms with this now is totally my problem," she assured, certain it was true. She'd made the decision to be here with him. She loved being here.

"But I want to help you come to terms with it. I'll answer anything I can. I'll tell you all my goofy parts, which I obviously have a lot of."

"You know, I never dreamed your goofy parts could be worse than mine."

"Oh, but they are. I have tons and tons of goofy parts."

Abby watched Nathaniel grin, as if a great weight had been lifted from his shoulders. He was happy right now – because of her – and that realization made her toes curl up inside her shoes. "So, am I really the only person who can see you when you're not solid?"

"You are. Everyone else looks right through me when I'm in my other world. I've grown quite used to it, actually. When I showed up at Rosemurtha's that first night, and you looked directly at me, I was so confused."

"Oh, right, the Madam. I almost forgot about her. Did she conjure you up with her magical soothsaying skills?"

Nathaniel chuckled. "No, I don't think old Rosemurtha is that good."

Abby sighed. "Yeah, I figured as much. But if she didn't summon you, then why were you there? Do you really work at her parlor?"

He sucked down the last of his soda, making slurping sounds with the straw. "No, I don't work there. I don't even know if you can call what I do *work*. I just went there because it seemed like a good place to start."

"To start what?"

"Well, I'm new in town, like I said. When I find myself somewhere new, the first thing I usually do is test out the emotions in the area. During the day, I went to the high school to get a sense of the students. At night, I looked for another place with a lot of people. I found this shopping center and I moved through it, sensing everything I could. That's when I felt you."

Abby's brow rose. "You *felt* me?"

"I did. Your emotions were very high that night," he explained, his warm eyes holding hers. "You drew me to you."

She licked her dry lips. "And what emotions did I have?"

"Sadness," Nathaniel answered, clasping his hands together on the table-top. "Some confusion, but mostly sadness. I felt your pain so deeply. You made it easy for me to decide to be solid for you. I haven't done that for many people. Not many at all."

"You aren't normally solid?"

"Almost never."

"Why not? Does it hurt?"

"It's...unnerving."

"But you've been solid for me at school. Every day during lunch."

"Yes, I have. For you."

Abby's heart tripped over itself. She worked to keep her focus, to not zone out to a place of psychedelic bliss where the only things that existed were her and Nathaniel and comfortable picnic benches. "So, you mostly stay in your other world, I take it?"

"Pretty much always. I think it's the reason I haven't changed physically from the teenager I was when I died. I still look the way I did in 1944, for the most part."

She examined him up and down, absorbing the form of his eighteen-year-old body, coupled with eyes full of wisdom far beyond those sparse years. She couldn't quite comprehend the reality of what he was just yet, but she did finally understand why he dressed the way he did. "And what did you do before you became a soldier in Normandy?"

"I lived with my family in Oklahoma. We had a farm."

"A farm?" Abby echoed. An image of Nathaniel wearing overalls and a straw hat popped into her head. She opened her mouth to ask a random farming question when their server returned to the table. She ogled the man – a college student by the looks of him – impatiently waiting for him to leave.

He asked if they needed anything right now, to which Nathaniel replied, "No, thanks." As Mr. College walked away, Abby exhaled in relief, reassured of her own sanity each time someone spoke to her delightful delusion. Other people saw him, which meant he really wasn't a figment of her imagination. But even with that assurance, her devious mind refused to grant her any peace. It conjured up a vision of Nathaniel in a field, planting and plowing, doing hard farm labor under a hot sun, his shirt off, his muscles tense, his skin damp and glistening...

"Abby?"

Her cheeks burned as she met his inquisitive gaze. "Yes?"

"What are you thinking about?"

"Um..."

"Do you find the waiter attractive?"

"No!" she protested in panic. "Why on earth would you think that?"

"Because you look...I don't know. Smitten, I guess."

She glared down at the tablecloth in utter mortification.

Nathaniel sighed. "I wish I could return to my other world for a minute."

Her eyes darted back to his. "God, please don't. Please don't leave me here talking to myself."

"Don't worry. I won't. It would simply be easier."

"Oh, damn," Abby cursed, just now realizing how much time they'd spent together tonight. "It must be hard for you to be solid for this long. I'm so sorry I didn't think about it sooner. Are you in pain? We should leave."

"No, that's not the problem," he assured, his eyes roaming over her face. "I feel fine. Except that I really want to feel what you're feeling, even if only for a few seconds."

"Feel what I'm feeling? Why?"

"Because it's frustrating not knowing."

"Maybe that's best," she mumbled under her breath.

Nathaniel sat back in his chair, watching her.

Abby fidgeted with her napkin. *You're gorgeous, okay? Is that what you want to know? That I'm still not sure you're real, but I can't tear my eyes off you?*

"Hey," he prompted, his voice edged with concern. "I know you're putting up a brave front here. But how are you handling all of this, really?"

"I don't know," she replied in truth. "Most likely, I'm crazy. But now, I'll throw in the possibility that I'm asleep and dreaming. Although I'm not sure which is worse."

"I think crazy would be worse."

"Yeah, but if I'm crazy, you'll probably be around for a while. If I'm dreaming, I'll be waking up soon."

"I see. And if you're neither crazy nor dreaming?"

She shook her head. "That's not possible. This can't be real."

"Can't it? Weren't you searching for something like this at Rosemurtha's? Some proof of life after death?"

"I guess. Sort of."

Nathaniel gave her an easy smile. "Well, now you have your proof."

Abby realized in this moment that his smile was as fascinating as the rest of his existence. "Tell me, please. What is your other world like?"

"It's a lot like this one, really. Everything looks basically the same to me, here or there."

"And the emotions? How do you sense them?"

He shifted in his seat. "The emotions are interesting. I have to concentrate to pick up on them. I can focus my energy on a group of people, to get a general sense of what is happening, or I can zero in on one or two individuals to understand very specific feelings. It makes them very colorful."

"Colorful?"

"Yes. Emotions have very distinct colors."

"So then, when you look at someone, they're all polka dots or rainbows?"

Nathaniel laughed. "Not exactly. Most people are only one or two colors at a time. It didn't take long for me to figure out which emotions went with which colors."

"You mean every emotion has a color you can see?"

"Yeah, pretty much."

"Wow. Will you tell me what the colors mean?"

"Of course. If you'd like that."

"God, I would love that. Although, on second thought," Abby amended, sitting bolt upright in her chair, "can I try to guess them, instead?"

"Sure," he said, leaning forward. "Where do you want me to start?"

"Um, at the beginning, I suppose?"

"The beginning? That would definitely be red, then. It was the first color I saw in my other world. It was everywhere."

"Red," she considered. "Well, you were in Normandy when you died. I take it you were still there when you crossed over into your other world?"

Nathaniel nodded slowly. "Yeah. I was."

"Okay. Then red has to be bad, right? I mean, you died in battle, so there must have been weapons, shouting, and blood. Does red mean anger, maybe?"

"That's very good," he praised. "A deep red, like crimson, is usually anger or fear. They go hand-in-hand. But a brighter red can be more like confusion or searching."

"Man, that is...that is actually really, really cool. I mean, except for the Normandy part. And the bloodshed. And the dying, of course."

She grimaced, yet Nathaniel only smiled.

"It's okay, Abby. I don't mind talking about it. It was a long time ago."

"But I don't want to bring up bad memories. I never want to hurt you."

"You don't. Trust me. Nothing hurts when I'm with you."

"Really?" she asked, even though she could see the truth of it in his eyes. There was no pain in his bright, clear blue. Not right now.

"Really," he assured. "Now, do you want to keep going with this?"

"Yes," she said, not sure if he meant the color game or something else entirely. But she did know that her answer wouldn't change either way.

"Then would you like to try another?"

"Please. I'm more than ready."

"Okay. How about the color green?"

"Green," she echoed, working to refocus on the game. "Well, green reminds me of trees, grass, and mountains. And they all feel very calming."

"You're right. Green is peaceful."

"But what about people being green with envy?"

"No, envy is more of a mustard yellow."

"That's weird."

"Yeah, tell me about it," he laughed.

Abby relished the sparkle in his eyes. "Can we do another one?"

"Okay. How about, um...how about black?"

"Black, huh? Well, I know there are black holes in the universe. And I remember that the plague was called 'the black death'. Which makes me think it has something to do with emptiness, or maybe death."

"Yes, black can mean death. Or deep sickness, physical or psychological."

She shook her head, wanting a different emotion. "Is there another color?"

"Sure. Blue is pretty distinct."

"Blue? I like blue. I mean, who doesn't? There's the blue sky, the blue ocean, and..." Abby stared into his stunning blue eyes. "I imagine it has to do with something deep and profound. Is that right?"

"It is. Blue shows when someone is in thought, or has just come to some kind of understanding. You're really good at this, Abby. I'm impressed by the way you've reasoned these out."

She smiled with her whole body. "Are there any more?"

"Well, uh..." Nathaniel glanced down to his hands, unclasping them to drum his fingers against the table.

"What? What's next?"

"Well, there's, um..."

"Oh, please tell me. I love this game."

He looked back to her face. "Okay, then. There is purple."

"Purple? That's my favorite color."

"Yes, I'm well aware."

Abby studied him as he sat across from her with his all-too-innocent grin. "This is actually a hard one," she admitted. "I mean, what is purple in life? Grapes? Or flowers? Or maybe..." her voice trailed off as she considered the fact that a person could probably turn purple – that is, if they were embarrassed enough – like when her cheeks caught fire earlier as she'd imagined Nathaniel-the-farmer with his bared, heated chest.

"Do you give up?" he prodded.

She watched his eyes glimmer in the dim lighting, watched them focus on her mouth when she moistened her lips. "No, I don't give up," she declared, summoning all her courage. "Does purple have to do with attraction?"

"Yes, it does." Nathaniel's gaze lingered on her lips for a moment before shifting back up to her eyes. "Attraction, excitement, desire. There are other words, but you get the idea."

"Yeah. I get the idea." Abby focused entirely on the sight of his delectable mouth. She thanked the stars that he wasn't in his other world right now, since he would see her in every shade of purple. Her skin would probably ooze purple. She might actually be able to pee purple.

The waiter showed up at their table again, saving her from the perils of her vile brain. "Is there anything else I can get you guys?" Mr. College suggested.

"Are there desserts?" Nathaniel asked.

"Sure. Ice cream, chocolate cake, apple pie..."

"Apple pie, please. Two slices," Nathaniel jumped in. A second later, he looked to her. "I mean, if that's okay with you."

Abby nodded. "Yeah, fine."

"Okay," Mr. College said. "Be right back."

Once the waiter stepped away, Nathaniel practically shook with anticipation. "Oh, man. I can't believe I get to have apple pie tonight."

"I guess you've had apple pie before?"

"My mom used to make it all the time. I haven't had apple pie in..."

Abby did the math. "Well over sixty years?"

"Yeah. That long." He peered over at her plate. "You didn't eat much pizza. I know I'm probably to blame for your lack of appetite, but I hope you'll have some pie with me."

"Of course. I'd love to."

The waiter returned before she knew it, before Nathaniel had the chance to calm down. He nearly salivated when the plates landed on the table. Abby thought Mr. College might lose a hand if he didn't pull away fast enough.

She exhaled when their server escaped unscathed. "You don't have to use utensils if you don't want to, Nathaniel. You could just dive in, face first."

He met her eyes across the table. "You wouldn't mind?"

"Not at all."

Abby was half-relieved and half-sad when he picked up his fork. She watched in amazement while he devoured the apple-filled creation. "Why are you even here?" she wondered aloud. "Because, unfortunately, I don't think it's just to eat."

Nathaniel paused his ravenous consumption to look at her. "I don't know why I'm here. I follow...I mean, I get drawn to places. I was drawn to your high school. I've been at several others in the past."

"Always high schools?"

"To start with, yes."

"Do you go to high schools because you were a teenager when you...when you changed over to your other world?"

"I suppose that's part of it. Also, high school kids have a lot of emotions. I can always find someone who is hurting and in need of help."

"And here comes Nathaniel, the spiritual policeman?"

"Yeah. That's me, I guess." He finished the last of his pie, struggling to collect the remaining crumbs on his fork.

Abby observed his pitiful attempt to shovel scraps of crust into his mouth. "Here," she said, taking a bite of hers and handing him the rest. "Have this."

"Are you sure? You didn't eat much."

"It's better when you eat. More enjoyable to watch."

He grinned before taking her plate and shoving another bite in.

Abby settled back in her chair, content to watch him eat for the rest of the night. "So, tell me, spiritual policeman. What happens when you go to someone's rescue?"

"Mmm," he mumbled between mouthfuls. "I don't always have to. Sometimes, I just hang around a school for a while and nothing happens. But there have been several times when I found a person who needed help. Then, I did what I had to do."

"Like what?"

"Well, it all started a little over twenty years ago. That was the first time I realized I could turn solid."

"Twenty years ago? But it's been well over sixty since Normandy. What did you do for the first forty or so?"

Nathaniel chewed the final pie morsel and set his fork down. "When I first woke up in my other world, still in the middle of a battle, I was completely confused. I saw my body lying in the sand, and I figured I had died, but I didn't have any clue about what I was supposed to do next. I still don't know, really, but I've learned a lot since then. Soon after Normandy, I found my way to Oklahoma and just stayed with my family."

"You stayed with your family? Did they see you?"

"No," he said, staring sadly at the second empty plate. "They never did."

"I'm sorry," Abby offered, knowing it wasn't only the lack of pastry that upset him. "It must have been really hard for you to see them when they couldn't see you."

"It was hard, but I got used to it. I didn't know any other way to exist, so I stuck around them and watched as they grew old. I finally made the decision to leave Oklahoma in the 1980s."

The far-off look in his eyes flustered her. "You don't have to talk about this, you know. Not if you don't want to."

After a quiet, unsettling moment, Nathaniel refocused on her. "The first years aren't much to talk about. I'll start from the '80s. It was such a weird decade, so different from when I grew up. If you think high school is bad now, you should have seen it then. Girls in cut-off sweatshirts and leg warmers. Boys in popped-collar polos and blazers. Everybody's hair all puffy. Yeesh."

Abby laughed at the disgruntled picture he drew.

Nathaniel gave her a lopsided smile. "Anyway," he continued, "I eventually found my way to a high school in Kansas. At first, the air was so charged with emotion that I would simply stand in the halls and absorb it. I watched everyone's colors change from moment to moment, and I tried to figure out human nature, but I wasn't any good at it. Instead, I just tried to see who had the most on their plate, so to speak. After a few months, I honed in on one girl: Maria."

"Maria? Was she in trouble?"

"She was. At first, I didn't know what was wrong. Her colors swirled in shades of red and even some black, and she always looked so sad. Finally, one day, I followed her home. I had to stay at her house for nearly a week before I figured out what the problem was."

Abby's gut filled with dread. "What was it?"

"Her dad beat her. He beat her mother, too. I was there one night when he got drunk. He had the worst look on his face and his body glowed in a deep, blood red. Even his eyes looked red to me. I could see the sickness inside him as he beat Maria's mother until she nearly died. I felt entirely overwhelmed, sitting on the sidelines, not able to act. God, I didn't know what to do. I had no idea what I could do.

"As I stood there, totally helpless, Maria tried to pull her father away from her mother. She screamed at him and he turned and literally threw her across the room. Maria landed in a corner, making this awful thudding sound when she hit the wall. Then he started advancing on her, coated in red and black, like the devil himself. I pushed my body in between the two of them like a barricade and willed myself to stop him. That was the first time – the first time I ever appeared in solid form."

Abby couldn't feel her limbs. "Nathaniel, that is so horrible."

"Yeah, it was. I only wish I'd been able to do something sooner."

"What did you do then?"

"Well, her dad kind of freaked out when he saw me. For several seconds, he stared in shock. But then he came around and started hitting me. He really went at it for some time."

"Holy crap! I hope you hit him back!"

Nathaniel shook his head. "No, no. I didn't need to. I realized quickly that I could heal my body by returning to my other world. When my injuries got bad enough, I would simply change back and reenergize myself."

"But didn't it hurt when he hit you?"

"Hell, yeah, it hurt. He was like a boxer."

"Then why on earth didn't you defend yourself?"

"Because I was capable of other things. Whenever I disappeared, he would punch through air and stumble over. By the time he picked himself back up, I stood solid and fully healed in front of him, which made him even more confused. It felt like a long time, but it probably only took a few minutes before he realized something otherworldly was happening. When he finally seemed ready to listen, I looked him straight in the eyes and told him that if he ever hit his wife or child again, the wrath of demons everywhere would be upon him. And then I made myself look really mean. He sort of crumpled into a heap on the floor and started crying, so I guess he bought it."

A chill skittered down Abby's spine. "What happened to Maria?"

Nathaniel squeezed onto his fork. "She'd passed out when she hit the wall, so she never saw me. I only stayed solid long enough to call 911. Then I changed back and waited until the police got there. They arrested Maria's dad and took her and her mom to the hospital. I stayed for a few days to keep watch over them. They were okay, and her father was in jail, so I moved on."

Abby's eyes glazed over, unable to imagine all the wretched things Nathaniel had witnessed in his many, many years. She wanted to give him every slice of apple pie in the whole world. "So, that's what you do, then? You go from town to town, high school to high school, watching awful things happen and helping people you've never met, who can't even thank you?"

He shrugged. "I told you I don't have a manual, Abby. I'm not a hero. It's just the only thing that makes this existence of mine feel worthwhile."

"But, Nathaniel...you are a hero. Don't you see that?"

"No. I'm really not."

"Yes, you are. You're the most incredible kind of hero. And please let me be the one to finally say thank you."

"Thank you? For what?"

"For every person who never had the chance. Thank you from Maria, and from everyone else I don't even know about. It doesn't begin to do you justice, but thank you."

Abby reached her hand across the table to cover his. Nathaniel smiled as he threaded their fingers together. She sighed with the warmth of his skin, wishing she had more words – words no one had even come up with yet – to explain how phenomenal he was.

When the waiter returned with the check, Abby jumped. She yanked her hand away from Nathaniel's, as if she'd been caught doing something terribly wrong. But that couldn't be true, because touching him felt right in every way.

"Anytime you're ready," Mr. College said before leaving again.

"That guy sure does show up a lot," Nathaniel grumbled while reaching for the bill. "Maybe he's the one smitten with you."

"Oh, I think he's just doing his job. Besides, it's late and they probably close soon. And I highly doubt that he's smitten with me."

"Then he's blind."

Abby wanted to hold Nathaniel's compliment in both hands and dance with it, but she was caught off guard when he pulled out a large roll of cash from the pocket of his cargo pants. "Holy crap. Where did you get that?"

"What?" he asked with angelic innocence.

"All that cash?"

"Well, I asked you out to dinner, so I needed to be able to pay."

"But that's a lot of money."

He removed four twenties from the roll and set them under the check before pocketing the rest. "That ought to cover it," he said, rising from his seat to step toward hers. "Shall we go?"

Abby pinned his bright eyes as she stood to her full, albeit much shorter, height. "You're not going to tell me where you got the money from, are you?"

Nathaniel settled his hand on the small of her back, guiding her across the room toward the front door. "I've just acquired a few things over time. I assure you, it's nothing illegal."

She stared up at him as they stepped out into the cool night air. Her mind raced in a hundred directions – from the origins of the cash in his pocket, to the feel of his strong hand on her back, to everything in between. She chewed on her lip and her thoughts while they walked across the street and into the alleyway. "So, you've acquired things over time? What kind of things?"

"Oh, you know how you tend to pick things up. They're just things."

Abby barely registered the fact that they now walked through the same alley as the night before, when her entire life was turned upside down and spanked. "Yeah? And where do you keep these things?"

"I can carry a few things with me," he explained, leading her to the other end of the alley and out toward the row of stores connected to Rosemurtha's parlor. Thankfully, he steered clear of her father's auto shop. "It's really just pocket change, Abby. Are you worried I robbed a bank or something?"

"No! No, no, that's not what I meant at all."

Nathaniel chuckled as they arrived at her car. He reached down, pulling on the handle to open the driver's door for her. "Do you mind if I ride home with you tonight? Just to make sure you get there safely?"

"Yes, please," she answered, unsure of so many things at this moment and yet absolutely certain she wasn't ready for him to leave her yet. After she collapsed into her seat, Nathaniel shut her door and walked around to the passenger's side. Abby watched in giddy wonder while he climbed into her tiny car and folded his large body up on the seat.

She had to concentrate on turning the ignition and pulling out of the shopping center, since all her nerves were tuned to the gentle heat he radiated inside the cramped space. "I'm sorry I drive so slowly. It always makes Julie crazy. She calls me an old lady."

He reached out to pry one of Abby's hands from the steering wheel. "I don't mind at all. I appreciate the fact that you're careful."

She glanced over, marveling at the sight of his fingers winding into hers. She wanted to stare at that perfect vision while her heart pounded blissfully out of her chest. But instead, she forced herself to look out of the windshield and ask the question she truly dreaded. "Nathaniel, I know you haven't been at my high school for long, but have you been able to sense if anything bad is going to happen? I mean, you were drawn here to Charlottesville, which probably means that something terrible is going to happen to someone, isn't it?"

"That's not true," he assured, smoothing his steady fingers over her tensed ones. "I told you, sometimes when I go to a new place, nothing bad ever happens. And honestly, I won't know anything until I have a chance to pay more attention to the other students."

"Oh, right. I guess you paid most of your attention to me this past week. Sorry I took up so much of your time."

"Don't apologize, please. I love spending time with you."

"God, I love that, too," she admitted as she continued driving the familiar streets home. His fingers still drifted over hers, making it more difficult for her to concentrate. "But, um…what about when you weren't with me? Were you able to get any readings from anyone else at my school?"

"Yeah, actually. I did."

"And what emotions have you found so far?"

"A lot, actually. But that doesn't surprise me. So many teenagers are angry, confused, or depressed. It's hard to decide what's normal and what's unusual."

"But can't you just search for the reddest, the angriest, and follow them?"

"I wish it was that simple, but just because someone is angry doesn't make them bad. And some people are at their calmest right before they do the most unthinkable things. I wish what I did was an exact science, but I usually don't know what will happen until things are at a boiling point. Then I just try to do the best I can."

Tears stung Abby's eyes. Nathaniel had so much pain to bear, yet he did it without a second thought. He was the most incredible being ever.

She gazed blankly at the streetlights flashing by, distraught by the fact that he belonged to another world, and yet still thrilled to have him in her life in any form. She only wished it didn't have to be like this, with him waiting patiently for something horrible to happen. She didn't want any part of this miracle to be ruined by reality.

Nathaniel angled toward her. "Abby, can I ask you a question?"

"Well, I've asked you about a million, so I think you can ask me one."

He laughed. "Okay, then. How do you see emotions?"

"Wh-what do you mean?"

"I'm just curious about your method. I've told you how I do it – how I see the corresponding colors when I'm in my other world. But I'd love to know how you manage it as a living person."

"Um…" she stalled, wondering if she could pretend that she had no idea what he meant. Unfortunately, that probably wouldn't work. She'd called him out on the pain thing way too early and accurately. She knew it was a mistake at the time. Now, it was coming back to bite her in the buttocks.

Abby peered at him over her shoulder.

His eyes caught hers. "Does it have something to do with your dad?"

She looked back to the windshield with a watermelon-sized lump in her throat. She didn't reply. But she did manage to nod.

"It's okay," Nathaniel soothed, cocooning her hand inside both of his, "you don't have to tell me if you don't want to."

She definitely didn't want to. She would never want to. But after tonight, his goofy parts were hanging out all over the place. It would only be fair to have hers out there, too.

"Seriously, Abby. Don't worry about it."

She turned the final corner of her neighborhood, pulling her car into the driveway of her home. "I appreciate you letting me off the hook, Nathaniel. But you've answered all my questions, and I – I should be able to do this."

He remained silent as she put the car in park.

Abby took a steep breath. "I'm just scared to say it."

"Why are you scared?"

She studied the glow of her car's headlights against the brick face of her house. "Because the stuff with my dad, it makes me feel like a freak. Like I'm some kind of separate being who doesn't fit anywhere."

"Well, speaking as a separate being who doesn't fit anywhere, I hope you know you can trust me. You don't have to hide anything."

She risked a sideways glance into his eyes. She'd never hoped to find someone whose goofy parts rivaled her own, but here he was. "I was twelve the first time I read an emotion," she admitted for the first time ever, to anyone. Her mother knew Abby could sense things, but they'd never discussed it. Saying the words out loud made them sound even more bizarre. "But I can't start there," she amended, knowing Nathaniel deserved a real explanation, however painful. "I have to go back farther."

His hands gripped hers. "Okay."

She worried her lower lip with her teeth. "My dad was in the military." It sounded like such a simple beginning, but Abby knew it was the beginning of the end. "He fought in the Middle East. At some point, he got captured."

"Oh. I'm sorry."

"I'm sorry, too. But I wasn't even born yet. My mother told me that he was held for several months and then released, but he didn't come home right away. The Army sent him to a hospital after."

"That makes sense."

"Yeah, but it wasn't a medical hospital. It was a psychiatric hospital."

Nathaniel nodded. "That makes sense, too."

"I know it does. I know there's post-traumatic stress and all, but there was something deeper in the way he...transformed."

Abby sucked in another breath. "When he came home, Mom said he was happy at first. That was when she got pregnant with me. But once she was pregnant, Dad started changing. He did the strangest things. He would spend huge amounts of money one week and the next week say they were starving and couldn't eat. Sometimes he would tell my mom that spies were out to get him and he would have to leave for everyone's safety. She didn't know what was happening. She didn't know what to believe.

"Eventually, his Sergeant Major noticed enough bizarre behavior to have him committed back to the hospital. They diagnosed him with bipolar disorder and paranoia and even some schizophrenia. They put him on medication and it seemed to work. For a while, at least."

Nathaniel sighed. "Damn, Abby. I'm so sorry all of that happened."

"Yeah, well, I didn't know about any of it for a really long time. Mom always did everything she could to make my life normal. When Dad was well, she was the perfect wife and mother. And when he would go off his meds and spiral down, she would pick up the pieces and keep me happily in the dark. I had no idea there was even a problem until I was in sixth grade."

"What happened then?"

Abby's hand trembled inside his. "Mom and Dad were at a party at a friend's house and Dad had a vision – or more like a hallucination. He thought his friend, the person throwing the party, was the devil. Dad attacked the man right there, yelling at him and punching him. My mother somehow managed to drag him back home, but that didn't stop him. Dad tore through the house, ranting about his duty to kill his evil friend.

"I was in my bedroom and I heard everything. He sounded so insane. I didn't know what was going on, so I just stayed in my room, peeking around my door, scared out of my mind. Dad searched the house for one of his guns and loaded it up and left. Mom had enough forethought to hide the car keys, so he took off on foot. That gave me just enough time."

"Time for what?"

"To call the police. God, my mother was so out of it that day. Normally, she held herself together really well. But that time was different, maybe since I was there and I saw the whole thing, so she couldn't hide Dad's illness from me anymore. But I didn't care that she'd hidden it from me. I just knew I had to help her. It was one of the hardest things I've ever had to do – calling the police on my father. And holding my mother while she sobbed. And calling my dad's friend to tell him to lock his doors and hide in his own home."

Nathaniel remained quiet while Abby confessed. He sat calmly and supportively beside her, listening and holding her hand. His strength gave her the courage to continue.

"The police found my father on his friend's front lawn, screaming at that poor family hiding inside their home. At least, he went peacefully when they arrested him and didn't start waving his gun around or doing anything that would have gotten him shot. By the next day, he was back in the psychiatric hospital. It took several months, but they got him on the right meds, straightened him out, and let him come home.

"But this time, Mom didn't have to go through it alone. She told me everything that had happened since the war. From that moment on, we formed a united front. We watched over him like hawks. We made sure he took his pills every day. I obsessed about his every move, his every word, his every mood. That's when I started to be able to sense his emotions."

"Really? Did your ability show up out of the blue one day?"

"I don't know, exactly. I just studied him. Morning 'til night, everything he said and did. Most of all, I studied his eyes – their exact shade, how clear they were, how deep they went – and I imagined I could read the thoughts swimming around inside. After a while, I could tell when his eyes changed and I would warn my mom that something was wrong. I predicted every one of his hospitalizations and suicide attempts in an eerily accurate way."

Abby's voice trailed off. She could hear every beat of her heart as she waited for Nathaniel to either run away or disappear. He didn't do either.

"My God, you've been through so much," he said, gripping tight to her hand. "I truly wish you'd never had to experience any of that. But, at the very least, I think I know now why you can see me when I'm in my other world."

Her eyes darted to his. "Really? I'd love to hear the answer to that one."

"Okay. I think it's because of your dad."

Abby's shoulders fell. "It's because I've got his crazy genes, isn't it?"

"No," Nathaniel insisted. "No crazy genes, I promise. It's because you've developed a unique intuition from watching him over the years. People don't generally look that deeply into what's around them. You wanted to have that ability – you willed yourself to have it – so you could see what was happening to him. So now, you can see me when everyone else simply looks through."

She shook her head. "That figures. I have the ability to see otherworldly beings, yet I couldn't see what was happening right in front of my eyes."

"What do you mean?"

"My mom," Abby answered on a shaky exhale. "I wish I could have seen what was happening to her."

"I guess you didn't pay as much attention to her issues?"

"No, I didn't. I was too preoccupied worrying about his."

"Your father's illness must have taken its toll on her."

"Yeah, but she found a way to deal with it – alcohol. She drank all the time, especially at night. I knew she shouldn't, but I understood why. She needed it to get from one day to the next. She wasn't ever mean to me or Dad. She just couldn't sleep. She did so much for us, she had so much on her mind, and she needed to rest. I didn't even think it was a problem until..."

Abby turned fully in her seat, angling her body toward Nathaniel's to pin his clear blue eyes. "The reason I went to Rosemurtha's that night is because I wanted to find out about my mom's death."

He held her intent gaze without falter. "Do you not know how she died?"

"Not really, no. I've got the basics – there was a lot of alcohol, some sleeping pills, the two don't mix – that sort of thing."

"Why don't you know what actually happened?"

"Because I was at school. She was in bed that morning when I left, and when I got home, she was gone."

"Who found her?"

"My dad."

"And what did he tell you?"

"That it was accidental. That she didn't mean to do it."

"And you think it may not have been accidental?"

Abby wanted to look away from him, especially for this, but she couldn't. "I think it's a distinct possibility."

"Do you...do you suspect suicide?"

"Maybe. Or..." her voice trailed, the images in her mind making her numb.

Nathaniel hung his head. "Oh, no. No. It was probably the alcohol and the sleeping pills, like you said. That would explain it."

"Yeah, it would. But why would she have done that? Had she just given up? On Dad? On me? Or was there some other explanation? I mean, he did try to kill his best friend."

"So, you think your father..."

"...may have had something to do with it." A tear slid down her face.

"Abby. Holy hell. That is a horrible thought."

"I know," she whispered, slamming her eyes shut. "I'm a horrible person."

"No. No, you're not. That's not what I meant. Look at me..." Nathaniel reached to her, sliding his fingers down her cheek.

She opened her eyes, seeing him perfectly even through her tears.

"I meant that it must be horrible for you to live with him, day after day, with this thought in your mind. It's just the two of you, right? You help him at home? You take care of him?"

"Yes."

"Then how do you do it? How do you continue caring for him every day, with this question hanging over your head?"

Abby forced a smile. "Because he's my dad."

Nathaniel studied her for a minute. "Does he...has he...ever hurt you?"

"No. Not physically. But it does hurt."

"What hurts?"

"Knowing that I'm his daughter. I mean, I have his hair, his eyes, his sense of humor. Mom always said we were two peas in a pod. It just follows that one day I'll have the crazy things, too. That is, if I don't already. But he didn't get really sick until his mid-twenties, so maybe I have a few good years left."

Nathaniel exhaled. "Abby, you're not going to go crazy."

"You can't know that."

"Yes, I can. You're way too emotionally stable. You're not the crazy type."

"I love that you think that. It's very sweet."

"I'm not trying to be sweet, here. I'm telling you the truth – something you should have heard years ago. You are an emotionally stable, entirely sane person. I've spent over sixty years reading emotions, and I can honestly say that yours are some of the most centered, the most balanced, that I have ever come across. You're dealing with your past and your doubts in a very rational way. I wish you could see that."

Abby wanted nothing more than to believe him. But she'd spent too many years in fear to have it erased by a few beautiful words. "Thank you, Nathaniel. That really is sweet."

"Okay. I can tell you don't believe me. But one day, I'll convince you."

Her heart lit with hope even as she fell quiet, drained by all she'd confessed. Her gaze drifted down to the sight of her hand engulfed in his. She watched his fingers smooth across hers again and again. All she heard were breaths and heartbeats, their melodic tempos lulling her into a sense of blissful safety. She felt so at peace that she jumped when his voice broke the silence.

"I – I suppose I need to apologize again."

"What for?"

"For being so nosy," he replied. "You were right before, about me grilling you. I've wanted to know everything about you from the moment I saw you in that parlor. But in my desperation to learn, I've caused you pain. For that, I am truly sorry."

"Please don't be. You shared a lot with me tonight. That couldn't have been easy for you, either."

Nathaniel offered her a gentle smile. "I don't know how many times I've thanked you already, but I definitely need to do it again."

"Why do you need thank me? I haven't done anything."

His eyes widened. "Wow. Really? Do you really not know?"

"Know what?"

"My God, Abby. It's absurd that you don't realize what you've done for me. You have no idea how bizarre this has been – this inexplicable existence of mine. I've spent over sixty years sitting idly by, literally watching life pass before my eyes. I can't even tell you how much pain I've been in, how lost I've felt, how much I've needed friendship and found none. I was just watching. Always watching.

"And then I found you, and now here I am, doing things. I'm having conversations, eating at restaurants, and holding your hand. I can't begin to tell you what this means to me. I can't begin to thank you enough."

Abby clamped her lips shut to keep her jaw from falling on the floor. She couldn't believe this phenomenal being actually thought she was the one doing him favors. "Okay, then," she decided. "You can't be real, and yet you are real. So now, I have to accept this. You're a ghost and I can see you. Which means that kid from *The Sixth Sense* has nothing on me."

"Kid? What kid?"

"Oh, it doesn't matter. It's just a movie about a kid who sees ghosts."

Nathaniel's forehead crinkled. "Ghosts, huh? That sounds so negative, like I've got no chance at all. Do you think we can call me something else?"

"Sure. How about a spirit? All humans have spirits. I think it suits you."

"Are you saying you find me spirited?" he asked with an overzealous grin.

"Yes, I do. And I think you have a really incredible spirit."

"Good. Because I think you do, too."

Abby tried to hide her own overzealous grin by studying the fog collecting inside her car windows.

Nathaniel slowly extracted his fingers from hers. "Well, I guess I should walk you to your door now. And then I should definitely leave. It is a school night, after all."

School? What is that?

Before Abby could protest, he stepped out of the car and walked around the hood. She watched him through the windows, feeling lonely and cold until he opened her door and she got out to stand beside him. As they ambled up the sidewalk together, she kept her body within an inch of his at all times. Her mind grasped for something intelligent to say while they stepped up the stairs onto her porch. But all she could do when they came to a stop in front of her door was to look up at his stunning face and breathe.

Nathaniel stepped closer, so close that they nearly touched. His eyes met hers and held them. "Do you remember what you said to me in the alleyway last night, Abby?"

"Last night? Oh, God. Was it ridiculous? I bet it was ridiculous. I was such a basket case – I know I was. Did I say something incredibly awful?"

"No. Not at all, actually. You said something really wonderful."

"I did? What was it?"

"You said that I was too good to be true, and that I was sweet and caring and beautiful. Yes, I definitely remember you using the word *beautiful*."

Abby gulped as she stared up at him. "Well, my memories about last night are a little shaky. But that certainly sounds like something I would say."

Nathaniel raised his hand to her face, easing his fingers up the side of her cheek. "So, after everything you've learned since then, has your mind changed? Or do you still think all of that?"

Her body sagged into his touch. "God, yes. I still think all of that."

"Hmm. Then maybe I can see you again? Only if you want."

"I – I'd like that. I'd love it, actually."

"Good. I'll see you at school tomorrow. Although, I probably shouldn't be solid at lunch anymore. That was risky to start with."

Abby nodded, recalling the moment last week when Jason and Randy came out of the woods and stared at her like she had multiple heads. "I completely understand if you need to stay in your spirit form while we're at school. Honestly, it's fine if people see me talking to myself out at the picnic table. But I hope you'll forgive me if I don't speak to you in front of everyone in the hallways. I prefer not to be locked up, if possible."

"I can understand that," Nathaniel assured with a tender smile, "as long as I get to talk to you when we're alone. I'd like that. I'd love it, actually."

Abby held his soft, entrancing gaze. His fingers still traced her cheek, slow and steady. She took an uneven breath before glancing at his lips. They were so close and so amazingly perfect. She could only imagine how soft they would feel against hers.

She risked looking back to his eyes, which were definitely a shade darker than they'd been a minute ago. Nathaniel moved his hand to her hair, running his fingers through it, tucking a wayward strand behind the curve of her ear. The simple touch sent goose bumps skittering over her skin.

He stared at her mouth. He stared hard, his entire body in sole focus. Then he closed his eyes and exhaled. A bare second later, he dropped his arm to his side and stepped back.

"Have a good night, Abby. I'll see you tomorrow."

She stood and watched as he walked away.

Abby lay awake on her mattress. The subtle ticking of her wall clock resounded through her bedroom, reminding her that it was well after midnight. That infernal tick could hound her for as long as it wanted, but she wouldn't be falling asleep anytime soon.

There were so many reasons why she should be lying awake right now, after her date with Nathaniel. She should be thinking about his gorgeous eyes. Or remembering how warm his fingers felt wrapped in hers. Or obsessing over how tempting his lips looked when he stood in front of her on the porch and she'd thought, just for a moment, that he might kiss her.

Unfortunately, none of those wonderful things explained her current insomnia. Because the moment Nathaniel walked away, Abby realized the obvious. The reason he was drawn to Charlottesville – the reason he'd come to her high school – was *her*.

He'd told her tonight about how he spent his existence moving from town to town, searching for people in need. He was drawn to people in danger. And here she was, struggling to figure out if her father killed her mother, while still living under the same roof with him.

The stabbing pain in her stomach twisted her body into a knot against her bedsheets. Nathaniel was here to help her, just like he'd helped Maria. He didn't know it yet – or perhaps he wouldn't admit it out loud – but Abby knew. She knew the truth like she knew her own name.

She only hoped Nathaniel could help her before it was too late.

CHAPTER
FIVE

The next morning, Abby stood in the kitchen doorway, watching silently as her father fixed himself a sandwich. His movements were sluggish from working all night and his overalls hung loosely on his tall frame. She knew that he was too thin now, since neither of them had eaten well since the funeral, and that her mother would have fed him more.

Her mother had always loved her father, even through all of the sad, strange moments. Now, it was Abby's turn to take care of him. She owed that to them both, yet today the task felt heavier than ever. After all, if Nathanial was here to protect her, then it had to be her father he would protect her from.

Abby didn't want to be afraid of her father. She didn't want to question his loyalty to their little family. She knew how hard he worked to give her a happy life.

The words her mother had said so often echoed in her mind: *It's a chemical imbalance in his brain, Abby. He can't help it, and you can't hold it against him. Bipolar is a sickness, just like cancer, and it needs treatment to heal. There are good times and bad and you have to make it through together, as a family.*

Family. That's what they were, she and her father. He was the only family she had. She needed to hold her doubts deep inside, so he wouldn't see her fear. He didn't deserve that. She would be his loving daughter, no matter what. And if her intuition ever told her he was getting sick again, then she would do her best to help him and hope Nathaniel would stay by her side.

Abby steeled herself before stepping into the kitchen. "Hey, Dad," she said, her voice drawing his eyes. She studied them. Clear. Calm. Even.

"Hey, honey," he spoke as he yawned. "You look nice again."

"Thanks."

She stepped over to the cabinet to get his pills. She pulled out the three he needed and handed them to him, watching while he swallowed. He showed her his empty mouth.

Abby gave him a grateful smile, grabbed her granola bar and water bottle, and pulled her backpack over her shoulder. "It's Friday. What do you want to do tonight?"

"Movie?" he asked.

"Yeah, sounds good."

"I'll see you when you get home, then."

"'Kay." On her way out, she stopped and looked back to watch him standing, quietly and peacefully, at the sink. "Love you, Dad."

He nodded. "Love you, Abby."

ABBY TUCKED her sweater under her arm as she got out of her car and walked toward school. It was still warm out, but the extra clothing would keep her from feeling Nathaniel's cool air when he sat with her at lunch. After all, if she planned to spend her free time with a spirit who existed in another world, she needed to accept the challenges that went with it.

Bounding up the steps and into the main hallway, she tried not to look too excited about being in school. She kept her eyes forward while she walked to her locker, opened it, and grabbed a few notebooks. After snapping the door shut, she turned to move into the crowd. Then she saw him.

Nathaniel.

He stood on the other side of the hallway, vigilantly watching her, with his blue eyes glowing and his lips curved into a lopsided grin. Abby wanted to wave, or say hello, or walk over to talk to him. But no one else could see her glorious vision, so she had no option but to stand and stare. She only hoped that everyone else would think she was daydreaming.

In truth, he felt like a dream. She would probably still think he was, except for the very prominent physical effect he had on her. Even from across the hall, he could make her knees weak and her palms damp. Abby wondered if she had the same effect on him. She wondered if her presence had any effect on him at all. It probably didn't. Nathaniel most likely sensed every single person around him, even with his breathtaking gaze glued to her.

As Abby stood in the boisterous, congested hallway, she kept her focus entirely on him. And yet, from the corner of her eye, she still managed to spot Sondra Lawson – a beautiful girl with long, black hair and olive skin – headed his way. Sondra pushed through the crowd of teeming bodies, straight toward Nathaniel. Abby opened her mouth, trying to squeak out some kind of warning, but it was too late. He remained exactly where he was, with his eyes fixed to hers, while Sondra walked right through him.

Nathaniel's jaw fell open. He looked over at Sondra, who stopped cold after she emerged on the other side of his body. Sondra shivered from head to toe, so fiercely that the girl beside her, Holly Dayton, noticed.

"You okay?" Holly asked, combing her fingers through her cropped hair.

Sondra hugged her arms, rubbing her hands over her raised flesh. "I just had the craziest chill. So weird." She shrugged before the two girls moved on.

Abby's eyes bulged while refocusing on Nathaniel. He stared down at the ground, shaking his head, for several seconds. When he finally looked up, she could hardly believe what she saw. Her magnificent spirit was actually blushing. Unable to prevent the wild grin spreading her lips, she absorbed the glorious pink on his cheeks for as long as she could before slipping into class.

THE MORNING LASTED FOREVER. When the lunch bell finally rang, Abby sprinted for the back door. She power-walked through the field toward the distant woods, arriving at her favorite picnic table in record time and flopping breathlessly down on the bench. She pulled on her sweater and attempted to calm her nerves.

She knew Nathaniel would be in his spirit form when he came to sit with her today. That meant he'd be able to sense her emotions, in all their colorful glory. Abby couldn't possibly prevent herself from being purple – probably a ridiculous amount of purple – but she hoped she could also conjure up some other colors, like green and blue, so he wouldn't think she had a wretchedly one-track mind.

Fidgeting with her sweater sleeve, she grew impatient to see him after only a minute. She craned her ears, hoping to hear the stomping of his feet. But then she realized Nathaniel couldn't warn her of his arrival by being noisy, since he would be in spirit form with no sound available. She looked to the trees, but she didn't see him flailing his arms around in there, either.

Maybe I can try something else, she thought, remembering how he'd told her she had a unique intuition. She closed her eyes, settled her racing heart, and concentrated, wondering if she could sense his presence even before she felt his soothing chill. Amazingly, within mere seconds, she could practically hear his voice in her mind.

I'm here, Abby.

She opened her eyes. Nathaniel sat across from her on the picnic bench with his hands resting on the table. Had he been solid, she could have easily reached out and entwined their fingers. As it was, she contented herself with staring into his brightly glowing eyes.

Maybe I should tell him that I just hallucinated hearing his voice, Abby considered. However, she figured it best that she didn't. He could still disappear if – or when – he realized she was only seconds away from madness.

"Hi," she said, wishing she could control her fantastical grin.

He grinned rather fantastically on his own. "Hi."

"So, I see you met Sondra Lawson this morning."

"Who?"

"You know. The girl who walked through you in the hallway?"

Nathaniel cast his gaze down to the tabletop. "Oh, that. Yeah, I definitely need to pay more attention to my surroundings."

"Sorry you were...distracted," Abby offered, quite pleased with herself.

His sparkling eyes rose back to hers. "Yes, you are a danger to your fellow students. If I don't watch what I'm doing, they'll all think they've caught the heebie-jeebies."

Abby's head tilted. "Heebie-jeebies? Really?"

"Is that not a saying anymore?"

"Was it ever a saying?"

"I'm pretty sure it was. I don't know how long ago, though. Those things get lost over time. I have trouble knowing which phrases are in and which ones make me sound old."

"Well, I think we all just talk normal nowadays."

"I'm sure you do. But trust me, certain things you say now will sound ridiculous to you in twenty years. Can you imagine saying *jive turkey* or *gag me with a spoon* in conversation?"

Abby laughed at the thought of Nathaniel talking like a '70s polyester dude or an '80s Valley girl. "Man, it must be really hard for you – always trying to fit into new decades."

He shrugged. "I wouldn't know. I've never tried it before now."

"Oh. I guess you haven't, have you? Well, you certainly don't have to fit in for me. I'm perfectly happy with you just the way you are."

"I appreciate that. But if you let me take you out on any more dates, I want to seem like a regular teenager."

"You could never be regular," she insisted, meaning it as a compliment.

Nathaniel exhaled. "But I wish I could be...for you."

The sudden sadness in his voice incited Abby's late-night worries once again. She didn't want to ruin these few perfect moments they had together, but she couldn't stop her wayward thoughts. "You shouldn't have to do anything else for me, Nathaniel. You're already doing so much. I mean, I know why you're really here. We can just face the facts."

"The facts? What are you talking about?"

"The fact that you're here to protect me, just like you protected Maria back in the '80s. Because my dad is going to get sick again and I'll be in trouble. It's the only thing that makes sense, isn't it? It's the only logical explanation – that you're here because of me."

Nathaniel's glowing eyes fixated on her face. Abby knew he could read her emotions, and probably see right through to her soul, and there was nothing she could do to hide. It was terrifying to let someone look at her so undiluted and unchecked.

"Abby," he sighed, glancing to her hand as if he wanted nothing more than to hold it. "I don't know that for a fact. I don't know anything of the sort. You've had this on your mind all night, haven't you? I'm so sorry. I didn't mean to make you doubt your father like that."

"It's okay. I mean, I already doubted him. I just put two and two together. Here I am, worrying about how my mom died, and then you show up and I can see you when no one else can. I don't think it gets much more obvious."

"No. It's not obvious. I told you, sometimes I never find out why I'm drawn to a place, and nothing bad ever happens. I don't want you to think a situation with your father is inevitable. It's not."

"Perhaps not inevitable, but it's definitely possible. Even if you don't know for sure, you can't deny that it's possible."

Nathaniel sucked in a harsh breath. "Damn it," he cursed, squeezing his eyes shut. "Maybe this isn't a good idea."

"What's not a good idea?"

"Us. Maybe I was wrong to try to be with you. I don't want to hurt you."

"No!" Abby shouted, slamming her hands down next to his on the table. "God, please don't say that. You are not wrong. This is not a bad idea. I need you here with me. Desperately." She emphasized that last word, despite how painful it was.

Nathaniel looked back to her face. "Are you sure? Because I can't be one of these boys here at school. I can't walk with you in the halls, or sit by you in class, or make plans for any sort of a future. I can't be a normal, everyday guy."

Abby bit back her tears. "I know that. I know what you are – *who* you are. I just want every minute I can have with that amazing person."

He studied her for long, agonizing seconds before finally nodding. "Okay. But if we're going to do this, I have to know our relationship isn't hurting you. I don't want you thinking your dad is going to turn on you just because I'm here. God, Abby, being with you means more to me than I can put into words. I feel hopeful for the first time in forever and I can't imagine giving that up. Yet I would, in a heartbeat, if I thought I was doing you any harm at all."

No, no, no. You can't leave me now. Not when I just found you.

"You could never hurt me," she lied, fully aware that Nathaniel would hurt her one day, when he moved on to the next person he would save. But he wasn't hurting her now. "Please stay with me. For as long as you can."

He kept watching her, silent and somber, before his grin slowly returned. It pulled up one corner of his mouth, making him look like the eighteen-year-old boy he'd once been. With that comforting vision, Abby allowed herself to breathe again. Knowing for certain that Nathaniel wasn't going anywhere right this minute, she dropped her gaze down to the table. His hands lay between hers, looking perfectly normal despite the chill they generated.

Abby examined his skin for a moment before reaching her hand to the surface of his. She rested her palm against the cool air that existed where his flesh should be. Then she pressed her fingers through his, down to the wooden tabletop. It was an odd melding, seeing her flesh end where his began.

"You know, it's funny," she considered as she ogled the sight. "I figured I'd be able to see my hand when it moves through yours, since you're the one who exists in another world. But I can't see mine at all. It's like you absorb me."

She continued marveling at the strange image, until she heard him take a shaky breath in. She pulled her hand away immediately. "I'm so sorry, Nathaniel. Did I hurt you?"

"No, you didn't hurt me. Not physically, anyway."

Abby nodded. "I know exactly what you mean," she agreed, since the need to touch him overwhelmed all her senses. She didn't know how it was possible to require something today that didn't even exist in her life two weeks ago.

Nathaniel straightened on his bench. He looked all around them, craning his neck to the woods to stare into the trees. A moment later, he refocused on her face. Abby watched as his eyes changed, their bright glow transforming to a steady blue. She sighed as his cool air shifted to enveloping warmth.

He reached for her hand. "Is this okay? I don't see anyone else around."

Abby nodded as his solid fingers eased over hers. "It's better than okay."

Nathaniel took his time touching her, exploring the length of her hand and the creases in her palm, like he'd never felt them before. "Damn, I really missed this," he confessed.

"But it's...it's only been a few hours since the last time you touched me."

"I know, but time is strange for me. I've had years go by in minutes and I've had minutes last for years. Time doesn't mean anything in my world. Not unless I find myself needing to be somewhere, or needing to do something." He laced their fingers together as he spoke.

Abby absorbed the intensity in his eyes. She worked on sitting still, but it was difficult with her heart trying to claw its way out of her chest. At this moment, she couldn't believe she ever thought Nathaniel was a hallucination. No figment of her imagination could possibly be this stunning, or create this maddening rush of blood through her veins. He brought out her wild side – the part that wanted to jump across this table, fling her arms around his neck, and kiss him like a savage woman who'd been raised by apes in the jungle. But she knew he was just a sweet boy from the '40s, so she settled for holding onto his hand for dear life.

Nathaniel looked straight into her while his thumb moved against her wrist, drawing tiny circles on her heated skin. His blatant stare made her throat run dry, which forced her to lick her lips. That movement shifted his gaze instantly to her mouth. His body leaned closer to hers across the infernal table that insisted on keeping them separated. His free hand reached to her face, his bright eyes darkening as his fingers traced the side of her cheek.

Abby swallowed hard. She took back her sweet-boy-from-the-'40s idea. This was no boy. And the look he gave her was far from sweet.

The school bell rang, making her jump in her seat. She reluctantly pulled her hand away. "Saved by the bell, I guess," she muttered beneath her breath.

Nathaniel huffed out a laugh as he settled back on his bench.

Abby stood and grabbed her backpack. "Hey, so, will you do me a favor?"

He looked up at her with angelic innocence. "Anything."

"Will you please stay in your solid form while I walk back to class?"

"Yeah? Why do you want me to do that?"

She stared at the ground. "Because I don't want you looking at my color. Or colors, if by some miracle there's more than one."

"You know, you can always just tell me what you're feeling."

"Oh, well, I...I probably shouldn't do that right now." *Although I really hope it's the same thing you're feeling.*

Abby turned toward school and forced her legs to move. She looked back only once, to make sure Nathaniel's eyes were still a solid blue. When she saw they were, she breathed a sigh of relief.

MR. PURYEAR's horrific history class should have been the most difficult one to get through today, just like every day. But once Abby took her seat, and looked to the front of the room, she realized it would be the most interesting class ever. Not just because she could still feel Nathaniel's hand touching hers, even though it had been several minutes since that actually happened. And not just because she could still see his beautiful face in her mind's eye, or hear the perfect lull of his deep voice.

Abby realized this would be the most interesting class ever when she watched Nathaniel stroll through the classroom door behind the other students, as if he belonged here among them. Of course, he was in spirit form and no one else saw him. But that little glitch didn't matter to her. She couldn't stop grinning while he walked over to sit in the empty chair beside her, folding his hands on the desk, with his eyes fastened on the teacher.

Mr. Puryear's sleep-inducing monotone began the way it did every day, but Abby didn't pay it any mind. She simply sat and stared at her astonishing apparition. Nathaniel pretended not to notice her gawking at him, and everyone else probably thought she was ogling an empty seat for no particular reason. She had to clench her teeth to prevent herself from talking to him, afraid of what would happen if people saw her babbling to an imaginary friend in the middle of class.

Finally, Nathaniel's eyes met hers. "Pay attention," he mouthed, grinning even as he inclined his head toward the teacher.

Abby turned away from him to open her textbook, but she couldn't focus at all. Nathaniel told her at lunch that he couldn't ever sit by her in class. Yet here he was.

Her heart soared so high that she wasn't sure she'd ever be able to catch it. That is, until Mr. Puryear announced, "Today, we're going to discuss the Invasion of Normandy." Then her heart plummeted straight to the floor.

WHEN SCHOOL LET out at the end of the day, Abby pushed herself through the bustling hallways with slow, drudging steps. She did her best to avoid bumping into other people, but she didn't really see anyone. Not when she had the battle of Normandy raging in her head.

She could see the pale, sandy beach as platoons of soldiers descended on it, masses of them being killed before ever leaving their ships. She could envision their blood as it oozed into the ocean, turning the water a murky, crimson red. She could watch as the men who were lucky enough to make it onto the sand got picked off one-by-one by unseen snipers in the distance. She could hear the soldiers' screams as they lay dying on the once beautiful beach.

Of course, Mr. Puryear's rendition of the battle had been nowhere near that pained or gruesome, but Abby could only imagine it from Nathaniel's point of view. She could only imagine *him* there, watching the horror surrounding him, helpless to prevent his own death. And it didn't help at all that he sat beside her the entire time, stoically poised in his seat.

His face remained a mask through every minute of the account, as he listened to each detail leaving her emotionless teacher's mouth. The moment class was over, Nathaniel gave her a soft smile and walked away. She hadn't seen him since.

When Abby finally managed to drag herself through the halls, away from her locker, and out of the building, she sat on the front staircase and surveyed the parking lot. She wondered if her spirit would come to her again today. She needed to know that he wasn't curled up in a ball somewhere, reliving the terror of his own death. She couldn't bear the thought of him trapped inside those awful memories, especially not when he'd only been sitting next to her in class to reassure her that he could.

Abby scanned the street in front of her school, noting that the buses had already left, and the few remaining students now chatted amongst themselves before climbing into their cars. She examined everyone, aching to see Nathaniel, dejected and fearful when he was nowhere to be found.

"He must be here," she assured herself, believing deep in her heart that he would know how much she needed to see him at this moment. She closed her eyes and stilled her erratic breaths – working to concentrate like she'd done earlier at the picnic table – praying to feel the cool swirl of air that would accompany his otherworldly form.

Please, Nathaniel, she begged in silence. *Please be here.*

I'm in your car, Abby.

Her eyelids flew open. She stared at her car, which was easily a hundred yards away and parked behind a tree. She looked all around her and back into the school's hallways, verifying the fact that she couldn't see Nathaniel anywhere. But she swore she'd heard him.

"Great," she huffed. "I'm hearing voices now, too."

Abby wandered down the stairs and through the lot toward her car. She caught sight of her spirit as soon as she cleared the tree she'd parked behind. Nathaniel sat in her passenger's seat, looking perfectly ethereal with his glowing eyes and lopsided smile.

Holy crap, did I really just hear his voice? No, that's not possible. And I'm not about to open that can of worms – not when we have Normandy to discuss.

She fell into her driver's seat, pulling the door shut behind her while pivoting toward him. "Good Lord, Nathaniel. Please tell me you're okay."

His head cocked to the side. "Of course. Why wouldn't I be?"

"Well, I…I just thought you might be upset."

"You mean about the Normandy lecture?"

"Yes. That."

The easy smile on his lips didn't falter. "I'm okay, Abby. I've been hanging around high schools for over twenty years, and I've audited a lot of classes. I've heard that story many times, so I'm familiar with the modern-day rendition."

"And was…was that what it was like?"

"Kind of. People get the scenery right, but rarely the emotion that goes with it. Anyway, it was a long time ago."

"Oh. I suppose you get used to it somehow, since you've had other near-death experiences."

"I suppose so. I mean, I have had more than a few of those."

Abby's gut sank to her feet, overfilled with curiosity and dread. "How many more than a few?" she wondered. "I mean, I know about Maria and her dad. I know how badly he hurt you. But how many times have you actually died?"

Nathaniel managed to laugh. "Well, I guess I only died the one time. But since then, I've been beaten nearly senseless, stabbed repeatedly, thrown from a moving car – that was quite a thing – and been set on fire. So, I suppose the tally is around a dozen, because beatings and stabbings are pretty standard. But I was only ever shot once. That was in Normandy."

Abby barely managed to close her gaping mouth. She stared at his T-shirt-clad chest in all its muscular glory, presumably lacking in bruises, scars, or holes. "But how? How do you survive all of that? I mean, you're solid when it happens, right?"

"Yes, I'm solid when it happens. But as soon as I return to my other world,

I'm healed immediately. All I have to do is keep the presence of mind to turn back into a spirit."

"That has to be hard, though. How in the hell can you possibly focus when someone is stabbing you?"

"It's not easy," Nathaniel answered with a shrug, "but I've had plenty of practice. Being able to see emotions means I usually have some warning when things are turning for the worse. It gives me a little time to prepare myself."

Abby shook her head, astounded by his casual answers. He truly didn't seem to care about the pain he suffered for strangers. But she cared. She needed to hold him right now, to comfort him whether he needed it or not. Unfortunately, his eyes still glowed and his air still chilled her skin.

She groaned in frustration. "Nathaniel, can you please turn solid now?"

"You mean here, in the parking lot? There are still a few people around."

"I'm aware of that. And I don't care."

He held entirely still, observing her for another lengthy minute, before easing himself into her world. His glowing eyes remained fixed on her face while they transformed to a deep blue. His cool air shifted to a steady warmth. His flesh turned solid like stone.

Abby didn't wait another second. She crawled across the seat and plopped her bottom down on his thighs. She curled up in his lap, throwing her arms around his neck and pressing her chest onto his. Her forehead burrowed into his shoulder before he had any chance to stop her.

"I'm sorry," she whispered against his neck. "I'm so, so sorry."

Nathaniel reached his arms around her, spanning the small of her back with both hands. He held her as softly and gently as possible. "Don't be, Abby. It's my decision to do those things. I know what I'm getting into."

"But you do everything so selflessly and all you get in return is pain."

He rested his cheek on her hair. "Don't be upset, please. The last thing I want to do is make you sad."

She breathed in deep against his skin. He smelled like warm apples and cinnamon. "You don't upset me, Nathaniel. I just want to find a way to make things better for you this time."

"What do you mean by this time?"

"This time, this school, this experience. If you're here to save someone..."

"Which is probably not you..."

"...then I want this to be the best mission you've ever had."

Nathaniel laughed, the joyful sound rumbling through his chest and into hers. His lips moved beside her ear, grazing her skin. "It's already the best."

"Yeah? Why is that?"

"Well, I already mentioned that I get to talk to you and take you to dinner. I also get to see you at school during the day and drive home with you in the afternoon. And right this minute, I get to hold you in my arms. And this feels…pretty damn incredible."

Abby smiled against his skin. "This is only the beginning. I'm going to make things even better for you," she promised, lifting her head to see his face.

"Even better?" Nathaniel echoed, matching her raw stare.

His lips were maddeningly close and she couldn't prevent her eyes from latching onto them. "I didn't mean – I just meant – pie."

"Pie?"

Abby forced her gaze back to his. "Um, yes. I want to make you pie. And a whole dinner to go with it. If you want."

"I would love that. How about tonight?"

She realized then, as if for the first time, that she was sitting in his lap. She'd actually plopped herself into his lap without his permission, and now lingered here unapologetically, with her hands draped across his shoulders and her face mere inches from his. "Uh, what?"

His hand shifted over her back. "You want me to come to dinner tonight?"

"Yes," she said, nodding vehemently. "Oh, but, damn it. I can't, since my dad is off work for the weekend. It'll have to be Monday. If that's okay."

"Sure. I can wait until Monday. I won't like it, but I'll wait."

Abby heard most of what Nathaniel said, despite the excessive humming of her skin. She really had no reason to sit on his lap anymore, but she couldn't bring herself to leave. His heavy arms felt altogether too right, wrapped around her body like they belonged here.

Nathaniel didn't look at all upset by her lack of withdrawal. He watched her, his eyes roaming over her face, as their breaths mingled in the cramped front seat. He traced the line of her spine with his fingertips, moving slowly up and down, bringing shivers to her skin. She wriggled against his thighs, which caused him inhale sharply, which made her succumb to nervous laughter.

"Well, I – I guess I should get off of you now," she sputtered. "I mean, I should probably move back over to my seat. Since I'm the one who's driving."

"Anytime you want," he said, sliding his hand up to brush her hair over her shoulder. "There's no rush."

Abby could have sat in his lap for all eternity. But she figured she was probably crushing him and he was just too polite to complain. As she inched away from him to settle back in her own seat, she cursed the fact that she couldn't disconnect the nerves that made her blush.

She looked to the windshield, buckled up, turned on the ignition, and white-knuckled the steering wheel. She could feel his eyes boring into her while she exited the parking lot, yet she made every attempt to stare straight ahead. *God, he must think I'm an animal for flinging myself at him like that.*

"So, I'm not going to see you at all this weekend?" Nathaniel questioned.

Abby clearly heard the dejection in his voice. She tried not to be happy about it, since she never wanted to upset him. But it was still nice knowing she wasn't the only one whose feelings had gone haywire. "I'm sorry about that, but my weekends are pretty fixed. I always spend time with my dad on Friday and Saturday. I could change it, but I don't like leaving him alone for too long. Then on Sunday, while Dad is sleeping before work, I go to the mall with Julie. And Sunday night, I do all the homework I've been neglecting."

"It's okay, Abby. I know you have a life. I just hoped you could help me."

She pulled onto the road and gently accelerated. "Help you? With what?"

"I want to pick your brain about some of the students at school, to see if I can fit what you know with the emotions I see."

"Ooh, how exciting. Are you getting some readings on people?"

"You make me sound like Rosemurtha."

"Madam Nathaniel?"

"Yikes. I think I like spiritual policeman better."

Abby smiled. "Go ahead, then. Ask me your questions."

"Okay. What do you know about the girl who walked through me in the hallway this morning?"

"You mean Sondra Lawson?"

"Yes. She was very sad."

"Well, that's probably because of her boyfriend, Chuck Harding. He's the captain of the basketball team. I think he's fooling around on her with her friend, Holly."

"Is that the girl who was walking with her in the hall?"

"Yeah. Not a great friend, huh? Honestly, I don't know what either of them see in Chuck. He gives me the – what did you call it? Heebie-jeebies?"

"He does? Why?"

"I don't know. He just doesn't strike me as a good person."

Nathaniel rubbed his fingers across his chin. "I see. And what about the guy who sits behind you in history class?"

"Oh, that's Eric Nichols," Abby said, remembering how he'd laughed at her when Mr. Puryear caught her daydreaming last week. "He might seem a little off, but I think he's just trying too hard to fit in. His parents got divorced last year and it was pretty nasty business. He follows Jason and Randy around a lot. They're the guys who looked at me like I was crazy when they walked out of the woods last week at lunch. I don't know much about them, but I think Eric's pretty harmless."

"And what about the guy who has the locker next to yours?"

"That's Marcus Dixon. I imagine he seemed stressed out."

"Yes. Quite."

"It's because he's way smart. He drives himself mad trying to be the perfect student. You should see the inside of his locker. It's like a maid cleans it and a librarian organizes it. He seems nice enough, though. Just maybe a bit obsessive-compulsive."

"Interesting," Nathaniel sighed. "I have to say, for someone who keeps to herself, you certainly know a lot about people."

"Well, when people treat you like you're invisible, they say stuff around you they normally wouldn't."

"Yeah, I know exactly what you mean."

Abby's hands choked the steering wheel. "Oh, God, I'm so sorry."

Nathaniel shrugged. "Don't be. After all, I am invisible. What I cannot comprehend is how you are invisible. Especially when everything about you is so amazing."

She grinned at the road. "I don't know about that., I think you're just incredibly biased. If I hadn't been able to see you, you probably never would have noticed me."

"That's not possible. I'm certain I would have noticed you." Nathaniel reached over to the steering wheel, gathering one of her hands in his. "I believe I would have found you anyway. I would have realized what I was missing," he assured as he laced their fingers together.

Abby's foot slipped, revving the car slightly above the speed limit before she eased it back down. Part of her wished she would get used to the feel of his skin against hers. Another part was quite happy with her involuntary body flutters.

He traced her palm with his fingertips. "Does my touch bother you?"

"No. I mean, not in any bad way," she admitted.

"Mmm," Nathaniel hummed, his voice as gentle as his actions. "Tell me, please. Why do you choose to be invisible?"

Abby winced, since she'd never considered that she *chose* anything. "I don't know. I guess it started in middle school. Those were definitely awkward years. I don't think anyone is graceful during that time in their life, but I was particularly gangly and unfortunate."

"I can't imagine it was that bad. I bet you were adorable."

"Not so much. Trust me." She made a silent note-to-self to never let him see her photo albums.

"So, you think middle school was bad. But why not make friends now?"

"I wanted to. I really did, especially when we first moved here. I even tried talking to a few people last year, before Mom died. But after she was gone, I was just so sad all the time. It was probably too much effort for anyone to get to know me. And it's hard to let people in, since the stuff about my dad might come up, and that's a lot to share."

Nathaniel nodded. "Yeah. I suppose I can see that. And in case I haven't said it before, I'm really glad you shared that with me. I'm glad you let me in."

Abby pulled the car over five houses down from hers. "I wish you could meet my dad. He really is a good person, especially when he's taking his meds. I think you'd like him."

"I'm sure I would."

"I wish you could meet Julie, too. She's totally funny and sweet."

"You'll go to the mall with her on Sunday?"

"Yes."

"And will you tell her about me?"

"Well, I'll have to say something. She'll know I'm acting differently."

"For the better, I hope."

Abby risked meeting his eyes again. Damn, those gorgeous blues could melt her, even when they weren't glowing. "Yes. Definitely for the better."

Nathaniel ran his fingers over hers. "I meant to tell you earlier that you look beautiful today. I mean, not that you aren't always beautiful. I guess I'm just...I'm just really looking forward to our dinner on Monday."

She grinned so wide that her ears hurt. "I am, too. I will see you at school Monday morning, and after school, I will make you a home-cooked meal. Complete with pie."

"I absolutely cannot wait."

"Me, neither," Abby confessed, the endless possibilities of Monday night swirling in her mind. Would he stay with her after they ate dinner? Would they curl up together on her couch and watch a movie? Would she be able to focus on anything other than him? And dear God, would he ever kiss her?

She focused on Nathaniel's mouth now. She stared quite deliberately as she imagined how warm and strong his lips would feel against hers. Her grip tightened on his hand.

"Abby," he whispered, leaning toward her. He moved closer and closer, until she felt his warm breath against her face. He gripped her hand just as tightly. Yet he stayed for seconds only before he groaned and shook his head.

Nathaniel forced himself backwards into his seat. "Monday," he insisted as he pushed open the door and sprang out of her car.

Abby watched him turn to walk down the street, fully aware that he didn't have to see her one overpowering color to know how she felt. But she couldn't bring herself to be embarrassed about her emotions. She just desperately wished it was Monday, already.

AFTER WATCHING NATHANIEL LEAVE, Abby drove the short distance to home and parked her car in the driveway next to her father's truck. She bounced into the house and tossed her backpack on the couch. "Hey, Dad, how'd you sleep today?"

"Good," Mark answered from the kitchen. "Did you decide on a movie for us to watch tonight?"

A dreamy smile lit her face. "How about one with a superhero?"

"Cape or no cape?"

"No cape."

"Will do."

Abby peeked her head around the kitchen doorway to see her father sitting at the small table in the corner. "Just give me a minute to call Julie and then I'll start dinner," she told him before scurrying into her bedroom. She grabbed her cell phone from her pocket as she flopped down on the bed. Kicking the door shut with her foot, she dialed Julie's number and waited to hear the bubbly voice she knew so well.

"Hey, Abs!"

"Hey, Jules! Whatcha doin'?"

"Taking my shoes off. I swear I can't breathe with socks on. Toes need air."

"That is entirely true. So, how are you and Peter doing today?"

"Off today."

"But you were just back on a couple days ago."

"Yeah, but today he irritated me again. We'll see about tomorrow."

Abby laughed. "Well, I hope you guys patch things up soon."

"Really? Why's that?"

"Because I thought maybe we could double date sometime."

The phone went dead for a long minute. Then Julie burst out screaming. "Oh, my God! No way! Seriously? Who? When? Where? What? How?"

"Okay, okay. Don't act so surprised. It's not like I have a disease."

"I know you don't, Abs. But you know you aren't always open to...oh, forget that. Tell me all about him!"

"Well, his name is Nathaniel. He's eighteen."

"Ooh, older. Nice. Go on."

"He's new in town and we just met a few days ago. He's really sweet."

"Yeah, and? What does he look like?"

The image of her hero flashed into Abby's brain, lighting her entire body. "Oh, man. He looks like one of those Greek god statues. Seriously."

"Wow. That is serious."

"Yeah. You'll like him, Jules."

"I will if you do. When can I meet him?"

"Um, I don't know. Soon, hopefully. But I have to go now, because my dad's waiting for me. I just wanted to make sure we're still on for Sunday."

"Of course," Julie said, her voice dropping to a gentler note. "And how's your dad doing today?"

"Oh, you know. The same."

"But no worse?"

"No. We're okay."

"Good. That's really good."

Abby could hear her friend smiling over the phone. "So, Sunday at our regular place?"

"Food court, milkshakes, noon. Be there."

"Yes, ma'am."

"I'm happy for you, Abs. About the guy, I mean. And I expect to hear a full report on Sunday."

"Sure. I'll see you then. Bye, Jules."

"Bye."

When the call ended, Abby stared blankly at her bedspread. As wonderful as it felt to be able to tell her best friend about Nathaniel, she was afraid her moment of victory would be overshadowed by unobtainable explanations. *Why can't he come to the mall with us? Why won't he meet your dad? Why doesn't he drive? Where are his parents?*

She could practically hear Julie's questions firing off, one after the other. Abby would have to think of some truly clever answers, although she feared they'd never be clever enough. Dreading the thought of lying to her friend, she dragged herself out of her room and down the hallway.

"What do you want for dinner, Dad?" she asked as she rounded the corner to the kitchen.

"Surprise me," he replied.

She held her breath until she saw his smile reach all the way to his eyes. Then she allowed herself to exhale.

CHAPTER

SIX

On Sunday morning, Abby stood in her kitchen, cutting up apples. She placed the slices carefully into a pie crust and coated them in spices. The comforting scents of apple and cinnamon made her think about how wonderful Nathaniel smelled. Of course, she didn't need pie ingredients to draw her mind to her otherworldly spirit. She'd thought of little else since he'd walked away from her on Friday afternoon.

Why is Nathaniel here? Why am I the only one who can see him? What does it all mean? Abby had asked herself a million questions in the past two days, coming up with very little in the way of answers. She only knew one thing for certain: he had to be here because of her.

Her spirit hadn't deterred her fears by asking about Sondra, Holly, Eric, and Marcus. Maybe Nathaniel had gotten some emotional readings from Abby's fellow students, but she knew he was only trying to ease her mind by deflecting her suspicions. He didn't want her to think he was here to protect her from her own father. He didn't want her to be afraid.

Abby tried to focus on the job at hand as she covered the pie filling with the top crust and crimped the edges. Gratefully, her fingers could perform the task on their own, since her mind remained fixated on her spirit. Nathaniel always put her feelings and needs above his own. The fact that he remained solid in her presence for so long was proof of that. He'd told her that leaving his other world felt unnerving to him, yet he still turned solid for her – so that he could spend time with her – so that he could touch her.

Goosebumps raised her skin as she thought about his arms wrapped around her body when they sat in the front seat of her car. She still couldn't believe she'd just plopped down in his lap like that. Not that he seemed to mind her boldness, but he also hadn't done anything but hold her.

"Well, maybe these pies will be so delicious, he'll have no choice but to kiss me," she whispered to herself as she cut more apples for the next one. "Although, maybe he doesn't think that kind of physical affection is polite behavior. Or maybe he's worried about our technical age difference. Or maybe he isn't sure if he should cross that line, because of his particular situation."

Abby pressed her lips shut with her disheartening thoughts. She didn't want Nathaniel to second guess himself. She wanted him as a boyfriend, as unrealistic as that may be. Was that even possible? Could a living person have a relationship with a non-living one?

Her thoughts shifted to the photo of her mother – the one she kept tucked into the mirror frame on her bedroom vanity. She talked to that photo every day. It was definitely a relationship, even if it wasn't entirely traditional. So, why couldn't she and Nathaniel have a nontraditional relationship, too? Yes, it would be radically nontraditional. But if they were both good with it, why should it be wrong?

"What are you doing?" Mark asked, his unexpected voice startling her into dropping an apple. "I thought you were going to the mall with Julie today."

"Yeah, I am," Abby said, picking the slice up off the floor and tossing it in the trash. "I just need to get these pies in the oven before I leave."

"Pies? Since when do you bake pies?"

"I, um, I wanted to try something new."

Her father stepped up to the counter, surveying her work. "And we need two of them?"

"Oh, you know. Go big or go home, I always say."

"I've never heard you say that."

"Well, then...there's a first time for everything?"

He observed her before nodding. "Okay. I'll be in my room. Let me know when you're leaving?"

"Sure," Abby answered as he walked away, knowing all too well what awaited him in his room. She turned her concentration back to the second pie, making sure the upper crust fit perfectly with the lower. She cut little slices in both tops and put them in the oven, hoping she'd done a good job. Her spirit deserved a decent dessert, at the very least.

After setting the timer, she washed her hands and exited the kitchen. She paused in front of the hall mirror, surveying her reflection. She'd spent a fair amount of time on her clothes and makeup today, and she cleaned up pretty well. Honestly, she looked happier and healthier now than she had in months.

Grabbing her wallet and keys from the hall table, Abby walked to her father's bedroom. She did her best to keep her nerves in check as she silently pushed the door open. Her mouth ran dry when she looked inside.

All of Mark's guns lay on his bed. Thirteen of them, as Abby knew well, since her mother always made her keep count. He stood beside his empty gun cabinet, methodically cleaning a revolver. She knew this was his happy place, although she couldn't understand it.

"I'm heading to the mall now, Dad. Will you take the pies out of the oven when the timer rings?"

"Sure. Have fun, honey. And tell Julie I said hi."

"I will. Have a good night at work. I'll see you in the morning." Abby turned away from him with a lump in her throat, rushing through the living room toward the front door. She hated seeing her father with a gun in his hand. It brought back too many horrible memories and way too many doubts.

She wanted it all gone – all her suspicions, all her worries. If she could only know for certain that her father had nothing to do with her mother's death, then she could let it all go. She could stop feeling guilty about doubting a man who did his best to love and care for her. And she could be with Nathaniel and not be afraid. That was everything she could ever ask for.

"You're not giving me much information on this guy, Abs. Is there something wrong with him?" Julie questioned with a scrutinizing stare.

Abby forced a laugh, hoping it managed to sound carefree. She'd spent the entire day being as vague and indirect with her friend as possible, had insisted on seeing a movie at the mall theater so she'd have more time to come up with plausible explanations, and was now attempting to drown her voice out at the bottom of a king-sized milkshake.

"Don't be paranoid, Jules. I just don't know much about him, since we only met last week," Abby explained, gazing around at all the other people sitting in the mall's food court. "What about you and Peter? Are things between you guys any better today?"

"Ah, Peter," Julie sighed. "That boy needs to learn how to treat a woman."

Abby smiled around her milkshake straw. She didn't have to worry about Nathaniel that way. He treated her like a queen.

"Ugh," Julie huffed. "Let's forget about Peter and go look at clothes."

They finished their shakes and tossed the cups in the trash. Julie grabbed Abby's arm to pull her toward the nearest clothing store, expertly maneuvering them both around the other shoppers who meandered through the broad halls. "So, we're resorting to shopping therapy again?" Abby asked while they stepped down an aisle to peruse the many shirts, jeans, and sweaters.

Julie laughed. "It works every time."

Her friend's smile appeared innocent enough, although Abby sensed another information attack coming. She braced herself by standing beside a mannequin and attempting to blend.

"So," Julie began her next interview as she thumbed through a clothing rack. "When are you planning to see Nathaniel again?"

This much Abby actually knew. "He's coming over to my house Monday night. I'm going to cook him dinner."

"Working the domestic angle. Nice. What will you do after dinner?"

"Well, I thought he could stay for a movie. If he wants."

"Wow. Have I mentioned lately how lucky you are to have your house to yourself five nights a week? Maybe if Peter could come to my house more often, we'd be doing better."

"Or maybe you'd drive each other even crazier."

"Yeah. That's also a distinct possibility." Julie tossed her bouncy brown hair across her shoulders. "So, you haven't mentioned where Nathaniel lives."

"Yeah, I don't, um..."

Julie stopped searching through clothing to search Abby's eyes. "You're being mysterious again, Abs."

"Well, like I said, I just met him."

"Yes, you've said that an awful lot. And look at you – all dolled up – with your hair curled and your makeup on. Are you sure he's not going to be here at the mall today? Because I know you love me, but you usually don't get all glamorous on my account."

Abby sighed. "No, I...I don't think he'll be here."

Julie inspected her for another formidable minute before turning toward a display of sweaters. Abby breathed easier with the momentary reprieve, although she knew it wouldn't last long. What would she say the next time her friend bombarded her with Nathaniel questions? She couldn't keep this under control forever. Honestly, it would be so much easier if he could simply be here, standing beside her. If she could call him and beg him to come, she could prove to Julie that she hadn't fabricated an imaginary boyfriend.

Is there any way to make that happen? Abby wondered, considering her options. Her spirit didn't have a cell phone. No bat phone, either. And she didn't possess Rosemurtha's talent for séances, so she couldn't simply conjure him up. Sadly, the only thing Abby was capable of was hearing voices. Or, at least, Nathaniel's voice.

That thought made her knees go weak. She grabbed hold of the nearest clothing rack to steady herself. *Oh, my God. I did hear Nathaniel's voice. Twice.*

She'd heard him at the picnic table during lunch on Friday, and again when she'd stood on the front staircase at the end of the school day. Both times, she'd just closed her eyes and concentrated on feeling his presence. Both times, he'd spoken to her. Of course, she'd assumed that the reason she heard his voice was either wishful thinking or utter psychosis. But now, she wondered if it was something else entirely.

"Look at this one," Julie said, holding a lilac sweater under her chin. "Take my bag, will you? I'm gonna throw this on and see how it looks."

"Okay," Abby said, taking the bag as Julie pulled the sweater over her shirt. *Holy crap! Can I talk to Nathaniel in my head? Is that even possible?*

Abby chewed on her lip, hoping she wasn't entirely out of her mind for even thinking she might be able to do it. Then again, stranger things had happened. Just in the past two weeks, in fact.

Julie stepped away to look in a mirror. When Abby was certain her friend was otherwise occupied, she closed her eyes. She breathed in deep, concentrating on the memory of her spirit's ethereal chill and glowing eyes.

Nathaniel, she thought, waiting a moment before asking, *are you there*?

She heard no reply at all. She lingered with her eyes closed for several more seconds, but absolutely nothing happened. She didn't know what she'd expected. Should this be some kind of mental phone call, perhaps? Or was it more like texting?

NATHANIEL! she tried again, screaming his name as loud as she could inside her head. *CAN YOU COME TO THE MALL, PLEASE? I'M HERE WITH MY FRIEND JULIE AND I WANT YOU TO MEET HER!*

Again, nothing happened. No response whatsoever.

Abby opened her eyes. She watched while Julie turned side to side in front of the mirror, surveying the new sweater she wore. Abby thanked the heavens her friend hadn't noticed her goofy concentration expression.

Closing her eyes one more time, she added, *I TOLD JULIE YOU'RE MY BOYFRIEND AND I DON'T WANT HER TO THINK I MADE YOU UP!*

Abby stifled a laugh then, since she'd screamed that last sentence entirely for her own amusement.

"So, what do you think?" Julie asked. "Is purple my color?"

It's definitely mine, Abby considered. *At least, whenever Nathaniel's around.* "Yeah, I think the sweater looks good on you."

Julie's nose crinkled. "I don't know. What would I wear it with?"

"Jeans, maybe? Or a skirt?" *Damn. He really didn't hear me.*

"Yeah, but I already have that other purple sweater. You know, the one we bought in Williamsburg that day we went to the outlet mall?"

"Oh, yeah. I remember." Abby heaved a sigh. *Not only am I crazy enough to try calling him with my mind, I am pathetic enough to hope it would work.*

"Hey, Abby," a deep voice spoke from behind her.

Her breath caught in her throat. She froze in place, focused solely on her friend, who stared past her. Did she just hear Nathaniel? Was his voice in her head, or did Julie hear it, too?

"This is a nice surprise," the deep voice continued. "I thought I wouldn't get to see you again until Monday."

A bizarre squeaking noise forced its way from Abby's lips, since this voice was definitely not in her head. It came from directly behind her. When Julie's eyes sparked to life, Abby slowly turned around.

Nathaniel.

He smiled as he closed the last few steps between them with easy strides. His face was just as stunning as she remembered – his grin the crooked one she loved – his eyes the clear blue of his solid form. Abby nearly fell over.

Nathaniel stepped up beside her and eased his arm around her waist, drawing her into his body to support her wobbly legs. He leaned down and pressed his lips to her hair. "It's funny, running into you like this."

Her mouth dropped open for a second before she managed to close it. *Was it possible? Had he actually heard her?* Her brain felt too overworked to even consider the option, since she could barely focus on the fact that he was here. Out in public. With his arm around her. Kissing her hair. With Julie in the same room. *Oh, God! Julie!*

"Um, uh, Jules," Abby fumbled. "This is Nathaniel."

"It's nice to meet you," he offered. "Abby has told me lots of good things about you."

Julie grinned as she drank in the spectacle. "Yeah, well...I pay her."

Nathaniel chuckled, making his warm body rumble beside Abby's. She wound her arm around his back and balled her fist in his shirt, needing all the support she could get. After all, she knew what her friend was capable of.

"So, Nathaniel, I've heard good things about you, too," Julie began. "Sadly, it's only been bits and pieces. I was hoping you could fill in some of the blanks for me."

"Of course," he said, running his hand down Abby's back. She figured he was trying to settle her frayed nerves. It had the opposite effect.

She glared at Julie, who paid her no attention. *Please be gentle, Jules.*

"Abby told me you're originally from Oklahoma, but she didn't say much else. Like why you left or why you moved to Charlottesville."

"My family owned a farm in Oklahoma," he answered without missing a beat. "But they sold it to a government-run facility that could bring in big machines and be more efficient. It was sad at first, losing our family business, but there were opportunities that came from it. I wanted to move here to establish residency, so I could have a chance at in-state tuition at UVA."

"Oh? And what would you study if you got in?"

Abby lifted her eyes to his, just as eager for the answers.

"I really like helping people," Nathaniel said, tucking her closer to his side. "So maybe health care, but I haven't gotten that far yet."

"Hmm," Julie considered. "Abby also told me you're eighteen. Does that mean you're a senior in high school?"

"Well, I had to help out a lot on our farm, so I missed several classes through the years. I'm technically still a junior, just like you two."

"I see. And where is the rest of your family?"

"Back home."

"Any brothers or sisters?"

"A little sister," he offered. "Hey, is that a new sweater you're trying on?"

"Oh," Julie looked down. "Yeah, Abby was just giving me her opinion on it. What do you think?"

"I think that's a nice color on you. Abby looks good in purple, too."

Abby peered up at him from under the crook of his arm. "You ought to know," she murmured, just loud enough for him to hear. His mouth curved into a grin as he met her eyes. She curled her fingers tighter into his shirt.

"Well, look at the time," Julie interrupted.

They both turned back to her.

"Do you have somewhere else you need to be?" Nathaniel asked.

"Regrettably," Julie said, one eyebrow arching as she glanced down from his white T-shirt to his brown cargo pants and black combat boots. "I have to help my mom with that, uh, that school project. You remember, right, Abs?"

"Uh…"

"Your mom goes to school?" he questioned.

"No, I mean *my* school project. Of course. She's like that, my mom." Julie pulled the sweater off and set it on a shelf. "I'm gonna think on that one."

Abby held her friend's mischievous gaze. "Are you really leaving now?"

"Oh, I imagine you can find something to do to fill the time." Julie winked while pulling her bag from Abby's hand. "It was cool to meet you, Nathaniel."

"You, too. Good luck with that project."

"Thanks. Catch you later, Abs."

Abby watched as Julie skipped away, looking back only once before disappearing around a corner. "Julie's not exactly subtle, is she?"

Nathaniel laughed. "Not exactly, no. But it's obvious she cares for you."

"Yeah, sorry about that. She asked questions you probably weren't ready to answer. I mean, I didn't even know you had a little sister. I think Julie could drag things out of FBI agents, if she wanted to. But you did really well."

"Thanks," he said, dropping his arm back to his side. "I just tried to be as truthful as I could."

Abby mourned the lack of his warmth until he stepped in front of her, so close that she could easily touch him. "Still, I apologize for the interrogation."

Nathaniel shook his head. "It really wasn't that bad. Honestly, I'd have to say the worst part was her eyesight."

"Her eyesight?"

"Yeah. She made quite a face when she looked at my clothes. I'm not in style, am I?"

"That doesn't matter. I really don't care how you dress."

"I appreciate that, but I should try to fit in. If you're going to introduce me to people, I should at least look like I'm from this decade."

Abby inched even closer. "You should do whatever makes you happy."

Nathaniel reached out, sliding his fingers down her arm. "Well, since we're in a public place, I suppose I'll have to settle for shopping."

His eyes sparked with his words. Abby had to remember how to breathe.

"So, will you help me pick out some new clothes?"

She nodded without thought, shamelessly aware that she would do anything he asked. She didn't resist in the slightest when Nathaniel laced their fingers together and tugged her toward the opposite end of the store. She walked beside him with her brain in a fog.

"Okay," he announced when they arrived in the men's section. "I am at your mercy."

"Uh..." Abby stalled, trying her best to not reply to that delicious statement in any sort of mortifying way. "Yeah, that's, um-hmm," she mumbled as she started searching the racks.

While she piled several shirts and pants into Nathaniel's waiting arms, she dwelled on every word he'd spoken to Julie. Did he really mean all those things he said to her? Did he want to finish high school? To go to college? To get a job and lead a normal life? And what about his family? Were any of them still alive? Did they know about his hopes and dreams before he joined the military and went to Normandy?

Abby wanted a thousand answers from him, yet one particular question took precedence above all others. It was a question she had to ask right here and now, even though it was an answer she couldn't imagine having. But she just had to know the truth.

"I suppose I should try these on now," Nathaniel suggested when the stack of clothes in his arms reached the height of his chin.

"Oh, sorry. Did I give you too many?" she fretted, realizing she hadn't paid much attention to what she'd been doing.

"It's fine, Abby. But we should probably head to the fitting room."

She nodded, toddling along behind him until they arrived in the very back of the store. An attendant allowed them into the changing section, which was gratefully empty. Nathaniel slipped behind a red curtain, dragging his haul of clothing in with him.

Abby took a seat on a bench outside of his changing room. She glanced down the short hallway beside her, making sure they were utterly alone. Once she knew there were no other humans present, she sucked in a steep breath. "Nathaniel," she began, uncertain of how to phrase this particular question.

"Yes?" his voice came from behind the curtain, like The Great Oz.

"Did you, um, did you hear me earlier today?"

"When, exactly?"

She licked her dry lips. "When...when I asked you to come to the mall?" Abby held her breath. If he hadn't heard, this was going to be really awkward.

Nathaniel's soft laughter drifted through the curtain, calming her wild heartbeat. "Yes, I heard you. You wanted me to meet Julie."

"Oh, my God," Abby mouthed, grateful the words didn't actually leave her lips. *This is insane. And unbelievable. And amazing.*

The curtain opened and Nathaniel stepped into the doorway, wearing a navy, long-sleeved shirt and blue jeans. The clothes were simple, but the way they defined his thick body was anything but. Abby's eyes clung to his solid form without any shame whatsoever.

Holy hell, Nathaniel. You are so damn gorgeous. If only I could have been in that changing room with you.

"Wait a minute!" she screeched in sheer panic. "If you heard me earlier, does that mean you can read my mind?"

His grin curved slowly upward. He remained silent for stretched seconds, just resting his shoulder against the door frame. "No, I can't read your mind," he finally admitted. "But I can certainly guess."

"Oh, please don't do that. Please."

He observed her in an all-knowing way before shaking his head. "Don't worry, Abby. First of all, I can't hear you when I'm solid."

"And when you're in your other world?"

"Even then, I can only hear what you want me to hear. Just the thoughts you specifically put into my mind."

"I see," she said, struggling to digest everything at once. "So, you were in your spirit world earlier and you heard me calling you?"

"Well, you were sort of shouting at me."

Abby hung her head. "I'm sorry. I tried to say your name normally, but nothing happened, so I figured it didn't work."

"I heard you the first time. I just didn't want to frighten you by answering, putting you in a situation where you'd have to explain your reaction to Julie. I was on my way here, but I also couldn't materialize into a solid being in the middle of the store. I was outside the mall, still a spirit, when you started shouting at me. You caught me so off guard that I panicked and materialized in the nearest stairwell. I scared an old lady on the stairs half to death. I'm just thankful she wasn't looking right at me when I appeared out of thin air or she probably would have had a heart attack."

"Oh, crap. I really am sorry," Abby apologized as she gazed up at him. "I just had no idea this was even possible. I mean, I thought I heard you in my head twice on Friday, but I wasn't sure. Why didn't you tell me we could talk to each other this way?"

"Honestly, I didn't know if you'd heard me, since you didn't say anything about it. It was only an idea I had – that we might be able to do it – but I didn't want to upset you if it didn't work. If you thought you heard me, why didn't you say anything about it?"

"Oh, you know," she answered with a shrug. "I just figured I'd started hearing voices. But I didn't mind so much. If I'm going to hear any other voice in my head, I'd prefer that it's yours."

Nathaniel's shoulders fell. "Good Lord. What am I going to do with you, Abby? You're so quick to consider yourself crazy. When will you accept the fact that you're amazingly intuitive? In all my years of roaming this earth, I've never met anyone who can do what you do. You understand wavelengths of the mind that normal people don't even know exist. That doesn't make you crazy. It makes you incredible."

Her heart skipped more than once. "Really? You think I'm incredible?"

"Yeah, I do," he answered with a soft smile before pulling the curtain closed behind him. "Now, let me try on the rest of these clothes and then I'll take you to get something to eat. Sound good?"

"Sounds great," she agreed, ecstatic over the idea of spending more time with him. She was even ecstatic over watching him eat again, in his uniquely ravenous way. She'd missed that about him. Along with his sweet smile. And gorgeous eyes. And deep voice. And warm, gentle touch. "Damn, how could I miss so much about a person in one single weekend?" she mumbled.

"What was that?" Nathaniel questioned from inside his changing room.

"Oh, nothing. I was...I was just wondering what you did this weekend."

"This weekend? I spent most of my time with Sondra Lawson."

Abby's face contorted. She shifted on her bench, trying not to be too jealous over another girl. Especially one who couldn't even see him.

"I only wanted to make sure Sondra was okay," Nathaniel clarified in the awkward silence. "Chuck Harding was with her a lot this weekend and I'm interested in their relationship because of what you told me. Chuck definitely has some personal control issues. And you were right – he's cheating on Sondra with Holly. Sondra doesn't know anything about it."

"Yeah, that's what I thought. Poor Sondra."

Nathaniel opened the curtain again. This time, he stood before Abby in a hunter green buttoned-up shirt paired with khakis. She made a conscious effort not to drool.

"So, what do you think of this outfit?" he asked.

She knew *yummy yum yum* wasn't an appropriate response, so she said, "Um, good," and tried to look normal. With another knowing smile, The Great Oz went back behind the curtain. But Abby didn't click the heels of her ruby slippers together, because she was perfectly happy being right here.

NATHANIEL EYED THE HALF-POUND CHEESEBURGER, preparing to pounce on the sesame seed bun. Abby sat across from him at their plastic table, giddily watching as he picked up his double-everything burger. He sank his teeth into it while his eyes rolled back in his head. Sixty years of not-eating was apparently a lot to catch up on.

Abby felt grateful to be back at the mall's food court, taking a break from shopping. Seeing her otherworldly spirit try on all manner of form-fitting shirts and pants wreaked havoc on her feeble mind. She couldn't even conjure up appropriate curiosity about the wad full of money he pulled from his pocket to pay for all the clothes they'd chosen for him.

Her eyes nearly crossed as she stared at him now while he chewed. Even the simple act of eating seemed fantastical when he performed it. "God, I just don't know enough about you," Abby sighed, not even sure she'd said the words out loud until Nathaniel stopped chewing.

"Don't you?" he asked, setting his partially devoured burger back on his tray. "I've tried to be as open with you as I can be."

"I know that, and I know we haven't been together long. But there's so much I want to learn about you. I mean, I don't even know your last name."

"That is odd," he agreed, wiping his hands on a napkin before setting his sights on her. "Especially since you told Julie that I'm your boyfriend."

Oh, hell. He heard every single word I shouted at him.

In her muteness, he grinned. "It's Dunnington, by the way."

Abby shifted in her food court chair. "Okay. Hello, Nathaniel Dunning-ton. Do you have a middle name?"

"Yes, I do. But I really don't want to tell you what it is."

"Why not?"

"Because it's...it's weird."

"Well, now you have to tell me."

Nathaniel shook his head. "Fine. It's Olaf."

Abby tried not to laugh, but a tiny giggle came out. "Sorry. That slipped."

"It's okay. You're allowed to make fun of the silly name. Everybody else did when I was growing up."

"Aw, now I'm really sorry. No one should make fun of you."

"I appreciate that," he said, sitting forward in the plastic chair that seemed far too fragile to support his large body. "But it's really not so bad, given the nod to my Nordic ancestry. When I think of it that way, I'm happy."

"Nordic," Abby considered. "Like Vikings." That made sense. He was built like a Viking. She could picture him in one of those gold helmets with horns sticking out of the sides.

"Yeah, like Vikings. And what about you? What's your full name?"

"Abigail Luann Forrest."

"Luann?"

"I know, right? My middle name is pretty weird, too. Honestly, I don't even know where Luann came from. I think my parents just made it up."

"Well, I think it's quite pretty," he offered, holding her gaze from across their little table. "And your last name suits you perfectly."

"Yeah? How so?"

"Forests are very green. Just like you are, deep inside. Calm and centered."

Abby's eyes widened at the preposterous thought. "Wow, Nathaniel. You see me differently than anyone else does, you know that? You even see me differently than I see myself."

"Is that a bad thing?"

"No, but I don't know if I can live up to it. I think my insides are a tangled, gooey mess. Calm and centered aren't words I would ever use."

"Then you'll just have to trust me on that one."

"Okay," she agreed. "I mean, you're incredibly easy to trust, aren't you? I've barely known you for two weeks, and yet I feel like I can rely on you for anything. I can't even imagine what you meant to your family. They must have missed you so much when you left for the military. I bet you were their rock."

Nathaniel's face fell, his calm expression transforming to one of somberness and regret. Abby wished she could take her words back.

"It was hard to leave them," he replied, his voice now low and aching. "My mother, especially, did not want me joining the service. But I did what I had to do, what felt right, at the time." He paused, looking down at his hands as they balled into fists. "My death tore open a place in her that never healed."

"H-how do you know that?"

"Because I saw it when I went back. After I found myself in my other world, and I went back to our farm, I stayed with her all the time. I was there the day she got the telegraph that said I'd been killed. I've never seen that kind of pain in anyone. Not up until that point, and not in the many, many years since. She was never the same."

"My God. That's so awful."

Nathaniel's soft laughter belied his obvious pain. "It's just crazy to me that it can still feel this raw after all these years. I've always felt responsible for her pain. After all, I was the one who made the decisions leading to that point. Had I only been more controlled…"

Abby leaned forward. "What do you mean by controlled?"

"Hell," he scoffed, staring blankly across the sea of mallgoers. "You talk about being a mess of emotions, Abby. But you should have seen me. I was such an emotional kid. I did everything, made every decision, with my heart and not my head. I was able to love very deeply, but I was also quick to jump to anger and even rage. I made my choices with my gut and those choices led me to that beach in France. Therefore, it was entirely my fault that I died."

"How can you say that, Nathaniel? You didn't have a choice in dying. You were a soldier. You had to follow orders."

"Yes, I had to follow orders, but I was only a soldier because I'd made the decision to be one. Being a soldier led to my death, and since my death was the cause of my mother's pain, I have to take responsibility for it. Damn, I tried to take responsibility. After Normandy, I tried to help her by staying with her for as long as I could. I wanted to believe that she knew I was there. I wanted to believe that my presence as a spirit reassured her. She used to sit in the kitchen sometimes and talk to an old picture she had of me. Those moments were so calming, feeling like she was really talking to me. But other than those few brief instants, I basically spent forty years watching her grow old.

"My dad died of a heart attack in his sixties. My little sister grew up and had a family of her own. And my mother went back to school to get a nursing degree. She cared for other people almost until the day she died. I think it made her happy, to some extent. But there was always that part of her – the part that was mine – that kept her from being truly at peace. She smiled, but it never reached her eyes. She was always in pain.

"I waited with her, right up until the very end. I was there with her when she died. And I expected, deep in my heart, to be able to see her then – to see her spirit in this other world – in this world I've been trapped in since the day I died. I just knew I would have that moment when she left her world and came into mine. But I watched as she took her last breath, and as her body stilled forever, and there was nothing. Nothing but the pain I knew I'd caused her. The pain I could never take away."

Nathaniel paused to take a shallow, stuttered breath. His distant gaze came slowly back to the present. His eyes fixed solely onto hers.

"I see that pain in you, Abby. I see the struggles you've been forced to endure: watching your father suffer beneath the weight of his illness, watching your mother drink herself to death, dealing with that death day in and day out. And caring for your father now, when he needs you most, even though your heart is filled with doubt and fear. I see your pain and I want to absorb it, to take it all away so you will never hurt again. Because you are so calm and so strong, deep inside, but you've never had the opportunity to enjoy the peace I see within your heart. My God, if I could have only one wish granted to me in this miserable existence I lead, it would be to take your pain away. I want to take all of that away from you and let you be at peace, the way you truly deserve to be..."

His voice trailed off into silence.

Abby could only stare at him.

Bodies moved around them, conversations continued, people carried on with their lives. But Abby sat, entirely immobile. She couldn't fathom how any of this was possible. Even if she'd had eighty years to deal with life and grasp its meaning, she would never understand the things Nathaniel did. She could never feel the extent of his emotions – the ones pouring through him every moment. She could never sacrifice herself so freely, existing only to save others. She could never be that good or that pure.

Abby knew of only one word that fully defined him.

Angel.

A tear traced a path down her cheek. Nathaniel reached out, catching the tiny drop with the backs of his fingers. "I'm sorry. I'm overdoing it again, aren't I? I can never tell when I'm just too much to deal with."

Abby made a noise somewhere between a laugh and a sob. "You're never overdoing it. It's just overwhelming – all you've seen and all you know. I want to understand. I want to be the best friend I can possibly be for you."

"Just be yourself, Abby. That's all I need. Just you. Just the way you are."

"I'm right here, Nathaniel." *Take anything you want.*

He smiled with her assurance, the lopsided curve of his lips bringing his boyish features back to life. He shook his head as if throwing off the past. Then he grabbed his cheeseburger and took another colossal bite, moaning in sheer pleasure.

Abby laughed through her tears.

"I know you have to go home to study soon," he said when he finished eating, "but I was hoping you could help me shop for one more thing."

"Yeah? What's that?"

"A brown leather jacket. Those are still in style, right?"

"Sure," she answered, not at all concerned about his clothes. He could be wearing a polka-dotted fur hat and leopard-skinned overalls, for all she cared.

"Fantastic. I always wanted one. Then we'll get you home, I promise."

She shrugged. "Whenever."

<hr>

Monday at lunch, Abby still wasn't quite right. She sat on her favorite picnic bench on the outskirts of school, gazing into the woods beyond, thinking of the confessions Nathaniel had made to her last night. Folded onto that undersized food court chair in the middle of the mall, he'd said words that affected her more deeply than any others she'd ever heard. Well, other than, "Your mother is dead."

Abby had only been told about her mom's passing. Nathaniel actually had to watch his mother die – a slow and painful process across years and years –

without ever being able to reach her, talk to her, or hold her. He was never able to tell her he loved her ever again.

At the very least, Abby had gotten to say those words. She'd been with her mom, as a friend and a confidant, until the very end. She never felt like she'd let her down. Sadly, Nathaniel couldn't say the same.

Abby didn't really understand why he blamed himself for his mother's pain, especially since he didn't die on purpose. He spoke of wild emotions, poor choices, anger and rage. She couldn't imagine any of that. The man who stood by and let Maria's father beat him over and over without returning a single blow was not a man of rage. He was her Nathaniel – a peaceful, perfect being – and she couldn't fathom his words or the anguish behind them.

She sighed as she waited for him to appear on the bench across from her. He'd ridden home with her in her car last night, giving her hand a reassuring squeeze before leaving her alone on her doorstep. He'd also smiled at her in the school hallway this morning, motioning to the new outfit he wore, as she made her way to class. But those tiny moments weren't nearly enough to satisfy her needs. Abby had to see him right this minute, to reassure herself once again that he wasn't a fantastical figment of her imagination.

Maybe I should just close my eyes and call him, she considered, curious to find out if she could use their mental connection to pull him to her. However, she didn't want to seem too anxious or clingy. After all, Nathaniel thought of her as calm and centered, and she didn't want to disappoint.

Abby settled for chewing on her lip and impatiently waiting his arrival. She stared into the trees, thinking he might appear there first, so he didn't scare her with his spirit stealth. But as she looked up from her bench toward the forest, an odd movement in the distance caught her eye.

Just beyond her small cluster of picnic tables, Abby saw four boys shuffling slowly into the trees. The first two were Jason and Randy, who often spent time in the woods, doing whatever they did at lunch. The third was Eric from her history class, tagging along behind them as he sometimes did. But the fourth boy was one she'd never seen before.

Number four walked behind the other three, ten feet back and yet obviously with them. He was tall, like Nathaniel, and also muscular, but with less bulk and more fluidity. This fourth boy looked a bit older than the others, although not too old. His dark brown hair pulled straight back from his forehead to rest at his shoulders. His eyes were shielded behind black sunglasses.

Abby couldn't stop herself from fixating on him. There was something about him – about the way his body moved – that felt out of place. She couldn't put her finger on it, not from this distance, but she couldn't look away until she did.

In an instant, he stopped walking. He stood deathly still for a long minute, letting the others wind their way into the woods before him. Then he turned. Toward her.

As the three boys disappeared into the trees, number four came straight at her. His footsteps flowed smoothly despite the unevenness of the ground. Abby couldn't hear his movements at all, which made her heart flicker uncomfortably in her chest. She wished he would take off his sunglasses, even if only for a few seconds, so she could get a good look at his eyes.

Straightening on her bench, Abby kept her spine stiff as a board while he approached. An icy burst of air preceded him, rushing over her skin with untamed ferocity. When he arrived, he neither asked to sit nor waited to be asked. He just sat down at her table, on the bench directly across from her.

The arctic air that gripped his body forced its way into her bones, sending a thousand slivers of frozen lightning shooting beneath her skin. She clasped her hands together on the wooden tabletop, as if she could form some sort of shield between him and her. Number four didn't speak to her at all. But he did reach up to his sunglasses, easing them slowly and steadily off of his face.

Abby's lungs seized in fear the moment she saw his eyes.

His eyes. Could she even call them that? They moved of their own volition – not the white parts, but the dark, muddied insides – like some evil, demonic sludge. With black irises and no discernible pupil, they changed shape and pattern like a thick, viscous oil that seeped and oozed across his field of vision.

His eyes settled onto her. They attempted to hold her in place even as they churned. Abby tasted bile in the back of her throat.

The boy smiled at her with a flash of perfectly white, straight teeth – a smile that would have been exceedingly handsome if not for his corroded, rotted eyes.

"Well, then," he said. "You must be Abigail."

SEVEN

Abby's whole body shuddered. She could have blamed her involuntary tremors on the appearance of another otherworldly being. The freezing air he generated could have easily been the culprit. But it wasn't. It was his eyes.

She couldn't pin them down. She couldn't make them come into focus. Years of reading her father's emotions through the clarity or cloudiness of his eyes had given her the uncanny ability to know when something was wrong. She didn't need to use that ability now. Anyone on the face of the planet would pull away from this roiling black oil staring straight inside them. The inherent need for self-preservation would make everyone everywhere recoil without thought.

Abby tried to fight her desire to run. She tried to stay steady and keep her wits about her. Yet her body still trembled.

He continued to smile. "So, you really can see us like this," he mused, his tone casual and smooth. "That's quite impressive."

Us? Does he mean him and Nathaniel? Or are there more of them?

"I'm Jonathan, by the way. Jonathan Fitzhugh. I'm an acquaintance of Nathaniel's. It's a pleasure to meet you. I'd shake your hand, but...well, I'm sure you understand."

Abby's gaze darted to his hand, resting on the table, grasping his black shades. She wished he would put his sunglasses back on. She didn't want to look at his eyes anymore. She also didn't want him sitting here. And she defi-nitely did not want to touch his hand. Never, ever.

WHERE ARE YOU, NATHANIEL?

Her spirit appeared instantly by her side. Before Abby could even finish screaming the question in her head, Nathaniel sat on the bench next to her. He brought his usual rush of chilled air with him, yet he actually felt warm compared to the blistering gusts blasting at her from across the table. His air swirled. Jonathan's assaulted.

Nathaniel's body turned solid in seconds. His hand reached for hers. Abby grasped onto him, gripping his arm and fingers, barely resisting the urge to crawl into his lap. She encouraged herself to take refuge in the strength of his presence, to slow her rapid breaths and focus on the problem sitting before her. Eventually, she calmed down enough to truly examine the churning pools of oil across the table.

Jonathan's eyes focused solely on her. Even as he spoke to Nathaniel, his rotted gaze never left her face. "Wow, Nate. You got here in about two seconds. That's a record, even for you. You keeping tabs on her that close?"

Nathaniel growled. "I don't think she's interested in your company, Jon."

Jonathan laughed – one of those deep, gorgeous laughs fit for the male lead in a movie – but it couldn't reach his eyes to contain the oil. "You aren't going to allow her to speak for herself, I see."

Abby huffed. She was perfectly happy being spoken for at the moment.

"Don't you have somewhere else you need to be?" Nathaniel questioned.

"Not really," Jonathan replied, finally turning his sights to the person sitting beside her. "But I will leave the two of you alone, for now. I can tell when I'm not wanted."

Nathaniel shook his head. "That would be a new skill you've acquired."

Jonathan grinned in amusement. An instant later, he looked back to Abby. His roiling eyes somehow managed to fixate on her face, examining her once again. It was unwanted – an invasion – and she grasped Nathaniel's hand harder and harder until her fingers went numb.

"Damn it, Jon..." Nathaniel warned.

Jonathan stood, the shifting of his large body causing no movement on the bench, and put his sunglasses back on. Abby breathed easier when his eyes were concealed. Until he spoke. "I will see you again, Abigail," he promised with a flash of teeth that she could only hope was intended as a smile. Then he strolled away into the waiting forest.

As soon as Jon left, Nathaniel turned fully toward her. "God, I'm so sorry about that, Abby. I'm so sorry about him."

She barely heard the apology. She pressed her hand against her heart, attempting to ease the intense pounding. *Don't cry. Don't cry. Don't cry.*

"Abby," he repeated, reaching to cradle her face in his hand.

She turned her attention to Nathaniel's eyes, witnessing the kindness and concern inside his clear blue. Her pulse began to settle. "Wh-who was that?"

"Jon is another...he's another spirit."

"Another one? How many of you are there?"

"It's just him and me. At least, as far as I know."

"You actually *know* him?"

"I do. Regrettably."

"How long have you..."

"A long time."

"And why didn't you tell me about him?"

Nathaniel's shoulders fell. "Well, I – I kind of did. I told you I only knew one other person here and I didn't like him. But really, that's only an excuse. I should have told you about him before now. I know I should have."

Abby frowned. "Then why didn't you?"

"Honestly?" Nathaniel asked, his fingers stroking her cheek.

"Yes, please."

He dropped his hand from her face and exhaled. "I was hoping that I was the only one you could see. I'm sorry. That was selfish of me."

His sudden sadness washed over her. Abby wasn't upset with him, since he was the most unselfish being she'd ever met. She slipped her fingers over his, wanting to take his regret away. "Hey, it's okay. All I really needed was to see you, and here you are. Besides, I think I can handle having another spirit in my life, now that I know about him. He just surprised me when he showed up here. I mean, he's very different from you."

Nathaniel huffed out a laugh. "Hell, I'd certainly like to think so."

Abby tensed, wanting to probe for more information, yet not sure how much she truly wanted to know. "So, you...you met Jon a long time ago?"

"Unfortunately. We've been around each other a lot."

"You mean at the different high schools you go to?"

"Yes."

"When did you first realize that there was another spirit in your world?"

Nathaniel glanced down to her hand, watching as he laced their fingers. "He was there in the '80s, at Maria's high school. That's when he found me."

"He found you? Did he help you with Maria? Does he help save people?"

"Help? Jon? Oh, no. He doesn't help at all."

"Does he...harm?" Abby asked, wondering how concerned she should be with this new spirit in her life. She didn't know much about Jonathan Fitzhugh, but she knew one thing for certain: he did not look at her gently.

Nathaniel sighed. "Jon just has a talent for searching out trouble. When I follow him, I'm almost guaranteed to find someone in need of help."

"You mean he's the reason you travel from one place to the next?"

"Usually. Yes."

"Oh. Then you're actually here now because of him," Abby realized, wishing the words didn't hurt as much as they did.

Nathaniel squeezed her hand. "No, that's not the reason I'm here. I mean, yes, I came here because of him. But now, I'm here because of you."

"Because you think you'll need to help me?"

"No, no. I honestly don't know who I'm here to help. But I do know that I want to be here because of you. I've never wanted to be with anyone else the way I want to be with you."

Abby smiled for the first time in forever.

Nathaniel reached up to curl a stray hair behind her ear. "Wanting you for myself blinded me to the fact that I couldn't keep Jon away forever. I should have told you about him sooner. I also should have been more vigilant about watching over you today. I should have been sitting right here on this bench, waiting for you when the lunch bell rang."

"I must admit, I would have loved it if you were here waiting for me. Is there a reason you weren't?"

"Sadly, yes. Things are turning worse for Sondra and Chuck. She's trying to pull away from him and I'm afraid he may become violent. They were arguing in the hall before lunch and I felt like I needed to stay."

"Oh, God. Of course, you were doing something heroic. And then you heard me mental-yelling."

Nathaniel chuckled. "Well, you do shout at me a lot."

"I know. I know," Abby sighed. "I'm sorry for yelling. Again."

"It's no problem. If I'm going to hear another voice in my head, even a shouting one, I'd prefer that it's yours."

Abby grinned wildly. "Thank you for coming to my rescue, by the way."

"Don't thank me, please. It only makes me feel worse. I should have already been here, especially since I figured Jon would try something today."

"Why did you think it would be today?"

"Because he found out about you this morning."

Her head tilted. "Really? How did he find out?"

"He noticed my new clothes."

Abby looked down, absorbing the navy shirt and jeans that fit Nathaniel so delectably in the changing room yesterday. They somehow looked even better on him now. "I guess Jon didn't believe you just decided on a change?"

"Yeah, not so much. I've been wearing the same outfit for over twenty years. He didn't have to be a genius to figure out that something unusual happened to me. But he is highly intelligent. I knew I couldn't lie to him, so I tried to tell him a partial truth – just that we met and you could see me – and then I worked really hard to not gush about you."

"Gush?" Abby echoed. "Would you really have gushed about me?"

Nathaniel's eyes sparkled. "Absolutely. I had a hard time holding it in."

"Wow. I think I'd like to hear all the gushing sometime."

"Well, I could do it right now, but you'd probably think me less manly."

"Hmm. I suppose we can't have that," she said, unable to hold back her laughter. She gazed into him, astounded that she even possessed the ability to laugh now, when she'd been terrified just minutes ago. How did Nathaniel take her worst emotions and turn them upside down, handing them back to her shiny and new? He was a miracle worker, and yet the only person who'd ever known that fact was someone who didn't even care – someone who was, apparently, the only other person in his life for many years.

Abby cringed with that revelation. "So, is Jon your...your *friend*?"

"Friend?" Nathaniel hedged, as if the word tasted bitter. "I, uh, I don't think that's the title I would give him. He's just the only other person I've had a conversation with for the last twenty years. I suppose it's like being trapped on a deserted island with someone. After a while, you get used to them."

She eased her fingers up to trace the straight line of his jaw. "I'm so glad you found me, Nathaniel. For both of us."

He turned his face into her hand and pressed his lips against her palm. Abby hummed with the feel of his mouth on her skin. It took several seconds for her to realize that the chimes ringing in her head were actually coming from school.

"Darn that blasted bell," she grumbled.

Nathaniel laughed. "My goodness, Abby. Careful with that language."

She begrudgingly pulled her hand away. "Are you going back to Sondra?"

"No, I can check on her later. I'm right where I need to be."

"Does that mean you'll come to class with me?"

"I promise I'm not letting you out of my sight for the rest of the day."

"Oh, man. That sounds absolutely wonderful."

Nathaniel rose from the bench and held out his hand. Abby accepted the offering as she stood, gripping onto him while they walked toward school. Nathaniel kept their fingers entwined until other students came into view. He shifted back into his other world then, but she knew he still moved in time beside her.

The swirl of air surrounding her spirit felt almost warm now. Abby smiled. It was all about perspective.

***

TEN MINUTES of history class passed by before Abby noticed anything wrong. Nathaniel had sat peacefully beside her from the moment they entered the room and took their seats, lulling her into a sense of security. However, the fact that Mr. Puryear still insisted on discussing Normandy made her hyper-tuned to everything around them. When Nathaniel stiffened in his chair and glared at the closed classroom door, she followed his gaze intently.

An instant later, Jonathan walked into the room. Abby's stomach lurched at the sight – not only because she had to see the oily-eyed spirit again, but because Jon didn't walk through the door like any normal person would. He actually walked *through* the door.

Abby whimpered quite loudly. She couldn't help it. Mr. Puryear paused mid-sentence to glare at her. She immediately looked down at her desk. *Please don't call on me.*

Nathaniel's serene voice drifted into her head. *Everything's okay, Abby.*

She smiled to herself, finding it much easier to breathe when she could hear her sweet spirit inside her muddled mind. As soon as she felt certain that the risk of being humiliated by her teacher had passed, she glanced up. Jonathan stood at the front of the class, meeting her gaze the moment she lifted her head. Gratefully, his sunglasses concealed his corroded eyes.

Jon acknowledged her with a nod, like they'd been friends for years. Abby's mouth gaped. She clasped her hands together on her desk and stared at them, praying he would find something else to occupy his time.

After another minute of Mr. Puryear lecturing everyone, Abby peeked sideways at Nathaniel. His eyes were downcast, yet the expression on his face was one of veiled amusement. She watched in wonder while his head shook and a tiny smile pulled up the edge of his mouth.

Holy crap, Nathaniel. Are you and Jon having a conversation?

Yes, Nathaniel replied, although he didn't look at her.

Really? What are you talking about?

His brow knotted. *Right now, I'm trying to occupy his mind so he doesn't focus on you. But I can let you hear our conversation, if you'd like.*

Abby risked looking up at Jonathan, who currently paced back and forth in front of Mr. Puryear. Did she really want to hear what was on Jon's mind? Even when she knew that curiosity often killed the cat? *Yes, I...I think I would like to hear.*

Okay, Nathaniel agreed. *I'll open my thoughts, but please don't say anything to me while he's here. I'd prefer it if he didn't know what you're capable of doing.*

I understand, Abby replied, gripping the sides of her desk while staring as hard as she could at her textbook. She waited only a moment before she heard another voice in her mind – one she could already identify from memory.

And what is it with this teacher? Jon asked, the irritation in his words resounding through her head. *He's as boring as the day is long. I swear he's even worse than that one back in Ohio. Remember the stupid science teacher who couldn't say the word 'anemone'?*

Yes, I remember, Nathaniel answered.

Any-money. Ani-mani. That guy was such an idiot. This one's no better. And what is it with his clothes? Doesn't he know tweed is out? And no one wears white pants after Labor Day, for Christ's sake. Man, I'm so grateful the girl finally got you to change. I thought I'd have to go through eternity staring at that same damn soldier outfit. How you weren't sick of yourself is beyond me.

Abby looked up from her desk, pretending to pay attention to Mr. Puryear. From her peripheral vision, she watched Jonathan walk around the edge of the classroom, staring at various pictures and graphs on the wall. A boy sitting near him shivered and wriggled in his chair. She could empathize with that unease, even from this distance.

With Jon currently distracted, Abby allowed herself to observe him in tiny, stolen glances. She found it amusing that he was so interested in other people's clothing. Although, to be fair, he could certainly wear his own. Form-fitting back pants, a black T-shirt, and a weathered, black leather jacket all showcased his body in the most sinful ways. His shoulder-length hair hung just so, slightly mussed yet perfect enough in its disarray to know it was no accident. His face was cut in angles, his skin tanned and smooth, his black sunglasses camouflaging his one physical flaw. From the way he carried himself – so differently than these high school boys – she guessed he was about twenty years old.

Abby grimaced, silently admitting to herself that Jon was physically stunning. She couldn't believe she hadn't noticed before, since it was so damn obvious. Then again, she knew his beauty only went skin deep. He couldn't possibly be a good person, since no decent, caring soul would spend eternity with churning oil for eyes. For all she knew, Jon was true evil.

That disturbing thought rattled her to her bones. She grabbed her pen from her desk, nearly strangling it with both hands. Nathaniel observed her for a moment before addressing the elephant in the room. *I think it's time for you to leave now, Jon.*

Jonathan spun around to stare him down. *Why?*

Because Abby doesn't like having you here.

Really? Are you reading her emotions?

You know I am.

Well, I know how much I like it when you read mine, so I can only imagine that it irritates the hell out of her.

Nathaniel smiled. *Sometimes.*

Abby bit her lip to keep from laughing.

So, what? Am I freaking her out? Jon asked with noticeable enjoyment.

You are, actually.

That's odd. I mean, most girls think I'm downright gorgeous.

Yes, I'm well aware. But you forget that Abby can see you as you truly are.

Hmm. Well, I saw the two of you as you truly are – when we were all sitting out at that picnic table. Hell, she looked like she was going to jump straight into your lap. Is that how it is between you two?

Nathaniel sat up taller in his chair, but he didn't reply.

How long has it even been since you've touched a person? Jon persisted.

A lot longer than it's been for you, Nathaniel retorted.

No, really. I want to know the truth. Have you touched anyone else since you died? And keep in mind that getting sucker-punched by strangers doesn't count.

Nathaniel pressed his lips together before offering a cautious reply. *No, I haven't touched anyone else since I died.*

Abby stared hard at a knot on her desk.

Jon huffed. *Well, then. I bet you're enjoying this. I suppose I can see why. She's pretty enough, and it must be interesting if she can see you all the time. So, how far have you gotten with her?*

Nathaniel bristled. *You're being crude now. Just drop it.*

Seriously, how physical are you going to get with this girl? What happened to that strict no-touching policy you've clung to all these years? Or was that just an oath of convenience, until you found something you actually wanted?

Damn it, Jon. You need to leave.

"Abigail Forrest?"

Abby heard her name called. She wasn't sure if it was Nathaniel or Jon.

"Miss Forrest?"

Crap. It's Mr. Puryear.

"Do you know the answer, Miss Forrest?" her teacher demanded.

"I'm sorry...could you repeat the question?" *Like that will help.*

"What was the code name for the naval portion of the Invasion of Normandy?"

Abby clenched her hands together until her fingers whitened.

Operation Neptune, Nathaniel offered.

"Operation Neptune," she repeated.

"Oh. Well. Very good," Mr. Puryear acknowledged before moving on to his next victim.

A bare second passed before Jon reacted. He laughed, deep and full, the raucous noise banging inside her head. *Well, butter my butt and call me a biscuit,* he drawled. *You gave her that answer, didn't you, Nate?*

She glanced nervously at Jon. He stared at her from behind his shades.

Hello, Abby, he said, his voice much louder in her mind. A devious smile crept across his lips as his thoughts – sharp and crystallized – pushed their way inside her. *Welcome to our conversation. Or have you been here all along?*

She forced her gaze down to her desk, hoping to feign ignorance.

Gosh, Nate. I don't know for sure, but I believe that feeding your girlfriend answers in class constitutes cheating. And no one could ever call you a cheater, could they?

Nathaniel's hands balled into fists. *You've worn out your welcome, Jon.*

Have I? I think I'll let Abby decide that.

She knew there was nowhere to run. There was no point in pretending not to hear. Jon already knew. *You've worn out your welcome,* she said.

Oh, yes. There you are, Abigail. My, my, my. Looks like I should have paid more attention to you before now. In my defense, I had no idea how impressive you are. No wonder Nate tried to keep you for himself. No such luck, though.

Abby raised her head to pin Jonathan's dark gaze. She found her voice without further hesitation. *I don't want you here, Jon. You need to leave. Now.*

He offered his million-dollar smile before bowing to her from across the room. *Very well, Miss Forrest. Your wish is my command.*

Jon disappeared into thin air. Abby jumped in her seat. She'd never seen Nathaniel do anything quite that spooky. It was incredibly unnerving.

Mr. Puryear cleared his throat. Abby glanced up to see him glaring at her from the front of the class. She refocused on her desk.

Is Jon truly gone? she asked once her teacher's droning resumed.

Nathaniel nodded. *Yes. For now. Are you okay?*

I think so. Jon is really irritating, though.

Tell me about it. But you did well. Incredibly well.

No, I didn't. He figured out that I could hear him in my head.

He would have figured it out sooner or later. But the way it happened was entirely my fault. I shouldn't have given you the answer to that question.

Well, I appreciated it, even though I guess it was cheating. It doesn't matter anyway, though, since I'll never pass this class. Too many distractions.

I can always tutor you, Nathaniel assured. *If there's one thing I know, it's history. And as an added bonus, it'll be a great excuse to spend time together.*

Abby smiled, already growing calmer and happier with her spirit beside her. She figured he must monitor her colors so he could do or say whatever was necessary to achieve a balance of blue and green inside her body. His capabilities were truly amazing, even though she'd never seen him walk through doors or disappear into thin air the way Jon did. She knew Nathaniel could do those things, but probably didn't want to freak her out by showing her. He always tried to act as human as possible, which she truly appreciated. Although now, she wondered if he could do more. Maybe he had the potential to do all sorts of things. Maybe he could help her in ways she never imagined.

Her heart swelled with possibilities as the bell rang. Abby stood and shoved her book into her backpack while Nathaniel waited in the seat beside her. When she started to leave, Eric Nichols tapped her on the shoulder.

"You okay?" Eric asked.

"Yeah, sure. Why wouldn't I be?" She sounded paranoid, even to herself.

He shrugged. "You just seem awfully jumpy today."

"Oh. Well, I'm good. Thanks for asking, though."

"Yeah, no problem," he said, moving past her. "See you tomorrow."

Abby nodded to him before turning toward Nathaniel. His intent eyes remained fixed on Eric until the boy fully exited the door.

Shall we? she asked.

Yes, we shall, Nathaniel agreed, falling into step beside her as they both walked out of the room. *Let's head to your next class.*

She looked to his face while they moved through the hallway together. Concern filled his eyes as he watched the other students scurry to their classrooms. Abby shook her head. *You don't really have to come to my next class with me, Nathaniel.*

His wandering attentions returned instantly to her. *But I promised I wouldn't let you out of my sight for the rest of the day.*

Yes, and I now release you from that promise. You should do whatever you need to do. I know you want to check on Sondra, and I highly doubt Jon will show up again. Even if he does, I can handle it.

Nathaniel's glowing eyes shifted over her face. *Are you absolutely sure?*

Yes, I'm sure. I'll see you in my car after school.

Do you believe me now when I say how strong you are, Abby?

Well, I guess we'll see.

Nathaniel leaned in closer. He slid the cool, airy surface of his hand over her arm, sending tiny shivers fluttering across her skin. *I already do*, he whispered beside her ear, just before he slipped away into the sea of students.

SETTLING INTO HER FINAL CLASS, pretending to pay attention to her teacher, Abby actually felt hopeful. It was an odd emotion, considering she'd just had a mind-conversation with a potentially evil spirit who said he intended to focus more of his time on her. Yet she was still hopeful, because if Jonathan Fitzhugh had certain powers, then Nathaniel might have them, too. And if Nathaniel had those powers, then maybe he could help her find out what really happened to her mother.

Abby did her best to concentrate for the rest of her class, but she wasn't very successful. Her eyes kept darting to the clock on the wall, watching the seconds tick by in slow motion. The instant the final bell rang, she practically plowed people over to escape the building.

She rushed through the halls and out the front doors, speaking to her spirit the moment she breathed the fresh outside air. *I'm on my way to the car.*

I'm already here, Nathaniel answered.

Abby reached her car in a flash, sank into her driver's seat, and turned toward the vision sitting beside her. Even with his glowing eyes and cool air, she'd never felt more comfortable around another person. Or more excited.

Hi, she said with an overpowering grin on her lips.

Hi, Abby. How was your last class?

It was fine. No problems, except that I missed you.

I missed you, too.

Well, then. I'm going to start driving, because there are too many people around for you to turn solid and I'd really like to hold your hand.

That sounds absolutely perfect.

She still smiled as she backed out of her parking space, nearly tempted to speed while driving toward the exit. *How am I doing with the mental-talking thing, by the way?*

Outstanding.

Good. I'm really working on not shouting at you.

Nathaniel laughed. *I truly appreciate that.*

The moment Abby turned onto the main street, the air in her car warmed.

She didn't have to look at the ethereal being beside her to know he'd turned solid. His hand reached for hers, winding their fingers together.

She sighed. *Damn, Nathaniel, you feel amazing. Every time you touch me, I swear it's like the first time I've ever been touched.*

Instant heat crept into Abby's cheeks. She cringed, mortified by her uncensored thoughts. She held her breath as she awaited his reply. Oddly, none came. "Oh," she realized in his silence. "I forgot."

Nathaniel's hand eased across hers. "What did you forget?"

"That you can't hear my thoughts when you're solid."

"Were you still talking to me when I transformed just now?"

"Um, yeah."

"Then I'm sorry I cut you off. What were you saying?"

Abby glanced out of her side window. "It's nothing."

"It doesn't seem like nothing. Will you tell me about it?"

"I think it's probably best that I don't."

"Do I need to turn back into a spirit and read your emotions?"

"Oh, God, no. Please don't do that."

"Then tell me," Nathaniel urged, trailing his fingers up and down her arm.

"It's really nothing," she maintained, trying like hell to not whimper with the warmth of his skin. "I just said that I like it when you touch me."

He grinned as he tugged her hand up to his mouth, turning it over to press his lips into her palm. "Mmm," he hummed. "That's definitely not nothing. I honestly can't think of anything better at the moment."

Abby needed to swallow insect repellent. The butterflies in her stomach were out of control. "I – I hope this isn't breaking the rules, Nathaniel. I mean, what we're doing right now, with the hands and the lips and stuff."

"Rules?" he questioned, eyeing her from the passenger seat. "What rules?"

"Well, Jon said something earlier about you having a no-touch policy."

"Oh, that," Nathaniel dismissed, sliding his fingers over hers again. "It was never really a policy. It was more of a personal belief. I haven't touched anyone since I've been a spirit, in a good way or a bad one. Not until you."

"Then you did break your rule for me. I feel like I should apologize."

"Please don't. It was all me. I didn't realize how much I missed human contact until I found you."

Abby stopped at a red light before meeting his eyes. "But if you missed it so much, why didn't you let yourself have it before now? I can see not touching anyone in anger, but what about good touches? If you could have them, why wouldn't you?"

Nathaniel held her searching gaze. "It's not that I wasn't tempted, believe me. When I found out I could turn solid, my first thought was to stay this way forever. I mean, how different could it be from actually living? If I can walk, talk, breathe, think, and love – and no one knows the truth about me – then who would ever realize I'm not actually alive?"

"Exactly. So, why didn't you do it? Why didn't you stay solid?"

"Because I'm *not* alive, Abby. Even if no one else knew, I would. I don't want to only go through the motions of life. I don't want to just pretend."

"Oh," she said, staring out of her windshield, working to digest his words. "Then you don't stay solid because you think it's immoral."

"Well, I always figured there must be a reason why I'm trapped in this other world. I never felt like I had the right to be solid, which is why I only did it when it was absolutely necessary to save someone. That is, until now."

"And what's different about now?"

"You, of course. You changed everything."

Her foot slipped on the brake and the car jolted. "This is all about me?"

"It is," Nathaniel confirmed, gripping her hand in both of his. "At first, I told myself you needed the contact, because you'd secluded yourself too much and you needed me to pull you back. But now, I realize it was the other way around. I needed you. I had no idea how much I needed you."

The light turned green then. Abby accelerated, feeling exhilarated by his confessions. She also felt like throwing up. "But what if you needing me is a bad thing? What if I'm no good for you? What if I'm actually a wicked temptress? A treacherous being who entices you to abandon your pure and virtuous ways?"

Nathaniel laughed so hard that his seat shook. "You're so funny – the way you see yourself sometimes. You are not a wicked temptress. I mean, you are tempting, but in positive ways only. Because of how incredible you are."

"Well, thank you." Abby smiled, truly relieved that she wasn't some trashy harlot. And amazed that Nathaniel needed her. And stunned that he had a polar opposite for a friend.

Her smile fell with the thought of the other spirit who'd entered her life today. "But, damn, though. That's really hard to believe," she muttered.

"What's hard to believe? The fact that you're so tempting?"

"No, that's...well, yes, that is hard to believe, although I'm grateful I can tempt you. But what I really can't believe is your friendship with Jon. I mean, here you are, trying to do the best you can with your unusual existence, yet he doesn't help you at all. And I'll bet he gets tempted by all sorts of things."

"If by things you mean people, then yes. But he doesn't only get tempted."

"What are you saying? That he actually does something about it?"

"Hmm," Nathaniel hemmed, as if he really didn't want to explore this particular topic. "There have been times when he's decided to live like a regular person. He's turned solid and pretended to be a student at several high schools, to get to know certain people."

"Would those certain people be women?"

"Primarily, yes."

Abby huffed, offended for every woman in the world. Although she had to admit she could see the appeal, in a purely objective way, if Jonathan was solid. And if he didn't have oily sludge for irises. "And do these girls really think Jon is one of them? I mean, he definitely looks older than a high school student. How old is he, anyway?"

"He was eighteen when he died. Just like me."

"Eighteen? Are you sure?"

"Yeah, I'm pretty sure. He only looks older because he's aged himself."

"Aged himself? How in the hell did he age himself?"

Nathaniel shifted in his seat, apparently uncomfortable with her current line of questioning. Yet he still answered. "When Jon became solid for extended periods, in order to pursue his affairs at different schools, he started to change. At first, he didn't realize what was happening to him. Time is nebulous in the spirit world, but when we turn solid, it always moves forward. Once Jon figured that out, he started limiting his time with the living. But over the last twenty years, he's spent a couple in solid form."

Abby choked her steering wheel in one hand. "My God, is that how all this works? Jon turns solid whenever he feels like it, just to get with these poor, unsuspecting women? While you sit alone, only turning solid to get the crap beat out of you, because you believed all this time that it would be wrong to allow yourself positive human contact?"

"I suppose you can look at it that way. Although I'm solid now for the sole purpose of being with you, so I can't really condemn his actions."

"Yes, you can. You can condemn him anytime you want."

Nathaniel's gaze dropped to her hand. He focused on his fingers as they traced tiny circles inside her wrist. Abby had to concentrate on not jumping on top of him right this second, while the car was still moving.

She pulled over down the street from her house, putting the car in park and pivoting in her seat. "Well, this makes it all very plain, doesn't it?"

He met her eyes. "What's that?"

"You are good and Jon is evil."

Nathaniel's body stilled. "I don't think anything is that simple, Abby."

I do, she thought. But when she witnessed the tense set of his jaw, she didn't say it out loud. "All I mean is I'm happy you're different from him. Honestly, the two of you couldn't be any more different if you tried."

"I'm glad you see how different we are."

"How could I not? Jon doesn't even enter a room the way you do."

"Yeah, I'm sorry about that, too," Nathaniel apologized. "Did he scare you when he walked through the classroom door earlier?"

"Only because I wasn't expecting it. If I had some warning, I'd be okay. I mean, if it's ever something you need to do in the future."

"Well, it's something I *can* do."

"And you can also do the whole disappearing-into-thin-air thing, right?"

Nathaniel tightened his hold on her hand. "Yes."

Abby tried to look unaffected. "That's cool. Where can you reappear?"

"Anywhere I've been before. Or with anyone I've felt."

"Felt? Felt how?"

"Anyone whose emotions I've read."

"I see. Is that how you always find Jon when he moves to the next school?"

"It is. He has a very distinct emotional pattern. I can find it pretty easily."

"Wow. You really are amazing, you know that?" she asked, staring at Nathaniel in actual wonder. She didn't know if she could ever fully wrap her mind around the reality of his world, but she certainly wanted to try.

He smiled softly. "It's possible you give me too much credit."

"It's also possible I don't give you enough," she countered, her mind latching onto the thoughts she'd had earlier today. Was there a way Nathaniel could sense her mother's emotions on the day she died? Abby desperately needed to ask him, but she couldn't just blurt the question out here and now. She needed to butter him up first, quite literally, with a belly full of food. "So, are you...are you still coming to my house for dinner tonight?"

"Definitely," he answered. "Wild horses couldn't keep me away."

"Don't worry. We don't have any of those."

His lopsided grin reappeared. "What time does your dad leave for work?"

"Six o'clock."

"I'll be there one minute later."

"Perfect."

Nathaniel ran his palm across hers, soft and slow. "Also, if you don't mind, I'd prefer to not talk about Jon tonight. I'd like for it to just be us."

Abby nodded with wild abandon. "Absolutely. Tonight is just for us."

"God, that sounds wonderful."

Her heart somersaulted. "I can't wait."

EIGHT

Abby moved with lightning speed, clearing dishes from the kitchen table the moment her father finished eating. She'd spent the entire afternoon preparing their dinner, hoping he wouldn't ask too many questions about the excessive amount of food she made. She plastered a smile on her face as she placed the leftovers on the stovetop to keep them warm.

"Do you need help with all of that?" Mark asked.

"No, it's fine. I can get it."

Her father milled around the kitchen, pouring coffee into a thermos. "Thanks for dinner, Abby. That was really good. You outdid yourself."

"I'm glad you liked it," she replied, holding out the lunch she'd packed for him. Her eyes shifted to the clock: 6:05. "You're going to be late for work."

"Okay, boss," he said, taking his lunch and moseying out of the kitchen.

I'm in your living room, Abby.

"Oh," she gasped, startled by the sound of Nathaniel's voice in her mind. As she followed her father to the front door, she saw her spirit standing beside the living room couch. He looked as perfect as ever, dressed in his navy shirt and jeans, holding one hand behind his back, with his eyes glowing.

Sorry if I'm a little early.

"It's no problem," she answered him, not realizing she'd said the words out loud until her father turned back.

"What was that?" Mark asked.

Abby stepped past Nathaniel to the door. His light, airy chill washed over her as she grasped the handle to pull it open. "It's no problem about me cleaning up in the kitchen," she told her father. "I'm going to do that now."

Mark's head tilted. "Well, thanks again for dinner."

"Sure, Dad. Have a good night."

"I will. You doing all right?"

"Yeah, yeah. I'm doing great."

"Okay. If you say so," he conceded as he walked through the door and onto the porch. "See you in the morning."

"Bye, Dad."

"Bye, honey."

The instant she shut the door behind him, she spun toward her spirit. Abby watched the glow of his eyes transform to deep, clear blue. She inched closer, until the warmth of his solid form soaked through her skin.

Nathaniel's hand remained concealed behind his back. "I really am sorry about showing up before your dad left. I was a bit overexcited to see you."

"I'm just ecstatic that you're here now."

"Good. Because I have something for you."

She forced herself to stand still while Nathaniel pulled his arm forward, producing a single red rose in his hand.

"My God," she breathed. "It's beautiful."

"I'm glad. I really wanted to bring you a flower. Actually, I wanted to bring you dozens of flowers. But I thought you'd have a hard time explaining them all to your dad, so it's only one."

Abby squealed as she took the stem. "It's perfect, Nathaniel. I love it."

"Wonderful. Although I promise I'll understand if you need to throw it out later, to hide the evidence of us having a date here."

The word *date* made her bare toes curl into the carpet. "Are you kidding me? I would never throw this flower out. I'd eat it first, before that."

"Well, it might be a little tough to swallow."

"Oh, I'd figure out a way. Maybe drench it in corn syrup or something."

Nathaniel laughed as he leaned toward her, slipping his fingers up the side of her face. "It's been hours since I saw you last. How was your afternoon?"

"Fine," she answered, contentedly melting into his touch. "Mostly, I just cooked and spent time with my dad."

"I really should have waited for him to leave before I showed up."

"That's okay. He was running late. Besides, I'd love to introduce him to you. Someday, I mean. If you ever want to meet him."

"Please know that I very much want to," Nathaniel assured, even as the brightness in his eyes dimmed. "But I can't, because I'm not..."

"Never mind about that," Abby cut it, well aware that it wasn't practical to introduce her spirit-boyfriend to her father. And she didn't want to waste time on the impossible tonight. She wanted to concentrate on the possible. "So, how did my dad's colors look when you saw him?"

"They looked good. Very green."

She exhaled in relief. "Thank you."

"You're welcome. But you already knew he was calm, didn't you?"

"I thought so, but it's nice to have a second opinion. From a professional."

Nathaniel ran his hand down her arm, catching her fingers inside his. "Please know that I would do anything in my power for you. But you should really trust yourself more. Your intuition is spot-on."

"I appreciate your faith in me," she said, hoping he really would do anything for her, especially after she buttered him up. "Are you ready to eat?"

"God, yes. More than ready."

"Then let's go to the table," she proposed, clutching onto his hand to tug his large body into the dining room. Nathaniel followed along like a puppy, standing eagerly beside her when she reached the table and pulled out a chair. "Here you go. Just have a seat and I'll get everything ready."

"Are you sure I can't help you?"

"No need. I just couldn't set the table before my dad left. I want you to sit and enjoy your evening. Tonight, I am Chef Abby."

Nathaniel took his seat, watching her intently while she bustled back and forth between the dining room and the kitchen. His eyes widened as she placed plate after plate of food in front of him, filling the table with pot roast, mashed potatoes, salad, mixed vegetables, dinner rolls, soda, and an entire pie. At the end, she added a vase in the center of the table and placed his rose inside. She lit a candle beside the vase and dimmed the lights in the room before finally settling into her own chair beside him.

He remained mute, staring at the feast before him, for the longest time.

"What do you think?" Abby prompted. "Do you like it?"

"Wow," Nathaniel marveled. "What's not to like? This is truly amazing. But you don't have your own plate. Aren't you going to join me?"

"I already ate. I hope you understand. If I don't eat with Dad, he gets worried. Tomorrow, when he sees all the leftovers gone, he'll either think I'm going through a bizarre growth spurt or I've developed a hole in my stomach."

"Well, I could eat less. If that will help."

"Oh, no. It'll be fine, I promise. After all, Dad is getting his own reward, since I don't normally cook this much for just us."

Nathaniel's eyes held hers. "Thank you, Abby. Seriously. Having a home-cooked meal like this, it means...it means more than I can say."

"You're welcome. Now, dig in, please."

"I'll try to go slow and enjoy everything."

"Oh, don't do that. I love the way you eat. It's ferocious."

"Like a rabid dog?"

"No. Like someone who's been far too deprived for far too long."

"In more ways than one," he agreed, his gaze slipping from her eyes to her lips before he looked back to his plate. Nathaniel picked up his fork and knife and attacked the roast.

Abby watched as he placed bite after bite onto his tongue, humming and groaning while he chewed. Seeing him eat was an unearthly experience, and she enjoyed it far more than she probably should. She couldn't even muster up concern over how rudely she stared at him.

"This tastes incredible," he managed to say when most of his meal was already gone. "Where did you learn to cook like this?"

"My mom taught me," she answered, hoping her mother was right when she'd said that the way to a man's heart was through his stomach. "She loved cooking, and even wanted to go to cooking school, but it never worked out. She taught me everything I know. It's been helpful, now that she's gone. I think Dad feels like part of her is still around when I cook for him."

"Well, you certainly do an amazing job. You take care of your house, too?"

"Yeah, as best I can."

"And then there's schoolwork. You take on a lot."

She shrugged. "It's not bad. I had a job earlier this year, but Dad asked me to quit after Mom died. He pays me an allowance to cook and keep up the house. I tried to refuse the money, but he says it's a job, same as any other."

Nathaniel buttered a roll while eyeing the pie. "What was your job?"

"I worked at a movie theater. I loved it."

"Are you a movie fan?"

"Oh, yes. I was raised on movies. I think Dad was disappointed I wasn't a boy, but thrilled that I turned into a fellow movie lover. We went to the theater all the time when I was a kid. We still have movie night here every Friday. We just don't eat popcorn anymore."

"No? Why not?"

"Because I had to clean the popcorn machine at work and that was totally disgusting. You should see what passes for butter there. I still can't eat popcorn, to this day."

Nathaniel smiled as he finished his meal. "No popcorn for dessert, then."

"No, silly. I made you pie, of course."

His gaze darted back to the pastry on the table. "Is that apple?"

"It certainly is."

"Did you make it from scratch?"

"I did. I haven't made a lot of pies, though, so I'm sorry if it's awful."

"It tastes perfect, Abby."

"But you haven't eaten any yet."

"Yeah. I know."

She grinned as she stood, gathering empty dishes from the table. He tried to help but she shook her head. "I've got it. Let me get you a dessert plate."

Abby's grin fell while she made her way to the kitchen, her nerves spiking to high alert. She'd buttered him up as much as she could, and now came *the question*. Grabbing a dessert plate from the cupboard, she gripped onto it as she moved back to the dining room.

Nathaniel watched as she sat beside him, his solid features even more striking than usual in the glow of the candlelight. Abby shoveled a slice of pie onto his plate and set it in front of him. He took a gargantuan mouthful, shivering while he chewed.

"How is it?"

"Heaven," he insisted. "You are a magician."

Her stomach fluttered before she cleared her throat. "I'm glad you think so. Since you're, um, kind of a magician, too."

He scooped another huge piece onto his fork. "Yeah? How's that?"

"There are just so many things you can do. Walking through walls, disappearing into thin air, and...and finding people through their emotions."

Nathaniel paused between mouthfuls. "It's sounds like you're going somewhere specific with this."

Abby gulped. "Yeah, I guess I am. I mean, with all those things you can do, I was wondering if you can do other things, too."

"Other things? Like what?"

"Well, you said earlier that you would do anything in your power for me."

"Yes, I did. And I meant it."

"So, then...I was just wondering...I mean, I was thinking..."

Nathaniel set his fork down and reached for her hand. "Abby. Please tell me whatever it is you have on your mind. I'm very close to turning into a spirit to read your emotions, and I don't want to do that to you."

She worked to maintain his intense gaze. "Okay. I was wondering if you could find a way to look back in time, to see what happened to my mom."

Abby stared into Nathaniel's eyes, witnessing the emotions warring inside him: support and caring, uncertainty and pain. He drew his fingers across hers as he exhaled. "You want to know if your dad had anything to do with it."

She nodded, grateful to not have to speak the words out loud. Nathaniel watched her for a long minute, his gaze stark and undiluted. Abby fought the urge to hide.

Eventually, he held tight to her hand and spoke. "I'm sorry you still have these doubts about your father. I know I don't know him, and I don't have the experiences you've had with him. But when I saw him tonight, when I saw his colors, I felt how calm he was. I know you felt that, too. Which makes me wonder if you truly believe he could have hurt your mother."

"I do believe it," she whispered. "Not because I think he's a bad person. I don't. But he's been through so much – going to war, being held captive, dealing with this disease that literally takes over his mind – and I don't know what any of that is like. I can't be inside his thoughts. I can't be sure that in a single moment of weakness something didn't go horribly, horribly wrong."

Nathaniel kept her hand wrapped in his as he stared down at their fingers. He fell silent for an eternity. "I don't know if I can," he finally admitted. "I didn't know your mother. I never felt her emotions, and what happened to her is in the past."

"Well, as far as her emotions, I thought you could get those through me and my memories. And as for the past issue, you told me that time is nebulous in the spirit world. So, maybe there's a way around it, if we try hard enough."

A tender smile tugged up the corner of his mouth. "You have a strong mind, Abby. I can see you've thought about this. Now, the question is not if we *can* do it, but if we *should*."

Nathaniel paused, lacing their fingers together as he considered.

She remained very, very still while she waited.

"Let's just say I could find a way to do this for you," he began again, his voice edged with sadness. "There are only two scenarios to be had. In the first one, we find out that your dad is guilty, and your life is worse. In the second scenario, we find out that he's innocent. But your life is still worse, because now you know your mother was to blame for her own death, and you feel even guiltier for doubting your father all this time."

Nathaniel glanced up as he finished speaking, searching Abby's eyes. She felt tears welling but she held herself steady, letting his words soak in. He slid forward in his chair, moving closer to her, before he continued.

"But even if you think this through – and truly consider what I've said, and decide that having the knowledge is somehow worth accepting either scenario – even then, I still wouldn't be able to do that to you."

"Why not?" she questioned. "It would be what I asked for."

"Yes, but even if I had the ability to show you what happened, I would never wish that on you. I would never wish on you the agony of watching your mother die before your eyes."

Abby's breath stuck in her dry throat. The vivid memory of Nathaniel's past rang in her mind, of the years and years he'd watched his mother grow old, the day he'd watched her die, and the hope of seeing her spirit – hope that deflated as her body did.

A single tear fell down Abby's cheek.

He reached out, smoothing the wetness from her skin. "So much pain already," he sighed. "I couldn't stand to think that I gave you more. I'd rather throw myself in front of a bus."

She fought back her tears, but more fell with his words.

Nathaniel took her face in both hands. "I can't recall ever being hit by a bus before, but I imagine it won't feel all that great."

Abby shook her head. "Don't get hit by a bus, please."

"Come here," he said, wrapping his arms around her back to tug her forward. He pulled her out of her chair and into his lap. Abby immediately curled her body onto his, burrowing her face into his shoulder. Nathaniel held her with one hand spanning her low back while his other hand wound through her hair. His fingers combed her blond strands at a leisurely pace while a few more tears fell down her cheek and onto his crisp shirt.

"I'm getting your new shirt wet," she sniffed.

"That's okay. I always have a spare white T-shirt."

A smile found its way onto her lips, even as she considered this new reality. For four months now, she'd obsessed over what had happened to her mother on that fateful night. She thought if she just had an answer, good or bad, she could deal with it and move forward. But maybe Nathaniel was right. Maybe an answer would be worse. Maybe she just needed to let it all go, and be here in this moment, with this amazing person in her arms.

Abby pressed the side of her face to Nathaniel's chest. She could hear his heartbeat beneath her ear. Stable. Strong. Solid. It calmed her, allowing her pain and confusion to dissolve into the warmth of his body. Nathaniel gave her peace. He gave her happiness. He was her friend in every possible way. And yet, she wanted much more from him than just friendship.

She stared at the buttons on his shirt, watching the slow rise and fall of his shoulders beneath the navy fabric. She placed her hand over his heart and spread her fingers wide. His breath hitched for a second before evening out. Abby nibbled her lip.

"Do you – do you have to breathe?" she wondered aloud.

"When I'm solid, yes."

"And when you're not?"

"I think it's optional, but I do it anyway. Habit, I suppose."

"I don't think you do it out of habit. I think you believe, even though you have powers in the spirit world, that it would be wrong to use them unless it was for someone else's good. You still try to do the right thing, even when you don't have to."

"Hmm. I'm pretty sure that was a compliment," he said, his deep voice rumbling beside her ear. "Which hopefully means you're not mad at me."

"Mad at you? Why would I be?"

"For not honoring your request about your mother."

Abby pressed her palm securely onto his chest. "It was only a thought. Besides, I can't be mad at you for trying to protect my emotions."

"I really would do anything for you. But I never want to hurt you."

She raised her eyes to his, absorbing the sincerity of his words. "Nathaniel, do you remember what you said to me earlier today? About not wanting to pretend to be alive?"

"Yes. I remember."

"Well, I don't think you're pretending. I think you're just *alive*."

He didn't say a word in reply. But he did wrap his arms fully around her, fastening her to his chest in a vice. He buried his face in her hair and inhaled steeply. A shiver ran the length of his solid body while every one of his muscles worked to hold her to him.

Abby snuggled even closer. She kept her hand over his heart, feeling the perfectly rhythmic beat beneath her fingers. She swore she could feel her own heartbeat working to match his.

Time slipped by as he cocooned her in his arms. All the while, the straightness of his collarbone stared at Abby past the undone top button of his shirt. She studied that small bit of exposed flesh, knowing she probably shouldn't reach underneath his clothes to touch it. But eventually, the maddening warmth of his body destroyed her pitiful attempt at rationality. Her tongue darted out to lick her lips as she slid her trembling fingers beneath the fabric.

Nathaniel groaned when her hand eased under his shirt, his heart thumping faster beneath her palm as she pressed it fully to his bare chest. "So, is...is your dad going to be gone all night?" he questioned, his voice hardened to a rasp.

Abby traced the line of his collarbone with her fingers, mesmerized by the smoothness and heat. "Yes. The whole, entire night."

"Then can I stay a while longer?"

"As long as you want," she said, needing all the time in the world to experience the feel of his skin. She only wished she had more of it to feel. Drawing her hand out, she played with the collar of his shirt for a moment before sliding her fingers down to tug on the next button.

"So, what do you want to do now?" Abby asked as she managed to pop the button open.

"Holy hell," Nathaniel cursed. In one swift motion, he uncurled his arms from her body, picked her up, and set her back in her seat. He steadied her in place before letting go. "What I *want* to do now is irrelevant. What I *need* to do is help clean up. And get my head on straight."

Abby hated the coldness of her chair. "You don't have to get your head on straight," she assured, moving forward with every intention of crawling back into his lap. "Not on my account."

Nathaniel held his hand up. "I – I can't do this right now."

Her brow crinkled. "Why not? I like being close to you."

He raked his fingers through his hair as he looked to the ceiling. "Abby..."

She poised herself at the edge of her seat. "Yes?"

His eyes returned to hers, their blue deeper and darker. "Please understand how much difficulty I'm having here. My feelings are so strong. Too strong. I've gone sixty years without touching anyone, and being with you is..."

"Awesomely fantastic?" she hoped.

"Yes, of course, but also overwhelming. Like I've been starving my whole life and you've walked in with plates of..."

"Pizza? Cheeseburgers? Pie?"

"All of the above, and more. And I honestly don't know if I'm capable of pushing away from the table. I need to go slow. I need to be a gentleman. I was raised to be a gentleman, believe it or not. You deserve that much, at least."

Abby thought that sounded terrible. She crossed her arms and huffed.

Nathaniel exhaled. "It would help if you didn't look so upset about it."

"I'm not trying to be helpful."

He chuckled, grasping his empty dessert plate off the table while he stood. As Abby watched him walk into the kitchen, she encouraged her heart to stop racing and her skin to cease its incessant tingling. She wondered if he even understood how her teenage hormones were attacking her – heaving large, blunt objects at various parts of her body.

She jumped up from her chair and followed him into the kitchen, where he now stood at the sink rinsing plates. "I can get the dishes, Nathaniel."

"Oh, I think I can manage to load a dishwasher. I've seen it done a few times. Besides, it gives me something to do with my hands." He glanced over his shoulder, looking her up and down with a spark in his eye. "So, to change the subject, how does your dad like being a mechanic?"

Her body sagged against the doorframe. "He likes it fine. He worked on machinery in the Army, so he figured out cars pretty easily."

"I've never heard of a mechanic working nights before."

"Those are the hours he wanted. The guy who owns Auto Pro, Kevin, is an old Army buddy of Dad's. He agreed to hire him for the night shift so Dad wouldn't have to deal with a lot of people. I think he feels safest that way. When Mom was alive, it didn't matter that he was gone all night. Now he worries about me being alone. Although I keep telling him I'm okay."

"So, he sleeps most days, and you guys have dinner during the week, and then he's home on the weekends and you watch movies together?"

Abby sighed while Nathaniel arranged plates and glasses inside the dishwasher. "Yeah, that's pretty much it."

"You know, I've only ever seen one movie."

"Seriously? Which one?"

"*Gone With the Wind*. I didn't like it. I never watched another one."

"God, I can't blame you. We really should make up for that experience. Do you want to watch a movie now?"

"Sure. If you want to."

"Well, if we're not going to do anything else…"

Nathaniel smiled as he finished the dishes and dried his hands on a towel. "You're incorrigible sometimes. Do you know that?"

"Maybe," she admitted while he walked toward her. When he stepped into her personal space, she raised her chin. She didn't miss the way his gaze slipped down to her lips before he took her hand in his.

"Let's go watch a movie," he said, pulling her toward the living room.

"Do you have any idea what kind you want to see?"

"None whatsoever. Will you show me the choices?"

"Sure," Abby agreed when they reached the entertainment center. She opened the cabinet to show Nathaniel her family's fairly impressive collection of DVDs. As he perused the movie selections, she took up residence beside him, leaning her shoulder against his arm.

"Hmm. Most of these are about space and aliens."

"Yeah. Dad loves his science fiction."

"Do you have a recommendation?"

"You should really watch them all."

Nathaniel turned to see her face, which was entirely too close to his own. "Is that an invitation to come back again?"

"A standing one," she replied, allowing her eyes to focus on his mouth.

He grinned as he turned back to the movies. "Incorrigible," he repeated.

"Too good for your own good," she grumbled.

Abby was pretty sure he heard her, but he pretended he didn't.

"Do you have the movie you mentioned the other day?" he asked.

"Which one?"

"The one about ghosts, and the kid who doesn't have anything on you?"

"*The Sixth Sense?*"

"Yes. Let's watch that one."

"But it really is about ghosts. Won't that be weird?"

"I don't think so. It'll be interesting to see how other people view it."

Abby's brow furrowed. "Okay." She hesitated a moment, then took out the disc and slipped it into the player.

Nathaniel stood and stepped to their overstuffed couch, settling his thick body down into one corner. Abby grabbed the remote control and walked toward him. She knew she should be a good girl and sit in the chair opposite him. She decided against it.

She sank down onto the cushion directly beside Nathaniel, curling her legs up and propping herself against his side. Abby waited with her heart in her throat, figuring he would either protest her intrusion on his personal space, or pick her up and set her on the other side of the sofa. When he lifted his arm, she prepared for battle. But then he draped that arm over her shoulder and pulled her in closer. She smiled and rested her head on his chest. This was good. She liked this.

The movie started, but Abby barely watched. She was in tune to Nathaniel's every move, seeing the characters for the first time through his eyes. She laughed when he laughed, jumped when he jumped, and found it fascinating that he could be so caught up in a story about ghosts. When the movie finished, she stayed right where she was.

"Wow, that was incredible," he remarked as the credits rolled.

"Yeah? What did you think of the ghosts?"

"Sadly, most of them were scary and mean."

"Well, I know better than that." She smiled up at him from her happy place in the crook of his arm. "Did you like the big twist at the end?"

"That blew me away. I never would have guessed it."

Abby laughed. "Well, if you couldn't guess, I don't think anybody could."

Nathaniel watched intently as her laugh eased into a smile. She fell silent, content to sit beside him forever. He didn't move a muscle for the longest time. He only stared at her lips with his gaze fixed and his jaw clenched.

Just when Abby thought he might actually do something ungentlemanly, he pulled his arm from her shoulder and shifted away. "Maybe I...maybe I should leave now."

Her shoulders dropped. "Do you want to leave?"

"No. Not really."

"Then I think we can figure this out together," she said, perching herself on the edge of the cushion beside him. "I mean, there has to be something we can do that won't violate your rules of conduct. Because I'd much rather have you here than not here."

Nathaniel clasped his hands together, locking his fingers in place on his lap. "Actually, there is something I'd love to have your help with."

"Yeah? What's that?"

"Can you tell me more about the students at school? I've read so many emotions, and it's been really helpful having your perspective on people."

"I can do that. Just tell me who you want to know about."

"Well, that's the problem. They aren't in your classes, so I don't know if you're aware of them. And I don't really know how to describe them to you."

Abby admired the serious set of his features, appreciating how determined he was to find the person he needed to help, as if he truly believed it wasn't her. "What about a yearbook? I have the one from last year. You could look through it to see if you recognize anyone."

"Yes, that's perfect. I knew you'd have an amazing idea. Thank you."

"You're welcome. I'll just go get it and come right back."

She extracted herself begrudgingly from his side to walk through the living room and down the hallway. Once she stepped into her bedroom, she headed over to her bookshelf. Abby thumbed through a few old textbooks until she found her small collection of yearbooks. She found last year's, grabbed it, and turned back.

Nathaniel stood in her doorway. He looked quite relaxed, with one shoulder resting against the doorframe and a leisurely smile on his lips.

Abby stopped moving altogether. This was odd, having him here. In her private space. In her bedroom. *Good Lord, is he breaking any of his own rules?*

"Is it okay if I come in?" he asked.

Currently rendered mute, she nodded her head.

Nathaniel eased away from the door to wander slowly around the edge of the room, looking at her things. Abby felt naked, as if he could see through her just by examining her possessions. It was a silly sensation, considering he could read her emotions whenever he desired.

After passing by her window, Nathaniel paused in front of her vanity mirror. "Is this your mother?" he asked, reaching out to touch the small photo tucked into the frame.

Abby hugged the yearbook to her chest. "Yes."

"She's beautiful. Like you."

"Thanks."

Nathaniel's hand moved down from the picture to the tattered, fabric-covered jewelry box lying on the vanity top. He eased his fingers over the lid before opening it. A faint hint of tinkling music began as a tiny ballerina figurine twirled in tune. He chuckled softly.

"Did you pick this jewelry box out?" he asked.

"Yeah. When I was really little."

"The ballerina is a pig in a tutu."

"Well, my dad tried to get a human ballerina, but I insisted on the pig."

Nathaniel looked over to her with a crooked grin. "You like pigs?"

"Of course. They always seem so happy, just wallowing in mud. I mean, it's only mud. But it's their mud, you know?"

"Yeah. We had pigs on our farm. I'd like to think they were pretty happy."

"You like pigs, too?"

"I do. I had a pet one. She was cute."

"Seriously? You had a *pet* pig?"

"I did."

"Oh, my God. What was her name?"

"Petunia. Mrs. Petunia Piggles, actually."

Abby laughed until she snorted.

Nathaniel's grin widened. "That was the reaction my little sister always had, too. It made her laugh so hard. I loved that."

"What's your sister's name?" Abby asked, blissfully unable to scrub the image of him and Mrs. Petunia Piggles from her mind.

"Marybeth. She was a wild, fiery little redhead, ten years younger than me. She's a grandmother now, silver-haired but just as fiery. She has twelve grand-kids, several of whom look like her. I check on them sometimes."

Nathaniel closed the top on the jewelry box and continued moving around the room. Abby couldn't peel her eyes off of him. His existence was unfathomable, yet she couldn't imagine being with anyone else, ever.

When he reached the corkboard hanging on her wall, he stopped to examine the papers and pictures pinned up by tacks. He flipped through several of the certificates. "Are these honor roll awards for your report cards?"

"Yeah. Mom always stuck them up there."

"You've made it every semester. Most of them all-A's."

"Well, when you don't have much of a social life, it's easy to concentrate on school. And it's less for Dad to worry about, which is easier for everyone."

"Or maybe you're just incredibly intelligent."

She smiled with his praise. "Well, we'll see about that this quarter. I'm pretty sure Mr. Puryear is going to fail me, just on principle. I've been so spacey in his class. He probably thinks I'm on drugs."

"But you knew about Operation Neptune. That's got to count for something, right?" Nathaniel asked as he continued examining her corkboard. He perused the few photos she'd pinned up – mostly of her and Julie, acting silly together. Then, his hand traced over the one embroidered sports letter. "You received a school letter for sports? Are you an athlete?"

"An athlete? Not in the slightest. I played soccer for a season in middle school. It wasn't pretty. You got a letter just for showing up."

"Ah. These would be the supposedly awful middle school years?"

"Uh, well, that's..." Abby fumbled, wanting desperately to change the subject. She held the yearbook out in front of her. "Here's the book you wanted. We can look at it together."

Nathaniel stepped toward her with a playful grin on his lips. He took the book from her hands and set it on her bed. "We can look at that later," he said, turning toward her bookshelf. "Right now, I'd like to see if there are any older yearbooks in here."

Abby stared at his broad back. "Why do you want older yearbooks?"

"Because I just have to see this awkward middle school Abby."

"Oh, no, you don't. Never. Ever."

He chuckled as he pivoted to face her. "Please?"

"Uh-uh. Nope."

"Pretty please?" he entreated, moving in close enough to touch.

She raised her eyes to his. "Absolutely not. And your charm will not work for this."

"Are you saying that my charm works for other things?"

"I, uh...wow," Abby stammered, her body already flustered by the nearness of his. "You can be frustrating sometimes, can't you?"

"Yes, definitely. Sorry about that."

"Don't be. I'm flattered that you'd like to know more about me, even if you are looking for pictures of my awkward younger years. But at the same time, I'm sad that I'll never see pictures of you when you were younger. Although, you probably never had an awkward phase, anyway. Not that I'll ever have any proof, one way or the other."

Nathaniel cocked his head. "Hmm. I think I did have an awkward phase. I suppose I could show it to you."

"Show it to me? What do you mean?"

"Well, since we can talk to each other mind-to-mind when I'm in my spirit world, I don't see why I can't put an image into your head. A memory, that is."

Abby's eyeballs nearly fell out. "Holy crap! Are you saying you'd let me see into your memories?"

"Of course. If you'd like that."

"Good God, yes!" she hollered, bouncing up and down on the balls of her feet, digging her bare toes into her bedroom carpet. "Yes, yes, yes!"

Nathaniel laughed. "Gosh, you don't sound certain at all."

"Oh, please don't make me beg. Although I will, if I have to."

"I'll never make you beg," he assured, slipping his fingers up into her hair. Abby licked her lips, drawing his eyes to the sight of her tongue. His hand fell to his side, but his body leaned forward. "You know, I should probably be as close to you as possible while we do this. Just to make sure it works."

"Yeah, um, good," she agreed, his warmth already overfilling the miniscule distance still separating them. She fisted her hands at her sides to keep herself from grabbing onto him like a wild beast. "I'll do whatever you think is best."

His eyes grew a shade darker. "I'll need to turn back into a spirit now, so I can let you into my mind. If this is truly what you want."

"It is. I want you. I mean, your memories. I truly want your memories."

Nathaniel shook his head even as he smiled. "Okay, then."

Abby held her breath while she stared up at him. She stood in awe when he transformed, his cool chill rapidly engulfing the heat between them. She shivered, but not from the cold. It was pure excitement.

He stood within inches of her body, looking on her with glowing eyes. "Are you ready, Abby?"

"Mm-hmm. So ready."

"What do you want to see first?"

"How about your family? And your farm?"

"Our farm? Okay. I'll try to think of a good memory."

Abby closed her eyes that instant, more than ready to see through his. Her entire body hummed as she waited for some sort of reception. She wondered if she would be able to hear as well as see, and if she would get colors, or only black-and-white.

And then the vision came, so clearly in her mind's eye, and she was there.

Her sights filled with the image of a gigantic brown barn, weathered and beaten, like it got into a fight with a bigger barn and lost. There was a field behind it, with tall stalks of grain waving gracefully back and forth, inviting her closer. Abby swore she could feel the breeze that filtered through the lanky stems, fanning her hair and cooling her skin.

She focused on the roughened exterior of the barn door as she walked toward it. Except she wasn't the one walking – Nathaniel was walking – and yet she swore her own legs carried her forward. Her vision panned down to her feet, to Nathaniel's feet, inside scuffed and muddied boots treading over the dirt ground. Abby wriggled her toes, feeling them squeeze onto the carpet in her bedroom, but she could also feel them inside his heavy, stained shoes.

When she looked up again, she stood in front of the barn. She reached for the barn door, watching as Nathaniel's hand tugged it open, hearing the rusty hinges creak before she stepped inside. Sunlight streamed through the glassless windows as she passed by several divided pens of animals: a gray horse, a white one, two cows. She got a whiff of something earthy and unpleasant, which made her nose crinkle. "Whew! What is that?"

"Can you smell the cows?" Nathaniel asked, his voice filling her bedroom.

"Yeah, I guess I can."

"That's interesting. I'm sorry I can't shut that part off. Everything is all mixed together in my mind."

"It's no problem. Where are you taking me?" Abby wondered as they walked farther inside. Then she saw the next stall – pigs – seven of them. "Oh, yes! The pigs! Which one is Mrs. Piggles?"

Nathaniel! Nathaniel! she heard a little girl yell. *I dressed up Petunia!*

Abby froze as Marybeth Dunnington ran into the barn. Two pigtails held back bunches of her strawberry blond hair, the bows pulled loose and the ribbons hanging to her shoulders. Her yellow dress was mud-spattered, her knees scraped. She had at least twenty freckles on her little button nose alone.

The image moved back to the pig stall, where one fat sow sat amongst the others with a yellow bandana tied around its neck.

Marybeth. You know you're not supposed to go into the pig stall by yourself. You could get hurt.

Abby smiled at the sound of Nathaniel's big-brotherly voice drifting through her mind. She saw Marybeth again, with her arms folded in front of her chest and a huge scowl on her tiny face. *Don't you tell me what to do, Nathaniel! You're not Daddy!*

Abby watched the little girl pout and stomp her feet. Within seconds, she noticed the strangest thing. Marybeth had a glow around her, like the haze around a candle flame, surrounding her body in one distinct color: red. Abby laughed at the sight.

"What's so funny?" Nathaniel asked.

"Marybeth was really mad at you in this memory, wasn't she?"

"Yeah, she was. She hated being scolded. Are you able to feel her feelings?"

"Actually, it's more like I can see them."

"What do you mean?"

"I mean I can see the color of her emotions. She has this glow around her, like the halo of a flame, lit up in the brightest red."

"Can you really see that, Abby? That is truly something."

Her eyes opened to meet his. "What is something?"

Nathaniel's glowing blue held her in place. "The fact that you're seeing this through me, through my mind. You're seeing emotions the way I do when I'm in my spirit world."

"Wow," she said, marveling at the possibility of knowing any part of his world. "That is so cool. Seriously. So cool. Will you show me more?"

He grinned as he nodded. "Of course."

Abby slammed her eyes shut again, working to concentrate with her whole body. She found herself instantly back inside his vision, walking past the angry, red little girl and out of the barn. Fresh, cool air hit her in the face as she stepped outside. She now walked along a dirt path that wound around several large grain silos, toward a small white house with a gray roof. As she approached Nathaniel's childhood home, the spiced scent of apple pie drifted through the open windows.

Abby stepped up onto the wrapped front porch, past a spider crafting an intricate web on the corner of the roof, and into the house. She stood in the kitchen, glancing over to an older woman who busied herself working at the stove. The woman had dark red hair swept up into a bun at the back of her head and wore a simple gray blouse and skirt with a blue apron tied around her waist. Her body was surrounded in a pure green glow.

Did you see your sister? the woman's delicate voice sang. *It's nearly time for supper and I'd like her to be here.*

Abby moved to the kitchen table and sat down in one of the four slatted wood chairs, although it was actually Nathaniel who sat. *I'm sure she'll be along shortly,* he answered his mother. *When she's had a chance to calm down.*

Did you do something to upset her?

Yes, although I was just trying to keep her out of trouble.

The woman laughed, bright and sparkling. *I believe you.*

"What's your mom's name?" Abby asked.

The woman in the vision turned and smiled, her warm, soft features full of love for her son.

"Her name was Diana," Nathaniel answered.

"She's lovely."

"Yeah, she was."

Clunking footsteps approached from the other side of the kitchen then. Abby watched a big bear of a man walk into the room, his overall-clad body suffused in a blue glow. He could easily have been Nathaniel, aged thirty years. He sat down at the table and looked straight at her.

"What's your dad's name?" she wondered as she stared into the man's pale blue eyes.

"His name was Clifford."

How are the horses today? Clifford questioned her, stern and formal.

Good, Nathaniel replied. *Billy's hoof is nearly healed. Roy's bite looks better.*

Will they be in shape for sowing?

Yes, sir. I believe so.

Clifford nodded before glancing to his wife.

The vision panned back to Diana as she brought food over from the stove. The smell of eggs and bacon wafted into Abby's nose while she looked around. Clifford sat to her right. Diana took a seat to his right. In the next chair over, another young woman occupied a space at the Dunnington breakfast table. She had naturally-highlighted blond hair lying softly around her face, high cheekbones, perfect rose lips, and clear blue eyes. And she was absolutely haloed in purple.

Abby's heart flip-flopped. "Nathaniel, is that...is that..."

The image turned dark the instant his mind disconnected from hers. She opened her eyes, disoriented for a moment when she found herself back in her bedroom. She pinned her spirit's glowing gaze with her searching one.

"My God," she breathed. "Was that *me*?"

Nathaniel gave her a sheepish smile. "Yeah. Sorry about that."

"Holy hell! Was I alive in the 1940s? Am I some kind of reincarnation?"

"No, no. You weren't really there. I was just thinking about you, and you showed up."

"Thinking about me? Are you saying you put me in your memory?"

"Well, you sort of popped in there before I could stop it."

Abby stared up at him, trying to reconcile the image he'd showed her with the one she saw in the mirror every day. "But that isn't how I look."

"Yes, it is. That's exactly how you look."

"Can I...can I see that again, please?"

"Sure, if you want."

Abby closed her eyes tight, eager to rejoin his mind. When the image returned, she barely recognized herself. Her skin was so smooth – her eyes like aquamarine gems – her lips a soft, enticing pink. This was Nathaniel's image, so this must be how he saw her. But the only part she thought was accurate was the devilishly purple glow clinging to her skin like a spandex bodysuit.

"Wow, Nathaniel. You see me as beautiful."

"You are beautiful."

"I've never looked like *that*."

"You always look like that."

Abby shivered again, but she definitely couldn't blame it on the chill of his spirit form. She reponed her eyes to focus on his glowing ones. "It's interesting to see myself through your mind," she admitted. "Although, I'm still not sure why you had me sitting at your kitchen table."

Nathaniel managed to blush, even while still in his other world. "I swear I didn't mean to. I was really trying to concentrate on sharing my memory, but I was also watching you here, in real life. You looked so damn adorable with your eyes scrunched shut and I just lost my focus for a second. The next thing I knew, you were sitting there beside me."

"Oh," she said, thrilled by the fact that he found her adorable, yet also petrified by all of her oozing purple. "Well, I liked seeing your home and your family. Thank you for showing me."

"You're welcome."

"Although I didn't actually see *you*, so I still have no proof that you ever had an awkward phase."

"Sorry. I couldn't really think of a memory where I looked in the mirror."

"I guess that would be hard," she conceded. "It was kind of awesome seeing myself there, though. Is that what I would have looked like in the '40s?"

"I don't know. That part wasn't a memory, just my imagination."

"Hmm. You have a really great imagination."

"I'm glad you think so."

"Oh, I do. Which makes me wonder if you could do that again."

"Do what again?"

"Imagine me in another place, in another decade?"

Nathaniel's brow rose. "You want me to imagine what you would look like in another decade?"

"Well, you've actually seen a lot of decades, right?"

"That is true."

Abby inched closer to his cool body. "Then I'll bet you can imagine all sorts of things about them. And then maybe you can share your thoughts with me, since I've always wondered what my life would have looked like back then, and I'd love to see it up close."

Nathaniel shifted his feet over her bedroom carpet. "Yeah, I...I suppose I could do that. If that's what you want."

"Oh, yes, please! It's just what I want! This is going to be so incredible!"

"Well, I'll certainly try my best," he assured, matching her overzealous smile. "Which decade do you want to see yourself in first?"

Abby bounced on her toes. "Man, there's so many. Maybe the '60s?"

"Do you like the '60s?"

"I've just always been curious about that time. Especially the flower children and Woodstock. Do you think you could put me there?"

"Sure. But it will only be my imagination – a fantasy – and not real life."

"Honestly, a fantasy sounds wonderful. I'm perfectly happy with that."

Nathaniel's eyes glowed brighter. "Okay, then. Are you ready?"

"Yes, yes, yes," she said, the giddiness in her voice a bare shadow of the excitement bubbling up in her chest. She fidgeted with her fingers as she closed her eyes, waiting eagerly for an image to form.

The moment Nathaniel opened his mind to hers, Abby saw herself lying in a field of fresh green grass, bathed in sunshine. A few people sat scattered around her, lounging on blankets, strumming guitars, singing and laughing. She saw herself through a light haze of purple, resting on her side on top of a fuzzy woven blanket. She wore a white poet's blouse with big, puffy sleeves and navy hip-hugger bellbottoms. Her hair draped loose and long over her shoulders, with a thin brown leather band tied around her forehead.

Abby nearly burst with joy at the sight. She struggled to keep her eyes closed, never wanting to lose this image from her mind. "Nathaniel, this is absolutely amazing! You actually made me a flower child! But where are you?"

"It's my fantasy."

"That doesn't mean you can't be in it. I want you with me. Please?"

He laughed, the bright sound echoing in the quiet room. "Damn, Abby. You certainly are difficult to resist."

"Good," she said, clasping her hands together and nearly strangling her own fingers. Within seconds, Nathaniel appeared beside her, lying on the woven blanket, with his body facing hers. He had shoulder-length wavy hair and a several-day-old beard. Brown bellbottoms hugged his hips while a matching brown leather vest draped over his bare chest. Abby whimpered, certain that if this was her fantasy, she would reach out to explore his bared skin. But for now, all she could do was watch as '60s-Nathaniel gently stroked '60s-Abby's hair.

"This is wild," she mused, marveling at the image he'd created for her. She tried to not be too embarrassed by the purple haze she generated across her entire body, fearful that the color would plague her in every decade. "Thank you so much for this. I truly love it."

"I'm glad. I like it when you're happy."

"Oh, I am. And this is beautiful, but I can't help wanting more. Would it be too much to ask you for another decade?"

"That's no problem at all. Which one would you like next?"

"Hmm. How about the '80s?" she suggested. She knew how much Nathaniel despised that particular decade, so she hoped he wouldn't see her in purple from head to toe if she looked like a Valley girl. Although, since she would definitely still want him regardless of which year they were in, she figured the violet vengeance would never leave her in peace.

"Seriously? The '80s?" he grumbled.

"Please? Pretty please?"

Nathaniel heaved a slow, arduous breath. "Okay, then. If you insist."

Abby grinned while she listened to the strummed music a bit longer, seeing her '60s-self bask in the warm sunshine while lying in the field. But then, the green grass morphed into a beige linoleum floor. The blue skies transformed to white ceilings with fluorescent lighting.

She looked around her now, at the various shops and raucous crowds, realizing she was inside of an old '80s mall. The image panned her surroundings – thrumming with boisterous music playing over loudspeakers and drenched in the bright, mismatched clothing of shoppers – until she saw a young woman standing in front of a neon store sign. The girl stood with her back turned, her blond hair sticking up in all directions, teased to twice its size. A purposefully torn sweatshirt in a hideous melon color hung from her shoulders. A purple sequined belt cinched her waist overtop a black miniskirt. Matching melon leg warmers completed the gruesome ensemble.

"Great hell," Abby swore as the young woman began to turn around. "Don't you dare let that be me, Nathaniel Dunnington."

His deep laugh filled her bedroom. "Well, you did ask for the '80s."

The image rotated fully, so the young woman faced forward. '80s-Abby smiled, somewhere beneath her glittering metallic-blue eye shadow, rose-powdered cheeks, and glossy pink lipstick. She chewed on a wad of gum until she blew a bubble that popped over her mouth. And, of course, she was still bathed in a tenacious purple glow.

"I cannot believe you did that to me," Abby muttered. "I would never tease my hair...and that makeup...and that outfit..."

"I think I've already mentioned how much I disliked the '80s."

"Yes, you did," she conceded. "I can see now that it was a mistake to ask for it. But can I at least see you there with me?"

"Sorry, but no."

"Nathaniel!"

"Nope. No chance. I have to draw the line somewhere."

Abby laughed as she watched her '80s-self blow another bubble. "I can't believe you're going to leave me there alone, dressed like that! Take me somewhere else, please!"

"I'd be happy to. Where would you like to go?"

Her eyes opened to find his staring straight at her. "I want to go somewhere with you this time."

"Okay. Anywhere but the '80s," he agreed with a teasing grin.

"Very well, then. Why don't you pick a decade? What's your favorite?"

"Hmm. I guess that would be the '50s. I always wanted to be a greaser."

"The '50s? Ooh, nice. Could we could go to a sock hop together?"

"Yeah, sure. I suppose I could think one up."

"Yay!" Abby sang, wriggle-dancing in place. She shut her eyes again, watching the '80s mall change before her – transforming from a neon-and-saxophones nightmare into a plain-looking high school gymnasium framed in bleachers. Several teenage couples twirled across the gym floor, the soles of their sneakers squeaking over the polished wood as they danced to an energetic song filled with loud trumpets and crooning voices.

Abby couldn't see herself yet, but she definitely saw Nathaniel. He stood in front of the bleachers in cuffed blue jeans and a white T-shirt with the sleeves rolled up, his dirty blond hair slicked back and his face clean-shaven. He looked young and just a bit roguish, cocking one eyebrow as he reached his hand out.

She watched her own image come into focus then, grasping his fingers and allowing him to pull her onto the dance floor. '50s-Abby wore a white sweater, buttoned once at the neck and hanging loosely over her shoulders, with a short-sleeve white shirt underneath. A fluffy pink skirt hugged her waist, cinched with a black belt. Her hair was pulled back in a ponytail, her face bright and smiling. She looked beautiful again, like she had in the '40s, and she stared at Nathaniel like he was the only person in the room, or in the world.

Everything about this vision – the gym, the people, her face – was bathed in a hazy purple. Thankfully, Abby could still see herself with Nathaniel as he twirled and spun her across the floor. She liked '50s-Abby; she was a pretty good dancer. And '50s-Nathaniel was downright gorgeous.

The lively music pounded through her chest until it changed, giving way to a soft, slow love ballad. All the other bodies on the floor came together one-by-one. She watched with her pulse racing as '50s-Nathaniel reached for '50s-Abby. They pulled toward each other like magnets, his hands moving to her waist and her arms draping over his shoulders. He led her in a gentle sway, her body drifting in time with his as their eyes locked together. Nathaniel raised one hand to her face, cupping her cheek to draw her in closer.

The image started to blur, steeped in a vibrant, overpowering purple. Abby struggled to bring the vision back into focus. She desperately wanted to know what that felt like. She wanted her arms around his shoulders, his hand on her face, his mouth coming closer and closer to hers.

An instant later, the image disappeared completely.

Abby exhaled in frustration. She didn't want to be back in her bedroom. She didn't want to leave the incredible fantasy he'd created for them. She didn't want to listen while present-day Nathaniel apologized for the allowing the dream to go that far. She didn't want anything to do with reality.

That is, until she realized the chill in the air was gone. And there was a very warm, very solid body standing directly in front of her. Abby opened her eyes to find Nathaniel's. They were the deepest, most intense blue she'd ever seen. His breaths came in shallow pants to his chest. Her breathing was no better.

He reached for her face, his fingers tracing her cheek. His thumb moved to her mouth, grazing across her lower lip. He studied the movement intently.

Abby leaned toward him, into his touch, his warmth. She licked her lips. His eyes sparked as he watched. Then his mouth was on hers, instantly molding to her shape. She reached for his shoulders, needing the support to keep her knees from buckling.

Nathaniel deepened the kiss, tilting her head with his hand, while she slid her body fully onto his. His tongue traced her lower lip. Abby moaned, but didn't have the inclination to be ashamed. She rose up on her tiptoes, locking her arms around his neck and running her fingers into his hair.

When his hands reached for her waist, she forgot to breathe. She pressed closer, desperate to feel him pull her body onto his. Sadly, he did not. He used his grip on her waist to push her gently away, easing their lips apart.

Abby knew what was happening, and she couldn't bear it. "No, wait," she breathed over his mouth, "not yet. Please just give me one more minute..."

She half-expected rejection. Instead, Nathaniel groaned in defeat and wound his arms fully around her. Abby sighed in relief and delight, closing her eyes while opening her lips. He practically crushed her against his chest, but she couldn't have cared less. She did her best to crush him back, holding on for dear life, never wanting this feeling to end. She risked a taste, tracing her tongue across his lips, causing a deep moan to rumble through his body and into hers.

Nathaniel really did pull away then. She knew he meant it this time, because his hands became iron jaws on her hips. He pushed her away from him, until she could no longer feel his warmth or smell his sweet breath. A second later, he took her fingers in his and held them entirely still. He held her steady, just waiting.

Abby didn't want to open her eyes – ever – yet she finally resigned herself.

Nathaniel looked straight into her. "I'm sorry," he apologized. "I shouldn't have gotten so carried away. I swore I wasn't going to do that, but then I got so caught up in those '50s images and you were just so..."

"Purple?" she supplied, grimacing with the forcefulness of her feelings. After all, he didn't have anything to be sorry for. Not when she'd practically attacked him with her singular, all-consuming color.

Nathaniel gave her a soft smile. "I was going to say *beautiful*."

"Well, thank you for that. I appreciate your gentlemanly response, but I think we can both acknowledge that I was just ridiculously purple. I mean, I could barely even see your vision at the end. I was like some freakish human plum. I can't imagine what you must think of me."

He chuckled while staring down at their joined hands.

"What?" she asked. "What's so funny?"

"Nothing."

"Come on, tell me. Please?"

Nathaniel raised his eyes to hers. "You weren't actually there, you know. It wasn't reality. It was a fantasy. My fantasy. My emotions. That was my purple. Just mine."

"Oh," she said. Abby swallowed hard as the truth sank beneath her skin. "But I...I could hardly see through that. It was overwhelming."

"Believe me, I'm well aware of it. Now, maybe you can see how difficult it is for me to keep being a gentleman with you. Maybe you can give me a break, and stop being so desirable all the time."

Abby grinned with the foreign concept. She didn't know if she could stop being something she never realized she was. Or if she even wanted to. "Wow. You were awfully purple."

"Yeah," he admitted. "Still am."

"Yeah. Me, too."

Nathaniel stroked her cheek with the back of his hand. "Then that's my cue to leave, I think. I've tested my limits enough for one night."

"Are you sure? I'm certainly willing to run a few more tests."

"Hell, Abby. Maybe I need to take back what I said earlier today. Maybe you are a wicked temptress."

"Hmm," she considered. "That does have a certain ring to it."

He smiled while shaking his head. "I'm going now."

"Okay, okay."

"I'll see you tomorrow," he promised, exiting her room with a crooked grin still clinging to his lips.

ABBY HARDLY SLEPT. Which wasn't unusual for her – not in over four months – but this time, her insomnia was for a good reason. Or reasons.

When she finally sat up on the edge of her bed the next morning, she could number all of her reasons for not sleeping. After all, she'd spent a lot of time on them through the night.

First, his lips. Second, his eyes. Third, his voice. Fourth, his hands. Fifth, his purple-ness. Sixth, his joy. Seventh, his kindness. Eighth, his lips. No, wait...did I say lips already?

It didn't matter. There were one hundred and twenty-nine reasons by her last count, but she could easily come up with more. Abby stood from the bed and walked over to her closet, pulling out the one purple shirt she owned. Today, she needed to show Nathaniel that he was not the only human plum.

She stepped over to her window, glancing out to watch the angry clouds glare back. The weather might be miserable, but Abby felt bright and bouncy and bubbly and lots of other B words she couldn't think of right at the moment. She couldn't wait to get to school and lay eyes on her spirit.

After quickly dressing and brushing her hair, she skipped down the hallway and into the kitchen. Mark stood by the countertop, making his morning sandwich. "Hey, Dad," she sang, grinning as she pushed up on her tiptoes to kiss him on the cheek. "How was work?"

"Fine," he answered between mouthfuls. "Why the good mood?"

She reached into the cabinet to pull out his pills. "It's just a great day," she said, watching him take the meds and swallow them.

He showed her underneath his tongue before turning to the fridge to dig out a soda. "Where are the leftovers from last night? I was going to have some more roast later."

"Oh, well, I...I got hungry after you left for work."

"Yeah? Hungry enough to eat that entire pot roast?"

"I'll make more soon," she deflected, grabbing her granola bar and backpack before stepping out of the kitchen. "See you after school?"

"Okay. Hey, wear a coat today. It got cold out."

She scurried over to the hall closet to grab her jacket. "Thanks, Dad."

Abby tried to prevent herself from grinning like a steroidal clown when she left the house, but it was impossible. She bounded down the stairs to her car, hoping to see her spirit already sitting inside. Despite her eagerness, she still jumped when she heard a deep, masculine voice ring inside her head.

I'm in your car.

Nathaniel, she sang in her mind, opening the driver's door and falling inside. She turned toward the passenger's seat, expecting to see the brilliant blue glow she knew so well. Instead, she met oil-black sludge.

Her shoulders sagged. "Oh, crap. It's you."

Jonathan smiled. "Hello to you, too, Abigail." His churning eyes worked hard to pin hers down. "I take it you were expecting someone else?"

"You know I was," she grumbled, pivoting away to stare out of her windshield. Jon's arctic frost made the temperature in her car unbearable, so she turned on the ignition, flipped the heater to full blast, and plastered herself against the door. "Will it do me any good to ask you to leave?"

He ignored her question without any pretense. "You're looking all bleary-eyed today. Did Nate keep you up all night?"

"No," she replied as she backed down her driveway. "I just couldn't sleep."

"You mean he actually left you? With your dad gone and the whole house to yourself? Damn, you two could have had the entire night together."

Abby scoffed at the suggestion, not wanting to admit that Jon's argument was the same as hers. "Well, at least Nathaniel is a gentleman."

"Are you suggesting that I'm not?"

"If the shoe fits..."

"You don't know anything about my shoes, Abigail."

"Nor do I care to," she fumed, recalling the things Nathaniel had told her about Jon's years spent as a solid being, entirely in the pursuit of innocent, unwitting girls. Abby tried to focus on the road while her insides twisted, knowing his churning eyes perused her as she drove. "Why don't you go spend time with some other woman, Jon?"

"Some other woman?" he echoed, his voice dripping with amusement.

"Yes. Someone who can't see the real you. Someone you can...woo."

"Woo? *Woo?* Is that the picture Nate painted of me?"

Abby remained frigid despite the blast of her car's heater.

Jon huffed. "If that's the case, it's no wonder you're being so rude."

"Rude? Me?"

"Yes, you."

"Well, what about you? I'd say you're the epitome of rudeness."

"Come on, now. I'm not as rude as Nate."

"Nathaniel? He would never be rude."

"Oh, really? What about reading a person's emotions without their permission, or even knowledge? Isn't that an intrusion? Isn't that rude?"

Jon's strike at Nathaniel stoked her anger. Abby wanted to turn to him and give him her evil glare that was never quite as menacing as she wanted it to be. However, she couldn't quite bring herself to look into those eyes again.

"Come on, admit it," Jon prodded. "Sometimes it drives you crazy – when Nathaniel knows everything you feel, the moment you feel it."

"At least he tries to help people. He can turn solid, and..."

"And you think I can't?"

I know you can, she thought, wondering how Jon's last girlfriend felt after he'd had his way with her and then left without a trace.

"Not to sound childish, Abigail, but if this is a contest, I assure you there is nothing Nate can do that I cannot do in a far superior way."

The words were still in a balloon attached to Jon's lips when a surge of heat pumped full-force into the car. Abby struggled to breathe, wondering if her car's heater had suddenly been possessed. When she reached out to shut it off, she realized that Jon's frigid swirl of air no longer accosted her from the passenger's side. His arctic frost was gone – replaced by scorching heat.

Oh, hell. He's solid now.

Abby had never actually seen Jon in solid form, but the differences between her two spirits continued to mount. Just as Jon's ethereal air was so much colder than Nathaniel's, his solid warmth was more like fire. She could only imagine how Jon might appear in the real world. What would his churning black eyes look like now? She couldn't bear to find out.

"So, what makes you so superior to Nathaniel?" she questioned, trying to delay the inevitable for as long as possible. She rolled her car window down to escape his blistering heat, resisting the urge to drive with her head sticking out of the window like a dog.

Jonathan fell silent. He sat nonchalantly beside her, just waiting.

Abby knew what he wanted. He wanted her to look at him. She refused.

"As much as Nate feels, I think," Jon finally answered.

"Yeah? What do you mean by that?"

"I mean that I'm a much better judge of what people are thinking. I spend my time working to discover explanations for how the mind functions."

"And that makes you superior?"

"I'd say so, since what I do is actual work. Nate just closes his eyes and breathes. He can't do what I can. He never searches that far into the world."

"You compare yourself to him a lot, you know that?"

"Yes, well, it would be hard not to. He's always there, isn't he?"

Abby gripped hard to her steering wheel, still too nervous to risk a glance at Jon's solid form. She was also too nervous to ask what he meant about judging thoughts. Could he read minds? And what on earth would that mean for her? She cringed, her body assaulted by sweltering heat on one side and freezing wind on the other – his body versus her open window.

"Speaking of Nate and his ever-presence, I've been meaning to thank you, Abigail. You've been one hell of a distraction for him, which means I've had some much-needed free time, for once."

I don't want to know what he's doing with that free time, she told herself as she pulled up to her school. She eased into a space at the very end of the student parking lot, as far away from prying eyes as she could get. Abby pulled the keys from the ignition and fisted them in her hand. "Goodbye, Jon," she said, waiting for him to leave first, since it was her damn car.

"Are you afraid to look at me?" his voice enticed, sending unwanted shivers crawling across her flesh.

"No," she lied.

Come on, Abby. You can do this. You have to look sometime.

With a steep breath, she forced herself to turn toward him.

Oh, crap. That's just wrong.

Abby now stared into the most delicious chocolate brown eyes she had ever seen. Perfectly still. Perfectly clear. Perfectly perfect. Jon had an astonishing body, an astonishing face, and now astonishing eyes. They were like chocolate icing on a chocolate cake topped with chocolate sprinkles.

She instantly decided that she would never eat chocolate again.

Steeling herself against the deviously delicious sight, Abby worked to calm her erratic pulse. "It's time for school, Jon. I have to go."

"I'll see you in class, then," he agreed, still lounging in his seat, daring her to flinch first.

Abby caved and groped for the door, staring into his eyes as if witnessing a hideous accident she couldn't tear herself away from.

He leaned toward her with a wicked smile on his lips. "Chocolate cake with sprinkles. I've never heard that one before."

Jon disappeared into thin air.

Abby sat with her hand still clenching the door handle, unable to move. She felt cold again. The outside air seeped in through her window, no longer fought back by his intense heat.

Damn it, damn it, damn it. She hadn't said chocolate cake out loud. She hadn't concentrated enough to think the words into his head. He'd picked them out. Out of her brain. Without her consent.

Jon could read her mind. And he loved the fact that he could.

Abby's breath puffed out in tiny white clouds before her face. She visualized the two spirits in her life: Nathaniel, with his sweet smile and Viking-farmer-soldier handsomeness; and Jonathan, with his devious grin and I-dare-you-to-watch-me desirability. They were complete opposites. Light and dark. Feeling and thinking. Good and evil.

She only had one word to describe Nathaniel.

Angel.

That made Jonathan's word quite simple.

CHAPTER
NINE

Raindrops smacked Abby in the face as she shuffled from her car toward school. *Chocolate cake with sprinkles. I didn't say it out loud. I didn't think it on purpose.*

Jon was so very, very wrong. Everything about him was wrong, and she had fool-proof evidence of the fact. As a spirit, his oil-slicked eyes made her stomach lurch while his cold blast of air froze her flesh into ice. And when he turned solid, the heat surrounding him was so intense that he may as well be engulfed in actual flames.

But if Jon is so wrong, how can other girls stand to be around him?

That question roiled in Abby's mind, even though she did understand the outward attraction. She didn't need art appreciation class to see that he was a physical masterpiece. Yet she truly couldn't comprehend how these other women could touch him without realizing that something otherworldly was happening inside his solid body.

Solid body.

Abby stopped walking just short of the front door.

Solid body. Jon was solid when he pulled chocolate cake with sprinkles out of my head. He was not a spirit, operating in a spiritual world, taking advantage of my mind from a spiritual plane. He was sitting right beside me, chocolate eyes, fiery heat, and all. Which means he can hear my thoughts anytime he wants.

Abby muttered every curse word she'd ever heard – in one continuous stream of foulness so unfortunate, she'd never thought herself capable.

How am I supposed to keep Jon out of my head now? How can I censure every thought that randomly explodes in my mind? How will I ever have any privacy if that devil can dance around inside my brain whenever the mood strikes him?

Abby stood in place, shuddering. She would never have moved from that one spot if rain hadn't poured onto her head. The cold, wet droplets uprooted her, propelling her into school along with all other parking lot procrastinators. Once she made it inside the building, she shook herself dry while glancing down the hallway. Everyone else moved along with their lives, chatting, rummaging through lockers, and making their way to class.

She knew she needed to do those things, too. She needed to pull herself together and act normal, because she chose this. She was the one who decided to have a relationship with a spirit. Nathaniel hadn't forced anything on her. On the contrary, he'd only ever tried to protect her – both physically and emotionally. He couldn't help the fact that Jon existed. He couldn't stop that narcissistic jerk from using women to fulfill his random whims.

Abby forced her legs to carry her down the hall. She'd always known Nathaniel was too good to be true. Now, she realized he came with a payment plan. If she wanted to keep her hero, she would have to put up with the villain.

Abby?

Nathaniel's gentle voice eased inside her mind as she reached her locker. She looked behind her, searching the crowd until she found him. Her spirit stood across the hall, leaning against a closed door, maintaining a careful distance from the many moving bodies. His eyes locked onto hers, filled with concern. *Are you all right, sweetheart?*

Oh, my God. Did you just call me sweetheart?

I did. Is that okay?

Yes. Hell, yes. It's wonderful.

Good, because it suits you. You have the best heart.

An effervescent smile demolished Abby's frown. *Man, I really missed you.*

It's only been a few hours since we last saw each other.

Yeah, well. Time is nebulous when you can't get enough of someone.

The glow of Nathaniel's eyes intensified. *I know exactly what you mean.*

Abby caught her lower lip in her teeth, easily recalling the sensation of his mouth pressed against hers last night. She watched his gaze drift down to her lips and she nearly fell over. *Please tell me you've thought about giving in to my wicked temptress ways,* she enticed.

Mmm. I've barely thought about anything else...

Abby prepared to drop her backpack on the floor and run straight at him.

...but you know why I can't, Nathaniel finished.

No, actually. I don't know anything of the sort.

He shook his head. *My beautiful, wicked temptress.*

My virile, virtuous Viking.

Nathaniel laughed so hard at the title she gave him that tears welled up in his eyes. The sight made her giggle out loud, which caused several people in the hallway to stare at her. "Just got a joke," she mumbled as the students eyed her while walking by.

Everyone in this school is going to think I'm crazy, she informed her spirit as she stuffed a notebook in her bookbag and shut her locker door.

I won't, he reassured. *Go to class, Abby. I'll be around.*

AFTER SHE SANK into her seat in Ms. Pennington's English class, Abby drew her eyes toward the windows. She'd spent the entirety of the morning wishing the rain would stop, but now she had to face the facts. This ongoing downpour meant she wouldn't be able to sit outside for lunch, which meant no stolen picnic bench moments with Nathaniel. She sighed in dejection, turning her head to observe the other students.

Marcus Dixon sat front and center, textbook open, pen in hand, and leg twitching. Jason and Randy strolled into class together, looking entirely uninterested as they wound their way to the back row. Eric walked in on their heels, trying to also look aloof but failing, before sitting down in front of Jason. Sondra Lawson sank into a chair a row over from Abby, setting her notebook on her desktop and resting her chin in her hand.

Once the last student filed inside, Ms. Pennington walked over to close the door. Nathaniel slipped inside just before she shut it. The teacher shivered with the cool air of his spirit form.

Lucky woman. What I wouldn't give to feel that chill on my skin.

Nathaniel stepped around Ms. Pennington to move to the windows, steering clear of the other students. He sat down on a window ledge before meeting Abby's eyes. *Hi*, he said. *How has your morning been?*

Lonely, she admitted. *How about yours?*

Interesting. Lots of emotions. But I haven't been able to move past yours.

Yeah? How am I looking today?

Quite colorful, he answered, the concern in his voice pulling at her heart. *I don't normally see you in red, but something was definitely bothering you this morning. Care to tell me what it was?*

"Today, we will study the Shakespearean sonnets," Ms. Pennington sang, hopping around the front of class on her tiny feet.

Abby opened her textbook as she debated her answer. She didn't want Nathaniel to feel guilty, but she also didn't want to lie. *Jonathan decided to hitch a ride to school in my car this morning.*

What? Nathaniel barked, his eyes flaring before he had the chance to calm himself. *Damn, I suppose I should have seen that coming. Do you want me to talk to him? I can make sure he keeps his distance from you.*

Abby considered the possibilities. Part of her really wanted to watch him expend some of his obvious strength on that jerk. The other part of her knew her angel would never willfully choose the bad-touch option. *No, I can handle Jon. But maybe you can ride to school with me tomorrow?*

Absolutely. I'll be sitting in your car before you ever leave your house.

That sounds perfect. Honestly, I was hoping I'd see you there this morning.

I'm sorry about that. I was a bit busy.

Yeah? With what?

Sondra, Chuck, and Holly.

Oh, Abby said, glancing over to Sondra, who doodled on her notebook. *How is she doing today?*

Not good. She found out about Chuck and Holly late last night and broke up with Chuck over the phone. She made the right decision, but it's killing her. And it's doubly painful, since Holly was supposed to be her friend.

Abby's heart ached for the girl she barely knew. *At least she's safe now.*

I think she is. Holly isn't, though. She hasn't behaved well, but she doesn't deserve Chuck's anger or retribution. I've been keeping close tabs on all of them.

Abby sighed as she gazed at her hero, astonished by his constant willingness to give to others.

Wait...listen to this, Nathaniel said. *Your teacher is about to quote something really incredible.*

Ms. Pennington cleared her throat while looking down at the book she held. Her squeaky voice never flowed smoother as she read. "Sonnet 18 begins, 'Shall I compare thee to a summer's day? Thou art more lovely and more temperate...'"

Nathaniel's eyes sparked with the words.

You know the sonnets? Abby asked, pulling his gaze back to her face.

Yeah. Shakespeare is one of my favorites. I mean, he's impressively emotional. 'But thy eternal summer shall not fade.' How can you beat that? I wish I could think up words like that for you. But no words ever seem to do you justice.

Damn, she sighed, staring Nathaniel down as he sat perched on the window ledge only a few feet away. *I really hate this rain today.*

Why is that?

If it wasn't raining, we could sit outside and you could be solid for me.

His brow rose. *And what would you do then?*

Abby smiled sinfully before closing her eyes. She conjured up an image in her mind, so quickly and easily. She envisioned the two of them sitting at the picnic table together. Her eyes held his as her fingers gently outlined his face. Then she hopped up from the bench and landed down on his lap, wrapping her arms around his shoulders. She leaned forward, tracing slow kisses up his neck until her mouth found his.

Abby focused fully on this fantasy she created, but she also drew on the memory of the kiss they shared in her bedroom last night. Her mind lingered on thoughts of his heat and strength and desire. She could practically feel his solid body against her now, his arms engulfing her waist as she ran her fingers down his chest to his...

Good God. Stop already, Nathaniel growled.

Her breath caught with his rough words, but she didn't feel guilty in the slightest. She peeled her eyes open to look over at the window ledge. Nathaniel stood there, staring straight into her, his glowing blue filled with all the potential of her fantasies.

Abby gripped the edge of her chair to keep from leaping out of it. *Don't look at me like that, Nathaniel. Or I will come across this desk at you, I swear.*

He laughed, deep and dark, with her feverish threat.

Oh, you may think it's funny, she said. *But I would have to leap over several people, probably injuring a few along the way. Then, I'd end up falling through you onto the window sill, and they'd throw me in the loony bin for sure.*

Nathaniel shook his head. *You wouldn't fall through me, sweetheart. I'd appear out of thin air to catch you, and everyone else would scream in terror, but I wouldn't hear them because I'd pick up right where your thoughts left off.*

Mmm. And then we'd end up in jail, I suppose?

I would think so. For indecent exposure, of course.

Abby grinned, covering her mouth to keep from laughing hysterically in the middle of class. *So? How are my colors looking? Any better?*

Definitely, Nathaniel confirmed. *You match your shirt now.*

I'm a human plum.

You're beautiful, Abby. Beautiful and perfect.

She exhaled in frustration. *You should probably go. Or jail awaits us.*

He smiled as he pulled away from the window sill. *Call if you need me and I'll be right beside you. I'm leaving now. Please don't watch if you don't want to.*

It's okay, she assured, unable to tear her gaze away as Nathaniel passed by Ms. Pennington and disappeared through the closed door. Abby's heart stumbled at the sight. She pressed her hand to her chest, incredibly relieved that she could touch him whenever he was solid. Otherwise, she would never believe he was anything but a figment of her overactive imagination.

With her spirit gone, Abby attempted to refocus on her surroundings by looking around the classroom. Marcus sat inches from Ms. Pennington's desk, his leg still shaking. Sondra slumped over in her seat, shoulders drooping. Jason and Randy smirked at each other, passing a piece of paper between them, ignoring everything and everyone else. Eric tried to peer behind his shoulder to watch the older boys, obviously desperate to be in on their joke.

When Eric looked back to the front of the class, he caught Abby's gaze. She wasn't sure how long she'd been staring at him. But he'd definitely caught her, so she glanced down to her book and tried to concentrate on the sonnets.

Shall I compare thee to a summer's day – Shakespeare's words, Shakespeare's emotion. Abby felt like she was caught in the middle of one of his plays now, with the drama surrounding her. In the months since her mother's death, she'd been entirely focused on her own drama. But now, because of Nathaniel, she could see so many other things in her world. She could understand the problems of so many other people, because he'd opened her eyes.

Nathaniel saw everyone, tried to understand everyone, wanted to rescue everyone. He was her virile, virtuous Viking. He was her angel – an angel with a nemesis.

Jonathan Fitzhugh.

Abby didn't mean to think his name so loudly or clearly. It just popped into her head, much to her dismay. She clasped her hands together over her textbook, hoping he hadn't heard her. When his arctic air swirled up in the row beside her a second later, she realized there was no hope at all.

She watched in mortification as Sondra shuddered and hugged her arms. Abby shut her eyes, refusing to watch the dark apparition form inside her classroom. She focused all of her energy on her teacher's warbling words.

Jon's laughter echoed in her mind, far too close for comfort. *What? You're not even going to say hello, Abigail? I know you're aware of me.*

She didn't respond. After all, it was bad enough that Jon could pick her thoughts out of her head. She certainly didn't want to volunteer any.

I could have sworn I heard you say my name, he goaded. *Were you thinking about me as you sat here in your class?* Jon paused for a response, as if expecting her to admit to some giddy, girlish fascination with him.

Only in a negative way, Abby retorted, wishing he would have plucked *that* thought from her brain, instead of ones that were none of his damn business. Honestly, she wished her thoughts didn't interest him at all. She gasped then, as a light bulb illuminated over her head. *I know exactly what kind of thoughts will deter Jon's thieving mind.*

Keeping her eyes shut tight, Abby created a surreal vision of Nathaniel inside her head. She imagined him clothed in bear hides, his muscular arms bared and bulging. A Viking helmet with two jutting horns crowned his head. He stood at the helm of a large wooden ship with a dragon carved into the bow, looking sternly across the ocean. Behind him, several long benches were filled with men who rowed oars through the waters. In the farthest seat sat a scrawny, bedraggled Jonathan, holding an oar in two blistered hands, breathing laboriously as he rowed.

Abby reopened her eyes to see Jon. He still stood in her classroom with a devilish grin on his face. He looked so smug, like he had more of a right to be here than she did.

His sunglasses covered his eyes, but it didn't matter. She knew the blackness roiling behind the deceptive shield, which meant he couldn't hide from her. She solidified the image of her Viking and stared it straight into Jon.

His forced laugh echoed through her mind. *Enough already, Abigail. I don't need to see any more of the mighty Nathaniel. Hell, I've seen enough of him for a thousand lifetimes. I guess I was mistaken. You didn't wish to have me right now. I can tell when I'm not wanted.*

Well, it's about time.

Jon smiled, his flawless grin far too delectable to be any good at all. *The mighty do fall,* he promised. *But you can call for me anytime.*

He stared the suggestion into her just before he disappeared.

Abby twitched in her seat.

The bell rang, making her jump and bump her knee under her desk. She glanced around to see if anyone noticed her awkward spasms. Eric met her eyes from the next row over and nodded to her. He even seemed concerned.

Abby smiled at him. The poor guy probably thought she was a freak, yet was still being nice. She waited for Eric to leave the classroom, along with Jason and Randy, before she gathered her things slowly in hand and moved grimly toward lunch.

THE CAFETERIA.

"Ugh," Abby groaned as she stared at the massive, artificially lit room in front of her, filled with multiple tables holding countless student bodies.

You will never find a more wretched hive of scum and villainy...

Abby giggled at the *Star Wars* quote floating through her mind. Anxieties aside, she admitted that this was not an actual gathering place for space creatures. But it may as well have been, because everyone looked like an alien to her. Or perhaps everyone was normal, and she was the alien.

She filed through the food assembly line like everyone else, gathering indiscriminate items onto her tray. As her unappealing meal stared up at her, Abby lamented how her father had done her the injustice of making her a sci-fi movie geek, on top of everything else. On the other hand, perhaps that was a good thing. After all, she'd learned to accept her current relationships with two different ghosts fairly easily. At this moment in her life, suspension of disbelief was her dearest friend.

After paying for her meal, Abby emerged from the lunch line like a lamb to slaughter. The teenagers gathered in odd swarms, positioned tactically at each table. She'd forgotten her armor at home. Luckily, she had her spirit.

Nathaniel drifted around the edge of the room, his eyes scanning the students. He noticed everything and everyone, yet still managed to keep constant vigil over her. *You doing okay, sweetheart?*

Yeah, I am. I'll make it through lunch just fine. But please tell me I'll see you in my car for the ride home.

Um, well... Nathaniel stopped moving to stand beside Chuck Harding's table. Chuck sat in the center seat, surrounded by his fellow basketball players. Holly sat beside him in Sondra's old place, his arm draped around the back of her chair. Holly's eyes were cast down, her fingers fidgeting on the tabletop.

It's okay, Abby amended. *You should stay by Holly to make sure she's safe.*

Nathaniel looked to Abby from across the hordes of students. *Only if you're okay with it. You're always my first priority. I need you to know that.*

I do. And as much as I appreciate it, I also don't want to take you away from your mission. Although I would really love it if you came to my house tonight.

I'll be there the moment your dad leaves for work. I promise.

Perfect, she told him, offering a reassuring smile before she turned to find a seat in the corner. While she walked toward the back of the room, she noticed Sondra sitting alone at a little table by the fire exit. Sondra stared at the wall in front of her, her body unnaturally rigid.

Abby walked straight toward the girl. "Do you mind if I sit here?" she asked when she arrived at Sondra's table

Sondra glanced up. "Um, no. I don't mind."

"Thanks," Abby said, setting her tray down and settling into a chair. "I hate eating inside. I normally sit out on the picnic tables by the woods."

"Oh, yeah," Sondra said, her voice as weary as her eyes. "I've seen you head out to those tables before. It's Abby, right?"

"Right. Hey, do you know what you're writing your paper on in English?"

"Um, no. I haven't decided yet."

"I think I'm going to write about the sonnets. They're pretty cool."

"Yeah, I guess. I kinda had trouble concentrating on classwork today."

"I figured. Do you want to talk about it? I'm a pretty good listener."

Sondra's eyes darted to hers. "Oh, God. Have you heard something?"

Abby shrugged. "I just noticed you looked a bit sad in Ms. Pennington's class. And you're not sitting with Chuck, like you normally do."

"That won't happen again," Sondra insisted. "He's a total jerk."

"I'm sorry."

"Thanks. At least I found out before I did too many stupid things." Sondra glanced over her shoulder, but not at Chuck. She eyed a group of seniors sitting several tables over. One of them – a boy with dark hair and a kind smile – stared back at her. "Do you see the guy in the middle of the table over there? Brett Simpson?"

"Yeah, I see him. He's looking at you."

"I know," Sondra said, hanging her head. "I wonder if he thinks I got what I deserved. I dated Brett before Chuck, and Brett was wonderful to me. But Chuck was...well, Chuck. He asked me out and I left Brett and didn't look back. I don't know why I did that. I mean, Chuck is the captain of the basketball team, and he's gorgeous and all, but I should've known better."

"Well, you shouldn't beat yourself up about it. Everyone makes mistakes."

"Yeah, but I already knew it was wrong to be with Chuck and I still couldn't stop myself. And now Holly's sitting over there with him, and I'm angry at her, but I don't want her hurt..."

Sondra continued talking, but Abby's hearing faltered the moment Jonathan materialized in the cafeteria doorway in all of his black-leather-jacket-and-sunglasses glory. He sauntered inside like he owned the place, stepped immediately toward a very pretty sophomore girl, and rested his shoulder against a wall beside her lunch table. An instant later, Jon turned his gaze to Abby and nodded.

She shook her head at him before looking to the other side of the cafeteria. Nathaniel still stood guard over Holly. But now, he also glared at Jon.

How is Holly? Abby asked, trying to distract Nathaniel from the intruder.

His gaze softened as it met hers. *She's nervous. How's Sondra?*

Hurting, but okay. Hopefully, it helps her to have someone to talk to. Although I thought Holly would be happy now that she has Chuck all to herself.

She already knows she isn't enough for him. He'll choose another one soon.

Abby saw several girls from her biology class walk past Chuck's table then, smiling and giggling as they gazed at him. *Unfortunately, I don't think he'll have too much trouble finding someone else.*

Nathaniel sighed. *Girls always seem to go for the bad boy. Why is that?*

Abby looked back to Jon, who appeared quite engrossed in the bouncy sophomore sitting in front of him. *I DON'T GO FOR THE BAD BOY,* Abby yelled into his head, hoping she somehow hurt his eardrum. When Jon shifted a bit comfortably on his feet, she felt satisfied.

She refocused on Sondra, who still worried out loud over Holly and Chuck. Abby wanted to reassure her that Holly had a guardian angel, but couldn't risk sounding insane. Instead, Abby sat quietly and listened. She'd forgotten how nice it was to have a girlfriend at school. Especially now, with her good and evil spirits staring at her across the vast space of aliens.

***

ABBY MADE it through the rest of the school day without another Jon-incident, so she was relatively calm as she walked to her car after her final class. Tonight, she would see Nathaniel again, and begin her quest to turn him into a fellow sci-fi geek. After all, if there was a chance he might meet her dad someday, it would help if they had something in common.

Her face lit up as she imagined the two men in her life becoming friends. Mark and Nathaniel – watching movies together, sitting at the dinner table together, spending holidays together. Even if the likelihood of those things was slim, the thought of seeing them one day made her happy beyond belief. Abby felt so hopeful that she didn't even notice the person already inhabiting the passenger seat of her car. That is, until she opened her door and immediately froze like a popsicle.

"Oh, for the love of all that is good," she grumbled as she dropped down into the driver's seat. Slamming her door shut, she pivoted toward the dark specter who lounged beside her. "Seriously, Jon. Why do you keep coming back to me?"

The smile curving his lips was downright stunning, although only because his shades still hid his eyes. "I know you don't want me here, Abigail. However, I need to ask you a favor, and I hope you will indulge me."

She looked away, pinning her gaze on her windshield as she started her car. Jon sounded nice and that made her nervous. "Tell me what you want and I'll decide if I can help."

He eased off his sunglasses, resting them on his thigh. "I want to know what you see when you look at me."

Abby winced, knowing his oily eyes were on her. "What do you mean?"

"I mean, what do I look like when I'm all *Casper* like this?"

"*Casper*? Isn't he supposed to be a friendly ghost?"

"Well, I am trying to be friendly. And you know what I'm asking."

She peeked into Jon's churning black sludge for a second only before putting the car in reverse. "Don't you already have the answer? I mean, we both know you can read my mind. I'm sure you've pulled plenty of thoughts out of my head, especially the ones about you."

He laughed. "Okay. I'll admit I've listened to some of your thoughts. But I would appreciate hearing it from your lips."

Abby worked to focus on the road as she eased her car out of the student parking lot. "Why, Jon? Why do you want to know what you look like to me?"

"Because I can't see myself like this."

"Seriously? You don't know what you look like as a spirit?"

"A spirit? Wow – that's one hell of a euphemism. And no, I don't know what I look like. I don't have a reflection and Nate and I don't discuss these things. I've never met anyone else who can see me like this." Jon shifted toward her, causing a rush of frigid air to careen through her cramped car. "I have to be honest, Abby. I'm quite used to drawing attention from women. They're intrigued by me. They're pulled to me. They desire me. But you...you recoil when I'm around. I want to know why."

She reached out to her dashboard, cranking up her car's heater to battle his glacial air. "Those women only desire you because they can't see what I see."

"And that is precisely what I'm talking about. What is it you see?"

Abby returned her hand to her steering wheel, gripping tight. "Well, you do know you're cold, right? Like, freezing cold?"

"I have noticed people shivering in my presence. But that can't be all."

"No. It's not all."

"What, then?"

She exhaled. "Fine, Jon. It's your eyes."

"My eyes? What about them?"

"They're...not right."

"Can you be a little more specific?"

Abby scooted closer to her door as she drove. "They're pitch black, like all you have are these huge, dilated pupils. And they move – constantly – like oil sliding across the whites."

"Hmm," Jon considered. "I see."

"You see? Really? Is that all you have to say about it?"

"Honestly, it's not as bad as I thought. And easily remedied…"

Abby had already reached over to switch off her heater by the time Jon turned solid. Sadly, she was getting used to his whims. Of course, he would want to fix the one thing she thought was wrong with him. He wouldn't tolerate anything less than perfection in his physical form.

"There," he said. "Is this all better?"

She glanced to the man beside her. Jon's body was once again faultless, except for the hideous heat roiling in waves from his flesh. His eyes were the exact same yumminess as before, much to her dismay. She rolled down her window, her entire being craving the cold outside air.

"Well, Abigail? Isn't this what you prefer? Chocolate cake with sprinkles?"

She scoffed at the amusement in his voice. Staring at the road ahead, she conjured up the vision of Viking-Nathaniel in her mind's eye. She easily imagined him helming his dragon-bow ship while wearing his horned helmet.

"Ugh," Jon groaned. "Give me a break with the Nordic fantasies, already. Just because he has a goofy middle name doesn't make him a Viking."

"If you don't like my thoughts, Jon, stop pulling them out of my head."

"Why should I stop? Nate does it, too."

"Oh, no, he does not. He only listens to the things I want him to hear – only what I specifically put in his mind."

"Seriously? Damn, that's so lame."

"Maybe Nathaniel is simply acting like a gentleman."

"Or maybe he *can't* do it. He never pushes the boundaries of our world. He never looks deeply enough to see what's out there."

"Well, he's certainly more polite about it than you are."

"We're dead, Abby. We don't have to be polite anymore."

The callousness of Jon's words made her stomach knot. "Funny, I get the feeling you were never polite," she mumbled, wishing she never had to hear anything from him ever again.

Perhaps he listened to that last thought, because he quieted for several moments. Or perhaps he heard her and still didn't care. "You know, snails crawl faster than you drive."

"Yeah, well. You can leave anytime."

"Nah. I think you'd prefer to have me hang around as long as possible."

Abby gritted her teeth. Jon was baiting her – again – and she was a fish on a hook. "And why exactly should I want you to hang around?"

"Because as long as I'm here, Nate's here. And when I leave, well...sooner or later, he'll feel the need to follow me."

Her entire body stiffened. *Oh, God, is that true? Nathaniel has always followed Jon in the past. But will that change now, because of me?*

"He may stay for a while, at first," Jon answered her unspoken question, his chocolate eyes latching brazenly onto her body. "I can see why he would want to, after all. But I assure you, Nate will leave eventually. Haven't you noticed his whole Boy Scout routine? He'll come after me. He'll always need to make sure I'm doing the right thing."

Abby's heart caved inward. She knew she'd lose Nathaniel one day, but this made it feel so much closer. *No. I can't do it. I can't lose my angel.*

"He's no angel, Abby."

"Damn it, Jon! Stop picking things out of my head!"

"Sorry. Habit."

She pulled the car to a stop several streets away from home. She didn't want Jon to know where she lived, even though he could probably see it in her mind. "So," she hedged, terrified of her next question yet still needing the answer. "Can you hear everything I think, every moment I think it?"

"Sure. If I want to."

Abby groaned as she turned to him. "And what about everyone else? Can you hear everyone all at once?"

"No. I told you, what I do is work. I actually have to concentrate..."

"Well, stop doing it with me. Just concentrate on someone else. Please."

Jon smiled then, forcing her to watch his deep brown eyes light up with unexpected flecks of warm gold. An unwanted image popped into Abby's mind: birthday candles on the chocolate cake. He laughed when that tempting vision pranced around inside her brain, and she cursed herself for not keeping her wayward thoughts under control.

"Why on earth would I want to concentrate on anyone else?" he purred. "When you're the most fun?"

Abby sat, frozen to her seat, while Jon reached his hand toward hers. She stared at him in gruesome fascination, fully aware that he intended to touch her. She couldn't react fast enough to pull away. Although, to be truthful, a part of her was morbidly curious to know how his touch would feel.

Jon drew his fingers across the back of her hand. Fierce, blistering pain shot up her arm in an instant. His flesh was on fire, branding her skin with white-hot flames, as she gawked at the ungodly sight. A whimper escaped her throat before she could think enough to save herself.

Abby yanked her arm away, sucking in an anguished breath. She expected to see his fingerprints seared into her hand. She expected to witness the angry red of fresh, violent burns. Yet her skin appeared perfectly normal.

She looked back to Jon with her mouth gaping, which only made him smile in delight. His self-satisfied expression didn't falter in the slightest, despite her obvious disgust. Abby sighed as she watched him, silently admitting to defeat. She'd tried fending him off using rudeness, inner strength, and her almost-evil glare, all for naught. Now, she would take her last option – pleading – and pray to God that it worked.

"Look, Jon. I'm sorry I've been rude to you. I know you and Nathaniel have a relationship I can't comprehend, and I'm not trying to interfere with whatever exists between you. But since Nathaniel is in both of our lives now, I think the best option you and I have is to stay out of each other's way. I would really like it if you just pretended that I don't exist. And I would especially appreciate you not showing up in my car anymore. Please. Pretty please."

Jon didn't move at all. He studied her for a long minute, looking genuinely disappointed. Eventually, his shoulders dropped. "Very well, Abigail. I will leave you alone. For now."

With those words, he disappeared into thin air.

Abby smiled at his empty seat, even though she knew her victory couldn't last forever.

"Here's your lunch, Dad. Just the way you like it," Abby offered, holding out the bag she'd packed. She tried not to act like she was pushing him out of the door, even though she was.

"Thanks," he said, leisurely gathering his keys. "You have plans tonight?"

She shrugged. "Just to watch a movie. And maybe eat some more."

"You've been awfully hungry lately."

"Yeah. Those wild teenage hormones, I guess."

Mark met her eyes as he took his lunch. "Okay, then."

Ridden with guilt, Abby almost caved under her father's non-existent scrutiny. "Yup, um...I'm all good," she fumbled, hoping a few little white lies were far better than the hideous mother-load of truth.

He finally stepped toward the front door. "Don't stay up too late, honey."

"I won't, Dad. Have a good night."

Mark winked at her, shutting the door as he left.

I'm behind you, Abby.

She heard Nathaniel's voice at the exact moment she felt his cool breeze flutter over her skin. Within seconds, his gentle chill transformed to perfect warmth. She pivoted on her heels and pounced on his solid body, all in one continuous motion.

"Whoa," he gasped as he caught her to his chest. "Happy to see me?"

"I'm thrilled and amazed and ecstatic and…"

Nathaniel wrapped his arms around her, lifting her up and dangling her mid-air. Abby squealed and buried her face in his shoulder. He twirled her in a circle before setting her down, steadying her while she regained her footing.

She grinned up at him, dazed with joy. "To answer your question, I am indeed happy to see you."

"Ditto," he said, tracing her face with his fingertips. "I want to hear all about your afternoon. What have you been doing since you got home?"

"Oh, the usual. Cleaning. Homework. Cooking. Talking to Julie."

"Julie? How is the young reporter doing today?"

"She's fine. Fine, but curious."

"Curious," Nathaniel echoed, his brow arching. "Did she ask about me?"

"Hmm," Abby hedged, since Julie had actually grilled her within an inch of her life. "Well, she knew I fixed you dinner last night, so she expected an update on how our evening went."

"Yeah? And what did you tell her?"

"I told her we had a nice night," Abby downplayed the conversation as her face heated. Honestly, she hadn't thought she could spend fifteen solid minutes discussing a kiss. As it turned out, she very much could.

He slid his hand into her hair. "Did I get a good report card, then?"

"Oh, yes," she hummed while his fingers massaged her scalp. "Julie wants to know if you have a friend for her." An insidious image of Jon popped into Abby's head then, making her cringe. "But I told her she should definitely stick with her boyfriend, Peter."

Nathaniel's arm dropped to his side. "You're upset again. Did you have another run-in with Jon this afternoon?"

"Yeah, I guess so. I mean, he showed up in my car after school."

Nathaniel's entire body tensed. He stepped back, putting far too much distance between them. "That about does it, I think. Will you excuse me for a few minutes, Abby? There's something I really need to take care of."

"No." She touched his arm. "Please don't. Jon is only doing this to rattle you. He wants to get under your skin, and if you go after him, he wins."

"But he's upsetting you. I can't stand it. I hate that being with me means you have to put up with him."

Nathaniel drew himself up to his full height, his muscles flexing beneath his shirt. His raw power stunned her, especially since he was normally so calm and gentle. Abby barely ever considered the fact that he was strong enough to wrestle a gorilla. Although, right at the moment, he looked like he could crush a person with his bare hands.

She laughed to diffuse his tension. "Hey, I can cope with Jon. You take the bad along with the good in life. I may only be seventeen, but I've learned that much. Anyway, I don't want to waste time talking about Jon. He's not worth ruining a single one of our moments together, especially when I have dinner ready for you." She closed the distance between them, reaching up to stroke Nathaniel's hard jawline. "You know how much I love to watch you eat."

"Dinner? Again? You spoil me rotten."

"You deserve it," she insisted, grasping his hand to pull him to the kitchen.

Nathaniel settled into a chair at the kitchen table. "I'm sorry to bring it up again, Abby, but if you give me a minute, I can straighten this out with Jon."

"There's no need. Really, there isn't. I already took care of it."

"You took care of it? How?"

She stepped over to the stove to grab one of several dishes she'd prepared. "I just made it clear that I want him to stay away from me."

"And what did Jon say to that?"

"He said that he would." *For now.*

Nathaniel met her eyes when she returned to the table. "Wow."

"What's wow?"

"You are. I'm impressed, yet again. Jon is not an easy person to stand up to. I've seen many people fail miserably at it. I'm just...I'm very proud of you."

Nathaniel's praise lit a soft glow inside her chest. "Thanks," she said as she moved back to the stove to gather more food. "But I'd prefer not to talk about Jon anymore tonight. I like it when it's just you and me."

"God, I do, too. So much."

Abby brought several more plates over before sitting down. "Then hurry up and attack your food. We have important business this evening."

"We do?" Nathaniel questioned with a playful smile. "This wouldn't be wicked temptress business, would it?"

"No, it's not. I mean, unless you want that. But either way, we have to watch *Star Wars*. We'll start with the original, and continue on with one episode a night, until you've seen them all. Honestly, it's sinful that you've been on this earth for over eighty years and not done this before."

Nathaniel grabbed his fork, wielding it like a weapon, before digging into his food. "I will do whatever you want, especially if you keep feeding me."

Abby rested back in her chair as she watched him eat, wishing with all her heart that his words were true. The threat Jon made in her car this afternoon – the promise that when he left, Nathaniel would follow – still sat heavy in her chest. She wanted it to be nothing but a lie.

Forcing her dismal thoughts to the back of her mind, she focused on her Viking while he devoured his dinner. He shared stories between mouthfuls: hysterical tales of his tempestuous little sister and the trouble she got into around their farm. Once he'd finished every bite of his meal, Abby watched from her chair while he did the dishes, insistent that she relax while he cleaned.

After Nathaniel finished clearing her kitchen, he took her hand and led her to the living room. She started the movie before snuggling up beside him on the couch. Over the next two hours, she paid much more attention to the enticing feel of his arm around her shoulders than to anything onscreen. When the ending credits rolled, she turned off the TV. "So? What did you think of your first *Star Wars* episode?"

Nathaniel met her inquisitive gaze with a smile. "I really enjoyed it. Although, I'm surprised that you're such a science fiction buff."

"Why are you surprised?"

"Well, I often see you in purple, so I figured you'd like romance movies."

"I've only been purple quite recently, I assure you," she said, shifting sideways to see him better while still occupying her happy place in the crook of his arm. "Besides, science fiction can be romantic. Take *Star Wars*, for instance. In the next movie, Han and Leia get together."

"Really? I thought she might like Luke."

"Wow. I forget you haven't seen this before. There's an even bigger shocker with Luke, but I won't go there yet."

"Or warn me about the spoiler, at least."

Abby absorbed his teasing grin. "So, you really did like it, then?"

"I did."

"Mmm. You and my dad would get along so well."

"He likes *Star Wars*?"

"It's one of his all-time favorites. He dresses up like Darth Vader every Halloween to give out candy. I always love seeing it, because I know if he feels good enough to do that, then he's doing okay. Honestly, with all that's happened this past year, I'm praying he still dresses up for Halloween. I wish you could see him in his Vader costume. It's really funny, since he does the heavy breathing and everything."

Nathaniel eased his arm from around her, pulling away to sit up at the edge of the sofa. "I know you want me to meet him, Abby. But it's just...if you and I have to be separated one day, as hard as it will be if that happens, I think it will be even harder if your dad is involved. I don't want to leave you in a place where you have to lie to him about why I'm gone."

She unfolded her body from the couch to sit up beside him. "It's okay. I know why you can't meet him. I'm sorry I keep bringing it up."

"Please don't be sorry," Nathaniel begged, taking her hand in his. "I wish I could give you that much. I wish I could give you everything. But I just can't."

Abby stood from the sofa, keeping his hand inside hers. "Let's not talk about what we can't do," she said, tugging on his fingers. "Come with me."

Nathaniel allowed her to pull him up. "Where are you taking me?"

She smiled slyly as she led him through the living room toward the hall. "I'm taking you to my bedroom. I want to concentrate on what we *can* do."

"Abby..." he groaned, although he didn't stop following her.

"Well, look who has the one-track mind now," she teased, guiding Nathaniel into her room and over to her bookcase. "I just thought we could flip through that yearbook you asked about yesterday, to see which of the other students in my school need your help."

He turned to face her. "Is that the only reason we're in your bedroom?"

She looked up to him with the most innocent expression she could muster. "Of course. I mean, unless you're rethinking the gentlemanly thing?"

He shook his head with determination. "No. I'm not."

"Yeah, I didn't think so."

Abby grabbed her yearbook from the shelf. She drew Nathaniel toward the bed, urging his large body down onto her fluffy comforter. She sat directly beside him at the foot of her mattress, yet she still scooted closer – as close as she could get without sitting in his lap. She pretended that the near-merging of their bodies was perfectly normal as she opened the book to the class photos section. "Now, show me the people you've gotten readings from, and I'll tell you if I know anything about them."

"Okay," he agreed, barely able to move his arm due to the proximity of hers. He flipped through the pages, studying each picture, but Abby didn't see anything but him. She wondered if using a partly-true excuse to get him onto her bed made her an official wicked temptress. Even if it did, she couldn't worry about that right now. Because something he said tonight gave her hope.

When Nathaniel spoke earlier about them being separated one day, he said *if*. He could have said *when*, but he didn't. He said *if* they had to be separated. And that one little word filled her with gobs of blissful, effervescent hope.

"This person is very sad," he told her, his gentle voice breaking the silence.

Abby glanced to the photo he singled out. "That's Charity Gibbons. She was a freshman last year, so she'd be a sophomore now. I don't know much about her, though. Sorry."

"It's okay." Nathaniel pointed to another picture. "What about her?"

"That's Jasmine Sinclair. I think she was dating a boy a year older than her, and then he moved out of town. I imagine she's pretty depressed about that."

He nodded, flipping through pages until he found pictures of Sondra and Holly. He finally settled on one of Chuck Harding in the junior section. "This one," Nathaniel said, tapping the basketball player's photo, "is trouble."

Abby heard him, although she wasn't listening entirely, since her mind reeled with possibilities. Could Nathaniel find a way to stay here? Could he find a way to truly live? Did he want to go to college, to get a job, to have a future? Would he do anything in order to be with her?

"I don't know why," he continued as he stared at the yearbook, "but some guys start so young. The way they treat women is disgusting. Chuck will never stop on his own. He'll definitely require outside assistance."

Abby gazed at Nathaniel. Could they have a normal life? Could they date, person-to-person instead of person-to-spirit? Could he meet her dad? Spend holidays with them? Be her boyfriend in every sense of the word?

"You would never do that," she assured.

Nathaniel turned his head toward hers, his lips so close now that she could smell his sweet breath. "I'd never do what?"

"You would never hurt a woman."

"No, I wouldn't. Not if I could help it," he said, his voice burning with pain and fear. "I don't ever want to hurt you, Abby. But I'm so afraid I will."

If he left. But maybe, just maybe, their fate wasn't set in stone.

She ran her hand down his arm, reaching for the book he held. "I think you would move mountains for me."

"I would," he declared without hesitation. "I absolutely would."

Abby closed the book and set it down beside them. She shifted up onto her knees, tucking her feet beneath her on the mattress, matching their heights. "You won't ever hurt me, Nathaniel. I promise."

His eyes overflowed with emotion. She could see his ever-present pain, but now it was tempered by something else – something lighter and easier – that belonged solely to her. She reached up to slip her fingers into his hair, watching his blue darken with her touch. Slowly but deliberately, she leaned in to place her lips on his. She allowed herself only a fleeting instant to enjoy the soft, blissful kiss before she eased back.

Abby sat beside him and waited. She had no idea what he would do now.

Would he stand, growl in frustration, and run from the room? Or would he stay right here, silent and willing, and let her do as she pleased?

Nathaniel grabbed hold of her. He gripped her hips and pulled her onto his lap. His arms encircled her waist. His lips found hers, smooth and effortless, without hesitancy or restraint.

Abby lost whatever meager control she possessed. She pushed into him, wriggling against his thighs, clutching at his shoulders. She could barely catch her breath between their heated kisses, but she still pressed her body harder onto his, crawling farther and farther into his arms until they both toppled over on the bed.

Nathaniel fell down beneath her against the soft comforter. Abby only had a fleeting second to feel him under her before he flipped them over. The instant she lay on her back, staring up into his eyes as he held his body suspended over hers, she tensed for the withdrawal she knew was coming. Astoundingly, it didn't.

His mouth found hers again. The heat from his body spread through her skin as his tongue slipped past her open lips. She tried like hell to calm her wild heartbeat, since the pounding was so loud that she was certain he could hear it. When he pulled slightly back, she panicked. But then his mouth trailed down to her neck, pressing over the rapid, sputtering pulse leading to her collarbone.

As his teeth nipped against her shoulder, every nerve ending in her body ignited at once. Abby closed her eyes tight. For a brief moment, she considered behaving herself. She dismissed the thought immediately. Her eager hands wandered down, exploring the strained muscles in his arms before working their way down the length of his spine. Once she reached the hem of his shirt, she balled the fabric in both fists. Nathaniel tensed the instant her fingers found the small of his back, but she was too involved to notice.

Abby hitched her leg up around his hip, securing him in place on top of her, fascinated by the intensity of her body's response to his. She drew her hands across the bared skin of his low back, absorbing the heat of his flesh while he shuddered. Her lips found the side of his face, pressing into his jaw. She breathed in deep, filling her lungs with his intoxicating scent.

Nathaniel allowed her trembling aggressions for one more minute before he groaned. He reached down to her leg, grasping onto her thigh to unwrap it from his waist. The instant he freed himself from her clawing grip, he wrenched his body off of hers and forcefully flopped over onto his back.

They lay side by side on her bed, staring up at the ceiling. Abby panted so heavily that she could hear nothing else in the room for long, drawn seconds. She would have been mortified by the noises she made, except for the identical sounds she heard coming from Nathaniel. Eventually, her crazed breaths and ridiculous heartbeat slowed.

As soon as she regained a modicum of control, she reached tentatively for his fingers. He grabbed hold of her hand and held on tight. "Abby – I swear I don't remember – how did we end up lying down on the bed?"

"Would you believe me if I said I lost my balance?"

"Would you believe me if I said I'm losing mine?"

"You? Never."

Nathaniel drew his fingers across hers. "Maybe you think too highly of me. I may not be this strong."

"Don't worry about it. I'm happy to take all the blame."

He turned on his side then, propping on his elbow to look into her eyes. "I assure you, I am a perfectly willing participant. Too willing, in fact."

Abby hummed with his admission, still in awe of the magnetic pull of her body to his. Her gaze drifted over his face before focusing on his mouth, recalling how strong yet soft his lips felt when pressed to hers. She reached up, outlining their shape with her fingertips, wetting her own lips as she worked to connect the smoothness she now touched with the solid feel she remembered.

Nathaniel grabbed her hand away from his mouth to flatten it against his chest. "Do you feel that?" he asked, pressing her palm over his surging heart. "*That* is about to beat its way out of my body. And if you keep looking at me like you are, and touching me like you do, I'm never going to leave this room."

Abby smiled, since that sounded like an awesome idea.

He dropped his forehead onto her shoulder. "That makes it official," he grumbled. "I can't come into your bedroom anymore. This is two-for-two. I obviously can't handle the temptation."

"Well, that's what wicked temptresses are for, you know."

"Hmm. I've never had one before. I do enjoy finding these things out."

"I'm always happy to teach you more."

"Abby..."

"Sorry. Please don't leave yet. Just stay right here."

Nathaniel sighed into her neck, his breath flushing across her skin. She closed her eyes and exhaled in contentment. He continued holding her hand against his pulsing heart until the warmth of his body spread through hers.

Abby felt joyful. Safe. Alive. And she never wanted him to leave.

But at the end of the night, when he did finally leave her room, she was okay. When he pressed his lips to hers one more time, gently and quickly, before walking out through her front door, she was happy. Abby couldn't be upset now. Because Nathaniel didn't say *when*. He said *if*.

CHAPTER

TEN

"I have an incredibly important question to ask you." Abby pinned Nathaniel's eyes as they sat together on her living room couch. "And I need you to take this super seriously, and truly consider your answer."

He nodded solemnly. "I promise I will."

"Okay," she said, inching closer to him. "Now that you've seen every Star Trek movie ever made, I have to know – Captain Kirk or Captain Picard?"

"Hmm," Nathaniel considered.

Abby absorbed his thoughtful expression, loving how he took the time to mull over something he probably didn't care much about. She loved how he'd sat with her, night after night for the past several weeks, watching her and her father's favorite movies. She loved how he humored her in every way.

"I'm going with Kirk," Nathaniel finally answered.

"Yes! I was positive you'd say that!"

He took her hand in his, aligning their fingers. "If you were positive, why did you look so worried?"

"Well, I guess I was nearly positive."

"And why does it mean so much?"

She shrugged, trying to ignore her heart's customary leaps and bounds as he focused on the way their hands interlocked so perfectly. "Because I'm a Kirk girl and Dad's a Picard guy, so I need a tie-breaker."

"What about your mom? Wasn't she a tie-breaker?"

"Nope. She always stayed neutral. We called her Mrs. Beige."

Nathaniel laughed. "Well, I'm with you."

"I figured you would be," Abby said as she wedged her body up against the side of his. She wondered what kind of physical contact he would allow tonight. He'd been so cautious these past weeks, after the two incidents in her bedroom. He'd vowed not to go back into her room, and he hadn't.

Since then, Abby had worked all the wicked temptress angles she could think of: subtle seduction, outright coercion, over-stuffing of his never-ending pit of a stomach, and pretending there was a large spider on her bed in need of removal. Nothing worked. Nathaniel hadn't budged from her living room couch, not even when she claimed the bed-spider was the size of a small cat.

"Spiders don't get that big," he'd countered.

"Oh, this one did. It's probably one of those wild Australian spiders."

"Australian, huh? Okay, then. I will take care of it, if you promise to stay glued to this couch until I return."

Her ploy hadn't worked in the slightest. "Darn you," she'd said.

Nathaniel had smiled as she'd pouted. He'd reached out to smooth his thumb across her lips, erasing her frown. And he'd kissed her – Good Lord, how he'd kissed her – but that was all. For the umpteenth time, Abby went to sleep alone, frustrated, and exceedingly happy.

In truth, this past month had been one of the best of her life. She only wished her mother was alive, so she could tell her all about Nathaniel. But aside from missing her mom, Abby thought her world was pretty great right now. She took care of her father, watching for downturns in his mood and finding none. She refocused on her schoolwork, now perfectly comfortable with the idea of ghosts auditing her classes. She ate lunch with Sondra almost every day at school, enjoying having a new friend.

Abby had even learned to live with Jonathan. Since that day in the car when she'd asked him to stay away, he hadn't clobbered her with his company. His lack of conversation relieved her, although she still questioned his ulterior motives. Jon hadn't spoken to her – or invaded her mind with his dark voice – but he was still present each and every day, strolling through the halls of her school. He nodded and smiled at her, and she actually got used to having him around. She imagined it was similar to what Nathaniel had experienced since the '80s; Jon hung out for so long that he simply became part of the landscape.

In the past month, both of Abby's spirits had kept their promises. Jonathan, happily, had not attacked her with his foul presence. Nathaniel, sadly, had not attacked her nearly as much as she would have liked.

That thought made her huff as she sat with her Viking now, cuddled up on her living room couch. She wasn't sure what she needed to do to break the chains he'd placed on their relationship, but she wouldn't give up trying. Especially now, when she knew for certain that he was a Kirk guy.

Abby shifted up onto her knees on the cushion beside Nathaniel, willing some unseen seductive power to come to her aid. She leaned forward to skim her hand across his back. She pressed her lips to his neck, running little kisses up to his ear, causing a shiver to course down his spine.

He cleared his throat. "You need to study for your biology test tomorrow."

Abby heard the longing and frustration evident in his voice, which only emboldened her. She threw one leg over both of his and slid over into his lap. "I'll be fine," she assured as she rested her chest on his.

Nathaniel settled back against the couch cushion, making room for both of them to be more comfortable. He even held her in place on his thighs, with his large hands covering her hips, although it was far too gentle to be considered angst-ridden. "But I keep you up late every school night, Abby. You shouldn't miss an honor roll because of me."

"Please don't feel guilty. It's my choice to stay up with you. I'd stay up even later, you know – if you wanted to do something other than study."

"You're relentless, aren't you?" Nathaniel complained with a teasing grin.

"Mmm. I wish you were," Abby whispered against his lips.

He ran his hands up the sides of her body and into her hair, cradling her head with his fingers. "The need I feel for you is relentless. You know that."

She melted onto him. "Then why fight it?"

Nathaniel pressed his lips to hers, hard and desperate, but only for a second. "Because I know I'm not thinking straight about this," he explained while his mouth moved to her jawline, dragging kisses farther and farther down her neck. "I swear, I can't think at all when I touch you. I've been tempted in so many ways during my many years, but I never let myself falter. Not once. And then I meet you, and my control is just gone."

Abby whimpered as he nipped her shoulder. "But you are in control."

"No, I'm not. What I am is indulgent. I can't stop touching you. I can't stop kissing you. I can't stop thinking about touching and kissing you. If I was in control, I would be sitting on the floor right now, keeping my damn wandering hands to myself, and helping you study for biology."

She ran her damn wandering hands down over the smooth lines of his collarbones. Her fingers fiddled with the buttons on his white oxford, popping two of them open. It was enough to slip her hand beneath his shirt, to rest her palm against the warm skin covering his erratically thumping heart. "This is kind of like studying biology."

"You're studying genetics. Not the actual act of reproduction."

Abby worked another one of his buttons open. "How about anatomy?"

With a deep growl, Nathaniel grabbed her by the waist and set her body five feet away from his, on the other end of the couch. He sat up on the edge of his seat, dropped his forehead into both hands, and exhaled. "I don't know why I ever imagined this would get easier," he spoke to the floor.

She combed her fingers through her mussed hair. "What do you mean?"

"I told myself a month ago that if I didn't go into your bedroom again, I would be okay. I thought I could have these...these *moments* with you, and I would somehow get used to it. I thought the craving would lessen."

"It doesn't," Abby sighed.

He lifted his eyes to pin hers. "It only gets worse."

Her toes curled into the cushions. "I'm so glad it's not just me."

"You've had a few years of wanting, sweetheart. I've had close to seventy."

With his words, she ogled him in stunned silence. Her hormones had only been on the offensive since puberty, yet her need for him plagued her constantly. Did Nathaniel feel a desire seventy years stronger? She honestly couldn't imagine that level of demand.

Abby started moving back to him, intent to provide some much-needed relief. He immediately shook his head. "No, please," Nathaniel begged. "I can't anymore. I'm sorry, but I've reached my limit for tonight. Tomorrow. I'll behave better tomorrow."

"But there won't be a tomorrow. Tomorrow's Friday, so we won't get another night together until Sunday. That's three whole nights away."

"It's really just two," he amended. "And that's perfect. It'll give me time to convince myself that I can be with you and not attack you."

Abby sighed in utter dejection.

Nathaniel chuckled as he stood and walked into the kitchen. He grabbed her backpack off the chair and took out her biology notebook. When he returned to the couch, he sat as far away from her as possible. "Now, we'll study for your test," he announced while thumbing through her notes. "Let's see...what year did Gregor Mendel's ideas on genetics get published?"

"1866," Abby answered.

"And what was Mendel's primary occupation?"

"He was a monk. But you don't have to be."

Nathaniel laughed so hard that the couch shook.

She grinned as she scooted over to him again, aligning the side of her body with his. He wrapped one arm around her back, pinning her in place next to him. "Okay, okay," she conceded. "I'll be a good girl and study. As long as you stay right here with me."

"I'll stay," he accepted her truce. "For as long as you want."

Abby prayed that was true.

"Do you mind if Brett sits with us at lunch?" Sondra asked.

Abby looked to her friend as they gathered their belongings at the end of their English class the next day. They'd been sitting beside each other in Ms. Pennington's room for the past month, which thrilled Abby to no end. "No, I don't mind," she assured while stuffing her notebook into her backpack. "So, are you two officially back together?"

Sondra slung her bag over one shoulder. "I'm not sure it's official, but he called last night and we talked for hours. We're going to the movies tonight."

Abby saw her friend's face light with both excitement and relief, which probably had a lot to do with the fact that Chuck was now solidly in her rearview mirror. "That's great, Sondra. Really great. Can I take a raincheck on lunch today, though? It's so pretty out, and I know it's going to get cold soon, so I thought I'd sit outside while the weather's still nice."

"Are you sure? I don't want you to think I'm ditching you for a guy, because I'm not. I really want you to meet Brett."

"I will meet him, I promise. But you two probably need some alone time right now, anyway. I'll see you in history class after lunch, okay?"

Sondra studied her before nodding. "Okay. See you then."

They walked out of class together. Sondra met Brett in the hall while Abby turned in the opposite direction, doing a full-body slam into the heavy brown metal door that led outside. Navigating her familiar path across the school's back courtyard, she watched the sunlight shimmer through the trees. The branches were nearly bare now, except for a few tenacious gold and red leaves. Abby remembered how the changing colors made the fall her mother's favorite season.

A familiar jolt of sadness kicked in along with that memory of her mom. However, Abby could tell the pain was getting a little lighter and a bit easier to endure. She knew Nathaniel was a big part of her healing. He'd come into her life exactly when she needed him.

Abby smiled with that thought as she passed several students kicking soccer balls in the field. She wound toward the picnic benches, fully focused on her destination, until she was finally able to ease down onto one weathered wood slat. Dropping her backpack onto the ground, she closed her eyes while she waited for her spirit. He would have to be in his other world today, but that was okay. She just wanted him beside her.

Nathaniel. God, she didn't just *want* him – she *needed* him. She needed him in every way she could imagine, which very much included physically. Yet he remained a perfect gentleman at all times, wrapped in unbending willpower and smothered in superhuman restraint. He'd denied himself human contact for so long, but he still wouldn't give in to her multitudinous and strenuous advances. If the shoe was on the other foot, Abby-the-spirit would have surely made Nathaniel-the-mortal her love slave by now.

That image made her laugh, even if her joy turned to frustration in mere seconds. Today was Friday, which meant that after this time together at lunch, she wouldn't get to see him for two more whole, entire days. She was probably the only teenager in history to ever despise the weekend, but the thought of living without him for that long felt tantamount to tossing her heart into a wood chipper. And she couldn't even imagine what a mess that would make.

As Abby slumped over onto the tabletop, a rustling sound in the distance pulled her from the little world in her mind. She glanced up, searching for the trespassers who'd intruded on her quiet. Her eyes honed in on Jason and Randy, who now headed into the woods for their routine lunchtime meeting. She watched Eric followed closely on the older boys' heels.

Eric looked over to her, offering a wave before stepping across the tree line. Abby waved back, seeing as he was always nice to her despite her history histrionics. She knew he'd had a rough year with his parents' divorce, so she hoped whatever Jason and Randy did in the woods wasn't too bad. She hated to think of Eric getting caught up in something that he couldn't get out of.

The three boys disappeared into the forest before Abby even noticed Jonathan drifting toward the edge of the trees. His movements were unnaturally smooth, as always, yet her heartrate remained even and steady. The sight of him didn't provoke an instant fight-or-flight reaction in her body anymore. He was simply in her life now, and to be honest, that was a good thing. Because as long as he stayed here, Nathaniel would stay, too.

Jonathan stopped at the woods' edge, staring into the forest. A moment later, he glanced her way. Even from this distance, his brilliant smile reflected the sunshine and caused her partial blindness. He nodded cordially and politely, which made Abby almost feel guilty for being so rude to him the few times they'd spoken. Her hand popped up to wave before she could stop it. She regretted the gesture immediately.

Jon turned away from the tree line to face her. He glided forward, thankfully with his sunglasses in place. Abby hung her head.

Damn it. My reprieve is over.

"Hello, Abigail."

The opposite bench at her table didn't shift at all, but she knew by the gust of cold air sweeping over her face that he now sat with her. "Hi, Jon."

"How are you doing today?"

She risked peeking up at him. "I'm fine."

Jon slipped off his sunglasses as his body morphed into solid form. His stunning chocolate eyes perused her from across the table. "That's good. I'm fine, too."

Abby shook her head. *What is this? Are we supposed to be friends now?*

"I thought we could be," he answered her unspoken question. "I mean, would it be so bad?"

"It will if you keep pulling thoughts out of my brain."

Jon's head cocked to the side. "Come on, now. It's been a month – exactly one month to the day – since you asked me to leave you alone. I figure that's enough time to get over anything."

"Well, maybe it would be, if you weren't still bound and determined to read my mind. And since when is one month the time limit on grudges?"

"Oh, it's not. At least, not for me. I can actually hold a grudge forever. But you're young and kind, so I figured that would be about your limit."

Abby couldn't help smiling. She allowed herself to truly look at him, despite her ongoing wariness. Without his oily eyes staring at her, she had to admit that Jon looked better than ever. He'd traded his black jacket and pants for a cobalt blue Henley and jeans, creating the unsettling image of an all-American model prepped for a glorious outdoor cover shoot. Such wholesome appeal unnerved her, being so at odds with what she knew about his character.

Hmm, Abby considered. *Maybe Jon is trying out his Halloween costume a few days early.*

"Do you like Halloween?" he asked.

Abby mumbled several curse words beneath her breath. "Do I have to conjure up my Viking fantasy again, in order to keep you out of my head?"

"God, please don't. I've had more of Thor the Mighty than I can take."

"Then stay out of my mind."

"Hey, I just asked a simple question," Jon defended, resting his elbows leisurely on the table. "Maybe I didn't even hear you wondering if I was trying out my costume early."

Abby shook her head. A huge part of her wanted to scream at him to leave her alone. The other part of her wanted to see where this newfound peace took them, especially if his continued presence here meant Nathaniel could stay indefinitely. "Well, the answer is yes," she admitted. "I do like Halloween."

"And why is that?"

"Because you get to be someone else, even if it's only for one night."

Jon's brow rose. "Why would you want to be someone else?"

"I think everyone wants to be someone else at some point. Don't you?"

"Hell, no. Not me."

"You've never wanted to be anyone else? Not ever?"

"Why on earth would I want that? I mean, look at me."

"Wow, Jon. Have you ever heard the term narcissistic?"

He drew back in feigned outrage. "Who, me?"

His eyes sparkled, and Abby laughed before she could stop herself. If anyone had told her a month ago that she'd be comfortable enough to joke with Jon now, she would have considered them demented beyond redemption. But here she sat, realizing that he actually had a sense of humor. And that he might not be pure evil, after all.

"Did you really think I was pure evil?"

Abby groaned at his constant mental invasion. "Maybe."

"But you don't now?"

"I'm not sure. The verdict is still out."

Jon leaned closer. "Why don't you just admit it? I grow on you."

"Sure. Like a fungus. Or maybe a lichen. Or one of those weird, spongy yellow molds that show up on wet mulch and look like vomit..."

He held up his hand. "Okay, okay. You're quite silly, aren't you? It's no wonder you like Halloween – all that dressing up nonsense."

"And I suppose you've never done anything that didn't make sense?"

His face fell with her question. "I never said that."

Abby watched as Jon turned to stone before her. She wondered what sort of things he'd done that didn't make sense to him, and wished she could pull answers out of his mind like he did with hers. On second thought, maybe she needed to be careful what she wished for.

"I suppose I can see the appeal of Halloween," he eventually confessed. "It might be nice to be someone else, just for a bit."

"Really? Who would you be?"

Jon thrummed his long fingers against the table. "If I could be anyone else for a night, then I would be Nathaniel."

"What?" Abby yelped. "Oh, let me guess. You'd be Nathaniel so you could finally see what it's like to be a good guy?"

"Yeah, sure. Maybe that's the reason," Jon purred, his gaze drifting to her lips for lingering seconds before dragging back up to match her stare. "But if you ever tell him I said that, I will deny it. Most vehemently."

Abby forcibly averted her eyes down to the table. She couldn't allow herself to be engrossed by the cute little dimple she'd just discovered in his left cheek. Damn, his physical appeal was dastardly unfair.

"Speak of the devil," Jon said, "here comes Thor now."

In an instant, Nathaniel's cool air wrapped around her body. He settled down beside her on the bench, his glowing blue eyes focused entirely on her face. *Hey, sweetheart.*

His deep voice inside her mind sent delightful little shivers down her spine. *I'm so glad you're here, Nathaniel. I missed you so much.*

I missed you, too.

God, I wish I could hold your hand. I wish I could kiss you.

Without a second wasted, Nathaniel turned solid. His hand found hers, lacing their fingers together. He leaned in to kiss her, his lips soft and smooth and utterly delicious.

Jonathan groaned. "Come on, you two. This is nauseating."

"Then you can leave," they responded in unison. Abby laughed with their like-mindedness. Nathaniel smiled at the sound.

But really, how can you stand it? Jon's words tumbled through her mind. *The guy hardly ever leaves you alone. Don't you need time to think? Time to breathe? Time to just be Abby?*

What I need is more time with him, actually, she answered her unwanted spirit as she gazed into Nathaniel's eyes. *Honestly, Jon, I bet you'd leave us alone if I just gave you a mirror. It would entertain you for days on end.*

Jon laughed wildly, the sound echoing off the line of trees beside them.

Nathaniel's steel gaze landed on his dark friend. "What's so funny?"

"Nothing," Jon replied. "Nothing at all."

Nathaniel turned back to Abby. "Am I missing something?"

She shrugged. "Jon just likes to read my mind without my permission."

"Does he? You'll need to stop doing that, Jon."

"Doing what, exactly?"

"Invading her mind. She doesn't want it."

Jon stared him down. "And are you going to stop me?"

Nathaniel stood from the bench. "Absolutely. Right now."

Abby whimpered, not wanting this anger between them. She reached up to place her hand on Nathaniel's chest. The touch was light and simple, yet he immediately sat back down.

Jon glared at him. "Are you going to let that tiny hand stop you?"

Nathaniel didn't hesitate. "Yes. I am."

Jon clenched his jaw as he stared at his own hands. "Whatever," he said, just before he disappeared from the bench.

Abby shivered when Jon evaporated into nothing, but she didn't give him another thought. She turned her attention back to Nathaniel. "You let me stop you," she said, marveling at how he'd responded to her lightest touch, even against his own judgment. She glanced to her small hand resting over his large chest – small but powerful. "Thank you, Nathaniel."

"For what?"

"For always being here for me."

"Not soon enough. I wish I never had to be away from you for a second."

"It's okay. I know you have things to do. I'm just glad you're here now."

"Abby, I'm so sorry about being away from you, and about Jon, and..."

"I don't want to think about any of that," she hushed, leaning in to rest her ear over Nathaniel's heart. She listened to it thump, slow and steady, lulling her into a blissful state of peace. "All I want is to be close to you for as long as I can."

His bear-like arms encased her, pulling her tight against his body. Abby willed away her bones in an effort to merge with him entirely. When Nathaniel eased his lips to her hair, showering her with tiny kisses, she closed her eyes and let the whole world wash away.

WHEN SCHOOL ENDED THAT AFTERNOON, Abby drove home alone. She pulled into her driveway, turned off the engine, and stared at her front porch, actively dreading the weekend. It wasn't that she didn't enjoy spending time with her father, but there was someone else in her life now. Not being able to discuss Nathaniel with her dad was getting tougher by the minute. Withholding that amount of information felt tantamount to outright lying.

"There are definitely downfalls to dating a spirit," she mumbled as she stepped out of the car. Mustering up her courage, she painted on a dutiful-daughter smile while she walked in the front door. She heard her father cough as soon as she entered the house.

"Dad? You feeling okay?" she questioned, dropping her backpack on the couch and following the hacking sound into the kitchen.

Mark stood in front of the cabinet where they kept their medicine, digging through the boxes and bottles stored inside. "It's just a cold," he croaked. "But I don't think we have any cold meds left."

"Here, let me look." Abby stepped up next to him, taking over the search, while her dad wandered away into the living room. She sifted through the numerous containers of pills sitting on the shelves, including Mark's psych meds and several random pain relievers. As she searched, an orange prescription bottle near the back of the cabinet caught her eye. She grabbed hold of the bottle, pulling it out to hold it in her hand.

Sleeping pills. Abby read the label several times, staring at her mother's name. She opened the drawer under the sink and held the bottle over the trashcan. Her fingers clamped around the container as she tried her damnedest to throw it away.

After several maddening minutes, Abby replaced the bottle in the back of the medicine cabinet and slammed the door shut. Pivoting on her heels, she exited the kitchen to search for her father. She found him in his bedroom, pulling a fleece hoodie over his head. "You're right, Dad. I don't see any cold meds in the cabinet. I'll run to the store to get some."

"You don't have to do that, honey. I'll make it."

"It's fine. We need a few groceries anyway. I'll probably be gone for a little while. Will you be okay until I get back?"

"Sure." He gave her a weak smile. "Thanks."

She nodded before moving to the living room to grab her keys and wallet from her backpack. She left the house and jumped into her car, rolling down her window the instant she sat. The crisp October air was a momentary reprieve from the fresh weight on her mind.

As Abby drove the familiar roads to the grocery store, she thought about the orange prescription bottle still in the back of the medicine cabinet. Were those the pills that killed her mother? She knew her mother was drunk on the day she died. Her mother was often drunk. But was an added sleeping pill all it took to end her life?

Abby didn't blame her mom for drinking. Living with her dad was a challenge – never knowing when his personality would change for the worse, but always knowing something bad would happen eventually. Alcohol was her mother's anesthesia, pure and simple. And Crystal was a happy drunk, if there was such a thing. The only person she abused when she drank was herself. At least, that was the excuse Abby told herself. It wasn't until after her mother died that she understood how much everyone would suffer for that abuse.

Abby had spent hours ridding their home of liquor bottles after her mother's funeral. She'd dug through every drawer and searched under every bed. She'd watched each drop of alcohol pour down the kitchen drain and pitched every container into the trash. She hadn't thought twice about dumping the booze back then, so why couldn't she throw away those sleeping pills now?

She'd seen the bottle many times before. She'd held it over the trashcan more than once. Yet she'd always made the decision to keep it. Why couldn't she let go of it? Was it the odd connection she felt to her mother when she read her name on the label? Was it a reminder that her mother actually existed? Or was it because she still needed to understand exactly what happened on the day Crystal died?

Abby shook her head as she drove, knowing she should lay that question to rest, just like her angel had encouraged. Besides, that bottle of pills couldn't tell her anything. Nathaniel couldn't, either. He couldn't endure watching her mother die – not after watching his own. And even if he was willing to do that for her, she wasn't willing to do it to him.

There were no psychics to give her answers, either. She'd tried that route and failed miserably. Now, the only thing Abby had left was to mourn her mother's death, and to wonder every day if her father had been involved. Had he had made the biggest mistake ever? Was he still walking and talking and living his life, all while knowing that his wife was in the ground because of him? And how could that not drive a person mad?

A tear hit Abby's cheek before she could stop it. She forced the wetness away with the back of her hand. She was so tired of crying.

The grocery store appeared before her, although she didn't fully remember driving here. She dragged herself from her car and grabbed a shopping cart on the way inside. Leaning against the cart rail, she moved sloth-like through the store. She lingered in every aisle, staring blankly at the colorful boxes and cartons of food.

Abby remained in a trance until she reached the medicine aisle at the back of the store. She forced the sluggish fog to the back of her brain, working to focus on the task at hand. She needed to take care of her father the way her mother would've expected. Strong. She had to be strong.

After choosing the best medicine for him, Abby made her way to the checkout. When she finally left the store, it was already dark outside. Streetlamps illuminated the asphalt with shadowy lights as she drove home. She turned up the radio, making herself sing along in order to clear her mind. Still, their driveway appeared far too soon.

"Be strong," she instructed herself as she parked and grabbed the bags. The frigid night air flooded her lungs while she walked up the driveway and into the house. The moment she opened the front door, she heard her father snoring. He lay on the couch in the living room, wrapped in his fleece hoodie, with one arm slung over his eyes.

Abby watched him for a moment, aware that he never got enough sleep while working the night shift. Slipping past the couch as quietly as possible, she brought the groceries into the kitchen. She planned to set the bags down on the table. But she couldn't, because the kitchen table was already full.

Abby stopped cold and stared. It wasn't the gun lying there that bothered her. She already knew about her father's guns.

It was the bullets.

Her entire body started to shake. She couldn't help it. She shook from the inside out, until she heard the bags banging against her legs. Abby released her clawed fingers. The groceries hit the floor with a thud as she stood and stared.

She needed to collapse into a chair to relieve her wobbly legs, but she refused to be that close to the little gold shells. It had been so long since she'd seen bullets in the house. She still remembered the odd way they gleamed, and how they seemed so small to be so deadly. And she definitely still hated them as much as ever.

Mark's snores reverberated through the kitchen. Abby's hand flew to her chest, pressing hard to keep her pounding heart on the inside. "This can't be happening," she breathed. "But it is, so you've got to pull yourself together. What would Mom do?"

Abby continued staring at the tiny gold shells as she debated whether or not to confront her father. His behavior these past few months seemed fine. She believed he'd been steady and calm, and Nathaniel had agreed. She hadn't seen anything unusual in Mark's eyes, which made her think she might be able to face him now without breaking open the dam that kept his sanity in check.

"Dad," she said, her voice far too small to wake him. "Dad! I need you!"

Mark stirred in the other room. "What? Abby? Are you home?"

"Can you come into the kitchen, please?"

"Yeah, sure. What time is it?" His words were slow and his footsteps heavy as he approached. He stepped up beside her, reaching to the floor to retrieve the grocery bags at her feet. "You're back already. I must have fallen asleep while you were gone. Do you need help putting things away?"

"Dad, please. I need you to look at the table."

He followed her eyes to the tabletop. "Oh. I forgot," he mumbled, reaching for his revolver. He popped open the barrel, extracting a bullet from the chamber.

Oh, God. It was loaded.

Mark gathered the bullets into his hand and tucked the empty gun under his arm. "I'm sorry, Abby. I was cleaning it and I got tired. I was only going to lay down on the couch for a minute. I didn't mean to leave it out like that."

"The bullets, Dad. Why are there bullets?"

"Yeah, I know. I should have put them away."

"The *bullets*, Dad. You're not supposed to have them in the house. You promised us – Mom and me. You said you wouldn't anymore."

"Hey, Abby, it's okay…" He reached out, laying his hand on her shoulder.

She worked hard to not yank her arm away.

Mark straightened his spine. "It's fine, honey. I'm not doing anything bad here. I'm taking my meds. You know that."

Abby stared into him, concentrating with all her might. She searched for something, anything, to give her answers. His pale blue eyes – the ones that matched hers perfectly – were even and clear.

He extended his hand toward hers. "Here. I want you to take them. Put them somewhere, or throw them in the trash. Do whatever makes you feel better. I'm not leaving you, Abby. I'm not."

Her gaze fell to the little shiny shells. They looked so benign, resting helplessly in his hand. She forced herself to grasp them from his palm and curl them into her fist.

"There," he said. "Is that better now?"

She nodded stiffly.

Mark gave her a weary smile. "I'll put the groceries away. I know you've had a long day. Why don't you go put your feet up? We could watch a movie."

Abby stood frozen in place while he picked up the bags and put them on the counter, setting the gun down beside them. The bullets dug little rivets into the palm of her hand, but couldn't unclench her fist. "Actually, I think I'll go to bed early tonight. I'm tired, too."

He turned back to her. "You sure?"

"Yeah."

"You okay?"

"I'm fine."

"Okay, then. I'll see you in the morning. Sleep well."

"You, too," she said, taking several steps backwards before scurrying to her bedroom. The instant she got inside, she shut the door behind her and locked it tight, turning the switch on the knob so hard that she feared breaking it. She stumbled over to her bed, slumping down to sit at the edge of the mattress.

Abby stared at her hands as they lay in her lap. Her room was dark except for the glow of streetlamps outside the window, but Abby could still see the whitened knuckles of her clenched fist. She urged her hand open, coercing her fingers to finally unlock.

The shells fell loose in her palm, making a tinkling sound that assaulted her ears. Pain radiated from the center of her chest, sharp and stabbing. She allowed the tears to stream freely from her eyes. She couldn't have stopped them, anyway.

I can't do this again. I definitely can't do this alone. Not without Mom here.

Abby imagined her mother's face, which made her tears flow harder and faster. They tried their best to drown her, so she clung to the only thought that gave her hope. *You are not alone anymore.*

She didn't consciously make the decision to call him. She just couldn't do anything else. Clamping the bullets inside her palm, Abby closed her eyes.

Nathaniel, can you please come here? I really need you.

She felt his chill immediately, turning to warmth almost as fast. She felt his solid body as he kneeled on the floor before her, his strong hands moving to her arms. She heard his clear voice, edged with panic and pain.

"Abby, what's wrong? What's going on? Are you hurt?"

"No, no. I'm okay. Physically, anyway."

Nathaniel gripped her forearms, nearly shaking her. "Open your eyes, please. Let me look at you."

She did as he asked, slowly, her vision blurred by tears.

He still knelt before her in front of her bed, looking both sweet and utterly terrified. "I need you to talk to me. What happened?"

Abby wanted to answer him. Sadly, the words just wouldn't come out. Instead, she opened her hand and held it out to him.

Nathaniel glanced at the shells in her palm. "Where did you get those?"

She whimpered.

"Do they belong to your dad?"

Abby nodded, swiping at her tears.

"Hey, it's okay. I'm here." Nathaniel pulled himself off the floor to sit next to her on the bed. He wrapped his arm around her shoulders, drawing her in. "Everything will be all right. I'm here, sweetheart. I'm here…"

She leaned her stiff body against him, urging the pain away. She thought about breathing, in and out, as his warmth battled the cold fear stationed in her mind. His presence calmed her moment by moment. Eventually, she stopped crying and the room fell silent.

After several minutes, his deep voice rumbled beside her. "Are you okay?"

"I am," she assured, even as another shudder moved across her shoulders. "Thank you so much, Nathaniel."

His hand slipped down to rub her tight back. "Don't thank me until I've helped you. Tell me what to do. Let me do something."

"You're here. That's all I need."

"Let me give you more, please. Tell me what happened tonight."

"Okay," Abby agreed, drawing an achy breath. "This afternoon, I found out that my dad has a cold. I went to the store to get him some medicine. When I came home, there was a gun on the kitchen table and…and these bullets."

"You told me he has a gun collection."

"But not any bullets. He's not supposed to keep them in the house."

"Why not?"

She stared down at the shells in her palm. "When I was fourteen, I got home from school one day and heard my mom's voice coming from my parents' bedroom. She sounded panicked and hysterical, so I ran to her. As soon as I entered their room, she pushed me back behind her. I peered around her shoulder to see my father standing by his nightstand, holding a revolver to his head. He was crying and his hand was shaking so hard. I thought the gun would go off any second, right into his brain. I heard my mother begging, 'Please, Mark, please don't. Stay with us. Stay with me. Stay with Abby. We love you, honey. Stay. Stay…'

"I didn't know what to do, so I just nodded, again and again. God, I was so scared. I had no idea how long they'd been standing there like that, but Mom just kept begging him to stay, over and over. Finally, he lowered the gun. He let it slip out of his fingers onto the bed. Mom ran over to him then. She grabbed him in a giant hug and they both collapsed on the floor, sobbing. I stood there forever, watching them, until she reached her hand out to me. I went over to them and knelt down to wrap my arms around their shoulders. We all sat there together, and we all cried."

Abby sniffled with the memory, sucking in another shuddering breath.

Nathaniel's hand eased across her back. "What happened then?"

"Once my mom was able to stand, she got her phone and called 911. The ambulance came so quickly. Damn, I hate ambulances – they always take him away from me. And they did. They took him away for several months that time. It was a long hospital stay, but he came back in pretty good shape, all things considered. I wasn't sure if we would ever even talk about what had happened before he left. But then one night, soon after he came home, Mom called a family meeting at the kitchen table. She made us sit there together while she made a new rule. Dad could keep his guns, but never any bullets. She'd already gathered the ones she could find in the house and they were sitting on the table. I remember staring at them, thinking how small and simple they looked. Then she stood up, threw them all in the trash, and made Dad promise never to get any more. And he promised. He *promised*."

Nathaniel sighed. "Until today, when he broke that promise."

Abby turned her face into his collar, nodding against his warm skin. Nathaniel drew his hand down her arm, all the way to her clenched fingers. He pried her fist open to gather the bullets from her palm into his. Leaning over, he set the little gold shells on her nightstand. When he settled back into place beside her, he took her empty hand in his and wound their fingers together.

"Do you think your dad is having trouble again?" he asked, his soft voice filling her dark bedroom. "Medically, I mean?"

"Not that I can tell. He's been okay. You said so, too."

"You're right. I did."

"Will you check on him for me? Tell me what he's feeling?"

"Absolutely. Do you want me to do that now?"

She begrudgingly released her tenacious grip on his hand. "Yes. Please."

Nathaniel stood, reaching out to graze his fingers across her cheek before he left. Abby looked down to the ground, currently unable to stomach the sight of her spirit disappearing. But she still knew the moment he'd gone, because any sense of security she had disappeared with him.

Turning toward her nightstand, she glared at the bullets lying there. She rose from her bed, grabbed her trashcan, swept the little shells into it, and shoved the can back under her desk. She swiped the excess wetness from her eyes before striding across the room.

Abby stood in front of her window, staring up at the star-dotted sky. "It's those damn guns," she muttered. *What is it about them? Why does Dad need to have them in the house? Why does he still cling to them, even after leaving the Army? Why does he spend every Sunday caring for them like children?*

A rush of cool air flushed over her spine.

I'm back now, Abby.

"How is he?" she asked, not turning her eyes from the window.

"It's hard to tell when he's sleeping, but he seems fine. It looks like he took the cold medicine you got him and fell asleep on the couch. I can't read much emotion from him at this point. I can check back later, if you want."

She nodded, grateful for Nathaniel's help but too preoccupied to focus.

He stepped up behind her, his body solid and warm as it came flush with hers. "What are you thinking, sweetheart?"

"I'm thinking that I don't understand the gun thing," she admitted. "When Mom died, I was so worried about Dad. I felt my own grief, but I was consumed by his. I thought he was going to cave in, or implode, or something. His guns were the one thing he could focus on. He worked on them constantly. That's how he got through. But I just don't understand it."

Abby drew her gaze from the window, turning to fully face Nathaniel. "Have you ever held a gun?" she asked, watching his eyes darken in pain. "Oh, God, I'm sorry. What am I even saying? I know you've held a gun. You were in the military."

"Yes."

"That's so strange to me. I really can't imagine you with a gun. And my father's attachment to his guns is more than just a hobby. It's a need. He actually needs them, which I can't imagine, either. Can you?"

Nathaniel cleared his throat. "Kind of."

"Did you ever like having a gun?"

"No."

"Did the other soldiers like it?"

"Most of them."

Abby heard his carefully guarded answers. They weren't nearly enough. "Nathaniel, I need you to do something for me. Please."

"What do you need?" he asked, reaching to touch her face.

"Tell me about the war. Show me. Give me your memory."

His fingers paused against her cheek. "You're under a lot of emotional stress right now. I don't think you really want to see that."

"Yes, I do. I need to watch this, to feel and understand it, in order to understand my dad. I can't do that now, because I'm just too…too young. I haven't seen enough of the world."

"You've seen plenty. You don't need to be a full adult this minute."

"But I do. I have to. I'm practically the parent in our house, and I need to take care of him. I need to understand him. You have the knowledge I want. You have those memories. You share the same experiences he does."

Nathaniel hung his head. "I know you feel responsible for your father, but I can't imagine that this will actually help you. Besides, I don't share his experiences. I was never captured."

"No, you were killed. I think that qualifies."

His hand slipped from her face, falling down by his side. "God, Abby. You don't know what you're asking for. I can't turn off the emotions that go with that memory."

"I don't want you to."

"And you already know about Normandy. You studied it."

"You told me they got the scenery right, not the emotions."

"Your dad's war was fifty years after mine. The weapons were different."

"But the experience, I'm sure, was much the same." Abby stepped closer to him, to rest her hand over his heart. "In here."

Nathaniel covered her fingers with his, pressing her palm against his chest. "Please," he breathed. "I don't want to do this to you."

"You're not doing anything to me. I'm asking you for this. I'm actually begging you, because I worry every day about what's going on in his mind. I worry about when he's going to go crazy on me again – and what in the hell I'm going to do about it – and it's because I can't understand him. Please let me have this. Let me understand, even just a little."

Nathaniel clutched her hand. "I need you to realize that if I do this, it will be the same as when I gave you the memory of my family's farm. You will be inside my mind, doing what I did. You will see what I saw. You will feel what I felt. I can't turn anything off. It's all warped together."

Abby nodded solemnly. "I'm well aware of what this means. I also know it won't be easy for you to cope with those memories. Honestly, I'll understand if you tell me you can't. I never want to hurt you, Nathaniel. Never."

"Remembering it won't hurt me. Lord knows, I've relived those moments in my mind a thousand times already. You're the one I'm worried about."

"Don't be. Please."

Nathaniel studied her forever. When he spoke again, his voice was low and raw. "Are you absolutely certain that this is what you want?"

"Yes. Absolutely certain."

He released his grip on her hand and took several steps away. When he reached the center of the room, he swore under his breath. Abby knew he was at war. She knew she should probably back down now and tell him to forget the whole thing. But she couldn't. She had to know.

Just when she thought he might deny her, Nathaniel's body transformed. She felt his chilled air even at this distance. "I was at Omaha Beach," he began, turning to face her. His eyes glowed with ethereal brilliance in the shadowy room. "Do you remember what you learned about that wave of the assault?"

Her knees weakened. "Yes. That was the worst – the most miscalculated."

"That's right. I was in a personnel landing craft. We were launched far off shore. Too far, actually. We were sitting ducks for German gunfire. Even for those of us who survived the trip across the water, it was no easy feat to get to the beach. There were huge wood and steel obstacles, like tipped-over crosses, sticking up out of the ocean. They were constructed to rip the hulls out of ships, so the landing craft could only take us so far. We had to wade in the rest of the way, being shot at the entire time by men in trenches and firing pits and pillboxes. It was utter chaos. Utter fear."

Nathaniel stared the words into her, as if expecting her to change her mind. She didn't. Eventually, he closed his eyes again, dimming the light in her room. "Are you ready, Abby?"

"Yes. I'm ready."

"I'm doing this against my better judgment."

"I know you are. Thank you."

Nathaniel exhaled before stilling his body. Abby didn't move any closer, but she did remain facing him. She closed her eyes and opened her thoughts, anxious to accept anything he was willing to share. Her mind stayed blank and dark for the longest time. Then an image formed inside her brain, slowly and tentatively, like tiny bits and pieces of a memory.

At first, she could only see the color gray. Moment by moment, as his vision came further into focus, Abby realized the gray was the sky – a sky filled with huge, roiling clouds that blotted out the sunrise. Airplanes flew over her head, splitting the clouds in two, although she couldn't hear them at all. She looked ahead, across the murky water, watching the beach loom closer and closer. The eerily silent image became blurred by a haze of deep, crimson red. She knew the color well. It was Nathaniel's color of fear, anger, and pain.

Abby could see everything through his eyes now, filtered through the color of his emotions. But his other senses weren't present yet. She could only look at the white sands in the distance. She could only stare at the monstrous wood-and-steel crosses jutting out of the water. She could only squint at the trenches dug far up from the shoreline.

She understood that he was trying to keep the worst of this war away from her. In truth, she appreciated how much Nathaniel wanted to protect her. But she also wasn't unhappy when his control eventually slipped. His true memory took over then – breaking free to open a floodgate into her mind – attacking all of her senses at once.

Airplanes zoomed forward to drop bombs on the beach, their thunderous explosions tearing into her ears. Arctic winds froze her skin, transforming her shallow breaths to white puffs before her eyes. Ocean sprays burst up to slap her in the face, the gritty taste of saltwater mixing with the acid in her throat.

These were Nathaniel's thoughts. They were his sights, sounds, and tastes. Yet they all felt real to her – as real as the sick fear churning her gut.

Abby realized now that she stood on a personnel landing craft. She looked to the men alongside her, rows and rows of them, each one standing as stiff and straight as possible on the floor of the rocking vessel. Every soldier wore green camouflage pants and jackets, with bowl-like helmets covering their heads and rounds of ammunition draped across their chests. They each clenched a gun in their hands, held like armor in front of their body. She swallowed hard as she stood in the middle of the fearful throng, absorbing the red and black halos surrounding every figure.

A young man's voice cut through the icy air. *So, if I don't see you again, it was good getting to know you.*

Nathaniel responded to him in a deep rasp. *Yeah. Same to you, Steven.*

Abby's heart broke at the sound of her angel's voice – so drained and beaten. She watched the image shift to the person standing at her side. He was a rail-thin boy, barely eighteen, with freckled skin and eyes sharp with panic. Even haloed in red, he still looked pale.

And if I do see you again, Nathaniel told him, *maybe you'll take me to Kansas to meet your family.*

Yeah, sure, Steven answered, fingers quaking against the barrel of his gun. *We can find some gals to go dancing with, right? And we can stay at my parents' house for a few days, and then maybe get back to Oklahoma to see your folks.*

Yeah. We'll do that. We'll definitely do that.

Nathaniel sounded exceptionally calm, given the deep, treacherous ache Abby felt inside his chest. Of course, he would try to put the other boy at ease. He always helped people, even in his own state of fear.

Abby tried to smile at Steven, until the piercing sound of sailing bullets split the air beside her. The tiny missiles came from nowhere and everywhere, striking several men who stood on the landing craft with her. The soldiers collapsed then – folding like unanimated puppets – one five rows up, one three away to the right, one two rows behind. She heard the heavy thuds as the hard metal floor met their falling bodies. Another boy on her row, the one standing closest to the railing, vomited over the side.

The remaining soldiers struggled to stay upright while the floor beneath them shifted with the ocean current. Steven hummed anxiously as he clutched his gun closer to his chest. The soldier in front of her hit his head, over and over, into the butt of his rifle.

Abby looked down at her arms – at Nathaniel's arms – expecting to see a gun in his hands, too. She didn't. She could feel a weapon strapped to his back, resting hard and cold against his spine, but he didn't reach for it.

Instead, he reached to one of the many pockets in his pants. Nathaniel yanked open the snap and dug his fingers inside, pulling out a small, heart-shaped gold locket. It was beautiful, shimmering, and delicate, with tiny swirls carved into the front and back.

He fumbled with the clasp until he managed to pop it open. Abby stared at the tiny photos nestled inside the two hearts. On the left was his mother, Diana, with her kind eyes and loving smile. On the right was his sister, Marybeth, with her toothy grin and glint of mischief. He ran his calloused, dirt-stained thumb across the photos as another bomb exploded in the distance.

The craft struck something in the water, something hard and unforgiving, and all the men lurched forward as the vessel stopped cold. The locket knocked loose from Nathaniel's fingers, falling soundlessly down. The men around him yelped and cursed, but Abby barely heard them. She lunged to the floor, grasping and searching across the slick metal ground, desperate to find the locket. Thankfully, she did. But she also found a dead body. The other soldier's face lay cold and lifeless against the deck only a few feet away, his dull, glazed eyes staring straight through her.

Nathaniel! Get up here! Steven barked. Abby's fist curled around the tiny gold heart. She forced herself to stand back up. *We stopped, but we're still so far away from shore. Why do you think we stopped?*

I don't know, Nathaniel answered his friend. *Maybe there's something wrong with the hull. Try to stay calm. We'll find out soon enough.*

Steven huffed. *Yeah, sure. Calm.*

Abby looked down to the locket in Nathaniel's hand. He stared at the photos for one more second before clicking the two hearts shut. He secured the gold trinket into one pocket before reaching to a different one. Abby tried to focus on the contents of this other pocket, but her thoughts were derailed by another airplane ripping through the thick clouds. More bombs crashed up ahead on the beach while the boy standing to her right rubbed the side of his rifle like a genie's lamp.

Nathaniel shifted his eyes away from the sight. He pulled several objects out of his pocket to hold them in his palm. They were coins – most of which Abby had never seen before – of all shapes, sizes, and denominations. His trembling fingers turned them over one by one, heads and tails, heads and tails.

The raucous noises around her dulled to a soft roar as he concentrated on the small metal tokens. Slowly but surely, his riotous pulse began to stabilize. For a few precious moments, Abby actually felt calm.

A man's voice bellowed orders into the frigid air, but she didn't hear.

Hey. It's time, Steven said, nudging her with the butt of his gun.

Abby looked to the boy, taking a second to register his words, before she nodded. She returned the coins to her pocket, securing them inside while staring straight ahead. She watched as the large front metal gate of the landing craft collapsed forward, becoming an open plank into the ocean before them.

Every man in her vessel gripped their weapons in front of their chests while Abby stood with empty arms, stiff and silent.

She waited an eternity, praying for Nathaniel to reach around his back and grab onto his gun. She needed to hold that weapon in front of her – to display it like some invincible shield to protect her from the inevitable – yet nothing happened. The hardened steel rifle remained right where it was.

Here we go, Steven announced weakly.

Abby took a sharp gulp of salty air. The oceanwater swirled around her boots, up her calves, and onto her thighs as she propelled herself into the icy sea. She trudged forward within the oddly synchronous hoard of men, looking around her to see the other soldiers holding their weapons above their heads to keep them dry. She prayed again that Nathaniel would reach for his gun. Yet still, nothing happened.

She refocused on the monstrous wood-and-iron crosses tipped on their sides several yards in front of her. Waves smashed against her waist as she waded closer to the hull-rippers, looming larger and more terrifying with each drag of her sopping boots over the sandy ocean floor. Another raining hail of bullets descended around them all, striking many of the men from her troop. Garbled, choked cries filled her ears while a dozen soldiers collapsed into the water. Their blood seeped out, turning the oceanwater red against her uniform. The crimson halo of Nathaniel's emotions deepened, slurring everything she saw.

Abby lunged toward the hard cross that now lay just a few feet away. She grasped at the rusted metal, using it as a momentary lifeline, clinging with all her might. Steven coughed and wobbled in the waters beside her, struggling to maintain his balance against the charging waves. She reached out, grabbing him by the arm to drag him closer.

Hang onto this for a minute, Nathaniel instructed. *Get your breath back.*

Steven followed orders without question, hugging onto the unforgiving steel. A third soldier from their troop clung with them, fighting for life against the current. Abby looked out to the shoreline, so close now. She watched the assault tanks roll forward out of the ocean and onto the sand, firing at the snipers in the distance. She saw man after man drop like flies all around her. The crimson red continued to seep into the water and into her mind.

Can you move? Nathaniel asked Steven.

Yeah. I think so.

Stay behind me. Keep low in the water. We're almost there.

The moment Steven nodded, Abby launched herself forward. She ducked back into the waves, crouching as far down as she could, while the ocean mercilessly pummeled her spine. The blaring noises rose by deafening degrees: the crashing of bombs, the whirling of bullets, the splashing of downed bodies, the screams and gurgles of the fallen soldiers. She crouched lower and lower while she pressed on toward the beach, until the water was too shallow to maintain her position.

Run! Now! Nathaniel commanded.

Abby took off at full speed with Steven behind her, moving in alongside other soldiers who'd found their way onto the sand. She made it about twenty feet onto the beach when she heard the bullet sail past her ear. Abby heard Steven grunt, sharp and hard. A thudding sound came from behind her before she turned to see him.

Steven lay on the sand, blood seeping out onto his uniform from the bullet hole in his shoulder. Abby dropped to her knees beside him. *Steven, get up!* Nathaniel yelled. *Can you hear me? Get up! You have to keep moving!*

The boy gasped for air. *I can't. I can't move, Nathaniel. Go. Just go.*

No! You're coming with me! Get up!

Nathaniel grabbed his friend's good shoulder, hoisting him up by brute strength alone. He wrapped his arm around Steven's waist and dragged him forward through the sand, their progress slow and clumsy and labored.

This is too hard, Nathaniel. Just leave me. You have to save yourself.

No. No. We're in this together.

Steven tried to walk, struggling to match Nathaniel's long strides. He couldn't. He tripped and fell, taking them both down.

Abby grunted against the pain when her chest struck the unforgiving sand. She scrambled to sit up, looking to Steven, who lay flat on his stomach beside her. Nathaniel's hand reached out to grab the boy's arm and flip him over. Steven flopped onto his back, the blood from his shoulder saturating his shirt and staining the sand beneath him.

Come on, buddy, Nathaniel groaned. *Come on, you can do this.*

Steven gave him a resigned smile. *I would've liked seeing Oklahoma.*

I still want to see Kansas.

Blood gurgled in Steven's throat. Nathaniel pressed his hand against his friend's wound, trying pointlessly to stop the bleeding. Bombs exploded around them. The last men in their troop fell, one by one, onto the beach. The crimson halo of his vision blackened.

A sizzling sound caught inside Abby's mind – the lightning-fast whirr of a bullet – an odd noise she was now unnervingly familiar with. She looked up to the bunkers in the distance, to the men who fired continuous rounds from automatic weapons. She sat back on her heels and exhaled.

Her vision went dark.

She was back in her room now. She'd actually never left, although it felt like she had. It felt like she'd lived through those moments, like she'd seen hell – all red and black, all screams and terror - and returned to the comfort of her home. But Nathaniel hadn't.

Abby opened her eyes. Her spirit still stood in the center of her room. His eyes still glowed, lit with perfect clarity and yet dark with anguish.

"Are you okay?" he asked, his body turning solid as he spoke.

She watched as the glow transformed to an even, stable blue. "Yes," she answered, her voice tiny and thin in the dimly lit room. "Are you?"

"I am. I just can't show you the final part of the memory. I don't think it'll be good for either of us."

Abby took a step toward him. "That was when you were shot, wasn't it?"

"Yes."

"And did you...did you die right away?"

"No. The bullet hit my stomach. It took a while, maybe twenty or thirty minutes. I'm not sure. It could have been less than that. Time was warped."

Abby shut her eyes again, blocking that image so she wouldn't collapse where she stood. She didn't know how Nathaniel survived all this pain, let alone how he still managed to be so selfless. "That was amazing, you know – how you tried to save that other soldier."

"It didn't work."

She looked back to him. "Yeah, but you tried. Were you always a hero?"

His fingers twitched by his sides. "I'm not a hero. Believe me, I'm not. I just did what I thought was right at the time."

"And Steven died, too?"

"Yes. We died together, lying on that sand. We were pitiful."

Abby hugged her belly, almost able to feel the gunshot. "Your memory was so vivid. I felt like I could touch, smell, and taste. I felt like I was there."

Nathaniel winced. "I knew it was going to be that way. I'm sorry."

"Please don't be. It just felt very fresh, like it happened only yesterday."

"Well, it is the last memory of my life – my real life. I will never forget."

She moved closer to him, wanting to erase the distance between them. Her footsteps carried her forward until she finally felt the warmth of his body flush over her skin. She needed that reassurance, reminding her that Nathaniel was whole and solid, here and now.

Abby looked up to his eyes, fixing onto them in the dim light. Her gaze held his for aching seconds before drifting down to his stomach, imagining how his blood had soaked through his uniform as he lay dying on the sand. The vile image sent razor-sharp shivers down her spine.

"Are you sure you're okay?" he asked when she shuddered.

"I'm sure. But will you...will you indulge me in one more thing?"

"What is it?"

"Will you take your shirt off and let me look at you?"

Nathaniel's brow rose. "Take my shirt off?"

"Yes, please. I need to see where you were shot. I mean, I'm grateful you didn't show me the exact moment you were hit, but the pictures in my head are still so gruesome. I need to verify with my own eyes that you've healed."

He stared at her, unmoving. Abby wasn't sure if he would honor her request. She probably sounded crazy, but she had to know that he was safe.

Nathaniel reached down to catch the hem of his shirt in his hands. He pulled the material up and over his head, balling it in his fist to hold it by his side. He stood still before her.

Abby's lips parted as she studied his perfectly unmarred chest. She inched forward. "Where...where did the bullet go?"

"Here." He pointed to his left side, just under his ribcage.

She reached out to him. Her fingertips traced across the non-existent wound. His skin was on fire.

With her cautious touch, Nathaniel sucked in a breath. Abby glanced up to his face. "And the other times you've been hurt? Where were they?"

He clamped his teeth together, causing the muscle in his jaw to twitch. "I've been stabbed multiple times around my shoulders and chest. The pavement tore all the skin off my arm when I was thrown out of the moving car. My ribs have been broken more than once."

Abby's heart sank to her feet. She refocused on the brick wall of his body, her fingers exploring each place of insult, drawing across his smooth skin and over the tight ridges of muscle. His arms, shoulders, and chest were all completely healed – all strong and hard beneath her hand.

"Do they still hurt?" she questioned.

"No. Not anymore."

"Which one was the worst?"

"Normandy. Definitely Normandy."

"Because that's when you died?"

Nathaniel shrugged, the motion shifting his heated flesh beneath her palm. "I suppose. Maybe the others were easier because I knew I could transform back into a spirit and heal. Or maybe it was the bullet. I'm not looking forward to getting shot again."

Abby's eyes darted back to his. "Do you think you will be?"

"I've always known it's a possibility, in my line of work. Honestly, I haven't really minded any of the other incidents. I mean, they hurt like hell at the time, don't get me wrong. But they were just water under the bridge. That gunshot wound was horrifying. I don't ever want to go through that again."

"Then don't!" Abby demanded, the strength of her voice startling them both. "Don't ever stand in front of a gun again. I think that's pretty simple."

Nathaniel gave her a pained smile. "It won't be a choice, you know. I'll have to do whatever is necessary, if the situation arises." His fingers eased to her face, gently stroking her cheek, before he stepped away. He pulled his shirt back on as he moved to stand in front of the window, facing the clear night sky.

Abby followed on his heels, needing him close to her now more than ever. She stopped just shy of his body, wishing his shirt was still off so she could examine his back, too. Instead, she slumped forward, pressing her chest against the length of his spine, reassuring herself of his solidity. She snaked her arms around his waist and rested her head against his shoulder.

"Thank you," she whispered, wishing she could take his hurt away with a few simple words. "Thank you for sharing your memory with me."

"You're welcome. Although, I don't know that it did you any good."

"It did. I promise. Now, I can understand something of what my dad went through. I can feel some of his pain. It's a start."

Nathaniel's hand eased onto hers, pressing her palm against his stomach. He stood quietly in place, allowing her to absorb his strength. He obviously knew exactly what she needed right now. Unfortunately, Abby knew what he needed, too – he needed to leave her, so he could check on everyone else.

She pressed her forehead into his spine, scrunching her eyes shut tight. Dear God, she didn't want to let him go. Not tonight.

"Nathaniel, can I ask you to do something else for me?"

He pulled away from her embrace, only to turn and face her. The light from the window shadowed his features, but she could still see his haunted eyes. "Ask me anything."

"Will you stay with me tonight? I just really want to hold you."

His face fell. "Abby, I don't... I don't know if that's a good idea."

She figured that would be his answer, but she still couldn't fight the sting of rejection that landed in the pit of her stomach. "It's okay. I understand. I mean, it's not like you expected to be here with me. I know you need to check on other people." She shifted from one leg to the other, her feelings too raw to bear. "Is Holly doing okay? I think about her a lot. And how are the other people you're watching over? Do you think you've missed anything important tonight? I hope not. I hope everyone is safe."

Nathaniel took a step closer. He cupped her cheek in one hand, tilting her face up to his. "You want me to stay the night with you?"

Abby's chest swelled with hope. "Just so I can be close to you. That's all."

"Okay, then. I'll stay."

Her eyes widened. "Really? What changed your mind?"

"The fact that you're worried about other people after the night you've had. You shouldn't care in the least how the others are, but you do." Nathaniel dipped his head, giving her a soft kiss before pulling back. "You amaze me."

Abby smiled so hard that it hurt. "I'm so happy you're staying. And I promise I'll be good. I will not tempt you, not in the slightest. Also, you can leave whenever you need to leave. I mean, if you can wait until I'm asleep, that will be great. But if you need to go sooner, I completely understand. I just want to hold you for as long as I can."

"And how is that not going to tempt me?"

"I'm really going to try to not be tempting at all."

"You've already failed. But don't worry. I'll be good, too. We'll manage."

"Okay, then. I guess...I guess we should get in bed together."

Nathaniel chuckled. "Wow. You really stink at this not-tempting thing."

Abby grinned. "You know what? Just give me a few minutes to get ready."

"Take your time, sweetheart. I'll be here."

She scurried over to her dresser and reached into the bottom drawer, pulling out an old pair of pajamas. "See you soon," she promised, exiting her room to pad quietly down the hall and into the bathroom. She brushed her hair and teeth and changed her clothes. Then she snuck back, hearing her father's snores resonating from the living room couch.

She tiptoed into her bedroom and locked the door behind her. When she turned around, Nathaniel already lay on one side of her double mattress with the covers pulled to his waist. He was fully clothed, which Abby figured was probably best.

"What do you think?" she asked while approaching the edge of the bed.

"About what?"

"About my pajamas? They are the oldest, frumpiest set I own. Winnie the Pooh, no less. Completely non-form-fitting. No temptation at all."

Nathaniel rose up on one elbow to stare at her in the soft light. "Good Lord. That is the sexiest pot-bellied, honey-loving bear I've ever seen."

Abby choked with laughter. "Well, if you find this sexy, there's nothing else I can do to prevent it." She crawled into bed beside him, easing under the covers to snuggle against his chest.

"You're right," Nathaniel agreed, circling his arm around her waist to draw her closer still. "There's nothing else you can do. It's a good thing I've got willpower in spades."

"Yeah. Tell me about it."

His laughter rang clear and perfect beside her ear. Abby rested her head over his heart, her weary body honing in on his even breathing. As tired as she was, her mind still managed to toss and turn.

"So, Nathaniel...is this a typical night for you?"

He brushed her hair away from her face. "Holding onto my favorite person while lying in bed? This isn't typical at all, sadly."

She smiled against his chest. "No, I mean the emotional stuff. I've felt everything I'm capable of today, and it has completely exhausted me. Do you go through this every day?"

"Not every day. It depends on who I'm focusing on and what they're bringing to the table. But some days it gets bad. It can be difficult to control."

"I don't know how you do it," she said as his memories flashed through her muddled mind. She tensed, her fingers fisting against his chest.

"What's wrong?" he asked, smoothing his hand across hers until it relaxed.

Abby tried to focus on breathing along with him. "Nothing's wrong. I just remembered some of the things you showed me tonight."

"Yeah? Do you have any questions?"

"God, so many. Although, only one at the moment."

"What is it?"

"Why did you have coins with you that day?" she asked, latching on to Nathaniel's one moment of calm during his horrifying ordeal.

"Oh, that. I used to collect them, back in high school. I liked seeing how many different ones I could get."

"But why did you pull them out when you were about to go to shore?"

"Because I always found it calming to flip them over with my fingers. I figured I needed to feel calmer then, for all the good it did me."

"I see. Do you still collect coins?"

"No, not anymore."

"Then what do you do now, when you need to feel calm?"

His hand drifted up her arm. "Well, for these past few weeks, I just have to think about you."

"Mmm, I get that," she agreed, focused entirely on the warmth of his skin shifting over hers. "Most of the time, I'm calm when I think about you. But sometimes when you're in my head, I'm the complete opposite of calm."

"Damn, Abby. I thought you said you weren't going to tempt me."

"Was that tempting?"

"Yes. Very."

"Well, maybe you're just overly temptable."

"I don't think *temptable* is a word, but you're probably right."

"I mean, if Winnie the Pooh looks sexy to you…"

"Yeah, yeah, I get it. I'm the weakest link, here."

"No, you're not. You're Mr. Frickin' Willpower."

Nathaniel's laughter filled her soul as she inhaled the sweet scent radiating from his skin. He fell quiet then, so the only sound she heard was the steady thump of his heart. Abby allowed her eyes to close and her body to sink down, entranced by the feel of his fingers now playing over her back. Another memory eased into her mind, so close to a dream.

"What about the locket?" she whispered. "The gold heart locket you carried with you all that way?"

"Did you like it?"

"Oh, yes. It was so pretty. The swirly pattern was just perfect."

"I'm glad you think so. My mother gave it to me when I left to train for the war. She told me to remember the women who loved me, and to bring the locket back home one day. She wanted me to replace those pictures with photos of me and my sweetheart. She meant it as a gift to her future daughter-in-law."

Abby hummed in contentment as she thought of how many times he'd called her sweetheart. But he'd never made it back to his mother and sister. At least, not in any real way. "Sweetheart," she murmured, pressing her hand against his chest.

Nathaniel leaned in to kiss her forehead. "Sweetheart."

Abby wanted to say more, to talk to him all night, but she didn't have any strength left. Her mind drifted off, filled with images of little gold hearts holding pictures of Nathaniel. They floated around her, keeping her safe. She didn't dream of anything else.

⸻

THE SUN CREPT in through her bedroom window, warming the side of her face. Abby didn't want to open her eyes, since she dreaded facing the morning without her angel. But as she rolled over, she realized something amazing – she could still feel Nathaniel's warm, solid body beside her.

What is happening right now? Am I dreaming?

Unsealing one eye, she risked a peek. There he lay, sound asleep next to her. She rose slowly up on one elbow, careful not to disturb. Her gaze drifted over his face, absorbing how boyishly handsome he looked while fully at peace.

Abby savored the sight of her sleeping spirit, until she noticed the oddest thing. Nathaniel had the shadow of a beard. She resisted the urge to touch it, even though it fascinated her. She'd never seen his physical appearance change before, other than his clothes. But today, he looked a little different. It was only one night, yet his body had aged – all because of her.

That thought lit a fire in her chest, enticing her to press her soft cheek against his stubbly one. She touched her lips to his jawline, running tender little kisses across his scratchy skin. When Abby eventually sank her mouth onto his, she wasn't entirely surprised that Nathaniel responded to her. But she was surprised when he flipped her over onto her back and weighed her body down beneath his own. He continued what she'd started, kissing her for lengthy, leisurely minutes, while she sank farther into the mattress.

"Mmm," he hummed over her lips, "you can wake me like that any day."

"Stay every night and I will," she said, coiling her arms around his neck.

He nudged the tip of her nose with his. "Didn't you promise me last night that you weren't going to tempt me?"

"Yeah, but that was last night. Today is a whole other story."

Nathaniel chuckled, which shifted his chest deliciously over hers. "Then maybe I shouldn't have stayed. I've awakened my wicked temptress."

Abby gazed up into his eyes. "Why did you stay? I thought you'd have to leave before morning, to check on everyone else."

"I stayed because you asked. You are my most important person," he assured, propping on his forearms to run his fingers through her mussed hair.

She chewed on her lip. "Do I look like Medusa?"

"You look beautiful, as always."

"You're only saying that because I'm your most important person."

Nathaniel grinned. "Yes, you absolutely are. And that has me thinking."

"About what?"

"About how you said my memory of Normandy was good for you. You said it helped you understand your dad, and I can't tell you how much it means to feel like I gave you something you wanted. And I know you also want me to meet him, so I...I want to."

Abby grabbed his face in both hands. "Oh my God, Nathaniel. Really?"

"Really. I was wrong to think that not meeting your father would be the best thing for you if something happens to separate us. He's your family and you need him like he needs you. He should know about us. That way, he can support you if anything happens to..."

"You want to meet my dad? Seriously? You'd do that for me?"

"I would do anything for you, Abby."

"Holy crap. How about tonight?"

"If you like."

"Yes. That's perfect. Six o'clock. Be here at six."

"Okay. Six o'clock." Nathaniel nodded, giving her a crooked grin before his eyes shifted down. He stared at her lips as if he wanted nothing more than to kiss them again. A groan escaped his throat before he pushed himself away to sit up at the far edge of the bed.

Abby couldn't muster the energy to be upset over his withdrawal, even though she missed the weight of his body on hers. She scrambled up to sit beside him. "Thank you so much for doing this, Nathaniel."

"I'm happy to do it. Are you going to be okay until I come back?"

"Yeah, sure. Dad and I need to talk, to work out some issues, but I can handle that now. Sharing your memories truly helped me."

"Good. Then I guess I'll see you tonight."

"Tonight," she agreed, shutting her eyes so she wouldn't have to watch him disappear. She held entirely still, waiting for that moment to pass. But then, she felt Nathaniel come closer.

The warmth of his body drifted over her skin as he pressed his mouth to hers for a brief, blissful instant. "Sweetheart," he murmured against her lips.

Abby kept her eyes closed, imagining she could still feel him, even when she knew he'd gone.

CHAPTER

ELEVEN

Abby stayed in her room for a long time that morning. She spent most of the time thinking about how perfect it felt to have Nathaniel beside her through the night. She spent the rest of the time thinking about her mother and father.

Sitting quietly at her bedroom vanity, she stared at the photo of her mother tucked into the mirror frame. Her father had been so sad since her mother's death. He ate less, slept more, and barely ever laughed. Abby knew those were signs of grieving, so she'd tried to reassure herself that it was all normal. But now, with the bullets back in the house, she wondered if he'd been thinking about taking his own life. And if he had, then perhaps Nathaniel was actually here to save her from losing another parent.

"I wish you were still here with us," Abby whispered to the familiar, comforting picture of her mom. "And I wish you could be with us tonight, when Nathaniel comes over for dinner."

That last thought managed to put a smile on her face. She took one last fortifying look at the photo before she rose from her chair to step toward the door. *At least you'll have the two men in your life together tonight,* she assured herself while walking out of her bedroom and into the hallway.

Abby reached the kitchen in no time at all. Her father stood by the sink, staring out of the window at the sparse trees in the backyard. She listened to him cough as she slipped into a seat at their kitchen table.

"You okay this morning, Dad?"

Mark turned to her. "No. Not really."

"Is your cold worse?"

"It's getting a little better, actually," he answered while resting back against the counter. "I'm not okay because I did something I shouldn't have."

Abby's entire body tensed. "What did you do?"

"I betrayed your trust by bringing bullets into the house."

Her shoulders relaxed. She looked to his eyes. They were tired but steady.

"I wasn't thinking when I did that," Mark continued, looking down at his hands. "I wasn't thinking about how I made you that promise, just like I made it to your mother. You were younger then, and I guess I still think of you as my little girl. But you're not, are you? You're practically an adult now. Less than a year, and it'll be official. Honestly, you take on more responsibility than a lot of adults I know. I tell myself that it's good for you, that it makes you strong and capable. But I know you haven't had a great childhood."

"That's not true," Abby insisted. "You and Mom have always loved me. You've always worked hard to give me a good life. I don't mind having responsibilities. You're right – it makes me stronger."

"But you're strong enough, honey. You're strong enough."

She leaned her arms on the tabletop. "Dad, about last night..."

"Let me finish, please," he interrupted, his voice firm but gentle. "I broke a promise I made to you. That was wrong of me. I know you're down to one parent, and making you doubt me was stupid. But I want you to know that I really am trying, here. I'm trying to be the best father I can be."

"I know you are. You're doing a great job."

Mark shook his head. "No more bullets, I promise. And as for the guns... well, they're my hobby, but I also know how much they bother you. So, I'll get rid of them all. If that will make you more comfortable."

Abby studied him as he spoke. She appreciated his offer to give up his guns, but she had a different understanding of them now. She'd stood on a landing craft moving toward the shore of Omaha beach. She'd been on a battlefield, seeing the men around her fight for their lives. She'd felt their pain and tasted their fear. She'd wanted a gun in her hand in that moment. She'd wanted to grab Nathaniel's rifle and cling to with her entire body.

"It's okay," Abby assured her father. "I understand about the guns. I really do. But just never any bullets, please."

"Never again. I promise. That's your promise, honey. Just yours."

"Thank you," she said, clasping her hands together on the tabletop. "I can't tell you how much that means to me."

"You're welcome," he replied as he glanced to her twitching fingers. "Now, why don't you tell me what else is on your mind?"

"Oh, well, I, um..."

Mark cleared his throat. "Please just say it, Abby."

She laughed, aware that her father could read her just as well as she could read him. "Okay. I was wondering if I could have a friend over for dinner."

"Sure. Which friend? Julie?"

"No, I didn't actually mean a friend. Well, he is my friend. But he's also my...he's my boyfriend."

Mark observed her before mumbling a word that sounded like *finally*.

"What was that?" Abby questioned.

"Oh, nothing. So, a boyfriend. What's his name?"

"Nathaniel."

"Does Nathaniel go to your school?"

"Um, yeah," she hedged. That wasn't a lie. He did go to her school. Quite frequently, even. "He's new here, from Oklahoma originally. He's really nice – a good person."

"I can't imagine you picking anyone who isn't. When is he coming over?"

"Six o'clock."

"You already invited him?"

"Yeah, I hope that's okay. I figured you'd say yes."

"Of course. I'm looking forward to it."

Abby sighed in utter relief. An instant later, she knotted her fingers together. Now that tonight's meeting of men was official, she couldn't tamp down the fresh swarm of butterflies beating against the walls of her stomach. And she definitely couldn't silence the voice in her head that told her maybe, just maybe, this dinner might not be such a good idea after all.

ABBY COOKED for most of the day, marinating chicken, dicing vegetables, and creating apple pie masterpieces. At least, she hoped they were masterpieces. She wanted everything tonight to be seamless and perfect.

Thirty minutes before Nathaniel's arrival, she changed into a nicer outfit. But not too nice, since she didn't want to look like she was trying too hard. She dragged a brush through her hair while wondering how insane she was for introducing her spirit-boyfriend to her questionably-stable father.

Good God, is it too late to back out now? she asked her reflection. *No, Abby. You don't need to back out. This is going to be a good night. It has to be.*

She tamped down her prickly nerves, set her brush on the vanity, and walked out into the hall. She wandered over to Mark's bedroom door and peeked around the corner. He stood in front of his mirror, staring at his shirt. "You doing okay, Dad?"

"Yeah." He gestured to his clothes. "Am I presentable?"

"Of course. You don't have to make a fuss."

"I think I do. I mean, you've never brought a boy home before, so I figure he means something to you. Besides, your mom would have made a fuss."

"Well, just don't show Nathaniel any pictures of me in middle school, and we'll all get along fine."

Mark chuckled. "Promise."

Abby nodded before moving back to the kitchen. She busied herself with the dishes, setting three places at the dining room table. Shuffling back and forth from the kitchen, she managed to set out the glasses, silverware, and napkins before she heard the doorbell ring.

"Huh. That's funny," she thought aloud. *Nathaniel never rings the bell.*

"What's funny?" Mark asked from the living room.

"Um, nothing. He's here."

Abby forced a smile, reminding herself to watch her words. Her father didn't need to know that Nathaniel spent nearly every night here. Or that he was still here with her when she woke up this morning.

"What kind of a car does he drive?" Mark asked as he stepped to the door.

"Uh..." she grasped for an answer. *He just materializes* was definitely the wrong one, so she clamped her mouth shut.

Her father peered out of the window. "Oh, it's a Jeep. Nice."

Abby's eyes widened. "A what?"

"He drives a blue, two-door Jeep. Looks to be a few years old," Mark-the-mechanic analyzed. "Have you never seen his car before?"

"I...I usually drive?"

"Okay, well, I guess I'll let him in."

Abby sprinted out of the kitchen and over to the living room window. She stared outside, gawking at the blue Jeep sitting in her driveway. *What the hell? When did Nathaniel get a car? Does he even have a license?*

Her nerves came entirely unraveled then. They'd been tightly wound, they'd been partly frayed, and now they were utterly unglued. She would never be able to lie well enough to survive this night. She didn't know what she'd been thinking.

"You must be Nathaniel," Mark announced, his deep voice pulling her attentions from the window. Abby watched in awe as her father let her spirit walk in through the front door.

"Good evening, sir. It's a pleasure to meet you," Nathaniel offered as they shook hands.

She stared at the two men in horror. *Holy crap! This isn't five minutes at the mall with Julie! This is an entire night at home with my father!*

Mark motioned to the living room. "Come on in."

"Thank you."

Nathaniel turned to step inside. His eyes fastened onto her instantly – sparkling bright and clear and solid – and Abby felt his soothing energy overtake her body. She could almost read his mind: *Relax, sweetheart. Everything will be okay.*

She smiled up at him when he came to a stop in front of her. "Hi."

Nathaniel smiled back. "Hello."

Abby wasn't sure how the word *hello* could be the most amazing word ever, but it was. "Um, you guys can go sit in the dining room, if you want. Dinner is almost ready."

"Can I help you with anything?"

"No, thanks. I'm good."

"This way," Mark instructed, leading Nathaniel to the dining room. He waited until their guest was seated before settling in at the head of the table.

Abby hurried back to the kitchen. She began pulling pots off the stove while simultaneously craning her ear toward the adjacent room. Her father spoke first.

"That's a nice Jeep you've got, Nathaniel."

"Thank you, sir. I find it very dependable."

"Yeah, they are. Good resale, too. Do you know the history of the name?"

"No, sir. I don't."

"You know, it's okay if you call me Mark."

"Thank you, sir. Mark."

"Not Sir Mark. Just Mark."

Abby giggled while walking into the dining room with several serving dishes. As she placed the food on the table, she caught Nathaniel's eye. A hint of nervousness dampened his otherwise brilliant blue. "Go ahead and dig in," she encouraged, knowing how food always made him happy.

"The Jeep was originally a military vehicle," Mark explained as he piled chicken and vegetables onto his plate. "It was a general-purpose vehicle, which got shortened to GP, which became Jeep. They're great for all-terrain driving. I've driven them a few times. Did Abby tell you I was in the military?"

Nathaniel nodded while filling his own plate. "Yes, she did."

Abby placed the rest of the food on the table before sitting down on the chair between her men. "I told him we moved here after you retired, Dad."

"And now you're a mechanic?" Nathaniel asked.

"Mm-hmm," Mark said between bites. "I like working on cars. Do you?"

"Unfortunately, I'm not very good at it."

"Well, if you ever need any help, just let me know. I like Jeeps."

Abby glanced between the two of them. They were both a little anxious, yet doing well. Her lips curved into a smile as she ate.

"So, Nathaniel, tell me about yourself. You're from Oklahoma, right?"

"Yes, si...Mark. I grew up there. My family had a farm."

"A farm? Really? My grandparents had a farm in Minnesota. I used to go there when I was a kid. That's hard work, farming."

"It can be. But I don't mind hard work."

"Good. That's good. Do your parents still have the farm?"

Abby swallowed her mouthful of chicken and waited for the answer.

"Um, no. My parents passed away last year. Car accident."

"Oh." A flash of pain crossed Mark's face. "I'm sorry, Nathaniel."

"Thank you. I appreciate it."

Mark glanced to Abby before turning back to their guest. "Do you have other family?"

"I have a sister. She's...much older. She still lives in Oklahoma."

"Then how did you end up here in Virginia?"

Nathaniel gripped onto his fork. "Well, after my parents passed, I needed a change of scenery. I decided to plan for college. I'd really like to go to UVA, if I make it in, so I thought I'd come here to establish residency ahead of time."

"That's good thinking. Who are you living with? Distant relatives?"

"No, actually. I have my own apartment."

Abby's head shot up. *An apartment? Did you really get your own apartment?* She stared the question into Nathaniel's eyes, wishing he could hear her thoughts when he was solid.

Mark's brow arched. "You live by yourself?"

Nathaniel hesitated to answer. "Yes, I...I do."

Abby turned to her father. He was in deep thought now. Well, not all that deep. When he met her eyes, she could pretty much tell which questions were on his mind. She wanted to jump up and shout that she was not having sex with Nathaniel, no matter how many opportunities they'd had. But instead of creating that spectacle, she decided to change the subject to something much more palatable. "Nathaniel likes movies, Dad. A lot."

"Really?" Mark mumbled. After another deadly silent moment, he looked back to their guest. "Abby and I like to watch movies, too. What's your favorite genre?"

"I pretty much just watch science fiction," Nathaniel replied.

"Oh, you're a sci-fi buff. See, Abby – I told you it wasn't just us."

"Yeah, Dad. We are not alone."

Nathaniel chuckled, which soothed her beyond measure.

"That's good," Mark said. "It's good that you both like the same things."

"Well, don't get too comfortable, Dad. He's a Kirk man."

"No. Say it isn't so."

Abby nodded. "Oh, yes."

Mark pinned Nathaniel's eyes. "Kirk over Picard? Why?"

"I guess because Kirk is so much more emotional. I'd like to think it's brave for a man to show his feelings like that."

"Yeah, yeah, emotions. But Picard is such a leader, don't you think?"

"Don't badger him, Dad. He's made up his mind."

Mark smiled. "Well, I guess it's best. You're a Kirk person, just like Abby."

She grinned with her father's acceptance. She'd always known that sci-fi movie nights with Nathaniel were a good idea, although she hadn't dared to dream that this night would ever be possible. Both Dad and Nathaniel looked more relaxed now, and they all ate together in peace while discussing their favorite scenes from *Star Trek*.

By the time they finished the main course, Abby was practically beaming with joy. She got up from the table to clear the dishes and bring in desert, setting slices of apple pie in front of each of her men before sitting down between them. Grabbing her fork, she sighed in contentment as she took her own cinnamon-y bite.

"Abby just started this new pie-making hobby last month," Mark noted while he ate. "Do you like apple pie, Nathaniel?"

She instantly stiffened in her seat. *Oh, no! Don't answer! It's a trap!*

"Yes, absolutely," Nathaniel gushed. "It's my favorite dessert ever."

Mark stared him in the eye. "Mm-hmm," he hummed, slow and knowing.

Abby choked a little on her pastry. She gulped down her water, understanding her father's inflection all too well. Her eyes rose when Nathaniel stood from the table.

"If you'll excuse me, I need to use the restroom," he said.

She watched, utterly confused, while her spirit left the room.

"I guess he already knows where the bathroom is," Mark surmised.

Anxious laughter bubbled up from her chest. "Yeah, well...yeah."

Mark looked back to his dessert, chewing on his pie and his thoughts.

Abby? Are you okay? Nathaniel's voice eased into her mind.

She glanced up, but she couldn't see him anywhere. *Yeah, I'm okay. Did you really have to use the bathroom?*

No, I just needed to check on your dad's emotions. I shouldn't have said that about the pie. He obviously knows I've been coming here for weeks and weeks.

Well, he probably figured that much, anyway.

But now he's certain I've had countless hours alone with you. I never thought I'd be nervous meeting my girlfriend's father, but here I am. I'm a big chicken.

Abby stared down at her pie to keep from giggling. *No, you're not a chicken. You just needed some reassurance. How are Dad's emotions?*

Mostly calm, actually. More than I would have imagined.

See? You have nothing to worry about. However, I would like to say that I am not calm at all!

No? Why not?

Because I have so many questions! About the Jeep! And the apartment!

Oh, right. It was a busy day.

A busy day? That's all you have to say about it?

Abby waited impatiently for explanations, until Nathaniel walked back into the dining room and took his seat beside her. Her shoulders drooped when she realized she would have to wait even longer for answers. The room fell uncomfortably silent as they all resumed eating.

Desperate for a change of mood, Abby woofed down the rest of her pie Nathaniel-style and set her fork on the plate. "So," she boomed, startling both men, "should we go sit in the living room? I can make coffee."

"That sounds nice," Mark said.

"Yes," Nathaniel agreed. "Thank you for dinner, Abby. You're incredible."

She didn't miss the look Mark shot him as they left the table.

Abby made the coffee quickly, poured two cups, and joined the men in the living room. They hadn't spoken to each other at all since they'd left the table. "You know, Nathaniel's very good in school," Abby blurted out as she handed a cup to her father.

Mark took a sip while he sat. "He is?"

Abby handed Nathaniel his cup. She started to take her customary seat beside him on the couch, but thought better of it. "Yeah. He helps me out in history a lot," she explained as she planted herself in the chair across from him.

"Hmm," Mark considered. "I have to admit, you don't exactly strike me as a high school student, Nathaniel. How old are you?"

"Eighteen, sir. Mark."

"There's just a year's difference between us," Abby chimed in.

Mark shrugged. "Just an old soul, I suppose."

"An old soul?" Nathaniel questioned.

"Yeah. Abby's mom used to say that there were old souls in this world – people who've been around for longer than one lifetime. As opposed to the new ones, who are obviously here for their first run. But you strike me as an old soul, just like my Abby." Mark turned to look at her with pride in his eyes.

Nathaniel nodded. "She definitely knows who she is."

Abby chose not to argue with either assessment, not when the two of them were actually agreeing on something.

"That being said..." Mark's face fell, his tone turning solemn. "I think it's my duty to let you in on some secrets."

"Secrets?" she asked. "What secrets?"

"Yes, what secrets?" Nathaniel seconded.

Mark turned to him and smiled. "She's a biter."

Abby's stomach sank to her feet. "No, Dad. Not that. Please."

"But it's true. She bit a dog once."

"Oh, my God," she grumbled. "Do you have to tell this story? Really?"

"Hey, I'm the father here. It's my right to tell embarrassing stories, isn't it? Especially since I've been banned from showing middle school photos?"

Abby caught Nathaniel's smile from the corner of her eye.

"I would like to know more about this dog-biting thing," he prompted.

"Please don't encourage him," she pleaded.

Mark turned back to Nathaniel. "Well, when she was four years old, we were over visiting a friend who had this little Shih Tzu. Abby loved animals, so she ran off to play with the dog and we didn't think anything of it. Abby was a small thing, with white-blond hair and cute, rosy cheeks. You would have thought she wouldn't hurt a fly. But then, we heard the dog yelp from the next room. A second later, we heard Abby crying her eyes out."

She slumped forward in her chair, holding her head in her hands.

"Her mom and I ran into the next room," Mark continued. "And there was our little girl, sitting on the floor, holding a plastic ball in her hand, with her mouth full of dog hair. Abby cried and cried, so we kept looking her over, thinking she'd been hurt. But when she finally calmed down, she told us the dog wanted to take the ball away from her – and she knew it was going to bite her – so she bit it first."

Mark chuckled with the familiar tale. Nathaniel laughed hysterically. Abby groaned, knowing she was too big to fit under the couch, although that was the only place she could imagine being right at this moment. "Okay, okay, Dad. Are you done now?"

"Oh, not at all," Mark said, the amusement in his voice appealing even in her state of distress. "I just want Nathaniel to know how strong you are."

"Yeah. She really is," Nathaniel agreed, holding her gaze from across the room. She focused in on him – on how he looked at her like she was the most beautiful, most intelligent, most courageous person he'd ever seen – even after that awful story.

"So, what other tales should I tell?"

Mark's voice pulled her mind from her blissful Nathaniel-world back to the living room. She thought to protest further humiliation, but decided against it. Both of her men were happy, and that made her happy, too.

Abby forced herself to sit and listen – even though she couldn't help fidgeting from time to time – as her father regaled Nathaniel with story after story of her tempestuous youth. She thought they all made her sound like an untamed beast of a child, especially when told in succession. She preferred to think that she was just a headstrong kid, at least until her life utterly transformed the day she found out about her father's illness. But that younger-Abby was definitely still inside her. There was no way she could date a ghost, let alone invite him to dinner with her father, if she didn't have some iota of willfulness left.

"Well, it's getting late. I'm heading to bed," Mark eventually announced.

"Yes, I should probably go home," Nathaniel offered as he rose from the couch. "I really appreciate you having me over, Mark."

"You're welcome, Nathaniel."

Abby looked to her father. "I'm just going to walk him out, Dad."

"Okay," he agreed before wandering off to the kitchen.

She stood to join Nathaniel at the front door. They stepped out onto the porch together and Abby pulled the door closed behind them. She filled her lungs with the chilled night air and shivered.

He stepped up to her, running his hands over her arms to warm her skin. "How are you doing, sweetheart?"

"I'm good. How about you?"

"So incredibly good. That was the first real family dinner I've had in...in forever." He wound their fingers together as his voice hitched. "Thank you, Abby. For everything."

She absorbed the emotion in Nathaniel's gentle gaze. "You're welcome, although I should be the one thanking you."

"Really? Why?"

"Well, for starters, you met my father. What do you think of him?"

"I like him. He's intuitive and intelligent, like you. And he's a good dad."

"I like to think so. And I love that you had dinner with us. But that's not even the most impressive thing you did for me today."

"It isn't?"

"No, it isn't. You also went out and bought a car."

Nathaniel glanced at the Jeep in the driveway. "What do you think of it? I wanted something that said stable and sound, not capable of recklessness, able to weather difficulties, not too old, but not too new…"

Abby laughed. "Wow. That's a lot of talking for a car."

"Yeah. Maybe so."

"And what about the apartment? Did you actually go get one?"

"Well, I just wanted to have the ability to lie as little as possible tonight. I mean, I had to manipulate the truth about my folks, of course. I also knew I couldn't show up here without transportation. And I definitely couldn't tell your father that I didn't require a roof over my head. So, I just set out to make things as right as I could. Like I said, it was a busy day."

Abby shook her head as she stared up at him. "I can't believe you did all of that for me. But there are still so many things I don't understand."

"Like what?"

"Like *how*? How did you get a car? Do you have a driver's license? How did you get an apartment? And where does the money come from? I mean, do you have some sort of spiritual credit card?"

Nathaniel grinned. "Those are all good questions. Well, except maybe that last one. But they are better answered another time, I think. Right now, I really need to check on some people."

"Oh, man, I'm sorry. I'm being selfish with you again, aren't I? I know you have work to do. I just wish sometimes that I could have you all to myself."

"Mmm. That actually sounds amazing."

"It really does," she agreed, clinging tight to his hands. "So, who are you protecting tonight? Is it Holly?"

"For one. She and Chuck are out on a date right now, and I'm nervous for her. But I'm also nervous for Marcus."

Abby pictured her uber-intelligent, next-door-locker neighbor. "Marcus? Is he not doing well?"

"School's hitting him pretty hard this year. He's thinking about ivy league colleges and trying to be the perfect student. His father's being really hard on him about it. I'm worried he's not coping well."

"Oh," she said, struggling to wrap her head around the world outside of her own. "You should go, then. But maybe I can see you tomorrow? It's Sunday, so I'm going to the mall with Julie, but I'll be home at night."

Nathaniel stepped toward her. "You know what? I'll try to make it to the mall with you and Julie. Chuck and Holly talked about going, so I should be able to accomplish two things at once. God, I really am sorry that I have to divide my time like this. But if you ever need me, I'll be by your side immediately. You know that, right?"

"I do. I'm just really looking forward to seeing you tomorrow."

"I am, too. But can you do me a favor until then?"

"What's that?"

He smiled slyly. "Can you try not to bite anything while I'm gone?"

Abby's cheeks heated. "Oh, hell. I can't believe my dad told you that stupid dog story."

Nathaniel's eyes sparkled in the porchlight. "I'm glad he did. Although, I'm not sure what could be so bad about a tiny little Shih Tzu."

"Hey, you weren't there. That thing looked vicious."

He kept smiling while tugging her closer. "Then I'm glad you defended yourself," he said, bending down to ease his lips onto hers. When the soft, warm kiss ended, he reluctantly pulled away. "Damn, I miss you already."

Abby could only respond by whimpering. After Nathaniel stepped back, she had to concentrate on maintaining her balance. She watched in a blissful stupor while he lumbered down her porch steps, climbed into his Jeep, started the engine, and pulled onto the street. She stood in awe as she watched him drive away, too giddy to consider how odd it looked.

Once her angel disappeared from sight, she turned back to the house and entered the living room. Mark stood in the kitchen doorway, watching her. Abby walked toward him with a nervous grin. "So, Dad? What do you think?"

"I can see why you like him," he answered, resting against the doorframe. "Nathaniel has a kindness to him. And you must feel a connection, since he knows what it's like to lose a parent."

"Yeah. There is that."

"Yeah, there is. But just because he doesn't have a family, doesn't mean you have to be that for him. I don't want you to feel like you need to be everything he's missing."

Abby stopped a few feet away from her father, shifting from one leg to the other. "I don't feel any pressure from him, if that's what you're wondering."

Mark nodded, looking down to the ground before refocusing on her. "Speaking of pressure from boys, I know your mom is gone, but I'm still here if you need to talk about..."

"Nope. Don't need to talk," Abby insisted, never wanting to have the sex discussion with her father. She had no idea what manner of birds and bees would be involved. "Mom and I used to talk a lot, so I'm all set."

"Are you sure? Maybe I need to rethink working nights again. Maybe I should be home with you instead."

"That's not necessary, Dad. Nathaniel's a gentleman. Really. And you can trust me, anyway. Right?"

Mark stared at her before nodding. "Yeah. But I'm here if you need me."

"I know. Thanks."

He turned toward the hall. "Well, I'm off to bed. That was a good night."

"It was," she agreed, frozen in place as he walked into his bedroom and closed the door. *It was an amazing night,* she realized. So many things had gone better than she'd hoped. She could even see the three of them sharing many more meals and stories together far into the future. That is, if Nathaniel had a future.

Abby chewed on her lip, struggling to think of a way for Nathaniel to stay here with her forever. She couldn't take back the bullet that ended his life, but there had to be something she could do to turn his half-life existence into a whole one. Because she couldn't fathom a world without him, and she would do just about anything to make sure she didn't have to.

THE NEXT AFTERNOON, Julie zeroed in on Abby's eyes as they sat across from each other at their favorite mall food court table. "He got his own apartment? Are you serious, Abs?"

Abby stiffened in her plastic chair, prepping for her friend's scrutiny. "Yeah," she answered, still amazed by Nathaniel's actions herself, although not for the same reasons. She couldn't believe everything she'd learned yesterday – how he'd spent the day buying a car and finding an apartment, all so he wouldn't have to lie to her father at dinner – and those realizations had caused her to float through today's mall adventure in a giddy fog.

Julie took another sip of her soda. "Man, Peter doesn't even have his own car. I can't tell you how embarrassing it is when he picks me up in the mommobile. And here you are, dating an adult with his own place."

"Yeah," Abby repeated, staring down at her tray, at the remnants of the cheeseburger and fries she'd demolished a few minutes ago.

"So, give me more details. When did Nathaniel get the apartment?"

"Um, yesterday."

"But hasn't he been here a while? Where was he staying before?"

"He…he was staying with a friend," she fibbed, glad she'd waited until the end of the day to bring up the apartment issue. Normally, she could side-step Julie's customary grilling with some semblance of grace. But today, Abby had far more questions than her friend ever could. Honestly, even if she could accept the things Nathaniel had done for her yesterday as normal, she still couldn't get his memories of Normandy out of her head.

Abby's gaze shifted to the other people sitting at the food court, anxiously scanning the many faces. Her spirit had said he would try to make it to the mall today, and she desperately wanted him to appear. She wanted to see him, touch him, and ask him a million questions. But there was only one question that truly mattered.

Can he stay with me always?

"Abby? You doing okay?"

Her friend's voice pulled her focus back to their table. "Sure. I'm fine."

Julie eyed her. "Are you waiting for someone? Is Nathaniel coming?"

"I don't know, actually. He said he might, but it's pretty late already. Are you still meeting Peter for a movie?"

"Yeah. He can wait for me, though. I certainly wait for him enough."

"But the two of you are on again now, right?"

"For the moment."

Abby smiled at her friend before she continued her search for Nathaniel. As her eyes scanned her surroundings, her ears filled with the sound of a deep male voice coming from behind her. Sadly, it wasn't the voice she'd hoped for.

"Abigail. What a surprise, meeting you here."

Her fingers clamped onto the table edge until her knuckles blanched. She pinned Julie's eyes, which were fixated above Abby's left shoulder. She forced herself to turn toward the spirit she dreaded. "Hello, Jonathan."

"Hello to you, too," Jon replied, his cocky grin igniting the birthday candles on the chocolate cake. He wore his black leather jacket again today, which was more in tune with his bad boy image, and also highly desirable to the right type of girl. *Or pretty much any girl*, she corrected herself as she watched Julie swallow back drool.

"Um, this is Jonathan," Abby introduced him as politely as she could.

Julie's smile overtook her entire face. "Well, hello there."

"You must be Julie. Do you mind if I join you?" Jon asked, already slinking down into the chair between them. He took Julie's hand to shake it, lingering obscenely longer than politeness dictated, before his fingers finally slipped away from hers.

"No…of course not," Julie fumbled, her flawless skin now blotched red.

Jon angled his body toward her, his broad shoulders squared, his dark hair perfectly misplaced. "I'm a friend of Abby's from school."

Abby huffed. "He's a friend of Nathaniel's," she corrected.

Julie set her forearms on the table, leaning closer to their intruder. "Oh. Are you the friend he lived with before he got his own place?"

Jon didn't turn his attentions away from her at all, not even when his voice pushed into Abby's head. *His own place? Did Nate actually buy a place?*

Abby grabbed onto her soda cup, sucking on the straw until her cheeks caved inward. *Just tell her yes*, she pleaded in silence.

Jon nodded at Julie. "Yes, that's me." *What is it? A house? An apartment?*

Abby studied her food tray. *An apartment,* she answered, knowing Jon would just pull it from her thoughts anyway.

Well, well. Isn't that interesting.

Julie ran one hand through her hair, dragging her long, dark curls forward. "Wow," she breathed. "That was so nice of you, letting Nathaniel crash at your place for so long."

Jon shrugged his shoulders beneath the clinging black leather. "What can I say? It just warms my heart to be able to do something good for someone."

Abby choked on her drink.

Jon didn't turn to her, but he did reach over to pat her on the back. "You okay there, Abigail?"

"Mm-hmm," she grumbled as the heat of his palm burned through her shirt. She coughed a few more times before sucking down the rest of her soda. Eventually, she only made slurping noises with her straw.

"Here," Jon offered, reaching for her cup, "let me get you a refill."

Abby raised her eyes to his as he stood. He had to pry the Styrofoam from her clawed fingers. *What game does he think he's playing right now? Being Mr. Gentleman to me, of all people?*

"And what about you?" Jon turned back to Julie, ignoring Abby's inner monologue. "Is there anything I can get for you, Julie?"

"No, but thanks. That's so sweet of you."

Jon winked at her before sauntering away.

Julie stared after him, thrumming her fingers against the table until he was out of earshot. Then her head snapped back and her mouth dropped open. "Holy crap, Abs!"

"What?"

"What? What! Have you even taken a look at that boy?"

Abby exhaled in defeat. "Yes. I have."

Julie threw her hands in the air. "My God! Why did I have to move away when I did?"

"What do you mean?"

"I mean a truckload of male models apparently got dumped on the front lawn of your high school. So why, oh why, can't I still be going there?"

Abby shook her head. "It's not a truckload. Besides, Jon's not all that."

Julie's forehead crinkled. "Um, yes he is."

"Well, I don't think so."

"That's just because you're blinded, Abs. Blinded by love."

"Love? Do you mean me and Nathaniel?"

"Yes, of course. Who else, silly?"

Abby's eyes widened. *Good Lord, is that true? Am I in love with Nathaniel? Sure, I think about him constantly and want to be with him every minute. I also crave every thought in his mind, every grin from his lips, and every touch of his body. But is that love?*

"I...I haven't known him all that long," Abby croaked in response.

"I don't think there's a time frame on these things. Sometimes, it's instant." Julie's gaze darted over to the dark spirit currently standing by the drink machine. "Like with Jonathan," she purred. "I mean, I may be in love right this second."

"Oh, hell, Jules. You are so, so not."

"I don't know, Abs. Maybe I am..."

Abby cleared her throat when she saw Jon approaching them. Even though she knew he could read Julie's thoughts, she didn't want her friend to feel embarrassed by her blatant fawning.

"What are you lovely ladies discussing?" Jon asked when he arrived at the table to hand Abby her drink.

She smirked up at him as she took her cup. "Oh, just the weather."

Jonathan chuckled, obviously having far too much fun with this. He sat down between them again, situating his body back towards Julie's, radiating all of his overtly male energy toward her. "So, Julie, tell me about yourself. Abby says you're the best friend ever, but I'm sure there's more. Other than your obvious beauty, of course."

Yeesh, Abby groaned inside her head. *Julie's not going to buy that, is she?* Abby glanced at her finger-fidgeting, hair-twirling, goofily-grinning friend. *Yep, she's buying it. Already paid for it. Taking it home in a shopping bag.*

Julie licked her lips. "Um, well, I...I like journalism," she stumbled. An instant later, she regained her footing and began regaling the intent Jonathan on all her future aspirations.

Jon nodded at Julie, and smiled at her, and seemed entirely focused on her, while she rambled on and on. Consequently, Abby jumped when his smooth voice assaulted her mind once again. *Do you see this, Abigail? I need you to pay attention to how your friend is acting right now, because I want you to realize that this is the proper way for a woman to respond to me.*

Abby stared out at the sea of mallgoers, knowing neither Jon nor Julie saw her. She rolled her eyes anyway. *Thanks for the tip. Sorry I disappointed you.*

Just keep it in mind, please. He smiled again, causing Julie's voice to crack.

Abby blew a stray hair from her face. *Damn it, Jon. Why don't you just leave Julie alone? You do know she already has a boyfriend, right?*

Yeah, and?

Well, doesn't that fact bother you?

Why should it? What's he going to do – kill me?

"So, Jon," Julie sang, balancing at the edge of her seat. "You seem older. Are you in college?"

"No, I'm a junior in high school, just like you and Abby."

"Really?"

"Yeah." He rested back over-dramatically in his plastic chair. "Man, it's been so hard. My dad's been in and out of work, my family moves around a lot, and I never get to complete a full school year anywhere. I've failed a few classes and I've been held back. It's a constant struggle."

Abby whipped her head around to stare at the side of his face. Was Jon actually attempting to play a sympathy card? And what kind of ridiculous story was he feeding to her friend?

"Oh, I'm so sorry," Julie offered, reaching out to slip her hand over the back of his. "If you ever need a tutor, I could certainly help."

"Would you?" His dark eyes lit with tons of birthday candles, like a tiny, tenacious forest fire. "That is so kind. I'll definitely take you up on that offer, if you're serious."

Abby cleared her throat as voraciously as she could, but Julie didn't notice at all. Jon had stepped over the line this time. At least, he'd stepped over Abby's line. She wasn't sure if he even had a line.

Leave her alone, Jon. This isn't fair. Julie doesn't know you.

You don't know me either, Abigail. But you have an open invitation to get to know me. Anytime you want.

She shook her head in silent but firm protest as Julie issued him a flustered invitation for Ultimate Tutoring. Abby turned away, looking to the other people around them, needing to focus on anything but Jonathan. While she stared out into the crowd, she saw Chuck and Holly sit down at a table on the opposite end of the food court. Abby's heart leapt with hope just seconds before she heard the soothing voice of her spirit.

"Hello," Nathaniel said, the warmth of his solid form brushing over her skin as he eased into the seat beside her. "Julie. Jon. *Abby.*"

Nathaniel lingered on her name while smiling with his whole body. Abby trembled with the effort of trying to sit still and not jump directly on him. She didn't think the flimsy chair would hold. "Hi," was all she managed to say.

He leaned forward, pressing his lips to hers for a quick kiss – far too quick. When he sat back in his chair, he gathered her hand in his. Jon grunted at their display of affection, but Abby didn't care about the festering hostility. Her angel was finally here.

Nathaniel looked her over for tender, lengthy seconds before turning to her friend. "How are you today, Julie?"

"I'm good, Nathaniel. You?"

"Good, thanks. I see you've met Jonathan."

Jon smiled. "That's right. I've been spending some time with the girls."

Nathaniel huffed. "Yeah. I'll bet you have."

Julie glanced between the two boys before setting her sights squarely on Nathaniel. "So, I hear you have a new apartment?"

Abby stifled a laugh, since only the unabashed harvesting of information could pull Julie away from her crazed hormonal response to Jon.

"Yes, it was time for me to get something more permanent," Nathaniel answered, squeezing Abby's hand beneath the table.

"Hmm, your own place," Julie considered. "Have you decorated it yet?"

"No, I thought my girlfriend could help me with that."

"Yeah?" Abby said, looking to him with eager excitement.

Nathaniel met her intent stare. "Of course. Any way you like."

She nearly melted into her chair.

"Well, that sure sounds like fun," Jon cut in. "But back to you, Julie. What were you saying about tutoring me? I'd love to set a date."

Julie nearly melted into her chair.

Abby straightened instantly. "Julie! We totally forgot the time! Aren't you supposed to meet Peter at the theater now?"

"Oh, God, I completely forgot," Julie said, glancing at the time on her phone before she stood from the table. "I'm sorry I have to go, Jon. But I'll see you around, I'm sure."

Jon slid his hand down her arm. "Yes. Absolutely."

An anxious laugh bubbled up from Julie's throat. "Yeah, that's...yeah. Um, bye, guys," she said before bouncing away.

The moment Julie disappeared into the crowd, Abby turned to Jon. She gave him the evilest eye she possessed. He looked back at her with an undaunted smile.

Nathaniel leaned toward him. "So, Jon. What are you really doing here?"

"What are you, Nate? My parole officer?"

"Yeah. Maybe I am."

"Wow. You're awfully judgmental for a dead guy with an apartment."

"That's none of your business."

"No, no, of course not," Jon scoffed. "But I'm just noticing how you're disregarding your own rules, here. I mean, weren't you the one with the no-contact policy? You've obviously obliterated that."

Nathaniel glared at him. Their eyes locked in a silent showdown.

Abby shifted uncomfortably in her seat. Part of this was about her. Part of it wasn't. Either way, their stalemate was deafening. It made the crashing boom of Chuck's voice that much worse.

"Look what you did, stupid!" Chuck's roar carried across the length of the food court, straight to their table.

Abby, Nathaniel, and Jon all turned to see Chuck stand from his table to swipe at the soda now soaking into his jeans.

"I'm so sorry," Holly told him, the meager words moving across her lips, barely audible from this distance. Holly fumbled to straighten the overturned cup on their small table, grasping for napkins to fix the spill she'd caused.

Chuck scowled at her, his face contorting in rage. Abby's heart ground to a stop as she watched the young woman who felt so far out of reach. Would Chuck do something terrible in the middle of such a public place?

Nathaniel angled himself toward the distant couple. Abby looked to her angel, witnessing his clenched jaw, fixed gazed, and thick body on the verge of attack. At this moment, she almost wished he would.

Chuck stormed away from Holly while she cleaned up the brown liquid with her head hung and her hands shaking.

"Well, look at that," Jon said. "Apparently, Mr. Basketball's getting close to losing his cool on the new girlfriend. I imagine it won't be too long now."

Nathaniel and Abby snapped their heads back to Jon. They stared him down with both incredulity and disgust.

"What?" he asked in innocent wonder. "Hey, don't shoot the messenger. Damn, you people are so serious all the time."

Abby's jaw gaped. Jonathan Fitzhugh had a complete and utter disregard for anyone but himself, and she couldn't fathom how he'd come to be this way. Only the feel of Nathaniel's warm hand engulfing hers enabled her to refocus. She looked into her angel's eyes – so clear and full of life – making her world right again. She caught her lower lip in her teeth as she imagined kissing him, here and now.

When his gaze fell down to her mouth, Jon groaned. "Yeah, I can't sit here and watch you guys make cow eyes at each other anymore," he complained. Jon jumped up from his seat, causing the plastic to scrape boisterously on the floor. "Later."

Abby imagined that last word was actually a threat. She didn't look directly at Jon, but still watched his retreat from her peripheral vision. She couldn't relax fully until the crowd swallowed him whole.

"Hey," Nathaniel said. "Are you okay?"

She couldn't help frowning. "Do I really have cow eyes?"

"You have exquisite eyes," he insisted, tucking a strand of hair behind her ear. "Jon's just trying to get under your skin. He's persistent, if nothing else."

"What do you mean?"

"I mean he always wants what he can't have."

Her brow furrowed. "Which is what?"

"Not what, who."

"Who what?"

Nathaniel laughed. "That's one of the things I love most about you, Abby. You have no idea how desirable you are, even though you really should."

Love. Her angel just used the word *love* in a sentence that contained her name. Right at this moment, she didn't care about anything else. "I hope I'm desirable to you," she fished.

"God, yes. But not just to me."

Abby exhaled in frustration, not wanting to think about Jon anymore. She especially didn't want to think about him wanting her. Because he didn't – not really. He only wanted to use her as an irritant for Nathaniel. She was absolutely, positively, almost sure of it. "Well, you don't ever have to worry about that, you know. Jon's putrid compared to you."

Nathaniel sighed. "Julie didn't think so."

"She's just confused. But I'm not." Abby rested her hand on his chest. "At least, not about this."

He covered her fingers with his. "All the same, if Jon ever bothers you, just let me know and I'll find a way to make him stop."

Abby watched a flash of anger cross Nathaniel's face. "That's not the first time you've made me that offer," she reminded him. "Tell me – have you two ever fought? Physically, I mean?"

His gaze wandered away briefly, toward Holly's pitiful form sitting alone at her table. "Let's just say that Jon and I have a long and sordid history."

"Well, no matter what's happened in the past, I don't want the two of you to ever fight over me. There's no reason. I'm just yours."

Nathaniel turned back to her, playing his fingers against her wrist. "I like the sound of that."

Abby fisted her hand into his shirt. "I could be yours tonight," she offered with a playful grin, although she was only half-joking.

"Ah, there's my wicked temptress. I always look forward to seeing her."

"Does that mean you'll come over later? My dad will be at work."

"You know I want to, but..."

"Please, Nathaniel? I really need to talk to you."

He glanced over to Holly again. Chuck had reappeared to sit beside her, his eyes shooting daggers at her head as she stared at the tabletop. Nathaniel's gaze eased back to Abby.

"Please," she reiterated, trying not to feel too guilty about begging. "You can leave every five minutes to go check on people, or you can check on them first and come over to my house later. It's just, after last night, I have so many questions to ask you. I could really use some of your time."

"Mmm," Nathaniel hummed. "How can I refuse you anything?"

"Then I'll be waiting. For as long as it takes."

CHAPTER

TWELVE

Nathaniel was taking too long. Every tick of the clock on Abby's bedroom wall struck a looming chord inside her brain. She stared out of her window into the dark night sky, not knowing what else she could do to make the time pass.

Since leaving the mall, she'd done everything she normally did on a Sunday night. She'd stopped by Auto Pro to check on her father, she'd come home and finished her homework, and she'd gotten ready for bed by changing into a comfy camisole and PJ bottoms. After doing all that, she honestly thought Nathaniel would be here already.

A yawn overtook her as she dreaded the possibilities of why he was late. Maybe her spirit had gotten into something he couldn't get out of. Maybe Chuck had lost his temper, just as Jon predicted. Had Nathaniel saved Holly from something horrible tonight? Was that part of his journey over? And if so, when would the rest of his journey be over?

Abby fidgeted with the tiny straps of her top, straightening them unnecessarily, working to keep her nerves at bay. She shut off her desk lamp, settling her bedroom into darkness until the faint moonlight carved out the shape of her window on the floor. When she finally resigned herself to move toward the bed, she heard him.

Do you still want me, Abby?

"Yes, Nathaniel. Please."

He materialized in the darkest corner of her room with his eyes glowing and his body stone-still. She stood in awed anticipation, waiting for her ethereal being to step out of the shadows and into her world. Yet he didn't move toward her at all.

Her head tilted. "Why aren't you turning solid?"

"I'm sorry," he sighed, "but I need to read your emotions first."

"Really? Why?"

"Well, you said earlier that you've been thinking, and you have questions."

"Yes," Abby said, not sure what emotions he thought he would find.

Nathaniel's body remained rigid. "I can see that you're still thinking."

"How? Do I have smoke coming out of my ears?"

He didn't return her lighthearted smile. "Actually, your aura matches your eyes. And that has me worried."

"Why are you worried?"

"I just...I just wonder if you've changed your mind."

"About what?"

"About me. About us."

Her whole body revolted. "Holy hell, Nathaniel. You are joking, right?"

"No, I'm not. I keep thinking that one of these days you're going to tell me to leave. I keep waiting for it, actually. I'm waiting for you to realize how selfish I've been, how I have no right to come over for dinner and meet your father and spend the night in your arms. I'm waiting for you to realize all of the things I don't give you – the things I can't give you – no matter how much I wish otherwise. You should ask me to leave, Abby. You should."

When he finished speaking, the room grew painfully quiet. Or maybe the pain was growing inside her chest, preparing to burst out of her like an alien with razor-sharp teeth, dooming the world. "Well," she said, forcing her voice to not shake, "just so you know, if I ever do ask you to leave, you can be certain I've gone off the deep end straight into Crazy Town. And you absolutely cannot leave me then, because I'll need you more than ever."

Nathaniel finally stepped out of the dark corner. "I wouldn't leave you. I'd just make sure you didn't see me anymore. But I would always stay close, for as long as I could."

Abby watched his eyes turn to a deep blue and felt his cool air transform to perfect warmth. She took two steps forward and threw herself into his arms. He caught her to his chest and buried his face in her hair.

Nathaniel cocooned her until the heat of his skin soaked fully into hers. "So, if you're not thinking about kicking me to the curb, what are you thinking about?"

"Mmm," Abby hummed, blatantly aware of how every inch of her body begged to be close to his. "Honestly, I'm not thinking at all. I'm just wanting."

"Wanting? That's a nice way to put it."

"You, too?"

"Yes. Undeniably."

With that soothing confirmation, she freed him from the vice of her arms and rested back on her heels. "I'm so glad it's not just me."

"It's definitely not just you," Nathaniel assured. He watched his fingers trace the side of her face, as if he needed to memorize her all over again. "Wanting aside, Abby, I know you have questions for me."

"I do. Lots of questions. Do you have time to answer them?"

"Some, at least. I would like to check on a few people in a bit."

"Holly?"

"For one."

"Did Chuck do anything terrible tonight?"

Nathaniel's eyes cast down. "Not physically, not yet. But he's doing all the things I expect. He doesn't allow Holly to have contact with her friends. He won't let her out of his sight when they're together. He tells her not to leave the house without him. It's typical, unfortunately."

"Typical for who?"

"An abuser. They isolate their victim as much as possible, so no one can see what's really happening."

Abby grimaced. "You have too much experience with this, you know. I hate that you have to see the worst things people do."

"It's not the experience I want to have, believe me. But it's important for me to be aware of the signs. That's the only way I'll be able to help."

She took his face in both her hands. "You're amazing, Nathaniel."

He dipped down, grazing his mouth over hers. "You don't know every-thing about me. You may want to reserve your judgment for another day."

"My mind won't ever change on that."

Nathaniel pressed his mouth more deliberately to hers. He drew her in, banding his arms around her body while he explored her lips. When he even-tually pulled away, he sucked in an unsteady breath. "I hope your mind will never change about me," he said as he rested his forehead against hers. "But if it does, I want you to remember that you mean everything to me – absolutely everything – and that will never change."

Abby's eyelids fluttered open. She watched him straighten, easing away from her, as she worked to grasp his words. She raised her hand and opened her mouth, but nothing came out.

Nathaniel ran his thumb over her lip. "You have questions," he reminded, dropping his hand, stepping toward the window, leaving her speechless.

What in the hell did he just tell me?

The word *love* crept into Abby's mind for the umpteenth time today. He hadn't said it, but she'd almost heard it. At the same time, it reeked of regret. But what did he regret? Was he afraid of something she might ask him? Did he really think he could give her an answer that would change the way she felt?

"I'll need to leave soon," Nathaniel prompted.

"Um, yeah, I'm working on it," she said, struggling to focus. "I had a list of questions I'd made in my head, but now you've gotten me all flustered."

He chuckled as he stared at the dark sky outside. "Sorry about that."

Abby concentrated on how their eventful weekend began, with bullets and Normandy. "Okay. I know where I need to start. Are you a pacifist?"

His back stiffened. "A pacifist? Why would you think that?"

"Well, you told me that when you have spiritual policeman confrontations with people, you never fight back."

"Yes, but I can turn into a spirit and heal whenever I need to. I think that's a better way to handle it, don't you?"

"I suppose. But what about Normandy?"

Nathaniel glanced back to her, his face stoic. "What about it?"

"You never touched your gun. Not once."

He smiled before turning back to the window. "You noticed that?"

"Yeah. I noticed." Abby stood in silence for several seconds, waiting for a response. When none came, she took a step toward him. "Why would you go to war if you never intended to use a weapon? Do you just not believe in violence of any kind?"

Nathaniel crossed his arms over his chest. "I was a boxer in high school."

Abby gawked at his profile, certain she hadn't heard him correctly. "Wait a minute. You were a *boxer*?"

"Yes. There was a gym in my town with several boxing rings. It wasn't professional, but I fought anyone in my weight class. I even fought men much older than me. I was...I was very good at it."

"And you *liked* that?" she asked in sheer bewilderment, since the thought of him hitting anyone felt absurd.

Nathaniel shrugged. "I believe I mentioned before that my emotions were quite volatile when I was younger. Boxing was a good outlet."

"You mean for anger?"

"Yes."

Abby bit into her lip. She'd never seen her angel angry. She couldn't imagine it. The way he saved people – women, especially – just didn't match.

Her mind screeched to a halt that instant. Nathaniel protected women so fiercely now, but was it possible that he hadn't always been so kind? Abby didn't want to believe it, but it would explain why he was so nervous about answering her questions. "Have you, um, have you ever..." she stumbled. "I mean, you wouldn't ever hurt a woman. Would you?"

Nathaniel turned to pin her questioning gaze. "Absolutely not. Never have, never will. Growing up, my mother and sister meant everything to me. In the '40s, women were treated much differently than men. I was raised to care for and protect them, and I always have."

"Of course," she said, guilt-ridden that the thought even crossed her mind.

"Will you please excuse me now?" he asked. "Just for a few minutes?"

"Yeah, sure."

"I'll be right back."

The moment he disappeared, Abby exhaled and sat down on her bed. This was more difficult than she'd imagined. She had so many questions, but no idea which were the right ones to ask. If her goal was to find a way for him to stay solid permanently, then she had to figure out why he was living this semi-life and what needed to be done to break the spell.

Her shoulders slumped. "What makes you think you can accomplish all of that?" she questioned herself in the quiet of her room. After all, Nathaniel had over sixty years to figure it out, and he didn't seem to have any more of a clue than she did.

"And why in the hell did you ask him if he'd ever hurt a woman? You know better than that. All he ever does is watch over everyone, all the time." Abby groaned as she wrenched her fingers together. "Damn, you're an idiot."

I'm on my way back, Nathaniel said, his voice easing softly into her mind.

The moment she heard him, she straightened on the edge of her bed.

Nathaniel reappeared in the corner by the window, turning solid instantly.

"Is everyone okay?" Abby asked.

"Yes, for now. They're all settling in for the night. I'll need to leave again in a few minutes, just to check on them one more time, if you don't mind."

"I don't mind. Honestly, it means so much that you're here now. I know it's not easy for you to be disconnected from your spirit world, yet you do it for me constantly. I want you to know how much I appreciate it – all of it."

He held her with the most tender, understanding gaze. "You don't have to feel guilty, you know. I'm not upset with you."

"About what?"

"About wondering if I've ever hurt a woman. It was a valid concern."

"God, no, it wasn't. It should never have crossed my mind."

"Don't be so hard on yourself, sweetheart. There are a lot of things you don't know about me."

Abby sighed, utterly grateful to him for giving her an easy way out. "Well, that's why I'm asking questions, silly," she teased.

He laughed – a sound so sweet and sparkling that she felt it all the way to her toes. "Okay, then. Ask me more questions."

"All right. Why don't we address the fun topics?"

"Which are?"

"The Jeep! And the apartment!" she shouted, bouncing on her bed until the comforter rumpled beneath her. "When do I get to be in them?"

"You can be in them any time you like. I'm serious about you decorating the apartment, if you want."

"Oh, I want. I want *a lot*."

A shameless grin spread Nathaniel's lips. His gaze shifted to her messy bedspread before drifting back to hers. "Not as much as I do."

Abby fisted her fingers into the covers. "I highly doubt that. And don't distract me with your unearthly charms, please. Where'd you get the Jeep?"

"At the car dealership."

"Ha, ha, very funny. You know what I mean."

He chuckled as he rested back against her windowsill. "I already told you, I needed to drive something to your house to meet your father. A Jeep was the last thing I drove before Normandy, so it felt like a good choice. Of course, the Army vehicles were a bit different back then."

"And do you have a driver's license?"

"I do."

"From 1944?"

"No. This one says I was born twenty years ago. But I'll need to update it again soon. I don't think I can get away with much past twenty-two."

Abby's brow crinkled. "How do you get your driver's license changed?"

"Oh, you can find people to do just about anything – new driver's license, new birth certificate, new Social Security number – it's not difficult if you have money to throw around."

"Money. Right. Exactly how much do you have?"

"Enough."

"Enough to do what?"

"To take care of things."

She huffed with his cryptic answer. "Okay, Nathaniel. You have to tell me where it comes from. You said you didn't rob a bank and I believe you. But where did you get those rolls of cash you always pull out of your pockets?"

His intent gaze didn't veer from hers. "Do you remember me telling you that it was just pocket change?"

"Yes."

"Well, I meant that literally."

Abby's mind reached to the boat in Normandy. "Your coin collection?"

"It was worth a little in the '40s. In the '80s, it was much more valuable."

"So, you carried it with you all that time?"

"I spent my first forty years as a spirit with my family, wearing what I wore in Normandy. My clothes looked the same as they did when I died."

Her stomach churned. "You mean they were soaked in blood."

"Yes, although no one saw them. Not until I confronted Maria's dad in Kansas, and discovered that I could turn solid. He was the only living person who ever saw me like that."

"And after you saved Maria, and realized you could turn solid, then you found all the coins in your pocket?"

"They were still there, just the same as that day in Normandy."

"Wow. They must have been worth a lot after forty years."

"Some were, but not all the money came from selling them. Hell, I suppose I should have just left them in my pocket. But as I told you once before, I was very tempted by things when I found out I could turn solid."

"I remember you telling me that. You wondered if pretending to be alive would be any different than actually being alive, if no one knew the truth."

"I wondered about that a lot," he admitted, raking his hand through his hair. "Money was a temptation for me, to say the least. I didn't have much of it growing up, so when I thought I might have a chance to be alive, I wanted all that I could get. The '80s were a very good time for the stock market. I forced myself to learn how to invest. I did pretty well."

"Holy crap, Nathaniel. You invested in the stock market way back then? Does that mean you're rich now?"

He shook his head. "To be honest, I don't know what constitutes wealth in this day and age. I've made a lot of money through the years, but it's not mine. At least, I don't think of it that way. I use it from time to time, out of necessity, although I have minimal needs. Back in the '80s, all I wanted was to change out of my bloody uniform. But people wore the worst stuff back then. I wasn't about to feather my hair or put on a pink shirt with a white blazer."

Abby giggled with that mental image of him. "So, I guess you decided instead on the white T, brown pants, and chunky boots combo?"

"I went to an Army surplus store and bought them out of that outfit. It was also helpful that the clothes meant I didn't really fit in with modern society. It reminded me that just because I could be solid didn't mean I was supposed to be. I told myself that I needed to turn away from the temptations of life, including money. But I also didn't want to leave what I'd made just sitting in a bank, so I had a trust set up for my sister and her kids. I have to contact the bank to renew my account every year, or all the money goes to her and her family. Anonymously, of course."

Abby didn't know how to respond. *This is wild. Interesting, but wild.*

Nathaniel stood from the windowsill. "Will you excuse me again, please? I'd like to check on everyone, just once more."

She nodded before he disappeared. Then she stared at the space he'd just occupied and thought about everything he'd said. Her angel was rich, but didn't act like it. He didn't flaunt or waste it. Hell, she'd even wondered once if he was poor. But he wasn't; he had plenty of options. Nathaniel could stay solid, living the life of a king, indulging without consequences. He was already dead, after all. What other consequences could there be?

But that wasn't his choice. He wasn't living it up in a mansion with cars and boats and Miss Oklahomas. Instead, he wore the same outfit for years on end, threw himself in front of violent jerks in order to save people, and ensured his money would go to his last remaining family. If he didn't contact the bank every year, his sister would become a very wealthy woman.

Abby hung on that last thought. *He has to check in every year. Why?*

I'm coming back now, Nathaniel warned a moment before he appeared in front of her window. Abby watched his glowing eyes transform to a deep, calm blue. "It's for good, this time."

She sighed in relief. "Is everyone okay?"

"For the night. Marcus fell asleep on his history book. Holly is in her room, eating ice cream. Chuck is passed out drunk on the couch in his basement."

"Wow. Chuck's a drinker, too?"

"He gets the booze from his folks. They either don't know or don't care."

"My God, Nathaniel. You live in too many different worlds."

"Believe me, I'm well aware of it."

Abby's face fell. "I'm sorry. That was a stupid thing for me to say."

"No, it wasn't. It's true." He continued standing by her window, much too far away for her liking. "Do you have any more questions for me tonight?"

"Um, yeah, if that's okay," she replied, fingers fidgeting with the comforter beneath her. "It's just, you said something funny before you left.

You said you had to contact the bank every year or your money will go to your sister."

"Yes, that's how I set the account up."

"But that doesn't make sense. I mean, why can't you just transfer the money whenever you're ready? Why create the one-year deal?"

Nathaniel held her eyes with a look of sheer pride in his own. "You see so much, Abby. That mind of yours."

She nearly vibrated with anticipation when he finally walked toward her. She didn't realize how much she missed his warmth until he sat down beside her on the mattress. They weren't touching, but she felt the energy surge between them, setting her nerves on a teetering edge.

"I told you I don't have a manual for this existence," he explained, the bedframe creaking beneath his weight as he turned to face her. "But that doesn't mean I haven't been trying to figure out what's going on, and when it will all end."

Abby shivered with his ominous words. "Do you have theories?"

"Some. At first, I thought it might all be over on one set day, like everything was on a timer and I was just waiting for that clock to run out. Part of me thought it would end the day my mother died, but it obviously didn't. Still, I never knew if I would just disappear at some point, so I wanted to make sure the money would get to Marybeth and her family."

"And do you still think you're on some kind of time limit?" Abby asked, inching closer, hating that he wasn't touching her. For all she knew, he could disappear right now and never return.

Nathaniel reached over to lace their fingers together. He must have known she needed to touch him. Somehow, he must have known. "No, I don't think I'm on a time limit anymore. Although anything is possible, I suppose. It's one of the many reasons I've been reluctant to fixate myself in your life. I know I shouldn't be doing all of these things – buying cars and apartments, having family dinners, and touching you again and again – but I just want to be with you so badly. I keep telling myself it's okay, as long as you want me, too."

"I do want you," she insisted, moving closer still, until the sides of their bodies aligned.

Nathaniel's gaze drifted slowly across her face. "But does that give me the right to want you back, Abby? Or am I supposed to know better?"

Her heart caved in. She knew what she needed, but what about him? He'd obliterated his no-touch policy for her, and now she couldn't imagine a life without that touch. She shook her head, not wanting to think that their beautiful relationship could somehow condemn his soul.

"What is it?" he asked, drawing his fingers up and down her arm.

"I was just thinking that it would be really handy if you had a manual."

"Wouldn't it, though?"

"It would. But maybe figuring out why you're here is part of the process."

"Well, I figure it must have something to do with emotions. I was such an emotional kid. My feelings always overcame my reasoning, and now here I am – not just dealing with my own emotions, but with everyone's. From the very first moment I became a spirit and found myself overwhelmed by the violent colors of everyone around me on that beach, I've believed that I must learn how to control my feelings. But I've done everything I can think to do. I've contained my anger time and time again. In all my spirit encounters, I've never fought back once. I honestly don't know how I can be any more controlled than I already am."

"Seriously," Abby agreed. "You are Mr. Frickin' Willpower, after all."

Nathaniel laughed, deep and full. She watched the boyish spark light in his eyes. It was all she could do to not pounce on him.

"Maybe you're wrong," she considered, although it was admittedly for her own benefit. "Maybe you're not supposed to be all willpower, all the time."

His brow rose. "Is this my wicked temptress speaking?"

"I'm just saying, maybe you were sent to me for a different reason. Maybe we're supposed to explore some other options, if you catch my meaning."

"I do catch it," he assured with a sinful smile. "But unfortunately, I don't think anything is that easy."

"Oh, you're probably right. Although you can't blame a girl for trying."

He looked down to his hand as he drew it from her elbow to her wrist. "I would never blame you for that."

Abby worked to keep herself still while he concentrated on touching her. "You know, maybe it really is the opposite of utter willpower, though. Maybe you're not supposed to stand there and get the crap beat out of you when you confront those horrible people. Maybe you're supposed to fight back. Instead of being a spiritual policeman, you could be a spiritual *boxing* policeman."

"Hmm. That is a thought."

"Do you have other thoughts?"

"Yes," Nathaniel admitted, treading his fingers back into hers before meeting her eyes. "There's a part of me that wonders about the guns."

"What about them?"

"Well, you know it's the one thing that actually killed me. That bullet in Normandy was excruciating. I can't imagine making it through that pain again – to even have the willpower to turn back into a spirit and heal. Maybe I won't be able to. Maybe if I get into a situation where someone shoots me, that will be the end of it."

She clenched onto his hand. "Then don't do it, Nathaniel. You told me before that it wouldn't be your choice – that you would do anything to save someone – but I think it *should* be your choice. I want you to promise me that you'll never get in the way of a bullet. I can't stand to think about it. I can't stand to think of you not being here with me."

He drew his free hand up to cradle her cheek. "But, Abby...don't you see? That's exactly how you *shouldn't* feel. I should never have worked my way into your life like this. I should never have forced myself on you."

"Forced yourself? You've done no such thing. You've been nothing but a gentleman. You've made sure that I'm safe, that everyone is safe. I mean, you spent half the night checking on other people."

"You're giving me too much credit again."

"I'm not."

"You are. Why do you think I keep checking on people? It's not because I want to. I don't want to leave you. I want to stay here and hold you and not care about anything else in this world. But aside from making me exceedingly happy, it won't get me anywhere. It won't get us anywhere. I have to go. I have to help people. Because something has to make a difference. Something will set this right and end this unnatural existence, one way or another."

Abby trembled all over.

Nathaniel's voice softened. "I know which way I want it to go, sweetheart. I want to end up right here with you, solid and real and alive. But I honestly don't know if that will happen. I don't know if it's even possible. My only hope is that someday, somehow, I'll do something good enough to deserve my life back. To deserve you."

His words filtered out into the still air, carrying the weight of the world. Abby ran them over and over in her mind. What else was there to do? What sacrifice had he not made? What horrid death had he not endured for the sake of saving another soul?

"You deserve everything," she whispered. "Everything you ever wanted."

Nathaniel smiled, slow and tender. "All I want is you."

Abby whimpered. She searched his eyes, waiting for something to happen. Wondering if he would just disappear now. Wondering if their time would come to a sharp, abrupt end. Or if he would get what he wanted.

When Nathaniel leaned closer, she let her eyelids fall. The warmth of his body wrapped around her as his scent filled her mind, but it was his mouth that melted her fears. His lips touched hers, intent yet cautious, erasing all her disturbing questions at once. She allowed herself the forbidden belief that nothing else mattered except the two of them.

Her anxiety jolted back to life when his mouth left hers. But he simply shifted his attentions to her face, trailing soft kisses up her jaw. She focused entirely on keeping her hands in her lap and holding her body stiffly in place, not wanting to give him any reason to stop.

Nathaniel threaded his fingers into her hair and urged her head to the side, allowing him access to the slope of her neck. His hand found the thin strap of her camisole top, drawing the tiny string down to fall onto her upper arm. His mouth eased across her neck and onto her bare shoulder. When his teeth nipped at her skin, goose bumps skittered across her flesh.

"Mmm," he hummed. "Are you cold?"

"No, I'm...I'm just right."

"Yes, you are," he agreed before lips found hers again. This time, his kiss was much deeper than before. It was torture for Abby to keep her hands to herself, yet she did. She let him work his magic, calming all her doubts and fears. But her body still responded voraciously to every sweep of his tongue over hers, which made her fingers twist together in a desperate attempt to keep from clawing at his chest.

Nathaniel pulled back just enough to rest his forehead onto hers. "You're not touching me, Abby."

"You're right. I'm not."

"Why is that?"

"Because I always get too carried away when we do this. And I really don't want you to run from me tonight."

"I see," he said, his warm breath fanning over her face. His fingers slid across to her other shoulder. Nathaniel urged the second strap of her camisole down her arm before replacing it with his mouth.

She inhaled sharply with the pressure of his lips on her bared skin.

"It is interesting to see you in such a passive role," he murmured against her. "But I have to admit, it only makes me crave your touch even more."

Abby didn't need to be asked twice. She reached for the hem of his shirt, bunching the fabric in both fists to tug him closer. The bare skin of his lower back lay beneath her fingertips, enticing her in the rudest way, so she dragged her nails across it.

Nathaniel groaned, raw and pained. He urged her backward onto the bed, his chest settling over hers. When Abby's comforter met her spine, she froze. She didn't know how much of this he would allow, so she waited for a sign that he would go no further. None came.

She dragged her eyes open to find Nathaniel watching her from above. He worked his fingers into her hair, examining the movement as if it was the most fascinating thing he'd ever seen. Abby tried not to notice that he was lying on top of her on her bed. If she paid too much attention, she would start to lose control. She couldn't afford that now. Not when he was giving her this much.

His fingers slid across her scalp, massaging, releasing tension she didn't even know she had. She closed her eyes again, trying to enjoy every sensation, yet she only wanted more. Very slowly, hoping he wouldn't quite notice, she flattened her hands against the small of his back. His skin was smooth and even, his muscles corded beneath her fingers. Viking, farmer, soldier, boxer – his body held brute strength, yet he was as gentle as she could imagine.

Nathaniel drew one hand from her hair to steady her face in his palm. He leaned down and Abby parted her lips in anticipation. His mouth hovered over hers for slow, painful moments, their breaths mingling together in uneven pants. She waited for him to kiss her, waited until she thought she would explode. Finally, she couldn't stand the torment any longer. She arched up, pulling against the heated skin of his spine, begging him without words.

He smiled against her lips before pressing his chest entirely onto hers. His full weight sank her down into the mattress. She sighed with the feel of him on top of her, warm and solid and heavy. Right now, his body was the only thing holding her to the earth.

Abby breathed in deep as he kissed her again, intimately aware of all the places they now touched. She moved her hands cautiously upward, tracing the straight line of his spine, until his shirt bunched to his shoulders. She wanted the offending fabric gone but knew there was no way to accomplish that without his participation.

A second later, Nathaniel's mouth left hers. She thought to protest, but instead, she watched in amazement as he arched up to yank the shirt over his head. He flung it onto the floor before settling back down against her. Abby slipped her hand onto his bare chest with stealthy speed. She didn't look into his eyes, afraid he might stop her from tracing the lines of his muscles.

Nathaniel allowed her explorations for lengthy, mesmerizing moments. She tried to not make any garbled or lewd noises as she absorbed the heat of his skin. Eventually, he made the garbled, lewd noises. Then he reclaimed her face in his palm, drawing her gaze to his. He didn't look upset at all. He looked as crazed as she felt.

Abby moaned when he brought his mouth back to hers. She forgot that she was supposed to be physically memorizing the definitions of his chest. All she could think of was the smooth sensation of his firm lips against her soft ones, of the way they melded together as if they were made to be like this. She lost all sense of time when his tongue traced her mouth, and barely heard the growl that rumbled through his chest when she eased her tongue onto his. And she completely forgot to breathe when he caught both of her hands in his and pinned them to the mattress above her head.

She didn't know if Nathaniel had trapped her hands so she wouldn't lose control or so he wouldn't. Either way, it didn't seem to matter. He kissed her for stretched, seamless minutes, his mouth erasing the whole world from her mind. There was only him. Only the heat of his skin. Only the weight of his body. Only the wild beating of his heart and hers.

When he finally dragged his lips away, cursing in defeat before burying his face into her shoulder, they both gasped for air. Abby worked one of her hands free to trace the length of his spine. She flattened her palm against the small of his back, working to hold him in place. She couldn't keep him with her forever, but she needed to try.

Stay, she thought, even though he couldn't hear her. *Stay right here.*

Nathaniel raised his head, propping himself up on one elbow, to meet her drunken gaze. His eyes illuminated in the glow from the window, although not quite as bright as the glow of his spirit form. He caught a strand of her hair in his fingers and twirled it in a circle. "You know we can only have so much of this. Right?"

Oh, God. Not reality. Not yet. "Um, why is that, again?"

"Well, you can call me old-fashioned, but I think mortality is a must for that kind of relationship."

She signed with the practicality of his statement. Leave it to her to fall in love with a spirit. *Love.* There was that word again, and the truth to go with it. Abby loved him. She loved him utterly and insatiably, without any doubt at all. That realization forced a giddy laugh to bubble up from her throat.

"What's so funny?" Nathaniel asked.

"Oh, nothing. I guess we're just going to have to figure out a way to make you mortal, because I don't know how much longer I will last like this."

"You'll make it. We both will."

Abby stared up into him, feeling full and free in her newfound knowledge. "Stay," she said, emboldened her emotions. "Stay with me tonight."

"You know I want to. But I'll have to leave before morning."

"That's okay. I just want you here for as long as possible."

Nathaniel nodded without hesitation. He still had her pinned beneath him, so she waited for him to stand so she could move to the head of the bed and get under the covers. But he did no such thing. Instead, he grabbed her around the waist, clamped her body fiercely onto his, and Army-crawled up the bed with her in tow. Abby laughed as he grunted with the effort, dragging them both together until they reached the top of the mattress.

"There we go," he announced once he'd rested her head against her pillow. He released his grip on her waist to grab the edge of the comforter and pull it over them both. "We're all ready for sleep now."

Abby smiled into his eyes. "You know, I could have thought of an easier way to reach the top of the bed."

"Yeah, but would it have been as much fun?"

"Uh-uh. Not at all."

Nathaniel matched her smile while he laid back and gathered her in his arms. Abby rested her cheek over his heart, listening to the melodic thumping that assured her he was alive, right here and now. "I promise I'll stay with you for as long as I can," he said, his soothing voice rumbling beneath her ear.

Abby wasn't sure if he was talking about tonight, or if he meant that in a forever kind of way. It didn't matter, though. What she wanted for them wouldn't ever change. "As long as you can, Nathaniel."

And by the way, I love you, her mind added, even though she knew he couldn't hear her.

"HAPPY HALLOWEEN, MOM," Abby whispered to the picture tucked into her mirror while she sat at her vanity the next morning. Her eyes brightened as she remembered how much Mom loved seeing Dad in his Darth Vader costume. Abby couldn't wait for him to dress up tonight. When she saw him put on that funny black helmet, she would know for sure that he was okay.

She brushed her hair a few more times before standing from her chair. Her eyes drifted to her bed, to where Nathaniel had held her the entire night until sunshine crept through the window. She smiled as the image of him Army-crawling her to the top of the mattress filled her mind. That smile remained firmly in place while she left her room and walked to the kitchen.

Her father stood by the counter, bleary-eyed and coughing next to a half-eaten sandwich. "Mornin', honey."

"Mornin', Dad. Happy Halloween." Abby gathered his pills from the cabinet and placed them in his hand.

Mark swallowed them all before showing her his empty mouth. "Halloween is today, isn't it? Seems like forever since the last one."

She nodded, knowing exactly what he meant. Since the day her mother died, everything had moved in slow motion. That is, until an unearthly spirit entered her life. "Would you mind if Nathaniel comes over tonight to help us pass out candy?"

Mark shrugged. "Sure. I think that would be fine."

"Thanks. I really appreciate it."

His head tilted. "You really like this guy, don't you, Abby?"

"Yeah, Dad." *I love him.*

"Well, then. Why don't you invite him over for Thanksgiving, too?"

Her eyes widened. "Seriously?"

"Seriously. He said he doesn't have any family in the area. I bet it would mean a lot to him. I think it means a lot to you?"

Abby threw her arms around her father's neck. "Oh, my goodness. Thank you, thank you, thank you."

Mark chuckled as her bubbly hug ended. "I'd do anything for you, honey."

"I know you would, Dad."

***

THE SCHOOL picnic bench felt like ice. Even with the sun beating down on her, the whipping wind froze Abby's skin. She really shouldn't have tried to sit outside for lunch today. With this frigid cold, it would be much more practical to sit in the warm cafeteria with all the aliens.

Thankfully, Sondra had forgiven her for not meeting Brett, yet again. Abby swore she would meet him tomorrow, so her friend had let the issue go pretty easily. Sondra probably enjoyed the alone time at lunch with her new-again boyfriend. Abby was thrilled that Sondra had found her way past Chuck, but scared that Holly hadn't.

Holly and Chuck. They were the reason Nathaniel had to leave her room so early this morning. Even despite the fact that he'd held her through the night, and kissed her before he left, Abby hated lying in bed without him. She just missed him so damn much.

She stared out into the forest beyond the picnic tables, her jaw clenched as she considered all the fears Nathaniel had admitted to her last night. When would his spirit life end? Would he just disappear one day, smiling at her one moment and gone the next? Or would it be a bullet, tearing through his body and making him incapable of healing?

Abby shook her head, refusing to accept either horrifying option, wanting to bend the entire universe to her will and keep her spirit here forever. She stared blankly at the knots in the wood tabletop, pushing the worst-case scenarios out of her mind. Maybe Nathaniel wouldn't be torn away from her without a moment's notice. Maybe his spiritual policeman work really would give him another chance at life – a long, full life with her.

"Good afternoon, Abigail."

She jumped, nearly toppling backwards off her bench. "Geez, Jonathan! Don't sneak up on me like that!"

"Sorry," he said, sitting down opposite her without any invitation at all. "You know, I didn't actually sneak up on you. You were just off in your own little world."

Well, that much was true. Normally, she would have sensed Jon's presence by his blast of arctic air. But today, it just blended in with the wind. She glanced to his trusty sunglasses, grateful they concealed his oily eyes.

Jon folded his fingers together on the table. "You waiting here for Nate?"

"Yes. I am."

"I'll wait with you, if you don't mind."

"And if I did mind?"

"Then I would wait with you anyway."

"Yeah, that's what I figured."

Abby glared at him, expecting him to respond to her in some way. She figured he must be preparing to offer her some unwanted advice, or planning to ridicule her for something she was or wasn't doing. But Jon didn't pay her any attention at all. He simply looked out into the woods that crept up beyond them, sitting in utter silence.

Abby gave up. She couldn't spend time trying to decipher Jonathan Fitzhugh right now. She had too many other things on her mind to deal with the confounding intricacies of his.

Refocusing on the knots in the tabletop, Abby returned her thoughts to the question of Nathaniel's half-life. He'd told her last night that he had to save people because he believed those actions might end his unnatural existence, one way or another. He said he hoped that meant coming back to life so he could spend it with her. But he'd already saved enough people to deserve his life back, hadn't he? What else could he possibly do as a spiritual policeman that he'd never done before?

He could save me, Abby considered. Would that be his final good deed? Would saving her be the thing that finally gave him back his life? And if so, what exactly would he save her from?

Her father's face popped into her head then. She couldn't help envisioning him in answer to her question, fearful of everything that might go wrong between them. They'd being doing so well lately, but no matter how stable their current relationship was, Abby knew she had to keep her guard. She'd seen Mark fall one too many times before – into the depths of depression or mania – in tragic days and months and years. She remembered how he looked the day her mother died. And how he looked when he handed her the bullets he'd bought just a few nights ago.

Abby could see his eyes right now, as if her father stood directly in front of her. She could see their clear, perfect stillness when he was well. She could see their strange, murky depths when he was sick. They were the windows to his soul, and she couldn't help but look through them.

"So, it's his eyes, then?" Jonathan's voice cut through the chilled air.

Abby's roiling mind screeched to a halt. She looked up slowly from the tabletop to Jon's face. Her heart pounded against her ribcage. "Holy crap, Jon. Have you been reading my mind this entire time?"

"That's beside the point."

Her brows shot to her hairline. *How dare he steal my thoughts! Is that why he came here today? Did he sit here, all quiet and peaceful, just to lull me into a sense of calm? Just so I would hand over everything in my brain?*

Abby finally found her voice. "You are the biggest jerk I have ever met!"

Jon smiled. "That's also beside the point. So, it's his eyes?"

"Good God! What are you even talking about?"

"I'm trying to figure out why you can see ghosts, Abigail. From what I've gathered today, you read your father's mood swings through his eyes. When he descends into bouts of insanity, you see it first. Your gift is intuition."

She crossed her arms over her chest and sealed her lips together.

Jon dragged his sunglasses off. "Does that about sum it up?

Abby recoiled from the vision before her. The dark, foul liquid of his eyes churned in thick, sluggish waves. She nearly retched on the tabletop.

"I see now why you respond so strongly to me, in a way no other female does," he concluded. "My eyes bother you on an entirely different level. You equate them to the dementia of your father, and you equate that with periods of great stress and pain in your life. I finally understand why you are incapable of being drawn to me when I am in ghost form."

"Jonathan, I want you to understand this, here and now. I am incapable of being drawn to you in *any* form. You are rude and arrogant, and I think the only reason you asked me what you look like as a ghost was because you were worried that you had horns growing out of your head."

He laughed, but she didn't miss the flash of concern in his dark eyes. "Don't be silly. I don't have horns. Do I?"

"No. But you may as well."

Jon rested his arms on the table. "You certainly are quick to condemn me, when all I'm trying to do is figure things out."

"Figure what out?"

"Whatever it is that makes you different. I mean, it's been quite a while since I died. During the many years of my afterlife, I've sought out tons of different people. I've hung around with Buddhists and Scientologists, Democrats and Republicans, and everything else in between. Yet you are the only person who has ever been able to see me like this." Jon grinned at her, putting his adorable dimples on full display. "Don't you find that odd? I certainly do."

Abby wished she had the ability to just disappear. He didn't seem to require her presence anyway. He seemed quite happy conversing with himself.

"You must realize that there are people everywhere in the world who search for proof of the afterlife," he continued. "There are numerous television shows devoted to it – wild adventurers hoping to acquire some evidence of the existence of ghosts. And here you are, a seventeen-year-old high school student, having conversations with them. At lunch, no less."

Jon huffed as he glanced to the trees. "Those shows always struck me as funny, anyway. These hunters go out searching for bizarre phenomena, yet the only places they look are creepy castles and old basements. Don't people realize by now that the strangest things on earth happen in high school?"

A laugh snuck past her lips, much to her dismay. "Why does it even matter?" she asked. "Why does it matter that I can see you?"

He looked back to her, pinning her wide eyes with his churning ones. "Because it does. It makes me want to know you. To *really* know you."

Abby worked to ignore the sick feeling in her belly. She fought against the huge, overbearing part of her brain that demanded she sprint away from him as far and as fast as she could. *You are not going to make me leave this bench, Jonathan. Not until I get to see my angel.*

Nathaniel appeared then. He materialized beside her, the weight of his body making the bench creak the instant he turned solid. The warmth of his skin formed a shield against the cold air as he reached out to touch her arm.

"Abby? Are you okay?"

"Fine," she bit out, glowering at the loathsome creature across from them.

Nathaniel's hand eased to her face, pulling her toward him.

She finally turned to meet his concerned gaze.

"Tell me you're okay, sweetheart. Please."

Her entire body eased with the tenderness of his words. "I'm okay."

"Do you really mean that?"

"I do now."

"Would you like me to remove Jon from this bench permanently?"

"Don't waste your time," Abby assured. "He doesn't affect me at all."

Jon laughed, deep and hearty, since he knew it was a massive lie.

Nathaniel's shoulders bunched at the ominous sound.

Abby focused solely on her angel. "I missed you so much this morning."

"I'm sorry I'm late. It's been a really hectic day."

"More problems between Chuck and Holly?"

"Yes. He's wound up more than usual today, and I..."

Nathaniel didn't get to finish his sentence – not before the shouting started. Abby looked to the trees beside the picnic tables, tracing their line up ahead to see Chuck and Holly in the distance. He loomed over the much smaller girl as he dragged her toward the forest line. Abby watched in morbid fascination while Chuck yanked Holly forward by the arm, muttering curses while she cried and struggled to wrench free. A second later, their entwined forms disappeared into the trees.

"Abby..." Nathaniel began.

"Just go," she told him.

His eyes fastened onto hers. "Don't leave this bench," he instructed before he disappeared.

Her jaw fell open as she gawked at the now-empty seat beside her. This was it. All this time, Nathaniel had been watching. Always watching. Now, he was actually going to do something. But what?

Jonathan stood from the table, his sudden movement startling her.

Abby looked up to him, witnessing the excitement scrawled across his face.

"Here we go," Jon said. "It's finally time."

CHAPTER

THIRTEEN

Abby stared at Jon with her heart in her throat. "Wait! Time for what?"

"Time for Nathaniel to take another beating," Jon said, already turning away.

She lunged across the table to grab his arm, but only grasped fistfuls of air. Her frantic actions caught his attention. Jon stopped cold and pivoted back.

"What are you doing, Abigail?"

She pinned his oily eyes. "I want to know what you're doing!"

"I'm going to watch. I never miss one of these. Not if I can help it."

"My God. Only *you* would enjoy watching that."

Jon slid his sunglasses back on. "Oh, come on. You know you're curious."

Abby breathed a little easier with the black sludge hidden. But then he placed his palms on the tabletop and leaned toward her. His devilishly stunning face came far too close.

"I'll tell you what," he prodded, the glacial air of his body wrapping over hers. "I'll keep my mind open to you and you can watch the whole thing."

She recoiled on the bench. "You mean...watch it *through* you?"

"That's exactly what I mean. I know you've been in Nate's mind before. You know how to do it. Feel free to reach into mine." Jon grinned deviously as he straightened. He turned and sauntered away, tossing one last thought into her brain. *I promise I won't bite.*

That was a threat. No question about it.

Abby stayed glued to her seat as she watched Jon glide smoothly into the tree line. She bit back the tears in her eyes – a mixture of fear for Nathaniel and fear of Jon. He'd given her a choice and she had to decide.

Did she want to watch Nathaniel confront Chuck? Yes, but only because she needed to make sure her angel was unharmed. Would it be going against Nathaniel's wishes? Technically not, since he'd told her not to leave this bench and she wouldn't – at least, not physically.

Abby stared down at her fingers while they twisted together. She knew Nathaniel wouldn't want her to watch. He would want to protect her from seeing something so awful. But she just had to know that he was safe.

Her gut clenched the instant she made her decision. She shut her eyes and forced herself to think about Jonathan. She had to picture the foul spirit with his sunglasses on, or wild horses couldn't drag her into his mind.

Abby told herself this would be okay. She would share Jon's thoughts for one specific purpose only. She wouldn't allow anything else in his head to affect her in any way.

Her mind reached out tentatively, not entirely sure of how to find his. Sharing Nathaniel's thoughts always came so easily, but Abby knew this would be different. For several moments, nothing happened. She didn't hear Jon's goading thoughts or inciting voice at all.

She concentrated harder, grasping for his mind with all her might. Yet despite her efforts, she still couldn't hear anything. Probably because she couldn't overcome her repulsion at the idea of being connected to him in such an intimate way.

Abby grumbled in frustration, fully aware that she needed to ask him for help. But before she even had the chance to call his name, everything changed. She didn't find Jon. He found her. He pulled her to him. He dragged her inside. He filled her thoughts with his own, rapid and dominant, drenching her brain.

All the air in Abby's lungs seized the moment he took control. Her mind reeled and thrashed, drowning inside his. *No, no, no, no,* she chanted.

Calm down, Jon instructed, his cool voice echoing through her head. *I'm not keeping you prisoner. You're here of your own free will. Remember?*

Abby wanted to run full force in the opposite direction. She wanted to tear her mind away from his and return to the bench. That would certainly be the safest choice.

Instead, she forced her lungs to move with slow, deliberate inhales. Jon was right – she was not a prisoner here. He was a dominating and daunting force, but she wasn't without her own powers. She could roam his mind however she chose, which meant that he was as much at her mercy as she was at his.

Are you with me, Abigail?

The pleasure in his voice rattled every bone she possessed. *You know I am,* she replied, shoving her anxieties down to concentrate on what she could find.

Physically, Abby still sat on a freezing slat of wood with her eyes shut tight. But in her mind, she saw through Jonathan's eyes, moving steadily with him into the forest. The two of them were unquestionably joined into one single being, as if her whole body had entered his and now walked the crooked, brush-strewn path through the trees.

The images before her were sharp. Crisp. Clear. Undiluted by feelings. She could simultaneously visualize the bark on the trunks, hear the flutter of a bird's wings, and inspect the distant movements of Chuck and Holly. All of these things registered at once, without paying attention to any of them.

He feels, I think. That was how Jon once explained the difference between him and Nathaniel. Abby understood that now.

She was used to Nathaniel's mind. She was used to the auras of colors, the soft tones, the blurred edges stemming from Nathaniel's emotions. She was used to knowing how the world made him feel each and every moment.

But this was Jon's mind. His involvement with the world was immediate and critical – quick, even, efficient. He dissected his surroundings with an intent, keen eye. Without emotional hindrance of any kind.

Abby now saw the defining line that separated her two spirits. Through Nathaniel's eyes, the world was rich with color and feeling. Through Jonathan's eyes, everything was desolate.

She shifted her gaze to the bark on the trees, seeing each tiny imperfection and break in continuity, but she couldn't appreciate its disjointed beauty. She heard the bird's wings flutter, but she couldn't take delight in the grace of its flight. She watched the scene between Chuck and Holly unfold in the distance, but she couldn't feel the torrent of emotions flowing between them.

In this moment, Abby understood the world as Jonathan saw it: hollow, bitter, and cold. She almost felt sorry for him. Almost. But then she saw Nathaniel, and nothing else mattered.

She focused entirely on her angel's thick body as he paced back and forth beside the furious boy and the withered girl. Nathaniel's fists clenched at his sides while Chuck glowered and screamed at Holly. Abby's heart reached out to her spirit, desperate to be closer. Yet Jon meandered through the trees with painstakingly slow steps.

Hurry up, Abby urged.

What's the rush? he retorted, his voice banging through her head. *Are you looking forward to seeing Nate beaten as much as I am?*

She huffed at Jon's crass words while he continued moving at a snail's pace. *Why are you taking so long to get there?* she questioned.

When Jon didn't give her an answer, she realized it was obvious. He was giving her time to be inside his mind. He wanted her here.

Abby swallowed back the bile burning her throat. She fixated on the scene unfolding before them, coming closer and closer with each step Jon took.

"It was *you*, wasn't it?" Chuck barked, his body edging closer to Holly's.

"I don't know what you're t-talking about," Holly stammered, attempting to side-step his large, overbearing form. When her back hit a tree, she dug her heels into the dirt ground. Tears streamed from her eyes.

Chuck shoved his finger in her face. "You told Sondra about us! I always suspected it was you! And today I heard those girls in the hall say it!"

Nathaniel stepped up to Holly's side. He stood next to her, still and stoic. But Abby could see the twitching muscle of his clenched jaw and the fearsome glow of his determined eyes.

Holly shivered. "I swear I didn't! It wasn't me! Please, Chuck, please..."

"Shut up! You're just...just trash!"

Holly whimpered. "No..."

Chuck stepped closer, pushing his face into hers. "*What* did you say?"

She shook her head side to side, again and again.

"I told you to *shut up*."

Her body trembled and her eyes pleaded, but she didn't make a sound.

A sick smile slashed across his mouth. "So, you're deaf now, too? Stupid. Deaf. Piece of trash."

Chuck balled his fist and raised his hand. Holly cowered against the tree with her eyes pinched shut. He pulled back his arm and struck out, slamming hard into flesh.

"What the..." he gasped, staring at the larger hand holding his in place.

Nathaniel stood solid beside him, blocking his fist. Chuck's eyes bugged while he ogled the man who'd appeared out of nowhere. Nathaniel forced Chuck's arm back down to his side and disappeared.

Holly still stood shrunken and trembling against the tree. She opened one eye to look up at Chuck, who stared blankly at the empty space where Nathaniel had been. She took her opportunity, tearing her body away from the trunk. Holly broke into a full run, stumbling across fallen branches as she struggled to get out of the woods.

Her clumsy escape yanked Chuck from his stupor. "Come back here!" he hollered, whipping his head around and sprinting after her.

Before he could take two full steps, he ran into a solid wall of muscle.

"Hey!" Chuck yelled, bounced backward by his own momentum. He stared at Nathaniel with his mouth gaping. "Damn you, man! Where in the hell did you come from?"

Nathaniel stood his ground, his piercing eyes boring into the boy's. "Didn't anyone ever tell you how to treat a lady?" he asked, the calm of his voice betrayed by his deathly glare.

"You – you need to stay out of my business!" Chuck yelped. He puffed out his chest in a ludicrous display of dominance before stomping forward with his hand clenched.

Nathaniel didn't move away. He held entirely still when Chuck's fist slugged into his jaw, knocking his head to the side. Chuck grinned with the directness of the hit even as he steeled his body for retaliation.

Nathaniel drew his head slowly back to center. Blood oozed from the corner of his mouth. He swiped at it with the back of his hand, glancing down at the red smear on his skin, before lifting his eyes back to Chuck.

"You don't speak that way to a woman, and you certainly never touch her in anger," Nathaniel instructed as he stalked forward.

Chuck held his footing, waiting for Nathaniel to strike. He waited with his face scrunched and his teeth clenched. But Nathaniel only stood in front of him with a fiery, determined stare.

Abby watched Chuck's eyes brighten with the realization that his adversary wasn't going to retaliate. A wicked smile spread his lips when he landed his second punch, this one into Nathaniel's ribcage. She saw her angel suck in a swift gasp of air with the feral blow, but he still held his ground.

Chuck cackled in exhilaration. He struck out again. And again.

Abby stared in horror, unable to do anything, as Chuck pummeled her hero's body again and again. She reached out to him, desperate to help, but felt only the cool air skimming over the picnic table. She stuck her fingers in her ears, trying to block the vile sounds of flesh striking flesh, unable to bear the pained groans that pushed from Nathaniel's throat with every pounding hit. But she couldn't block anything she heard, because the noises didn't come from her ears. They came from Jon's mind, and she was forced to experience everything just as he did, violently crisp and clear.

Please, Jon, she begged. *Can't you do something?*

What would you like me to do, Abigail?

Anything. Anything at all.

Okay, he said, pausing before he shouted, *You can do it! Go get him!*

Abby whimpered. *Which one of them are you encouraging?*

Jon's easy laughter rumbled through her head.

Chuck hopped back and forth in front of his target now, gleefully aware that he was untouchable. He landed gouging blows into Nathaniel's face and sides, until Abby heard the distinct crack of breaking bones. Nathaniel hunched over in pain, barely able to draw breath.

When Chuck approached him again, he swung full force into Nathaniel's cracked ribs. But this time, her angel disappeared before contact. Chuck's momentum spun him around in a circle. He lost his balance and tumbled down on the forest floor.

Nathaniel reappeared in solid form behind the boy. He straightened to his full height without wincing at all. The blood on his face had vanished entirely.

Chuck pulled himself up from the dirt and turned around. He stared, dumbfounded and crazed, at the fully healed man standing in front of him. "H-how did you do that? How did you just disappear? Wh-what are you?"

Nathaniel advanced on the boy with his face drawn and his jaw fixed. "You will never touch another woman in anger as long as you live," he growled. "Do you *understand* what I'm saying to you?"

Chuck shuddered in fear, but didn't say a word. Nathaniel growled again, edging closer, his eyes darkened beyond anything she'd ever seen.

Look at that anger, Jon pointed out, as if Abby could miss it. *Now, that's the Nate I know. He doesn't look like Mr. Morality now, does he?*

Abby stared straight ahead, fixated on the man she loved, aware of just how different he appeared at this moment. His face was never so pulled, his body never so tense, his voice never so sinister. He moved relentlessly forward as Chuck cowered away. The boy staggered backwards until he tripped and fell onto the ground.

Nathaniel stood over him with eyes blazing. "Do – you – *understand*?"

Chuck barely managed to nod.

"If you ever do this again, there will be *hell* to pay," Nathaniel seethed. "I am *watching* you."

Abby felt the coldness of her angel's words and the insidious way they burned. Her mind grasped for images of the Nathaniel she knew – the man who always tried to save the world. She wanted to see him as everything kind and gentle and right.

Jon decided to disconnect from her then. He severed their connection as quickly and shockingly as he'd started it. The vision in front of her turned black. Abby's mind went entirely blank.

The deviant spirit reappeared on the picnic bench in front of her. "Well, that sucked," he said.

Abby blinked several times, working to reorient to her surroundings. "What...what are you talking about, Jon?"

"That basketball player. What a wimp. I mean, he's a pretty big guy. I thought he'd do more damage than a bloody lip and a couple of cracked ribs."

She gawked at him. In this moment, Jon was an absolute stranger. She couldn't believe she'd ever considered feeling sorry for him. And she couldn't believe she'd actually allowed her mind to join with his.

Her stomach knotted at the sight of the creature in front of her. Abby needed her angel with her now. *Nathaniel!* she screamed, desperate to see the peaceful, hopeful, loving person she knew.

Her angel appeared in an instant, sitting next to her on the bench. He transformed into solid warmth before she even had the chance to ask. He met her eyes with gentle assurance, his smile soft and handsome.

A tear fell down her face. Nathaniel cupped her cheek in his hand. "Abby? What's wrong?"

Jon sat opposite them, grinning wildly. "I let her watch," he answered.

Nathaniel's whole body went stiff. His head whipped around, his eyes pinning Jon's across the table. "You did *what*?"

"I. Let. Her. Watch."

Nathaniel's fist balled against his thigh. "Goddamnit," he cursed through gritted teeth. "You and I will deal with this later."

Jon chuckled in dark delight. "Eventually, I imagine."

Abby couldn't take this anymore. She'd witnessed all the acts of male bravado she could handle for one day. The only thing she cared about now was knowing that her angel was unharmed.

Reaching her unsteady hands to his face, she traced the straight line of Nathaniel's jaw and drew her fingers across his full lower lip. Chuck had hit him so hard that he'd drawn blood, but it was gone now. No lumps, no bruises, no scars or stains.

Nathaniel's earnest gaze drew back to hers. "Abby..."

"Are you hurt?" she asked, blinking back more tears.

He shook his head. "Not physically. But I didn't want you to see that."

Her hands still shook when they fell from his face to his chest. What she'd seen in the woods felt so much worse to her than Normandy. It was here and now, and she should be able to see broken bones and blood.

Abby unzipped Nathaniel's jacket, pushing it open to get to his shirt. She reached for his collar, struggling to undo the buttons, needing to see his bare chest. She didn't care about the freezing wind or the fact that Jon shot flaming arrows from his eyes. She needed to see her angel in the flesh, to make sure he was truly safe and sound.

"Good God," Jon scoffed at her. "That's completely unnecessary."

She doubled her efforts, popping open one shirt button after another.

"Yeah, I can't watch this," he announced before evaporating into thin air.

Abby barely noticed Jon's disappearance. She continued her task with frantic determination until she reached the last button. When she managed to get it undone, Nathaniel caught her hands in his.

"What are you doing, sweetheart?"

She peered up to his face, absorbing the tenderness in his eyes. She opened her mouth to reply, but was silenced when she saw movement in the distance. They both turned to watch Chuck run full force from the woods with a look of sheer horror on his face. He hurtled himself back toward school, barely keeping his feet underneath him.

Abby wanted to gloat at the sight of such a horrible man reduced to a simpering child, but she didn't have it in her right now. She refocused on Nathaniel's chest, grasping the sides of his shirt to spread them open wide. She stared in speechless astonishment at his bared flesh.

"Abby, you do realize you're undressing me on the picnic bench, right?"

She ignored the question. "I heard your bones break. I know I did."

"But I'm healed now. I promise."

His words weren't enough. Her hands flattened on his chest, the warmth of his skin shielding her from the frigid wind. With shaky skill, she explored from his neck to his collarbone, over his heart, across each of his ribs, and down to the tight flesh of his stomach. Not a scratch, a bruise, or a cut. Nathaniel was as perfect as always.

Abby's shoulders slumped in relief. She sank against him, pushing her hands underneath his shirt to wrap them around his back. She buried her face in his neck and breathed in deep.

Nathaniel's arms encircled her body, drawing her in closer. "You saw the whole thing, didn't you?"

"Yes," she admitted.

"Damn it, Jon."

"Don't be angry, please. It was my choice. I needed to see, to make sure you were okay." She raised her head to see Nathaniel's face. "I knew what would happen, but actually watching it was so different."

His eyes brimmed with sadness. "Did I frighten you?"

That was a loaded question. He'd definitely been frightening, but he was supposed to be. Chuck needed to be frightened. "I know why you did what you did. I also know you would never talk to me that way."

Nathaniel shook his head. "No, I wouldn't. That person you saw in the woods today – that's not who I am. At least, not anymore."

But he had it in him. Abby could see that. All his talk about how angry and emotional he'd been as a kid – it was still inside him. If he'd let his anger run free today, he could have snapped Chuck in two like one of the dried twigs lying on the ground. Yet Nathaniel had done nothing of the sort. If anything, he'd nearly allowed the reverse.

Abby could still envision the blood seeping from Nathaniel's mouth. She leaned her chest against his as she trailed slow, gentle kisses across his jaw. When she reached his lips, she hesitated. "Will it hurt if I kiss you, Nathaniel?"

He smiled softly. "Yes. But not in the way you're thinking."

Abby returned his smile before pressing her mouth to his. She kissed him carefully at first, but then much stronger, pulling at his bare back with needy hands. His lips smoothed across hers, his encasing arms creating a world just for the two of them. Abby knew she was safe here. Her angel would never hurt her. He would never hurt anyone.

She kissed him deeper, relieved when he didn't resist in the slightest. After several minutes, a shiver ran the length of his body. She pulled back, suddenly guilt-ridden about undressing him in this frigid wind. "I'm so sorry," she apologized as she looked to his bare chest. "You must be cold."

"I feel rather warm, actually. I suppose that has something to do with the company I keep."

"Still, I should probably button your shirt back up."

"If you must."

Abby's face heated while she refastened the buttons. When she finished, she smoothed his shirt down and pulled the edges of his coat in tight. "You're wearing the jacket I helped you pick out at the mall."

Nathaniel glanced down. "Yeah, I am. I didn't get blood on it, did I?"

She inspected the brown leather before meeting his eyes. "I don't think so. Are you really worried about your clothes?"

"I hate bloody clothes. And frankly, the rest of me heals quite easily."

Abby bit into her lip, nearly drawing her own blood. She wouldn't call anything she'd seen *easy*. "I'm not letting you go for the rest of the day," she told him, her arms turning to steel vices around his neck. "You're just going to have to carry me with you everywhere."

"Well, that might look a little funny when you head to class."

"I don't care. Everyone will have to deal with it. I need you in my arms."

Nathaniel sighed. "I really didn't want you to see what happened in the woods today. I don't want you to ever be afraid. Especially not of me."

"I'm not afraid of you. I'll never be afraid of you. But I hate seeing someone beat you like that. Because I know it hurts you, and because it reinforces the fact that I can lose you at any moment and there's nothing I can do about it."

He traced her face with his fingertips. "I'm sorry, sweetheart. I'm sorry for all of this."

"Please just don't leave. Stay here on this bench with me forever."

"But you have to get back to school now."

"No, I don't. I'm pretty sure the bell rang a while ago, so I've already missed most of my next class."

"That's why we need to go. Your life should stay as normal as possible."

Abby giggled at the preposterous thought. "Normal? Really?"

"Don't laugh. We'll study extra hard to make up for what you missed."

"Okay, fine. But I've already skipped most of this class, so just let me hold you until the next bell rings. Then I'll go back...grudgingly."

Nathaniel attempted to give her a stern look. A moment later, he broke into a lopsided smile. "Damn. It's wrong how much I enjoy giving in to you."

"Does that mean you'll come to my house tonight, too?"

"I thought your dad was staying home for Halloween."

"He is, but I asked if you could hand out candy with us, and he said it would be fine. You'll love seeing him in his costume. It's hysterical."

"That does sound fun."

"He also said you could join us for Thanksgiving dinner."

Nathaniel's body stilled. "I can come for Thanksgiving?"

"Yeah. If you want."

"My God, Abby. You have no idea what that would mean to me."

She did. She absolutely did. She fell back onto him, letting his arms cocoon her again, making the whole world slip away.

ABBY SWORE she couldn't breathe right for the rest of the day. Even though Nathaniel checked on her constantly during the last of her classes, the scene in the woods still played on a repetitive reel inside her mind. She just couldn't bear the pain he suffered at the hands of so many loathsome people.

All Abby could do to forge through class was to think about how silly her father would look in his costume tonight. She used that happy image to endure the end of the school day, the walk to her car, and the drive home. When she finally got to their house, her dad was still asleep. She thought he would already by awake, since he'd taken tonight off from work, but she figured he needed the extra rest to get over his cold.

With Nathaniel busy checking on Holly, Abby searched for a way to distract herself until the evening. She did her homework, straightened up the house, and poured Halloween candy into their big plastic witch's cauldron to set by the front door. She refused to waste another second thinking about Chuck or Jonathan or the things she'd witnessed in them today.

Eventually, Abby decided to make dinner. As she stood in the kitchen, preparing a giant pot of chicken and dumplings, her mind barraged her with forbidden questions. Now that Nathaniel had saved Holly, would he move on like he did after saving Maria? Would he follow Jonathan to their next destination, and involve himself in yet another life in need, continuing on as he always had? And would Abby's heart ever beat again if he did?

"God, stop thinking about it," she muttered to herself as she stirred the pot on the stove. "You probably don't want the answers, anyway."

The grandfather clock in the living room chimed once, refocusing her attention. It was 5:30, which meant the trick-or-treaters would start arriving soon. Abby strained her ears toward her father's bedroom, relaxing a bit when she heard him fumbling around inside. She sat down at the kitchen table, waiting patiently for him to emerge in costume. If she could just see him in his black helmet and cape, breathing laboriously, she would breathe easier.

Seconds later, Mark walked into the kitchen. He wore his work clothes.

"Hey, there," he said, reaching into the refrigerator.

"Hey, Dad."

He closed the fridge and popped open the can of soda he'd found. "I see you made dinner already. I'm not really hungry right now. I'll have leftovers when I come home in the morning, okay?"

Abby placed her hands purposefully on the tabletop. "What are you talking about? You're supposed to have off work tonight for Halloween. You're supposed to dress up and help pass out candy."

Mark rested back against the counter. "I'm not staying tonight, honey."

Her fingers clenched. "But you always stay for Halloween. You always dress up. You said this morning..."

"I know what I said. I'm sorry, but I'm not ready for that. Not this year."

Abby stared up at him with her eyes wide.

"Besides, you don't need me," he assured. "You've got Nathaniel coming over. He can keep you company. I'll be home in the morning. Have a good night, and tell Nathaniel I'll see him for Thanksgiving."

Mark took his drink and headed out of the kitchen. Abby stood from her chair to follow him into the living room. He exited through the front door without looking back at all.

Abby's heart sank to her feet. *Oh, God. This can't be happening.*

Halloween was supposed to be her one distraction – a moment of comfort in this bizarre world. She wanted to pretend for one single night that she was a normal girl with a normal boyfriend and a normal dad on a normal holiday.

The entire day crashed down around her then. An ocean of tears poured from her eyes as Abby collapsed on the couch. She fisted her fingers as she sobbed, wishing she had even the tiniest bit of control over anything.

"Get it together, get it together," she chastised, scrubbing her hands over her face, struggling to contain the flood. The doorbell rang, startling her for an instant only. Then she leapt up from the couch and hurled her body toward the door, praying her angel had come to save her from herself.

Before she could make it across the room, Nathaniel started singing from the other side. "Trick-or-treat, smell my feet, give me something..."

Abby yanked hard on the handle. The door swung open to reveal Nathaniel standing on her front porch. "...good to eat," he finished his song with a sweet, schoolboy grin. A second later, he took a good look at her, and his face fell.

"Oh, man," Nathaniel sighed. "Don't the kids sing that song anymore? I thought it was fairly standard for Halloween. Or is it my voice you don't like? I can't carry a tune in a bucket, can I?"

Abby laughed. Then she cried some more.

"Hey, hey, what's wrong?" he questioned as he stepped inside, reaching for her while kicking the door shut behind him. "Is my voice really that bad?"

She giggle-sobbed.

"What is it, Abby? Tell me, please."

She dropped her head onto his chest. "My dad, he – he went to work tonight. He said he couldn't dress up. He said he wasn't ready."

"Oh, sweetheart. I'm sorry." Nathaniel's arms banded around her back. "The holidays can be really difficult when you've lost someone. I'm sure he just needs time to heal."

"Yeah, I guess I should've known better. It was stupid to think he would be my Darth Dad this year."

"No, it wasn't stupid. It was hopeful."

Hope? Is there any of that anymore? For Dad? For Nathaniel? For me?

Abby's tears returned with a vengeance.

"Hey, shh, it's okay," Nathaniel consoled. He didn't seem to know what to do with her. In truth, she didn't know what to do with herself.

"Come here, let's sit on the couch," he instructed after several more dramatic sobbing moments. Abby swiped at her leaky eyes while they moved as one unit to her sofa, sinking into the cushions together. Nathaniel steadied her face in his hands, holding her anxious gaze with his solid one. "I know you're sad that your dad isn't here, but this is a lot of tears. Is there something else bothering you?"

"Yes," she confessed. "I just can't help it. Every time I close my eyes, I see you and Chuck in the woods. I see him hitting you over and over again."

Nathaniel exhaled. "I knew how much that would upset you. I'm sorry."

Abby shook her head. "It's my fault, totally my fault. You didn't want me to watch. You tried to save me from that, but I did it anyway. And now it's haunting me, because there's so much about it that doesn't make sense."

"Yeah? Like what?"

She blinked to clear her vision, trying her best to focus on his eyes. "Like I know why you do it, but why do you do it?"

Nathaniel's head tilted. "I'm not sure I understand the question."

Abby turned on the cushion to face him fully. "I mean, why do you put yourself in situations where you get beaten and broken like that? I understand helping out a girl in need, but why do you have to be hurt so badly?"

"Well, Chuck is a pretty strong guy."

"I know he is. But I saw you disappear after your ribs broke. He'd hit you so many times that you were in serious pain. Then you changed back into a spirit, and he just fell over."

"I changed back when I needed to heal."

"Yeah, I get that. But why didn't you disappear every time he tried to hit you? I know you could. If you wanted to, you could avoid all of that pain."

The light in Nathaniel's eyes dimmed. "You're right. I could avoid it."

Abby absorbed the guilt written across his face. A vision popped into her brain – of medieval monks flogging themselves, torturing their bodies to save their souls. She swallowed hard against the words in her throat, afraid to say them out loud. "So, you...you were punishing yourself. Weren't you?"

Nathaniel huffed out a laugh. He glanced to the floor for a moment before looking back to her. "You know, Abby, sometimes I'm truly amazed that you can see me. Because you see through me like no one else ever has."

She winced with his acknowledgement. "Then why? Why do you let those awful men beat you? Why do you punish yourself like that?"

He held her searching gaze without flinching. "For the same reason anyone punishes themselves. To atone for sins."

"You have sins?"

Nathaniel released his hold on her, backing away to the other end of the couch. He folded his fingers carefully together in his lap. "Yes," he said, looking down to his hands. "I definitely have sins to atone for. There are things in my past – things I've done that I've never told you about."

That truth made her whimper.

"I should tell you about them now," he continued, his shoulders crumpling inward. "Even if you never look at me the same way again, I still need to tell you how I..."

"Stop," Abby demanded. "God, just stop. I don't want to know."

Nathaniel looked to her in confusion. "But you need to know what I've done. It's not right for me to keep it from you any longer. I never should have kept it from you in the first place."

Abby shook her head as she studied him. Part of her actually did want to know what his sins were, since it might explain why he was doomed to live this half-life as a spirit. Another part of her didn't want to know about them at all, because she couldn't handle any more bad news today. But the biggest part of her simply didn't care, because she believed that the person sitting with her now had the purest soul in the whole world.

She scooted forward, closing the gap Nathaniel had placed between them. She covered his hands with hers and looked deep into his eyes. Abby didn't have to concentrate all that hard to see the pain within him. It was the same pain she'd seen the first time she'd looked this far inside. But now, she could also see his profound doubt and fear. He truly believed he could tell her something in this moment that would change the way she felt about him. He believed his sins were so great that he needed to suffer – to be beaten, stabbed, and burned – just to make up for them. But she only wanted her angel to see himself the way she did.

"I know you want to do right by me, Nathaniel. I know you want to give me complete honesty, but the truth is that I don't care about what happened in your past. It doesn't matter to me, because I know who you are, right here and now. You are the most amazing person. Your spirit is bright and strong and wonderful. You're a hero."

"I'm not, Abby. You're wro..."

"No. Don't tell me I'm wrong. Not this time. I saw what you did in those woods today. Whatever anger you felt in that moment was completely justified. You saved a girl. *Really* saved her. And who knows how many future

Chuck-girlfriends you also saved by scaring the pants off that toad. You're a hero and I won't listen to you say that you're not."

Nathaniel watched her, silent and pensive, for torturous seconds. Eventually, he sighed in defeat. Abby saw the remorse in his eyes, but she wouldn't budge. She eased her fingers onto his chest, taking a moment to relish the feel of his heartbeat, before slipping her hand up to his face. "Honestly, the only thing that concerns me right now is why you're still here."

"What do you mean?" he asked.

"I mean that you sacrificed yourself again today. You saved yet another innocent person. But you're still a spirit, aren't you?"

"Yes."

"Do you feel any different at all?"

"No. I don't."

Abby nodded, acknowledging the truth she'd accepted long ago. She straightened herself on the couch as she held his face in her hand. "Then maybe Holly isn't the person you're here to save. Maybe it's me."

"God, Abby. Please don't think that way."

"But listen. Just listen. If I'm really the one you're meant to save – if rescuing me is what you're supposed to do here – then when it's over, I hope you get your reward. I hope you go to heaven, or to some awesome tropical island where all the angels go to retire. I think you've earned it."

Nathaniel managed to smile. "I love that you think I deserve a heaven. And it does sound nice, but you know it's not what I want. Maybe if I do enough good while I'm a spirit, then I'll get to be solid permanently. Maybe I'll get to live my life again, and change, and grow old. Maybe I'll get to be with you and have everything I ever dreamed of."

A glimmer of hope flashed in his eyes. "That sounds perfect, Nathaniel."

"Yeah. It really does."

She returned his smile as bravely as she could. "Will you hold me now?"

"Always, sweetheart."

Abby crawled onto his lap and curled into a ball against his chest. Nathaniel's arms came around her like a shelter. She pinched her eyes shut and pressed her face into his neck.

Her body sank peacefully onto his, but her mind continued to reel. Nathaniel had tried to make her feel better by allowing her the hope of a real future between them, but Abby understood that he was already dead. No matter how much she wished otherwise, people simply didn't come back to life. When her angel finally saved her, his work here would be done. And when his work was done, he would move on forever.

That realization devastated her, but it wasn't a shock. She always knew she would have to let him go one day. As perfect as Nathaniel's body felt against hers right now, he was a spirit and she was alive and this could never be perfect.

Abby reached for the collar of his shirt, bunching the fabric in her fists. She felt his arms cradle her tighter, felt his fingers ease up and down her spine. Her mind wandered to her mother, wondering if she'd ever known this kind of blissful safety in the arms of the man she loved. And if she did, would she have changed anything that happened between them? If she'd been told on the day they met that he would eventually get sick, would she have forgone the happiness they shared in order to protect herself from the sickness that would eventually end it all?

Abby knew the answer to that. Her mother would have never chosen another life. Mom always said that Dad's illness was just like any other, and families got through sickness together.

A family is love, Abby, and love means taking everything as a whole – the joy and the pain, the smiles and the tears.

Abby shifted inside Nathaniel's arms so she could rest her cheek over his heart. It pulsed strong and steady beside her ear. She concentrated on the warm cocoon of his body, trying to hold onto this moment and keep it with her forever.

She understood how she had to look at Nathaniel's spirit life. He had an illness, so his time here was limited. But being sick didn't change who he was. It didn't change the sweetness of his heart, or make him any less kind or giving. Abby refused to regret a single moment they spent together, even though she would eventually have to let him go. She just needed to appreciate every second she had with her flesh-and-blood angel, knowing his final act would be one of heroism. Then he would find his perfect place, his place of peace, just as he deserved.

And all she could do was love him every moment of every day until.

Abby finally worked up the strength to raise her head from his chest and look him in the eyes. "Hey," she said.

"Hey," Nathaniel echoed. "You okay?"

"Yeah. Sorry about my crying fit. You must be pretty tired of them."

He wound his fingers into her hair. "Nothing you do will ever upset me."

"Not even if I soak through another one of your shirts?"

"I just have to remember to bring spares when I come over."

"Well, I can clear out a drawer in my room and you can keep a few here."

"That is a thought. But what if your dad ever found that drawer?"

"Hmm," she considered. "Yeah, scratch that. Bad idea."

Nathaniel smiled, but it didn't reach his eyes. "Are you really okay?"

Abby wanted to be brave, so she nodded. She remained right where she was, sitting on his lap, studying his face in order to commit every curve to memory. That is, until she heard the doorbell ring.

The chiming sound was accompanied by little giggles coming from the front porch. "Oh," she gasped, having almost forgotten that it was Halloween night. "I guess it's time to give out candy."

"Let me do it," Nathaniel offered, transferring her body carefully off his lap and onto the cushion beside him. As he stood to walk across the living room, Abby shifted in her seat. She leaned over the back of the couch to watch while he opened the door.

A little boy, no more than three years old, stood in her doorway dressed in a frog outfit. He held out a pumpkin-shaped basket with great expectation. "Twick-or-tweet," the tadpole said at his mother's urging.

Nathaniel grinned as he offered up Abby's cauldron of goodies. The boy grabbed a handful of candy, which amounted to two pieces, and shoved them inside his pumpkin.

"Say thank you," the mother instructed.

"Tank you," the boy parroted.

"You're welcome," Nathaniel replied, nodding to the point of bowing.

The little frog giggled with excitement as he waddled away.

Nathaniel closed the door behind the tadpole. He turned to Abby with bright eyes. Then he fell to the floor.

"Nathaniel!" she screamed, overtaken by utter panic the instant his thick body collapsed on the ground. She lunged over the back of the couch to find him, gripping onto the cushioned edge for balance. She barely kept herself from toppling over on her head, only to find him crouched down on all fours and smiling up at her.

"Holy hell!" she yelled. "You scared me to death! What are you doing?"

"Ribbit," Nathaniel replied.

"*What?*"

His playful expression turned serious. "Abby, did I ever tell you that I am a master impressionist?"

"Um, no."

"Well, I am," he insisted, just before he hopped on the carpet. "Ribbit."

Nathaniel hopped again. And again. And again.

Abby collapsed back on the sofa to watch her Viking-farmer-soldier-boxer spring around her living room, croaking and grinning. "Good Lord, Nathaniel. Are you really acting like a frog right now?"

"That would be a *master impressionist* frog," he amended.

The doorbell rang again and he hopped over, only standing to answer it. This time, Little Red Riding Hood greeted him. Red took her candy from the cauldron he offered and said thank you. When she left, Nathaniel closed the door and turned back to Abby.

Without saying a word, he ran into the kitchen. He returned a moment later with a red dish towel. He stuck it on his head, holding the ends under his chin like a bonnet, and batted his eyelashes. She burst out laughing.

"Oh, Abby, what big *eyes* you have," he squeaked.

"All the better to see you with," she replied.

"And Abby, what big *teeth* you have."

"You know, I will totally bite you. If that's what you're into."

Nathaniel laughed until the bonnet fell off. "You aren't supposed to distract me from my impressionistic feats. This is very hard work."

"Oh, I didn't realize," she offered with a grin. "I'm so sorry."

The bell chimed again. This time it was Superman. The dish towel became a cape. Nathaniel leapt with a bound.

Abby sat on the couch and watched him for well over an hour, while he ran around her house performing one impressionistic feat after another. She cackled hysterically when he danced and twirled after a tiny princess came to the door. She laughed until she snorted as he banged his fists on his chest like the hairy gorilla they met.

Toward the end of the night, a little ghost showed up on the front porch. Abby's breath caught as she wondered how Nathaniel would handle this particular impression. He gave the tiny boy in the holey sheet his candy, then closed the door and turned around. He stared at her for several seconds before he shrugged and said, "I got nothing."

By the time the last doorbell sounded, Abby smiled so hard that it hurt. She couldn't remember ever feeling so drained, joyful, and relaxed, all at the same time. And she would never understand how he could make her feel this happy after such a horrible day.

Nathaniel kept the door half-shut while he passed out candy to the last trick-or-treater. Abby couldn't see the costume, no matter how hard she craned her neck. When he closed the door, he pivoted toward her and grinned.

"Who was it?" she prodded, bouncing impatiently on the couch cushion.

Nathaniel walked over to the umbrella stand in the corner. He pulled out a huge golf umbrella and stuck it between his knees. Then he clip-clopped around the room, neighing and winking.

Abby sat, riveted to his every move. "Hmm. Are you a cowboy?"

He shook his head. The umbrella carried him to the kitchen and back. "Maybe Zorro?"

Nathaniel blew out a breath and shook his head again. "Clank, clank, clank," he chanted as he rode the umbrella back and forth behind the couch.

"Oh, wait. Are you a knight?"

He pulled to a halt and pumped his fist in the air. "Yes!"

"And the umbrella is your horse, then?"

"I believe the term is *trusty valiant steed*."

"My apologies. I obviously misspoke."

"Well, I guess I'll just have to forgive you," Nathaniel said, winking again.

Abby smiled up at him. "Since when do knights wink?"

"I thought it would make me look trustworthy."

"I don't know about trustworthy, but it sure makes you look cute."

"I'll take cute," he agreed, riding his makeshift steed to the couch before dismounting. He dropped the umbrella to the floor and collapsed down on the cushion beside her. "Wow. I am actually exhausted."

Abby tucked her legs up underneath her and scooted toward him. "I never thought I'd say this, Nathaniel, but you're just as silly as I am."

"Wow. That is the best compliment I've heard all day."

"Oh, really? Are you lacking in compliments? Do you need more?"

"I suppose *need* is a strong word. But from you? I could listen to your compliments forever."

"Okay, then. Where should I start?" she hemmed, not wanting to look ridiculous by listing a thousand things at once. "Well, you are a master of impressions, of course."

"Of course," Nathaniel echoed, the joy on his face making her heart skip.

"And you're the kindest person I've ever met," she continued. "And your hands are so strong and warm, and your voice is so clear and honest, and your smile is absolutely adorable, and I love you, and you have the most gorgeous eyes, and..."

All of his muscles tensed at once. "Wait a minute. What was that last one?"

Abby fidgeted with her fingers. "You have the most gorgeous eyes?"

"No. The one before that."

She tried her best to relax. "I...I love you."

Nathaniel closed his eyes for a long moment, barely moving at all. When he reopened them, he looked straight into her. "I love you, Abby."

"Please don't feel like you have to say it just because I did."

"Are you kidding me? Do you know how long I've waited to hear that? I was so afraid I'd freak you out if I said it first."

"Really?" She inched forward until her knees bumped into Nathaniel's leg. "How long have you felt this way?"

"Weeks and weeks," he said, grabbing her waist to pull her onto his lap.

Abby grinned as her thighs encased his hips. "Since when, exactly?"

"Since the moment I saw that pig ballerina in your jewelry box."

"Seriously? But we'd only been together a few days at that point. How could you already know you loved me?"

He shrugged. "If you haven't noticed, emotions are kind of my thing."

"Wow. I love that jewelry box. I love that pig ballerina."

"I love you, Abigail Luann Forrest."

"I love you, Nathaniel Olaf Dunnington."

"Can I tell you that is the first time I ever liked hearing my middle name?"

"Can I tell you I've never been happier than I am right now?"

Nathaniel leaned forward, pressing his lips to hers. "Let me stay tonight," he whispered against her mouth. "I don't want to be anywhere else. I don't want to think about anyone else. I just want to be with you."

"I take back what I just said. I've never been happier than I am right *now*."

He grabbed hold of her, clamping her onto his chest before standing and stomping down the hall toward her bedroom. Abby giggled uncontrollably, clinging to his body with all available limbs, bouncing up and down with every step until he crashed them both onto her mattress. His sudden, full weight on top of her was breathtaking in more ways than one.

Nathaniel kissed her a hundred more times, fast and furious. He teased her with tiny, ticklish nips across her neck and shoulders while uttering the occasional "ribbit" in her ear. Abby smiled with her whole body and held him as tight as she could.

Eventually, when his kisses changed from teasing to intent, she loved it even more. She loved the scent of his skin and the warmth of his lips moving over hers. She loved that he allowed her to remove his shirt without complaint and gave her all the time she desired to trace the lines of his chest. She loved knowing that despite the abuse he'd suffered today, his body was now healed beneath her hands.

In truth, Nathaniel wasn't just healed – he was perfect. She committed every last inch of his bared skin to memory. She memorized the sensation of his fingers gliding across her arm, over her ribcage, down her stomach and thigh, and onto to her calf. She memorized how it felt to have him hitch her knee up over his hip and hold it there, while his lips never left hers.

She wasn't sure why her clothes didn't spontaneously combust and burn off her body, but they didn't. Honestly, that was probably for the best. She remained fully clothed and he remained in control of his willpower, even while allowing her to touch him to her heart's content.

Nathaniel gave her all the physical reassurance he could without crossing his preset boundaries. And he told her he loved her, over and over, whispering the sweet words in the darkness of her room. Abby felt so safe and cherished that she couldn't bring herself to regret the moment he tucked her into the crook of his arm and settled them both down to sleep. She understood that he had to stop at some point, and she was far too happy to be difficult about it. Especially not now, when she loved him and he loved her and she knew there were people who never got the chance to feel this even once.

She took shallow breaths for long minutes, not wanting to disturb him as he fell asleep. She wanted to feel him resting contentedly in her arms while knowing for certain that he would stay beside her. Just for tonight, just for these moments, she wanted to feel like nothing could take him away. That thought allowed her to drift off to sleep with a permanent smile etched on her lips.

FOURTEEN

"Morning, sleepy head," Nathaniel whispered, smoothing his fingers across Abby's cheek.

"Mmm," she hummed. The sunshine covering her face created splashes of color behind her eyelids, although the feel of his solid body beside her was even more colorful. Purple. Lots of purple.

He shifted on her bed, his weight denting the mattress and pulling her closer. "I think your dad's home now. I should go."

Abby curled up against him, tucking her head into his shoulder. "It's certainly helpful that you can disappear at will. Much less explaining to do."

"Well, I wouldn't be able to stay all night otherwise, so I suppose this spirit-thing does have its benefits."

Her lips found the strong pulse on the side of his neck. She kissed him there, feeling his heartrate quicken. "Yes, it does. But it also has its restrictions, which is why all we're doing in my bed is sleeping."

Nathaniel buried his face in her hair to muffle his laughter. "Wow. Did you wake up with a one-track mind this morning?"

"How could I not? Lying beside you all night brings on quite the dreams."

"I wish I could have been there."

"Trust me, you were."

He placed a kiss on her temple. "You're in my dreams, too, you know."

Abby sighed with the scratchy feel of his morning scruff. "Am I really?"

"All the time," he assured, his lips skimming down her jaw.

"Hmm. Maybe we could share them sometime."

Nathaniel paused with his mouth against her neck. "What do you mean?"

"I mean that I'd love to share my dreams with you, mind-to-mind. I'd love for you to see what I imagine for us."

He stopped kissing her then. His forehead dropped onto her shoulder. "Abby, I...I don't think that's a good idea."

"Why not?"

"Because my dreams are overwhelming enough. If I had to deal with both of ours, I don't know if I could cope. I don't think you realize how difficult this restraint is for me."

She caught his earlobe in her teeth and nibbled. A shiver ran down his spine. "I don't know about that. Restraint seems altogether too easy for you."

Nathaniel raised his head. She felt his eyes drilling into her even before she dared to look up at him. Her heart flickered tenuously when she witnessed the raw emotion etched in his deep blue.

He grabbed her face in both hands, grounding her to him. "Tell me you're aware of how much I want you," he growled.

Abby froze in place beneath his immoral stare. The weight of his thick chest and the heat of his solid body robbed her of speech. Nathaniel wanted her. She wasn't sure she could comprehend just how much.

Minutes passed before she found her voice. "I-I'm aware," she stumbled.

His needy gaze dragged over her face for painful seconds, eventually settling firmly on her mouth. She lay mutely underneath him, mesmerized by the thought that he might actually give in to this, right here and now. She ran her hands over his back, urging him closer.

Nathaniel groaned with her silent encouragement. An instant later, he sucked in a harsh breath and shook his head. He placed a quick kiss to her lips before pulling his body away from hers to sit up at the edge of the bed.

Abby immediately wriggled over to sit beside him. "Thank you for staying with me last night," she said, not willing to lose him just yet.

"Thank you for letting me," he replied, staring out into the sunshine beyond her window. "Do you know what we should do this week?"

"What's that?"

Nathaniel turned to meet her expectant gaze. "We should decorate the apartment. Or rather, you should decorate the apartment."

"Seriously?"

"Seriously. Money's no object. You can buy whatever you like for it. You can make it a perfect place."

Abby bounced against her mattress. "And you'll come with me? We can spend lots of time together?"

"Of course. I want to check on a few people, but otherwise, I'm all yours."

"All mine? Wow. I like the sound of that."

Nathaniel smiled as he leaned in. "I'll see you later, sweetheart."

She nodded just before he kissed her. She breathed him into her lungs when the kiss ended. She kept her eyes closed while he disappeared.

The instant Abby sat alone on her bed, she folded her knees up to her chest and wrapped her arms around her legs. She could still smell him. She could still feel the warmth of his body on her sheets. It simply wasn't fair that he could be here one second and gone the next.

She tucked her chin to her chest, cocooning herself further into a ball. Yesterday had been overwhelming, to say the least, and she wasn't ready to face the morning. Last night, she'd accepted the fact that she would have to let Nathaniel go one day. But that didn't mean she had to like it. She could fight. She could do everything in her power to make sure that day was far, far away.

Abby raised her head to look up at her ceiling. The way she saw it, there were two things that could take her angel away from her. The first, sadly, was herself. If Nathaniel was here to save her, and saving her meant he could finally move on, then she had to make sure she didn't need saving. This would involve keeping a close eye on her dad. She would make sure Mark's pills were always swallowed – make sure he was well-fed and the house well-kept – make sure he felt like a cherished father – make sure he had no bullets.

Honestly, all of that was the easy part. It was the second thing that made her gut roil. Abby didn't want to think about it, but she didn't have a choice. In order to make sure she had every moment she could with her angel, she would have to deal with the one creature who had the most potential to take him away: Jonathan.

She heaved a sigh as she stared at the ceiling. Jon had told her that Nathaniel would always follow him, and for all she knew, Jon could walk away from here tomorrow. What would Nathaniel do then? Maybe he would try to stay. Maybe he would try like hell to divide himself between her world and Jon's new one, wherever that may be. But even if Nathaniel found some way to split his attentions, she understood that he would never be able to let Jonathan go for good.

Abby understood something else, too: Jon wanted her. She didn't know why, exactly. Nathaniel probably summed it up best when he said that Jon wanted what he couldn't have. But what part of her was that? As far as she was concerned, she wasn't available in any way, shape, or form. Everything belonged to Nathaniel. Especially her heart.

Her heart. Abby huffed quietly in the silent room. Her heart would be the one thing Jon cared nothing about. After all, it wasn't like he journeyed through his afterlife trying to get women to fall in love with him. Getting women to fall in *lust* with him was more like it. But he couldn't fool her. She saw his blackened eyes and felt his freezing spirit. She knew how horribly his solid flesh burned when he touched her.

So, what part of her did Jon want? If she asked him to stay, would he? Would he allow Nathaniel to remain here if she made a simple request? She certainly hoped he would. But with Jon, she doubted anything was that easy.

Abby squeezed tighter to her legs, remembering how safe and warm it felt to have Nathaniel's arms around her through the night. She would do anything to feel that love for as long as humanly possible. She would do anything in her power to keep her angel with her. Even if it meant looking into Jon's churning, oil-slick eyes and begging him to stay.

Abby shuddered at the thought, even though she knew she had to go through with it. "You need to get up now," she demanded, uncurling her legs and forcing her feet to the floor. "You've got a lot to do today."

Dragging herself off the bed, she yanked on her clothes while mentally preparing for the day's challenges. Taking care of her father should be fairly simple. Taking care of Jonathan would be another matter entirely.

She ran a brush through her hair before she left her room, wandering out into the hallway in search of her father. She didn't find him until she walked into the kitchen. Mark stood by the sink, holding a cup of water. He looked to her with tired, bleary eyes.

"Hey, Abby."

"Hey, Dad," she replied, moving immediately forward. She threw her arms around his neck and gave him her best hug.

He hugged her back. "Hmm. What's this for?"

Abby smiled as she pulled away. "I missed you last night," she said while reaching into the pill cabinet. "I always enjoy spending Halloween with you."

"I'm sorry about that, honey." He took his pills from her hand and swallowed them, showing her his empty mouth. "Didn't Nathaniel come over?"

"He did, but I still missed you. Also, he didn't get to see your Darth Vader costume. But we'll get to have Thanksgiving together, right?"

Mark nodded. "Sure. Thanksgiving will be good."

"Oh, I'm going to cook like a fiend. It'll be stupendous. I promise."

"You do everything perfect, Abby. You're the best."

She patted his arm before stepping away. "You sleep well, Dad. You need to get that cold all better. I'll fix you a nice dinner tonight, okay?"

"Okay. Have a good day at school."

"Thanks," she said, taking one last look into his eyes. They were calm, even, and still. Abby grabbed her backpack, walked through the living room, pulled on her jacket, and left through the front door.

The first day of November hit her with a blast of cold air. She jogged the few paces to her car and huddled into the driver's seat, cranking the heat up as soon as she turned on the engine. She sat in her driveway, waiting for the air to warm, concentrating on steadying her breaths.

Her father was okay. Abby could tell by the clarity of his eyes and the easy stance of his body. For today, all was well with him, which meant that she had her first problem under control. Now, she just needed to deal with her second problem. Her grotesquely huge problem. Her ungodly attractive problem.

With the heater in her car working at full strength, she gripped the steering wheel and backed out of the driveway. She grimaced as her car crept down the street, dreading the next thought in her mind.

Jonathan, can you please come here?

He appeared in the blink of an eye, lounging in her passenger seat like he'd been there all along. "Good morning, Abigail."

She flinched when his arctic air crashed over her. "My God, Jon. How do you do that?"

"Do what?"

"Show up so fast?"

"Well, I've been in your mind and you've been in mine. That gives us an unusually strong connection."

Abby glanced out of her side window, trying not to let his words get under her skin. "I'm sure you've had a strong connection with lots of women."

"No, actually, I haven't. No one else has ever known that I'm a ghost. No one else has shared the thoughts in my mind. It's just you."

She stopped at a red light and chewed on her lip.

Jon cleared his throat. "To what do I owe the pleasure of your summons?"

Abby shifted in her seat. "I just...I want to ask you a favor."

"Really? How interesting."

"Why is that interesting?"

"Because I was under the distinct impression that you wanted nothing to do with me."

She considered denying that statement, but what would be the point? It's not like she could lie to someone who could read her thoughts. She only wished she could read his thoughts, too. And she really wished that honking noise would stop.

"Abby, the light has been green for a while now."

"Oh. I guess it has." She accelerated, waving apologetically to the car behind her. "I suppose I'm a little distracted."

"You're also the slowest teenage driver in history," Jon noted. "What has you so distracted this morning?"

"Well, as you know, the problem with Chuck and Holly is over now."

"Did you not want it to be?"

"Yes, of course. I'm glad she's safe. But I figure it means you'll leave now."

"Why would you think that?"

Abby risked peering over at Jon, which was a terrible decision. His black eyes moved relentlessly, swirling like molten tar in milk-white pools. She turned back to the windshield, shivering despite her overworked heater.

"Isn't that what you do?" she questioned. "Don't you wait around to watch Nathaniel get beat up by someone, just to move on to another school afterwards and start all over again?"

Jon's sparkling laughter filled her car. "I do enjoy it when he gets beaten."

His callous words flipped a switch in her brain. "Damn it, Jon! This isn't just some eternal game you two are playing!"

"It's not?"

"No! Nathaniel is actually doing things for people, and you're just...just..."

"Just what?"

"Just being you! You're watching it all happen, and not doing anything except...except..."

"Except what?"

"Except wooing everything!"

"I think you mean every*one*."

"So, you admit it? You admit that you're only here to get girls in bed?"

"Does it really matter what I admit to and what I don't? You're already my judge, jury, and executioner."

Abby scoffed at his accusation, gluing her eyes to the road ahead.

Jon chuckled in her defiant silence. "So, then. Did you ask me here to lecture me? Is that the favor you wanted?"

"No," she grumbled, angry that he'd gotten her so rattled. She'd planned to act much nicer around him today, pulling out all the polite stops in order to lull him into agreeing to her request. But she'd already yelled at him now, so she figured she should just go ahead and ask. "The favor I want is your presence, Jon. I want you to promise you'll stay here in Charlottesville."

"You desire my presence?" he reiterated, angling his body toward hers. "I would have to say that is a surprising request, based on everything previously stated. Why on earth do you want me to stay?"

Abby stared out of her windshield. "Because I want Nathaniel to stay."

Jon fell silent. A surge of his freezing air blasted across the scant space between them. "I see. You're worried that if I leave, he'll follow me."

"Well, you did basically tell me that. Remember?"

"Yes, I remember."

Abby gritted her teeth. "Then will you stay?"

"Hmm," he considered while his fingers drummed against his thigh. "That depends, I suppose. What will you give me if I do?"

"What do you mean?"

"Come on, now. You're young, but not that young. You know you can't get something for nothing in this world. What will you give me in return?"

Oh, hell. I should have seen this coming. "Wh-what do you want?"

Jon didn't hesitate. "I want you to tell me about your mother and father. I want you to actually confide in me, so I don't have to pull it out of your head."

Abby's brow quirked. "Why do you care about my mother and father?"

"Because I want to show you that I can be your friend."

Those words rang like a death toll through her car. Abby felt his eyes on her even though she refused to look at him. She coughed against the constriction in her throat. *Friend.* Jonathan Fitzhugh wanted to be her *friend.*

"It won't be so bad," he assured, his voice now soft and lulling. "There can be many benefits to my friendship..."

"Stop right there," Abby commanded. "I don't want to hear about these supposed benefits. This is going to be hard enough as it is."

Jon shrugged. "Well, don't put yourself out on my account. I mean, we can just forget about the whole thing. Then I'll be on my way to the next school before you know it."

"Good God. Okay. Fine. What do you want to know?"

"Everything," he stated, staring her down from his seat. "Start with your childhood. I want to know the story of your family. Especially your father."

Abby's head shook before she even realized it. Her entire body revolted at the thought of confiding in Jon. She had no idea why he wanted this from her, but she was certain it couldn't be for any concerned or compassionate reason.

Can I refuse him? she considered, wishing it could be that simple. But refusing his request wouldn't get him to stay here. Besides, it really didn't matter if she decided to tell him or not, since he could extract the information from her mind whenever he desired. The only difference about this situation was that she would actually have to say the words out loud.

Abby drove up to the next corner and took a turn down an unnecessary street, prolonging her journey to school. If she was going to tell her life's story to Jon, she would need time, the distraction of driving, and an excuse to not look him in the eyes. She took a steep breath, reminding herself that she was doing all of this for her angel.

While her car rolled past rows of quaint suburban homes, Abby started talking. This wasn't like telling Julie. Julie had always been a true friend and had even lived through some of it with her. This wasn't like telling Nathaniel, either. After all, he actually cared about her. This was more like laying herself bare before an enemy and praying that they wouldn't stab an open wound.

As Abby confessed her family's secrets one by one, Jonathan pummeled her with questions. Every sickness of her father's, every hospitalization, every suicide attempt, every time she helped her drunken mother to bed after she'd passed out on the toilet – Abby answered each grotesque query as truthfully as she could. Honestly, the images were already in her mind and she knew she couldn't hide them. Her thoughts cascaded in a torrential stream until her whole sticky mess of a life was splayed out in front of him. She ended on the best note of all: her mother's untimely and questionable death.

"So, you think your mother may have committed suicide," Jon concluded.

"Yes," she admitted. "It's a possibility."

"I see. The other possibility is that your father murdered her."

Abby's stomach clenched as she finally turned onto the street in front of her school. She was terribly late, and the parking lot was empty of students. She pulled into the farthest space from the front door, turned off the engine, and stared at the keys in her hand. "Wow, Jon. Did anyone ever tell you that you have a way with words?"

"What do you mean?"

She raised her head to look into his churning eyes. "I mean that saying *murdered* is pretty harsh. This is my mother and father we're talking about. I love my father. Did it ever occur to you that I don't want to hear that word?"

Abby stared straight at him, awaiting a response. For whatever reason, Jon chose this moment to transform himself into a human. His suddenly solid body sent waves of heat crashing over her. His eyes shined bright and clear and disastrously perfect.

"I'm sorry if I offended you," he said, believably enough to be sincere. "I just figured, since you were already thinking it, that you wouldn't mind it being verbalized."

Abby observed him as he spoke. Under any other circumstance, in any other place in the world, she would have been amazed that such a beautiful creature was trying to get to know her. But this was Jonathan. She'd been in his mind. She knew all about that cold, hard, emotional void. He wasn't trying to know her. He was studying her. Like an insect under a microscope.

She fisted her keys. "Tell me something, Jon."

"Anything, little ladybug."

Abby shook her head. He hadn't missed the insect thought. She wasn't sure why she even bothered to speak out loud. "I'm just curious...do you even have feelings?"

"Of course. I feel irritated all the time."

"Irritation is not an emotion."

"It's not? You could have fooled me."

"No, actually," she sighed. "I don't think I could fool you."

Jon smiled as he watched her. "You are an intelligent thing, aren't you?"

His compliment brought an unwanted flush of heat to her cheeks. Abby silently chastised herself, knowing she shouldn't care what Jon thought about her mind. Or any other part of her.

"Are you done grilling me now?" she spit out. In truth, she couldn't believe he'd made her share so many horrible memories with him today. It was basically emotional blackmail.

"I didn't blackmail you, Abigail. We're friends now. Friends get to know each other."

"*Friends*," she repeated, trying to get used to the idea. "Okay, then. If you and I are going to talk like friends, then I want you to tell me about you..."

"What about me?" he cut in with a dastardly, stunning grin.

"I want you to tell me about you *and Nathaniel*," she finished.

Jon's grin fell. "Oh. You only want to know about him."

"Yes, I want to know about him. When did the two of you first meet, spirit-to-spirit?"

"Hell, I don't know. I think it was Kansas. Somewhere back in the 1980s."

"When he saved Maria?"

"Who?"

"Maria. You know, the girl with the abusive father? The first person Nathaniel ever saved, during the first time he ever turned solid?"

Jon shrugged. "Sure. I guess it was around then."

"You guess? Did you not know that he saved her?"

"Yeah, he mentioned it. But what I really remember is when he told me how her father beat the living crap out of him. He said the man was like a boxer, pummeling him over and over until he was nearly dead again. I made sure to never miss another one of his encounters after that."

"Good Lord, Jon. I can't believe you don't remember poor Maria, but you do remember Nathaniel getting beaten up by her dad."

"Well, her dad was interesting. I would've enjoyed examining *his* mind."

Abby ogled the creature sitting beside her. "How can you say that? How can you actually find that monster interesting?"

A slow, deviant smile spread across Jon's lips. "You know, a thing does not have to be good to be interesting. In fact, I find some of the most interesting things on earth are quite bad. Don't you agree?"

"Um, *no*. I definitely do not agree."

"That's just your age talking."

"Yeah, well, I don't think getting old means getting jaded and crotchety."

His brow rose. "Are you calling me jaded and crotchety?"

"Yes. I am. Even though you're not all that much older than me."

"Correction – I don't *look* that much older than you. But if we're going by birthdates, I'm actually much, much older. Although I don't think that means we can't be friends."

Abby shivered with that word. *Friends*. God, how did she get here?

"Shall we shake on it?" Jon asked.

She looked into his perilously chocolate eyes. "Shake on what?"

"On this new pact of ours? To be friends?"

Jon held his hand out to her. A swirl of flaming heat accompanied it, stealing across the tiny space between them, reminding her of how uncomfortable his touch felt on multiple levels. He may as well be offering her a red-hot branding iron, straight from a firepit, and asking her to cradle it like a baby.

He chuckled at her thoughts. "Get a hold of yourself. It's only a hand."

Abby's jaw clenched tight as she flexed her fingers. Slowly, with goose bumps crawling across her flesh like spiders, she moved her arm toward his. The instant she came close enough, Jon clasped their hands together. He wrapped his fingers fully around her wrist.

Her skin caught fire. Invisible flames rippled over her palm and seared up her arm. Abby cried out in desperation, yanking her hand back to wrench herself free of his grasp.

Jonathan studied her as she rubbed her wrist to soothe the lingering pain. "You really don't like it when I touch you, do you?"

It feels like a lightning bolt tore through me, she thought, although she didn't say the words out loud. She couldn't admit such a thing, even to him. She didn't think anyone should have to hear that they were untouchable.

Jon continued examining her for silent moments. She expected him to be upset by the musings in her head, yet his deep brown eyes sparkled with confidence. "Based on my past relationships, Abigail, I can assure you that being touched by me can be quite a pleasurable experience."

His words caused an unwelcome shiver to course down her spine. "And these past relationships would be with the living girls you've seduced whenever you've had a whim to be solid?"

"You make it sound as if I've done something wrong."

"Can't you see that it was wrong, Jon? Don't you think it bothered those girls that you seduced them and then disappeared without a trace?"

"They were bothered, all right. But not in any bad way. I'm very skillful with the bothering part."

"Ugh. I don't want to hear about that," she insisted, imagining how privileged those girls must have felt with such a gorgeous specimen fawning all over them. She imagined the charms Jon wielded for their momentary benefit, feeling sickened by the liberties he took.

"Oh, and Nate is taking no liberties with you?"

Abby held up her hand. "Nope. Do not go there. My relationship with Nathaniel is not open for discussion. If you and I are going to be friends, that is a basic ground rule."

Jon smiled. Far too quickly. "Okay, then. I'm glad you and I are going to be friends. It'll be a new experience for me."

"Why is that?"

"Because I've never tried being friends with a girl before."

Abby cringed with his admission. There it was: verification that she was an experiment. She was merely an insect under his microscope.

Jon chuckled. "I guess I will call you my little ladybug, then."

"Please don't," she groaned.

"Why not? Don't friends give each other pet names? I believe that's common practice."

"Well, maybe I'm not going to be very good at this friend thing. You may want to reconsider," she said, even though the idea caused instant panic. *I just need you to stay in Charlottesville. Please.*

"Don't worry about it, Abigail. Even if you're a bad friend, I'll still stay."

"You will?"

"Yes."

"Why?"

"Because there are other things here that interest me."

With that announcement, Jon gave her the most scandalous grin she'd ever seen. A second later, he disappeared without any warning at all.

She blinked as she stared at the empty seat beside her. Did she want to know what Jon found interesting here? Probably not. She only wanted a single moment of peace, restful in the knowledge that she'd accomplished her goal. Jon would stay, which meant that Nathaniel would stay, too.

Abby pulled herself from her car and trudged across the parking lot. She attempted to only think of her angel, but her mind betrayed her. She couldn't wrap her head around the fact that Jon wanted to know so much about her life. Something would come of this new friendship of theirs. There would definitely be consequences. She just didn't know what they were yet.

As she stepped through the front door of school, the bell rang to signal the end of first period. She attempted to blend in with the crowd of shuffling bodies in the hallway, although she felt more singled out than ever before. Could anyone tell she'd just made a deal with the devil?

"Hey, Abby, what's going on?"

Sondra's cheery voice surprised her. Abby jumped sideways, bumping into a random, innocent person. "Sorry," she apologized to the offended sophomore before turning back to Sondra. "What do you mean?"

"Wow, you're jumpy. I just meant hey, what's going on?"

"Nothing's going on. Just school. Being in school."

"Oh...kay."

Abby forced a smile. "So, how are you?"

Sondra shrugged. "I didn't sleep very well last night. Brett and I went to a slasher film for Halloween, and I had bad dreams. What'd you do last night?"

"Just stayed at home and gave out candy to the kids."

"Cool. You sitting with us at lunch today? It's like twenty degrees out."

"Yeah, no picnic bench today."

"I'm glad." Sondra smiled and Abby returned it, joining her to walk through the halls together, still somewhat amazed that she'd found a new friend this year. Correction: she'd found several friends. Nathaniel. Sondra. And now, Jonathan.

Abby gripped hard to the handle of her backpack. Maybe the cafeteria wouldn't be so bad today. After all, Jon couldn't show up there uninvited. At least, not in the flesh.

"Hey, Abby," a voice called, pulling her from her thoughts.

She looked over to see Eric standing by his locker. "Hey," she replied.

The "twins" Jason and Randy stood beside Eric. They glanced at her before looking away to talk to each other. Abby knew these boys wouldn't get their time in the woods at lunch today, any more than she would get her time on her bench.

Eric smiled at her as she passed by. "See you in English."

Abby nodded. "Yeah. See you then."

As soon as they were out of his earshot, Sondra turned to her. "Do you like Eric Nichols? I mean, do you *like him* like him?"

"Oh, well. He's nice, but no. Why do you ask?"

"Because I think he likes you."

Abby shook her head. "He's just being friendly. We have a lot of classes together." *And he's seen me spasm like a freak more times than I can count.*

"Sure," Sondra said with a knowing smile. "That must be all it is."

Abby glanced behind her shoulder. Eric still watched her as she walked away. She turned back around, tucking her chin to her chest while she moved toward class.

ABBY SHIFTED the purple pillow with embroidered white flowers a little to the left. She stood back from the ivory couch and studied the pillow's placement. She moved it an inch back to the right. "There," she said aloud, even though she was alone in Nathaniel's living room.

She looked around his apartment, surveying all of the items she'd chosen. Only a few weeks had passed since he'd invited her to decorate this place, but she'd made it fairly presentable. The eat-in kitchen had an oak table set with square purple dishes and complementary lavender glasses. The bedroom held cherry furniture and the queen-size bed looked fluffy and inviting, with a steel gray comforter over ocean blue sheets that matched Nathaniel's eyes. About thirty different rubber ducky decorations swam around in his bathroom, because she knew it was important to be cheerful when getting ready in the morning and nothing said happy quite like bright yellow ducks with neon orange beaks.

The hardest part of the decorating process had been picking out his living room furniture, even though she'd enjoyed visiting several stores with her angel beside her. She'd finally decided on an overstuffed ivory couch and loveseat. His entertainment center held a flat-screen TV and the best electronics she could get her hands on. She'd even started his movie collection with a few of her favorites.

Abby loved everything she'd chosen for this place, although the curio that stood in the corner of the room was her favorite by far. She walked over to the curio, crouching down in front to gaze through the glass at the illuminated shelves holding the figurines she'd collected. A pewter frog, a porcelain Little Red Riding Hood, a plastic Superman, a pink princess with glass slippers, and a metal knight in shining armor all sat side by side. More trinkets filled the second shelf: a little glass sculpture shaped like a crystal ball, an artfully painted ceramic pizza slice, a single red porcelain rose, and a Captain Kirk bobble head.

She smiled as she stood, knowing her touches were all over this apartment. This was their home, Nathaniel's and hers. At least, that's what Abby liked to pretend.

Shopping with him over these past weeks had been wildly fun. Nathaniel spent countless hours succumbing to her every decorating whim, yet still managed to keep tabs on her fellow students and her father. He was checking on her dad this very moment, in fact. Mark normally spent Sundays like this one hanging around the house while she went to the mall with Julie, but Abby still worried about him. Probably because she could hardly accept how well everything was going right now.

"Enjoy this moment," she told herself. "Things are good."

In truth, things were more than good. The people at school were doing very well. Abby had grown to love her lunches with Sondra and Brett, and she never felt like a third wheel, since Brett was funny and could name all the *Star Trek* movies in order. Abby was happy to see that Holly now steered clear of her ex-boyfriend, ever since the forest incident. And Chuck was currently single and apparently not looking for a new girlfriend, probably for the first time since his infancy.

Even Jonathan was currently behaving himself. Abby hadn't had any run-ins with him since the day they'd agreed to be friends. He smiled at her a lot in the halls at school, but she couldn't ask him to stop doing that. He just hung around like a pretty picture on a wall – something she saw so often that it didn't occur to her to think it was unusual. For now, she was perfectly happy with that arrangement.

"Is everything to your liking?"

Hearing a voice in the empty apartment should have scared the crap out of her, but it was Nathaniel's voice. She turned to face him as he materialized in the center of the living room. He was everything an angel should be – bright, serene, and stunningly beautiful.

"You're to my liking," she answered.

His glowing eyes sparked even brighter. "Thank goodness for that."

She took a step closer. "How's my dad looking today?"

"Fine. Calm. No problems."

"I appreciate you checking. Are you still coming over for Thanksgiving dinner on Thursday?"

"I wouldn't miss it."

Abby watched his eyes deepen as he transformed into a solid being. He closed the distance between them and slid his fingers up the side of her face. She leaned into the warmth of his hand, turning to instant mush, like one-minute oatmeal. "You feel amazing, Nathaniel."

"So do you."

"Mmm. But tell me honestly – are you dreading today's mall adventure?"

He chuckled. "I think I can handle Julie and Peter for one meal."

"And a movie. Don't forget the movie."

"I'm not. I promise."

Abby smiled despite her apprehension about their plans. Julie had hounded her relentlessly for a double date until she finally caved in and asked Nathaniel. He was gentlemanly when he accepted, although he'd never met Julie's boyfriend before. Peter was a seventeen-year-old skater dude. Abby didn't know what he and Nathaniel could possibly have in common.

"I really appreciate you coming," she thanked him for the millionth time.

"I think it'll be fun. I don't often get to act like a normal teenager."

"Well, don't act too normal. I like you just the way you are."

A smile lit Nathaniel's face. "And what about the apartment? Do you like it just the way it is?"

"Of course."

"Good, because I have a gift for you." He pulled a small box out of the pocket of his jeans, smoothing over the lid before he held it out to her.

"Ooh. What's in it?"

"Open it and see."

Abby grabbed the box and tore off the lid. Her fingers delved inside, pulling out a tiny metal chain holding a single key along with a charm.

"It's the key to the apartment," Nathaniel explained. "*Your* apartment."

Her brow creased. "My apartment?"

"Yes. I added your name to the lease and paid it up for the next six years. I figure that will get you through college. After that, you can stay here or move on to something else. I mean, I don't actually expect you to live here. I just want you to have a place to go that's always safe, no matter what."

"My apartment," Abby echoed, unable to hide the sadness in her voice.

Nathaniel hesitated. "Are you unhappy? I thought you liked it here."

"I do like it. I love it. With *you*. Because of *you*."

"But I'm right here with you."

"Yes, for now." She stared down at the key in her hand. "But this feels...I don't know. It feels like you're saying goodbye."

Nathaniel grabbed her by the arms, pulling her body onto his. "I'm never saying goodbye. Not if I can help it. I love you, Abby. I just want to give you something solid and grounded, something you can see and touch. You've been so unbelievable to put your faith in me and I want you to have a place where you can know that this is real – that *we* are real."

She wrapped her arms around his back and rested her head on his shoulder. She belonged here. Always. "*Our* apartment," she corrected.

"Yes, ma'am," he said with a laugh. "Our apartment."

Nathaniel eased back, looking to her eyes before leaning down. He touched his lips to hers in soft, heavenly reassurance. Abby arched up on her tiptoes, eager to return the kiss, but he pulled away before she had the chance. She couldn't help frowning with his retreat.

He ran his thumb over her pouted lip. "Aren't we supposed to be somewhere?" he reminded.

"Oh, right," she conceded, knowing they couldn't stay in this apartment together forever, even if that did sound like the best idea ever. When Nathaniel released her, Abby held her new keychain up to dangle in the light. "Look at that. There's a pig charm on here."

"Yeah. It reminded me of the ballerina in your jewelry box."

"Hmm. I think I'll name her Mrs. Petunia Piggles the Second."

"That is perfect. Just like the apartment. Just like you. Now come on," he encouraged, lacing their fingers together. "We have friends to see."

Abby toddled along beside him as his compliments soaked into her skin. He guided her through the living room to the small hallway that led to their front door. As they approached, the doorbell rang.

Nathaniel stopped cold. "That's odd. Are you expecting someone?"

"No," Abby answered. "I haven't given this address out to anyone."

His eyes narrowed as he stepped forward. He grasped the handle and pulled the door open. Jonathan stood in the doorway, wearing his usual black leather jacket and cocky smirk.

"Hey there, you two," Jon greeted.

Neither of them responded.

"What?" he questioned, looking past Nathaniel to focus on her. "Aren't you going to invite me in to see the new place? I am a *friend*, after all."

Abby cringed when he used the "F" word. *Nothing like a little blackmail on a Sunday afternoon.* "Come in, Jonathan," she offered. "See the new place."

"Why, thank you, Abigail." Jon stepped across the threshold, punching Nathaniel in the arm when he walked by. "How ya doin' there, old pal?"

Abby saw Nathaniel's bicep flex as she turned toward their guest.

Jon's chocolate eyes scanned the kitchen and living room before darting down the hall to the bedroom. "So, is this where the magic happens?"

"*Jon*," Nathaniel growled in warning.

Abby shifted on her feet. "What are you doing here, Jon?"

"Oh, I just wanted to see where you two are playing house."

"Damn it," she grumbled. "I am not playing house."

Jon laughed. *Yes, you are. And you know it.*

His cool voice echoed in her mind. Okay, maybe she was playing house. A little. Or a lot.

"Anyway," he continued. "I brought a gift." He held out his hand, presenting her with a small leafy green plant. "It's for your playhouse. It's a playhouse-warming gift."

"It's wonderful," Nathaniel spoke through clenched teeth, extracting the offering from Jon's grip and walking it into the kitchen.

Jon turned to Abby the moment they were semi-alone. "It's a plant."

"Yes," she said. "I can see that."

"I think that's a pretty standard gift for this type of situation."

Abby's shoulders fell. As odd as it was, Jon seemed to truly be working on this friend thing. "It's perfectly acceptable, Jonathan. Thank you."

"You're welcome. You know, when I picked it out, it had a ladybug on it. That's supposed to mean good luck."

The ladybug reference made her freeze. Was he studying her now? Of course, he was.

Jon smiled at her thoughts. "So, what are you two crazy kids up to today?"

Abby wondered if she could make it for two minutes without a picture of the mall popping into her head. She didn't even last two seconds.

"Ah, the mall," Jon confirmed. "I figured as much, what with it being a Sunday and you being such a creature of habit. I was headed there myself."

"Sure, you were."

"No, really, I was. Even if you weren't going. But now, I'll see you there."

Not if I see you first, Abby thought.

A wicked grin curved Jon's lips. *Do you actually think you could run away from me, ladybug?*

She glared at him in fitful silence.

Although it might be fun to watch you try, he suggested, his eyes flaming gold inside the chocolate. *Maybe we'll play that game sometime. A little cat and mouse, just you and me?*

Abby's insides twisted for more than one reason. "Well, look at the time. Are you ready to go, Nathaniel?"

"More than ready." Her angel pushed past their unwelcome guest to stand by her side. "We'll see you later, Jon."

"Yeah, sure, Nate. Nice place, by the way. Chez Dead Guy. I like it."

Jon's laughter resounded in her mind long after he disappeared from their living room. She shivered until Nathaniel's arms encircled her. "I'm so sorry about that, Abby. Is there any way for me to apologize for him?"

She forced herself to smile. "Just remember this when you're halfway through a conversation with Peter and you're ready to choke him."

"Honestly, I don't think a million Peters could equal one Jon."

"You may be right," Abby considered. "I say we go find out."

"Sounds good," Nathaniel agreed, taking her hand as they exited their apartment together. He stood right by her side while she locked the door behind them with her key.

"Dude, a Jeep? Really? That's awesome," Peter declared, dipping another French fry in soft serve ice cream before shoving it in his mouth. "My older brother, Joey, has a Jeep. He loves messing with it. You doing any work on yours?"

"Not at the moment," Nathaniel replied, settling back into the plastic chair at the mall food court. The four of them sat at a table together – Nathaniel, Abby, Julie, and Peter – finishing up their meals after watching a rom-com at the theater. Nathaniel eased his arm around the back of Abby's chair so he could run his hand across her shoulder. She did her best to not moan out loud in front of her friends.

"You should put a lift on it and get massive mud tires," Peter continued.

Nathaniel's brow rose. "Is that street legal?"

"Who cares? It would look crazy awesome. Besides, even if you don't do that, you gotta do something to it."

"Yeah? Why's that?"

"Because it's a Jeep. You do know what that stands for, right? Just Empty Every Pocket. That's what Jeep people do – they put more stuff on their Jeep. It's all about the love, man."

"Wow," Nathaniel said. "I had no idea."

Julie rolled her eyes at her boyfriend. "You know, *dear*, it's just a car."

Peter whistled, low and slow. "Damn, babe. Be careful what you say. Joey told me that every time someone calls a Jeep a car, a kitten dies."

Abby burst out in giggles. Nathaniel chuckled. Julie did not look amused.

"Anyway, I know tons of stuff you can buy for it," Peter restarted, focusing his energy back on Nathaniel, which had been the case nearly all day.

Abby met her friend's eyes across the table as Peter continued talking. Julie gnashed on a french fry, and Abby didn't require telepathy to read her mind. She often wondered what Julie saw in Peter, although they were pretty good together. After all, Julie liked to ask questions and Peter liked to talk. Plus, he was always happy, basically normal, and really did adore her. Abby figured Julie must see potential in him, otherwise she wouldn't keep coming back. Although, as Peter started making engine-revving noises at their table, Abby wondered if Julie would break up with him again right here at the food court.

Julie threw her hands in the air and sank back in her chair.

"You all right, babe?" Peter questioned.

Julie glared at him. "Yeah. I'm great."

Peter missed the sarcasm. He patted her on the thigh and returned to his conversation with Nathaniel. Abby watched her friend reach dejectedly for her milkshake, curious if Julie regretted the decision to have this double date. She'd obviously had no idea how instantly attached her boyfriend would become to Nathaniel. Abby probably should have warned her that it was difficult to *not* become instantly attached to him.

Abby turned in her seat to look at her angel. He immediately met her eyes, always tuned in to every move she made. She smiled at him, which drew his gaze down to linger on her mouth. Peter kept rambling on, but Abby couldn't hear him. Not when every cell in her body screamed at once, demanding that Nathaniel do unseemly things to her in the middle of the mall.

"Dude! What time is it?" Peter's voice managed to break through Abby's mental-rioting.

"Why?" Julie huffed.

"Man, we gotta go. My mom will be really pissed off if I don't get the minivan home soon."

Julie glanced sheepishly to Abby. "I guess that's that."

"It was fun," Abby assured her. "I'll see you back here next Sunday?"

"Same time, same place." Julie stood and grabbed her coat.

Peter looked to Nathaniel. "Next time we double date, we should go out riding in your Jeep."

"Absolutely. It was good to meet you, Peter."

"Yeah, man. You, too." Peter turned to Julie. "You ready, babe?"

"Sure," she said, nodding to Abby before taking Peter's hand.

Abby watched the pair stroll away together. As soon as they disappeared into the remaining horde of mall shoppers, she turned back to Nathaniel. "Well? How was it today?"

"It was fine. Peter is a decent guy."

"He is, isn't he? Although, he could never be you. No one else in the whole world could ever be you."

Nathaniel smiled softly before he leaned in to graze his lips over hers. The kiss was so light and quick that Abby barely had a chance to curl her toes. "Mmm," she hummed against his mouth. "Not enough."

"Nothing will ever be enough. Not with you."

She whimpered, wishing they weren't in such a crowded public place right now. She needed time alone with him. So much time.

Abby groaned at the growing volume of random voices surrounding them. "Why don't we go shopping?" she suggested, hoping she'd be able to lure him into a dressing room where they could have a bit more privacy. Perhaps she could even convince him to model some underwear for her – or a swimsuit, at the very least.

"Sure," Nathaniel agreed. "Let's go shopping."

She stood so quickly from the table that she nearly knocked her chair over. Grabbing him by the hand, she curled their fingers together and tugged him forward. Nathaniel allowed her to drag him away from the food court, across the mall corridor, and into the clothing shop where he'd first met Julie.

Abby led him to a corner of the men's section, to a place where it was only the two of them, and started thumbing through the racks. "Let's see what we can find," she hemmed, not wanting to make an obvious beeline for the swimsuits just yet. The thought of Nathaniel modeling skimpy clothes for her lit her eyes. But then her face fell entirely, since she realized that it was November and there would be no swimsuits.

His gaze roamed over the clothing displays. "I don't think I need anything here, Abby. I mean, you haven't soaked through any of my shirts lately."

She looked up to him. "Are you missing that?"

Nathaniel focused on her eyes. "No, I'm definitely not missing it. I love it when you're happy."

"I am happy," she confirmed. In truth, she'd been happier in these past few weeks than she'd been in years. Knowing that Jonathan had agreed to stay in town and that her father was doing well, she could think of no foreseeable reason for Nathaniel to leave. She hadn't needed to worry about letting him go one day, because that day was far, far in the future. She'd been able to spend every moment simply enjoying their time together.

Abby redirected her attentions to her angel. She stepped toward him, lining their bodies up and placing her hand over his heart. She felt his pulse surge beneath her palm.

Nathaniel's eyes sparked with her touch, yet he didn't touch her back. Abby searched inside his bright blue, working to understand the unearthly restraint he'd had with her lately. Since Halloween, he hadn't slept a single night at her house. They'd spent tons of time together at their apartment, yet he'd never once laid down with her on their bed. Even today, in the movie theater, he'd only held her hand. She understood his cautiousness about moving forward with their physical relationship, but she couldn't comprehend why they now seemed to be moving backwards.

He tilted his head. "What are you thinking about, Abby?"

Her fingers curled into his shirt. "I'm thinking about how happy I am with you. And about something that will make me even happier."

"What will make you happier?" he asked, easing his hand into her hair.

His simple yet perfect touch was the last straw. "I want to be with you tonight," she blurted out, not bothering to sugarcoat it. She refused to act as if her feelings were pure and innocent. They weren't. "You haven't stayed an entire night with me in so long and I really need to hold you. I need to touch you so badly."

With her declaration, Nathaniel dropped his hand back to his side.

Abby exhaled in frustration. She glanced around the store, grateful their small section was deserted, since she preferred not to beg in front of strangers. "Will you please stay with me tonight, Nathaniel? Please? My dad will be at work. We can go back to our apartment, just the two of us. We can spend the whole night together."

***

NATHANIEL STOOD, silent and watching, as Abby pleaded with him. From the outside, he knew they looked like any other normal teenage couple, standing in a store together, shopping for clothing. Yet they were anything but normal. This ache in his chest was anything but normal.

For the last sixty years, he'd had to cope with the emotions of everyone around him – from hellacious rage to heavenly ecstasy – but it still hadn't prepared him for the sheer volume of love, need, and desire he felt for her. They couldn't possibly be a normal couple, because any normal man who listened to her sweet words, and heard the longing behind them, wouldn't be able to resist. But he had to. He couldn't give in to this.

Nathaniel fisted his hands at his sides as Abby's eyes continued pleading with him. God, he wanted to touch her. He'd wanted to touch her for every minute since the night they'd spent together on Halloween. Yet he'd kept his actions very purposeful since then, being extremely careful with their physical contact. Being with her every day for hours on end had warped his sensibilities. It was far too easy to slip into the daydream of being a real, living person, especially while decorating a home. *Their* home.

He'd tried to convince himself that they were building a home together for Abby's good, to provide her with a place of stability, no matter what the future might hold. He'd attempted to ease his conscience further by giving her the key, assuring them both that the apartment was solely for her benefit. It was all a lie, of course. But it was a lie he had to believe. If he didn't, he would have to acknowledge how much he wanted the fantasy to be real. He would have to admit how much he wanted a home, and a family, and to come home every day to her smiling face.

Nathaniel huffed at his ungodly desires. He stood in silence, watching Abby as she watched him, painfully aware of how desperately he wanted her. He wanted her with a mind-numbing, overpowering hunger, and the constant struggle to keep his desires under control was damn near killing him. But he didn't have a choice. He'd never experienced that kind of physical relationship in his real life, but he understood what it would mean to both of them, here and now. He absolutely could not bind her to him in that way. He could never make those commitments. He could never assure her that they had years and years to be together, living this blissful lie.

Abby didn't belong to him. She couldn't. He wasn't alive – not like she needed him to be – and he couldn't take her for himself while knowing that he could be yanked away from her at any second. She had to be strong enough to go on without him, and that meant he could never truly have her.

Nathaniel's heart pounded ferociously in his chest as he drank in the sight of her face. During all his years as a spirit, he always hoped he'd been granted this half-existence as a means to make up for the sins of his life. He'd allowed people to beat, stab, and burn him in order to atone for his crimes, all while praying he might one day be given the chance to create a future of his own choosing. He'd experienced so much pain along the way, and yet nothing felt as raw, or ached as deeply, as wanting to be real for her.

Maybe this love that Abby and I share isn't supposed to be a gift, Nathaniel considered. Maybe this love was actually his punishment: to see his wildest desire, to talk with her and touch her and hold her, and yet always know she lay just out of reach. Maybe this half-life of his wasn't a chance at absolution. Maybe this was actually hell.

"Am I supposed to take your silence as a refusal?" Abby asked, her bright voice illuminating his dark thoughts. "You won't stay the night with me?"

Nathaniel plastered on a smile, thankful she couldn't read his mind or his emotions. He didn't want her to realize just how much pain her question inflicted on him. "I don't know," he hemmed. "How many of your wicked temptress skills are you planning to use against me?"

"How many wicked temptress skills am I allowed to use?" she asked, biting into her lip, chewing idly against that soft, pink flesh.

His eyes drew to her mouth. Nathaniel stifled a groan, forcing himself to remain still and not attack her in the middle of the store. "None," he replied. "No wicked temptress skills of any kind."

Abby shook her head. "I don't know why you're always so concerned. You've got more willpower than anyone."

"That is true. But with you, it may not be enough."

"I'm good with that."

"I'm not."

Her fist curled up tighter in his shirt, directly over his heart. He imagined she must be tired of this same old conversation, of his constant refusals. But he also knew she was tenacious, and he couldn't let his guard down for any reason.

"Fine, fine. I'll be sooo good," she submitted. "I'll be frumpy and irritating and I'll snort a lot, or something. You won't want anything to do with me. You'll actually have to force yourself to deal with my horrid disgustingness. Just as long as I get to enjoy every minute of it."

"Wow. How on earth can I refuse an offer like that?"

Abby laughed, pure and sparkling, an arrow stabbing in his chest.

"Come here," he said, allowing himself this much. She moved into his open arms as if there was nowhere else she could imagine being. He wrapped her up onto his chest while she flattened her hands against his back, infusing him with warmth inside and out.

Nathaniel was absolutely certain of one thing in this moment: *She belongs here.* And yet, that knowledge didn't make sense at all. How could this feel so perfect, but still be completely and utterly beyond his reach? He wanted to say it wasn't fair and that no one should be forced to endure this kind of torture. But he couldn't. He knew that hell was exactly what he deserved.

Abby sighed as her body melted into his. "I love you, Nathaniel."

"I love you," he replied without hesitation. He allowed himself to bury his face in her hair, to breathe in the scent of little flowers that swam around her. He memorized the contours of her body as they pressed against his, not caring that they stood in the middle of a clothing store, in the middle of a mall, in the middle of a world of strangers. All he wanted was to hold onto every moment he had with this amazing being in his arms.

Nathaniel could have remained like this for the rest of the day, content to never move. However, the noises in the distance would not be ignored. He pulled Abby in tighter as he strained his ears toward the growing commotion.

No. It can't be, he thought while the ominous sounds accosted his ears.

But it was. It was Normandy. All over again.

They were odd, firecracker-like noises. So strange. So unusual. They didn't belong here. They didn't belong anywhere, but especially not here. Not in this place, with Abby in his arms. They didn't make sense at all.

Then, Nathaniel heard the screaming.

Abby's muscles tensed against his chest. "Nathaniel, what is that?"

"It's gunfire."

She raised her head to meet his eyes. "What? Why?"

Another firecracker sound in the distance. Another scream. Closer now.

His heart raced. He had to stop this. He had to protect people. He had to protect *her*. "Abby," he said, grabbing her face in both hands. "I need to see what's going on."

Terror lit her eyes, but she still managed to nod. Nathaniel took her by the arm, pulling her toward the back of the store. He placed her behind a display of clothes and urged her onto the ground. "You stay here," he commanded. "Don't move. I'll be right back."

Abby looked up to him from her huddled position on the floor. She nodded again, her body trembling from head to toe. He didn't want to leave her, but he didn't have a choice. She was safe now and others weren't. His pull to these people was strong. The only thing stronger was his pull to her.

Nathaniel forced himself into his spirit world and materialized instantly in the food court. It was sheer chaos. People running. Falling. Crying. Screaming. Everyone glowing red with raw fear. He could barely see through the blistering colors of the panicked bodies around him. He struggled to clear his vision, to find the source of all this anguish. And then he did.

Randy Thorpe – a boy he'd seen a hundred times at Abby's school – drifted through the mall corridor with a sawed-off rifle in hand, firing at will. A serene smile pulled sickly at his lips. He glowed in black and crimson, and yet there was a bizarre calmness to his features.

Nathaniel's blood curdled. He searched his immediate surroundings, calculating the location of every innocent bystander. He could identify each of them, even those scattered and hiding, by their bright red halos. Thankfully, Randy couldn't see what he saw. Nathaniel knew he had only a few moments to save them all.

He pushed himself back to Abby. She was still huddled behind the clothes display, just as he'd left her. *Abby,* he spoke to her mind, not wanting to draw attention to her location.

Her eyes rose to his. Her cheeks were soaked in tears. He wanted to brush them away, to hold her and tell her everything was going to be okay, but there was no time.

Randy Thorpe is here. He's the gunman.

Randy Thorpe? The guy from my English class?

Yes. He's shooting at people. I need to help them.

Abby didn't respond. Nathaniel knew she was in shock. The thought of leaving her here alone made his entire body revolt, but he knew what he had to do.

Stay here, he instructed, staring the words into her eyes. *And call me if you need me. I will come to you no matter what. Do you understand, sweetheart?*

Y-yes.

I love you, he told her, just before he disappeared.

BULLETS. There are bullets.

Abby could hear them firing off at intervals, somewhere in the distance.

There are bullets, and Nathaniel is out there with them.

Her whole body shook. Uncontrollably. Until the shaking became painful. She pulled her legs up to her chest, crunching into a ball, rocking back and forth on the ground. *It's Randy Thorpe. Randy Thorpe from my English class.*

How many times had she sat in a room with him? How many times had she seen him entering those woods behind the school picnic table? A hundred? A thousand? Randy and Jason went into those woods so often. Randy and Jason – always together.

Abby's shallow, panted breaths ground to a halt. She stopped rocking when her mind focused on a single thought. *Oh, God. Jason. Jason Rathburn. Randy doesn't go anywhere without Jason. If Randy is here, then Jason is definitely here. And if Randy has a gun, then Jason does, too.*

Her head popped up, eyes staring blankly at the clothes hanging in front of her. *Will Nathaniel know that? No, he won't. He won't know to protect himself from someone he can't see coming. If he's focused on Randy, and turns solid to wrestle his gun away, he won't be able to defend himself against Jason. Nathaniel won't be able to avoid the bullets.*

Fear gripped Abby's heart in a vice, squeezing the life from her body. *It can't be a bullet. He won't come back from that. I'm not ready to let him go. I'm nowhere near ready to let him go.*

She stared straight ahead, having no idea what to do, but knowing she had to do something. Abby released her death grip on her legs and stood, working to balance herself as she peered over the clothing rack. Looking to the very front of the store, she could see that the entrance out to the mall corridor was empty. There were no other people anywhere in sight.

Her wobbly legs somehow carried her forward. She edged around the display Nathaniel had hidden her behind, forcing one foot in front of the other. Slowly but surely, she walked toward the store entrance.

A few steps shy of the door, she heard a familiar voice in her head.

Abby, what are you doing?

Jon? she questioned, looking across the short distance to the outer hallway, not seeing anyone at all. *Is that you?*

Yes, it's me. Where do you think you're going? Didn't Nathaniel tell you to stay behind that clothing rack?

Yeah, he did, but I've...I've got to help.

Help who?

Nathaniel. He needs me.

He needs you to stay alive. Your current behavior will not accomplish that.

But he's in danger. I can help him.

Abby, I hate to break this to you, but you are not immortal. You need to get back behind that rack and hide.

No.

Do it now, Abigail. Now.

No. I have to help.

Jon's groan of frustration echoed through her mind at the same moment a figure appeared in front of her. Jason Rathburn emerged from the hallway and stopped at the entrance to the store. Abby gasped when she saw him.

Her surprised sound caught Jason's attention. He turned fully toward her, locking their eyes together. Abby stood frozen in place. She'd seen his face more times than she could count, but she couldn't recognize it now. It looked twisted somehow. Yet, at the same time, it was calm and still.

God, does he even see me? she wondered.

Jason answered her by raising his sawed-off shotgun and aiming it at her chest. All of Abby's limbs went numb. But her vision stayed sharp as another person approached them from the mall corridor.

Jon walked up behind the gunman. He stopped cold a few feet away. He looked past Jason to stare at her with turbulent eyes of black sludge.

FIFTEEN

Bullets fired in the distance. Screams echoed through stores. People whimpered and sobbed from behind displays and beneath tables. But where Abby stood, grounded by the rifle that pinned her in place, there was only silence. Until Jonathan's voice seeped back into her mind.

Abby, can you hear me?

She wasn't sure. She could see Jon standing behind Jason, but only out of the corner of her eye. Her entire body stayed focused on the shotgun.

Abigail! Talk to me now! Do you know what's happening?

I...I think I'm about to get shot.

That's right, Jon confirmed. *Do you know what you need to do?*

No.

You need to call Nathaniel.

Abby shook her head. *No. This can't be happening. Jason knows me. He won't do it.* She glanced up to the boy's face. His eyes were dark, dead. She didn't know if he recognized her at all.

You're wrong, Abby. Jason will shoot you.

You don't know that.

Yes, I do. I can read his mind.

She struggled to grasp the concept. *Am I going to die now, Jon? Is this my time to go?*

No. This is not your time. Call Nathaniel. He will take this bullet for you.

Jon's calm, even words resounded in her mind. Nathaniel would save her.

He was always meant to save her. But from *this*?

Yes, Abby realized. This was it. Her angel's final act of heroism. This wasn't her time –it was Nathaniel's. Time to leave his half-existence. Time to move on. Time to finally find peace. All she had to do was call him, and it would be done. All she had to do was let him go.

No! No! No! she screamed in caged silence. She couldn't call her angel to his death. She wouldn't.

What are you waiting for? Jon demanded. *This idiot has a gun pointed at you. He won't hesitate much longer. Call Nathaniel.*

Abby's eyes shifted to stare into Jon's turbulent oil. *No. It can't be a bullet. Never again.*

Who cares if Nate gets shot? He dies for a living. That's what he does.

But it can't be a bullet. He can't leave me. He can't.

Jon glared at her now, his shoulders bunched beneath his black leather jacket. *Damn it, Abby! Listen to me for once! I am reading this simpleton's mind and he is going to shoot you! Do you understand that?*

She'd never seen Jon show this much emotion before. She'd never heard him sound so angry. But she wouldn't back down. *Yes, Jon. I understand.*

Jason's hand gripped harder to the gun.

Jon exhaled slowly, steadying his voice before pressing on. *Abby. You call Nathaniel now. Do you hear me? Do it. Now.*

She stared down the dark barrel. Tears lit her eyes, but she still stated one word in her mind with absolute clarity: *No.*

Jason cocked the shotgun. His finger tensed against the trigger.

Jon stiffened his spine. His words weren't meant for her, but she heard them all the same. *Nathaniel, Abby is about to get shot.*

The firing of the rifle was so much louder than Abby remembered from Nathaniel's visions of Normandy. Those guns sounded more like firecrackers, like the pops she could hear now in the distance. This noise was excruciatingly loud – sharp – deafening. The sound tore through her ears just as the bullet tore into her heart. But not literally.

The bullet tore into her heart when it tore into Nathaniel.

He appeared at the exact moment Jon called him, the exact moment Jason pulled the trigger. If his actions weren't instantaneous, he would have been too late. Instead, he was exactly on time to get hit in the stomach with the shot meant for Abby's chest.

The lethal scrap of metal slugged into Nathaniel's flesh and dropped him to his knees. His thick body slumped to the floor. His blood began to ooze, soaking through the hole in his shirt.

Jason's eyes bulged from their sockets as he stared at the bloodied man who'd appeared out of nowhere. He cursed beneath his breath before he took off running. Abby paid no attention to his escape. She remained where she was, looking down at the ground. At her fallen angel. At his solid body, now drenched in a steady stream of dark crimson.

She fell to her knees beside him, quivering fingers suspended above his chest, not knowing where to touch. She finally reached for his face, laying her hand against his cheek. Nathaniel coughed, making his blood gurgle inside his throat. He stared straight through her with unseeing eyes.

Abby sobbed as she leaned down to press her lips to his ear. "Nathaniel, don't go. Please don't go. Turn back now. Turn back into a spirit."

A spasm wracked his body, the violence of it jolting her upright. She sat back on her knees, staring down at his broken form, as his arms quaked with tremors. Blood spread from the bullet wound all the way across his abdomen, pooling in the fabric of his shirt.

Abby's heart caved inward, her chest on fire. She felt so alone. More alone than ever before. Until someone came to stand beside them.

Her eyes rose. Jon appeared, dark and still, next to Nathaniel's dying body. He didn't acknowledge the tears soaking her cheeks or the look of sheer desperation on her face. He looked only to Nathaniel, completely focused on his near-lifeless form.

"What is this?" Jon asked. "Are you going for dramatic effect, old pal?"

Nathaniel coughed again. A stream of crimson seeped from the side of his mouth. Abby whimpered and grabbed his hand. She squeezed tight, but his fingers didn't reach back for hers.

Jon huffed in annoyance. "Change back, Nathaniel. Fix this," he barked, motioning to the curdling blood. "This is nothing. You've survived worse."

Nathaniel took an anguished gasp of air, making a hollow, scraping sound inside his chest. Several moments passed before he inhaled again, this time even more strangled and shallow than the last. Abby's tears fell from her cheeks to land on his sinking chest.

Jon widened his stance as he glared down at him. "Damn it, Nathaniel! Change back now! Heal yourself!"

Abby focused on Jon's eyes. Harsh, fitful patterns stirred in the black oil, burning with pain. She never thought a bond existed between him and Nathaniel. She was wrong.

Please, she begged, her throat too dry to speak. *Please help him.*

Jon turned his eyes to hers. His face held no emotion. No narcissistic self-congratulation. No smooth, lulling temptation. Just emptiness.

Please do something, Jon. Please.

He ignored her and looked back to man on the floor, studying the labored breaths that heaved against his ribcage. "Fine," he growled through gritted teeth. "Do what you want, Nate. You always do."

She watched in sickening wonder as Jon disappeared. He evaporated into thin air, leaving her and Nathaniel entirely alone. Abby looked out of the store and into the mall corridor. It was empty. Everything was empty.

Had everyone given up on them? Was there no hope at all? *No.* She wouldn't believe that. She wouldn't let go.

Abby looked back to her angel, lying deathly still in front of her. This was the one memory of Normandy that Nathaniel refused to give her: the moment the bullet hit him. He'd told her how he'd lived for twenty or thirty minutes after he'd been shot. But looking at him now, she didn't think he could survive that long. The blood on his shirt had already turned sticky. The blood seeping from his mouth had already stopped.

She tried not to look at the blood. She focused only on his face. How many times had she looked into his beautiful eyes – into the bright, perfect blue that saw her like no one else could? They didn't see her now.

Abby tightened her hold on his hand. How many times had she felt his fingers curl into hers, holding on for dear life? They didn't move now.

She could still feel the warmth of Nathaniel's skin, but it was fading rapidly. She couldn't hold it inside him. Even if she threw her body over his, she couldn't make the warmth stay. She couldn't make his arms band around her, giving her a reason to want to be alive.

Tears rolled down her face, landing against their hands. It didn't matter how many times Nathaniel had held her before now. It wasn't enough. It would never be enough. She needed him here. He was hers and she was his.

Abby pulled his limp hand up to rest over her heart. She leaned down to press her heated cheek against his cool one. She closed her eyes and concentrated, stilling every other thought in her mind, focusing all of her energy on her angel, needing him to hear her.

"Nathaniel," she said, her voice steady and clear. "Don't leave me. I love you. I love you so much. You can't leave me. Not yet. I need you. I need you right here. Stay with me, sweetheart. Please. *Please.*"

No air entered his lungs. No pulse surged through his body. No heat seeped through his skin and into hers.

Abby grasped his hand as hard as she could, willing her heart to beat for them both. *Stay,* she prayed. *Stay, stay, stay.*

And then there was nothing. She no longer felt his cheek pressed against hers. She no longer felt his hand beneath her own. Her fingers curled into her palm, gripping only air.

Abby arched back and looked to Nathaniel. His body rested on the floor beside her knees. His blue eyes glowed as he stared up at the ceiling. His chest remained still beneath his blood-drenched shirt.

She stared at his motionless form for an eternity. But then, he breathed. Deep and full, Nathaniel's chest expanded. His eyes glowed brighter and brighter, as if a steadily rising morning sun pulled away from the horizon and filtered through him.

He sat up in an instant, so swiftly that Abby fell back on her heels. She gawked at him, heart pounding, focused entirely on his eyes. She watched the ethereal glow deepen to a strong, solid blue. His body became full, radiating warmth she could feel to her bones. Her angel was whole again.

Nathaniel looked to his shirt, to the congealing crimson over his bullet wound. He cursed as he tore at the stained fabric, ripping it off of his chest and shoving it to the ground. He ogled his bared stomach, his hands probing to find the bullet's point of entry. His skin was smooth. The wound was healed. The blood was gone.

His eyes darted to hers. "Where...where am I?"

"Oh, God, Nathaniel. You're with me. You're still here with me."

He reached for her without hesitation, pulling her onto his lap and curling her inside his arms. Abby cried while she clung to him, mixed tears of utter relief and beastly guilt. Her angel was as strong, as solid, as real as ever. He didn't leave her, even though he should have.

A second later, he tried to push her away from him. She fought back, feeling so safe in his embrace that she never wanted to leave. Abby groaned when he succeeded in separating them.

Nathaniel held her at arms' length. His eyes searched her body with frantic intensity. His hands moved over her face and neck before trailing down to her heart. "Are you okay? Were you injured? Were you shot?"

"No, no. I'm fine."

"You're not dead, too?"

"We're still in the mall, Nathaniel. We're definitely not in heaven."

His face softened. His fingers traced over her lips. "Are you sure?"

He leaned forward, pressing his mouth to hers. Abby attacked him, clawing at his shoulders, desperate to know this feeling again. Nathaniel only pulled her closer and kissed her harder, clutching her fully to his chest.

She arched her body into his, fierce and strong, needing everything. She barely noticed the harsh voices booming in the distance. She didn't truly hear them until Nathaniel tore his lips away from hers.

"God, Abby, what am I doing right now? I have to get you out of here."

He didn't say another word. He grasped her by the arms, drawing her up to stand with him. He threaded their fingers together and pulled her behind a clothing rack at the front of the store.

She followed blindly, working to grasp her new reality. The joy she'd felt when he'd kissed her was quickly being obliterated by crushing guilt. Whatever happened to either of them now, she knew one thing for certain: she'd kept him here. He remained in this infernal half-life because of her.

Abby didn't know if there was any way to apologize for doing such an appalling, selfish thing, but she had to try. "Nathaniel, I...I..."

He tugged her down with him to crouch behind the display before he looked to her eyes. "Yes?"

Her lip quivered. "I n-need to say something. Something that's so..."

"Hey," he said, squeezing tight to her fingers. "It's okay. We can talk later. Right now, I need to make sure we're clear to leave. Can you stay here for me? I'll only be gone for a second."

She nodded without thought, watching as he disappeared from sight. She barely had the chance to miss him before he returned. Nathaniel transformed back to solid that instant, holding his hand out and pulling her up to stand.

"Police are everywhere now. They have Jason and Randy cornered. I can get you out through a stairwell around the corner. Can you walk?"

Abby nodded again, wanting to give him anything he asked for. He circled his arm around her waist and fastened her to his side. She flattened her palm against his bare spine as he led her forward.

"Wait," she said, reaching out to pull a fresh shirt from a nearby display. "You'll need this. Too much to explain otherwise."

"Wow, Abby. I'm amazed that you can still think so clearly." He shoved his head and arms through the fabric before taking her hand in his. "Come on," he encouraged, staying low to the ground, leading her quickly from the store.

She mimicked his movements, following him out to the mall corridor and down the hall to a back stairwell. Nathaniel forced the door open as quietly as possible and pulled her through it. They trampled down the staircase together, drawing to a stop in front of the exit door.

He paused for a moment, looking out of the small window to the crowd gathered outside the building. "There are a hell of a lot of people out there," he said as he met her eyes. "If anyone asks us any questions, we have to keep what happened tonight between us."

Abby swallowed hard. "I know I can't tell anyone what really happened. I just want to make sure Jason and Randy get punished for what they did."

Nathaniel winced. "It'll be okay. The police don't need us. There are lots of other witnesses, and besides, we have no proof that they did any harm."

Abby looked down to his clean shirt. "Right. I understand."

He tucked her hand into his side. "Stay close to me, sweetheart."

They stepped out of the thick stairwell door into maddening commotion. As soon as their feet hit the sidewalk, Abby could see the massive throngs of people lining the front of the building. Police tape held swarming onlookers in place while red and blue lights flashed from rescue vehicles, illuminating the black sky like a freakish lightning storm.

Nathaniel urged her around the side of the building, keeping them shielded from prying eyes. She looked over her shoulder while she toddled beside him, scanning the turmoil in the distance, straining to see the people who now fled from the mall's entrance. The emerging victims were huddled under blankets, some sobbing, some being strapped to gurneys and rushed through waiting ambulance doors. Abby wished she never had to see another ambulance as long as she lived.

Nathaniel guided her to the very edge of the crowd, slipping unnoticed past the onlookers who focused on the mall's front doors. He ducked them both under the police tape to blend in with the swarms. Abby felt the bodies surrounding her, saw the multitudes of gawking spectators, and heard the frenzied gossip, but all she could think about was her angel's hand entwined in hers. She still had him. For better or worse, he'd stayed.

He maneuvered them through the mess, fleeing the mall as fast as humanly possible. She couldn't have agreed more. She just wanted to be free of it all.

"Abby! Abby!"

She scrunched her nose in confusion before digging in her heels. Nathaniel turned with her to see Julie tumbling toward them from the edge of the police tape. The frazzled brunette dragged Peter along behind her.

"I was so worried about you, Abs! We hadn't even left the parking lot when it started. I was scared as hell that you were still inside. Are you okay?"

Abby hugged Julie with one arm, keeping her other hand grounded inside Nathaniel's. "I'm okay, Jules. Nathaniel got me out."

Peter stepped toward them. "Man, you two really scared us."

Abby smiled when she witnessed the look of relief in his puppy-dog eyes.

"We were shopping for some new clothes when we heard the gunfire," Nathaniel explained. "We stayed low and ran down a back stairwell when we could. We didn't see much. Have you heard what's going on?"

Julie shook her head. "No one has said anything, but I was terrified that something happened to you. I'm sorry, Abby, but I was so freaked out that I...I called your dad."

"Oh, my God, Jules. You did *what*?"

"I just didn't know what else to do. I'm so, so sorry."

Abby wanted to vomit. She knew her friend was only looking out for her, but she didn't want her father to witness this hellish mess. She had no idea what it would do to him.

"Abby!"

She heard her name from a distance. She turned to see Mark hurtling through the crowd. His mouth was drawn, his movements frenzied. She met his eyes across the mass of people as fresh tears streamed down her face.

"Dad..."

He ran to her and pulled her into his arms, gripping so tight that she thought her spine would snap. "Abby, Abby, Abby. Oh, thank the Lord."

She clung to him while tremors wracked his body, thankful he would never know how close she'd come to dying. "I'm okay, Dad. I'm okay."

Mark held onto her forever. When he finally pulled away, he had as many tears on his cheeks as she did. "You sure you're okay?"

"I am. Thanks to Nathaniel."

The angel keeping guard beside her stiffened with her words. Abby smiled through her tears. She may not be able to tell her father the truth, but she could make sure Nathaniel finally got the credit he deserved after so many years of rescuing people in anonymity.

"He saved me, Dad. He pulled me away from everything, hid me behind a store display, and got me out through a back stairwell as soon as it was safe. He's the reason I'm alive."

Mark stared at the man standing next to his daughter. He took two steps forward and pulled Nathaniel into a giant hug. "Thank you," Mark said, pouring his heart into the simple words. "Thank you for taking care of her."

Nathaniel's eyes welled. "Of course, sir. I would do anything for Abby."

Her father nodded as he straightened. "You're always welcome in my home, Nathaniel. Consider yourself part of the family."

Abby looked to her angel, her heart swelled to bursting. "Yes, you are," she seconded, absorbing the perfect blue of his eyes against the backdrop of this dark, strange night. Nathaniel looked to her with such love that she nearly forgot where she was. That is, until Mark took her hand to pull her away.

"Come on, honey, let me get you home."

Her gaze shifted to her father's face. "But I...I..."

Mark paused. "Do you need to stay? To give a statement or something?"

"No. No, I don't. I just want Nathaniel…"

"It's okay," Nathaniel assured. "Go with your dad, Abby. Call me later."

She couldn't stand the thought of being separated from him right now. But she still nodded, standing her ground while Julie and Peter took turns hugging her. They all said their goodbyes before Mark led Abby away from the crowd. She watched Nathaniel for as long as she could, until his solid body was consumed by the sea of strangers.

"WE MADE THE NATIONAL NEWS," Abby called to her dad as she sat on their couch, cocooned in a battered, hunter green chenille blanket, clasping a half-empty mug of hot chocolate.

"Oh, yeah?" Mark's voice came from the kitchen.

Abby flipped through the TV channels, trying to decide how long she needed to stay with her father before she could go to her room to call Nathaniel. Several hours had already passed since they'd come home. She'd scrutinized Mark's every move since, afraid of what her trauma tonight could do to him. She'd tried to convince him that she wasn't ever in any danger – that she'd only been a bystander – but it was difficult to reassure him when she could barely hold herself together.

Abby gripped onto her cocoa mug as everything played over and over in her mind: Jason's shotgun pointed at her chest; Jon's turbulent, muddied eyes; Nathaniel's body, limp and lifeless, slumped on the floor. The images were too fresh and far too painful. The more her mind churned, the more her body felt like it would cave inward, sucking into some unseen black hole where the bullet should have gone.

She stared blankly at the TV screen, listening to a woman speak in a distant and proper tone about the event she'd barely survived:

A mall shooting in Charlottesville today left twenty-seven people injured, two of whom are in critical condition at the University of Virginia Medical Center. No information has been released by police on the suspects, although sources report the two alleged gunmen were high school students who live nearby…

Abby huffed. She wondered who their sources were. She could have told the reporters anything they wanted to know. She could have told them that there were twenty-seven injuries and one *death*. She wanted to tell someone the truth, to make sure Randy and Jason paid for the full extent of their crimes. But she also understood why she couldn't. Jason hadn't actually killed

Nathaniel, because he wasn't alive to begin with. He hadn't been alive in over sixty years. He'd been trapped in a horrible half-life, waiting for it to be over.

Nathaniel had told her once that he believed a bullet might end his unnatural existence. Abby believed it, too. She believed it so much that she'd been willing to take that bullet. It wasn't really a conscious decision. Or a noble one. She'd been driven entirely by the fear of losing him.

Her shoulders shuddered beneath her old blanket as she acknowledged the truth: if Jon hadn't called Nathaniel when he did, she would be dead right now. She wondered if that would have somehow been better. Would she have turned into a spirit, free to roam the earth by Nathaniel's side? Would they have had forever to be together? Or would she have disappeared at the moment of her death, just like his mother did? Would she be gone forever, leaving him to an unbearable eternity with Jonathan as his only companion?

Abby didn't have any answers, but she knew one thing for certain: begging Nathaniel to stay with her was the most selfish thing she'd ever done. He should blame her entirely for keeping him here. He should be angry as hell that she stole his one chance to move on.

Mark entered the living room, startling Abby into nearly spilling her cocoa. She recovered quickly, settling back into the couch and slowing her breaths, attempting to reassure him of her non-existent stability. "Hey, Dad."

"Hey, honey. How are you?"

"I'm good. Cocoa and couch time were just what I needed. I'll be fine."

"I know you will. You've always been so strong, Abby. So strong."

She plastered on a smile. "Thanks, Dad. Do you mind if I go to bed now? I'm pretty worn out."

"Sure. I'll be here if you need me. You might have some bad dreams. I promise I won't mind if you wake me. I'll probably be up a while anyway."

"Don't worry about me," she said, hoping beyond hope that he wouldn't give any of this a second thought. The last thing Abby needed was for him to relive his memories of being held prisoner. Certainly not now. Definitely not because of her.

Mark studied her. "Well, I am your dad. That gives me the right to worry."

She straightened on the couch and set her mug on the table. "Yeah, I know. But nothing happened to me tonight, so I should sleep fine."

"If you say so. But I'm still going to stay home from work tomorrow. I want you to stay home from school, too. We'll just take it easy, okay?"

"Sounds good," she agreed, since the thought of going to school in a few hours felt bizarre. She stood and gave him a half-hug with her free arm. Her other arm maintained her chenille cocoon while she padded down the hallway.

Abby stepped into her bedroom, shut the door, and locked it behind her. She moved to her stereo and turned the music up enough to keep her father from hearing any voices. She closed her eyes and pictured her angel.

Nathaniel? Can you come here, please?

He appeared instantly beside her window, haloed against the darkness outside. His eyes glowed clear and bright, showcasing his inherent purity. She didn't know why he ever questioned the fact that he was a hero. Especially when her own faults were so glaring.

Nathaniel turned solid as he stepped forward. "How are you, sweetheart?"

Sweetheart. That one word gave her so much hope. "I'm better now that you're here."

He stopped just inches away. Abby tilted her face up to his. He smiled, calm and peaceful, and she breathed easier than she had all night.

Nathaniel reached out to her, running his fingers over her hair, down her shoulder, and onto the dilapidated blanket she clutched to her chest. "Is this a new fashion statement?"

"You mean my magic blanket? My mom gave me this when I was little. She said it could cure any cold, flu, or heartache."

"Yeah? How's it working for you tonight?"

"Not so good."

"Why not?"

Abby shrugged, not knowing where to begin her numerous apologies.

"I understand," he said, sighing as he held her eyes with his own. "I know why you're upset, and I need to tell you how sorry I am."

"*Sorry?* What on earth do you have to be sorry for?"

"For worrying you at the mall, after I got shot. I didn't mean to be so out of it."

"Nathaniel, you were *shot*. Anyone on earth would be out of it."

"Yeah, I guess. But I hope you know I'd never put you through something like that intentionally."

Abby watched him like a hawk, still terrified that he might disappear any moment. "I know you wouldn't. I'm sure you couldn't help it."

"I really couldn't. God, when the bullet hit me, I just couldn't cope at all. I remembered that excruciating feeling from Normandy. I couldn't pull away from that image, from the agony I felt on that beach. It was too difficult to turn back to the spirit world, too difficult to stay, too much pain to bear." He shuddered before a tiny spark lit his eyes. "But, as it turns out, this was a completely different experience."

"Yeah? Why is that?"

"Because of you. I heard your voice. I heard you say you love me. You asked me to stay with you, so I knew I had a reason to be here."

Abby's knees weakened and she swayed. Nathaniel stepped up into her, wrapping his arms around her waist. "Hey," he said. "Are you really okay?"

She clasped her blanket to her chest as she rested her head on his shoulder. "Yes. I just missed you so much these past few hours."

He pressed his lips to her hair. "I'm sorry I didn't come home with you right away, but I could see how much your dad needed to take care of you. Also, I had a few things to do."

"What things?"

"Well, for one, I needed to go to the hospital to check on everybody."

"How are they? The news said two people are in critical condition."

"They're better now. They have strong colors, and I believe they'll pull through. I don't think Jason and Randy claimed any lives tonight."

Abby raised her head. "I can't believe those two did any of this. I hope they both get locked away forever."

He held her determined gaze even as he grimaced. "They're in proper custody now. I went to the police station to make sure of it. And once I knew they were, I went back to the mall."

"You went back? Were you making sure that everyone got out?"

"No, everyone was safe already. I had to go back to the clothing store."

"The clothing store? Why?"

"I needed to get rid of my old shirt. And leave money for the new one."

Abby's brow arched. "Did you actually pay for the shirt we took?"

"Well, I've never stolen anything before. I certainly don't want that going against me now."

"Wow, Nathaniel. You were almost killed in that store. I think the least they could do is give you a complimentary shirt."

He laughed, the perfect sound rumbling against her. For a moment, Abby was happy. But then, his face fell.

"You know, I wasn't actually the one who was almost killed," he said, locking onto her eyes. "You were. How did that happen? I thought I left you safely behind a clothing rack."

Abby worried her lower lip in her teeth. "Yeah, you did. But I – I was coming to help you."

"Help me? Can you please explain how walking out, utterly mortal, in the middle of that mess, was going to help me?"

"Well, I just...I knew if Randy was there with a gun, then Jason would be there, too. I needed to warn you, so you'd know there were two of them."

"Good Lord, Abby. You do know that you are the one person I absolutely needed to remain alive, right? And that everyone I was able to help, and anything else I was able to do, was all pitifully secondary to keeping you safe?"

She blinked away her tears. "I understand. I panicked. It was stupid."

He studied her for another moment before heaving a sigh. "No. Not stupid. Brave. Most people wouldn't have attempted anything like that, not when their urge for self-preservation took over. I should have known to expect something different from you. You're never like anyone else."

Nathaniel gave her a gentle smile. She couldn't help returning it, even though she knew she wasn't brave at all. She was the exact opposite.

He took her face in his hand. "Where did your smile go? I want it back."

Abby wanted to oblige, but her muscles wouldn't cooperate. "Sorry."

"Don't be sorry. I just want to know what's going on in that mind of yours. Are you still thinking about what happened at the mall?"

"Y-yes."

"I bet you were terrified when you saw Jason."

"Yeah, I was. But not for myself."

"Really? Is that because you knew I'd protect you?"

She sealed her lips together and shook her head.

Nathaniel's fingers shifted over her cheek. "There's something I really need you to tell me, please."

"What is it?" she asked.

"Why didn't you call me when Jason pointed his gun at you? I heard Jon's voice, not yours. Why is that?"

Her heart did a weird, thudding thing, making her entire chest tighten. "Because I knew it couldn't be a gun," she whispered, dreading his inevitable anger when he realized just how weak she'd been. "I knew you couldn't get hit by a bullet – because you thought it would end your spirit-life – and I wasn't strong enough to let that happen. I wasn't strong enough to let you go, to let you finally be free."

She shut her eyes tight, waiting for him to bombard her with fury and resentment. Seconds passed in torturous silence. Then she felt his fingers on her chin, raising her head up until she looked back to his face.

Nathaniel met her eyes with nothing but love in his own. "Sweetheart, I need you to understand that you didn't keep me here. I mean, yes, I was able to transform when I heard your voice. But if it was really my time to go, then I would be gone. No amount of wishing would change that."

"But...but I'm supposed to love you enough to let you go."

"Well, I love you more than life itself, and I never want to let you go."

Abby shook her head, still too ashamed to accept the ease of his forgiveness. "But maybe if I hadn't been so weak – maybe if I'd encouraged you to be free – then you could be in a better place now."

Nathaniel sighed. "You're taking on way too much responsibility here. It's not your job to save my soul. It's mine."

"But I knew it couldn't be a bullet. I couldn't let it take you away."

"Forget about me leaving here, Abby. Forget about that bullet taking me away. You must realize that it could have taken *you* away. For good."

"Yes. But better that, than the other way around."

Anger finally lit Nathaniel's eyes. He grabbed her arms, holding her in place. "No, it wouldn't be," he insisted. "Listen to me, and hear me, please. You are all that matters. I don't want to be here if I can't be with you. I may have thought I was trapped in hell before now, but I would consider the past sixty years a cake walk compared to a single new day without you. Please tell me you understand that."

Abby smiled through her tears. "It would be the same for me, you know – without you."

Nathaniel held his breath as he stared at her, until his shoulders eventually slumped. He pulled her into his chest, wrapping her up in his arms. "I don't deserve this," he confessed. "I don't deserve you. I'm sorry your emotions are as trapped as mine. I'm so, so sorry."

She rested her forehead against his neck. "I'm not. Some people go their whole lives without ever feeling this way. I just hope you can forgive me for not wanting to let it go."

"There's nothing to forgive. I want this just as much as you do. More, even. If you're guilty of something, then I'll definitely be damned for it."

Abby trembled, not wanting her angel to be damned for anything.

Nathaniel held her tighter. "God, you've had such a long night. I can feel how exhausted your body is. Why don't we get you in bed?"

Her eyes shifted up to his. "Will you stay with me?"

"Absolutely. I'm not going anywhere."

With his assurance, Abby nodded her consent and allowed him to lead her across the room. He pulled back the covers and she crawled into bed, still wrapped in her magic blanket. She waited patiently as Nathaniel situated himself beside her. The moment he looked comfortable, she invaded his personal space, pressing her body against his from head to toe. If he minded, he didn't show it.

Abby set her hand on his chest, needing the reassurance that he was fully healed. She ran her fingers across the wall of his stomach, stopping to trace the small area that bled so profusely mere hours ago. "I haven't even thanked you yet, have I?" she wondered aloud.

"Thanked me for what?"

"For saving my life."

Nathaniel smoothed her hair down across her back. "You're welcome."

Abby snuggled closer. "I always believed you were here to save me," she murmured, her fingers still tracing the non-existent wound.

He took her hand, pulling it away from the phantom bullet hole to rest it over his heart. "Maybe you were right, Abby. Maybe you were always going to be at the mall today, and Jason was always going to have a gun pointed at you. Maybe I've spent the last sixty years just waiting to be here, to stand in front of you at that moment. And if that's true, then everything I've gone through has been worth it. Because you belong here. You deserve to have a long, happy, healthy life. You weren't meant to die today. I know you weren't."

A tear spilled down her cheek. "I love you, Nathaniel."

His arms tightened around her. "I love you. Always and forever."

Abby held onto those words with her whole body.

"Try to sleep now," he encouraged. "I'll be right here with you."

She nodded, wanting nothing more than to let her mind rest. She pressed her eyes shut and tried to think of happy things, like picnic benches and endless science fiction movies. But her brain refused to stop ticking.

Nathaniel had saved her today, but nothing about him had changed. Abby had honestly believed that if he saved her, he would move on to a better place. But he was still here and still a spirit, so what was left for him now? Was there truly no end to his unearthly existence?

Or...was he meant to save her from something else entirely?

Her body stiffened with the thought, her fingers fisting Nathaniel's shirt. She didn't want to think that there could be more than one threat to her life. But what if her father really had killed her mother? And what if he might one day turn on her?

Abby whimpered, unable to prevent her mind from spiraling into darkness. She held tight to her angel as a memory resurfaced. A memory of hiding in her bedroom, peeking out of her doorway, watching her mother and father argue...

"What are you talking about, Mark?" Crystal asked, stalking him through the hall.

"You know damn well what I mean," he growled at her. "Karl is the devil. I saw it in his face. Didn't you see him with that weapon in his hand?"

"He was using it to uncork a wine bottle, Mark. It was a party. Karl is your

best friend. And you attacked him. Right there, in front of everyone. You actually attacked him."

Abby froze as her parents disappeared into their bedroom. She heard her father's gun cabinet door click open. She heard her mother cry.

"Karl is the devil!" her father screamed. "If you can't see it, then I can't help you! Get out of my way!"

"No. I can't let you leave. Not with that gun."

Her father burst back into the hallway. That's when Abby saw it – the shiny black weapon in his hand. Her mother followed him, but he pushed her away before stomping into the living room. He made it nearly to the front door when he stopped and turned back toward Abby.

She still stood cowering behind her door, but she saw his eyes. His dark, sick, diseased eyes, staring straight at her.

That was the first time. It was the first time she could see the difference between her dad – a man full of love, joy, and kindness – and the monster of insanity lurking inside him. She saw it then, and she would never forget. Even when Mark stalked away that day, leaving their home with his gun in hand, Abby could still see his eyes.

It would be many more months before she would be able to predict her father's bouts of insanity. But that was the first day Crystal shared Mark's dark secrets with her 12-year-old daughter. It was the last day of Abby's childhood. In that moment, she understood that when her father's mind was gone, no one was safe. Not his best friend. Not his wife. Not his daughter. When his mind was that far gone, the only truthful images were the ones created inside his brain.

She remembered calling the police while her mother sobbed. She remembered hearing that her father had been arrested before he'd had the chance to kill his best friend. She remembered countless other phone calls in the next few days, while her mother worked tirelessly to have him transferred from jail to a mental health facility, where he could get the care he needed.

Crystal had spent most of her life making sure Mark got the best care possible. But did that matter when his mind was gone? What had she looked like to him on the night she died? A monster? A demon? Had he disposed of some horrid, evil vision? Or did she look like his wife, the mother of his daughter, the woman he loved? Had he cared for her and put her to bed, not realizing she'd mixed too much alcohol with too many sleeping pills?

Tremors washed over Abby's body. Nathaniel stroked her hair to ease the shaking, but she couldn't make her muscles still. Not with these questions careening through her mind like a freight train into hell.

There was no way for Abby to know the truth. She'd once hoped her angel could help her, but that was impossible. He didn't want to put her through the agony of seeing her mother die, and she couldn't ask him to watch. Therefore, she was stuck with nowhere to go. She couldn't know what truly happened that fateful night, which meant she would never feel safe.

Abby wanted to cry, to scream, to run. But then Nathaniel's hand was on her face, his fingers tracing from temple to chin. He leaned closer, pressing a kiss to her forehead. "Just try to let your mind go," he whispered in the darkness, his warm breath ghosting across her face.

She knew he couldn't hear her thoughts, but it didn't matter. He knew her. He knew what she needed him to be. He was everything and more. Abby only wished she could do what he asked. She wished she could finally let go.

An image of her mother's face jolted into her brain. She tensed again, balling her fingers into Nathaniel's shirt. He ran his hand across her shoulder and down her arm, smoothing over her fist until she finally uncurled it.

"I'm here, Abby. Let your body relax into mine. Let me be strong for both of us. Even if just for tonight."

His words smoothed over her, hugging her like her mother's soft, hole-ridden blanket. Abby closed her eyes and willed her heart to beat in time with his. Nathaniel's rhythm was so steady, so perfect, so promising. She knew she could find peace here. Even if just for tonight.

NATHANIEL WAS STILL with her when she woke up ten hours later. Abby put up a brave front, smiling and reassuring him that she felt better. She knew he wanted to get back to the hospital to check on everyone else. She figured he felt guilty for not doing more during the shooting, and probably for not being able to stop it altogether. And yet, his biggest concern was her safety.

He kissed her and told her he loved her before he disappeared. Abby fumbled into her clothes the second Nathaniel left her sight. She didn't want any time alone to think, especially not after the places her mind had gone last night. She didn't want to imagine that her safety would ever be an issue again, especially not with her own father.

Abby forced a smile as she left her bedroom and headed for the kitchen. She needed to be brave for Mark today. After all, she knew he was suffering from her hostage trauma just as much as she was, if not more.

He waited for her in the kitchen, anxious to fix her breakfast, even though it was nearly noon. He insisted she rest on the couch while he served her a heaping plateful of pancakes drenched in syrup. Abby willed her body to sink into the cushions as her father doted.

They spent the day together, just the two of them, watching movies and playing cards. Mark seemed fine, at least on the surface. His eyes were clear and still, so she chose to not torture herself any more than she normally did about his mental state.

Abby did her best to avoid thinking entirely. She spent hours rummaging through her mother's recipe box, planning Thanksgiving dinner. Mark insisted she didn't have to cook, but she wanted to. Organizing this meal was far easier than dealing with last night's memories, even with her mom's beautifully scripted handwriting staring back at her from the index cards.

When it was time to sleep again, Abby pecked Mark on the cheek and said goodnight before moving to her room. She locked her door, turned up her music, and called Nathaniel. He came to her in an instant, pulling her into a strong, comforting embrace. Then he tucked her into bed beside him and secured her body onto his, allowing her to relax more than she had all day.

Nathaniel spoke softly to her in the stillness of her room. He told her how much he'd missed her and how much he loved her. He assured her that everyone who'd been at the hospital last night was doing well now, and most were home with their families. He said the two critical care victims would recover and no one would die.

But they'll never forget, Abby thought, pressing herself harder against her angel. Post-traumatic stress disorder was a term the doctors tossed around quite frequently after her father's ordeal in the military, but she hadn't really understood it until now. She only wished someone, somehow, could have foreseen this disaster.

Abby's mind screeched to a halt for the first time the entire day. *Oh, God. Someone could have foreseen this disaster. Someone did know what Jason and Randy had planned. Someone could have stopped it before it ever started.*

Jonathan Fitzhugh.

Nathaniel's heartbeat remained steady as it pulsed against Abby's skin, but her own heart tripped and stuttered. Visions flooded her brain, memories of all of the times she'd watched Jon follow the future gunmen into the woods. He would definitely have read their thoughts. He would have wanted nothing more than to delve into the minds of two boys planning a massacre. He'd even told her – when she'd asked him to remain in Charlottesville despite her being a bad friend – that he would stay regardless, because there were other things here that interested him.

Holy hell! Of course, Jon wanted to stay! He wanted to see Jason and Randy's shooting spree! He wanted to watch all that sickness play out! And that's exactly what he did! He watched it all unfold and didn't do a thing to stop it!

Acid surged from her stomach up into her throat. She whimpered with the bitter taste in her mouth. Nathaniel rubbed her back, soothing her in the darkness, murmuring sweet words of love and hope. Yet Abby could only envision Jon's churning black eyes.

Jonathan Fitzhugh, her *friend*. How could he be so cold? How could he care so little? She wanted to tell him to get the hell out of her life and never come back. But she couldn't – not if she wanted to feel the comfort of Nathaniel's body beside her, holding her, lulling her to sleep.

Damn it, I still need Jon to stay. But will he? Now that the things he found interesting about this place have played out, will he remain here? Does our friendship hold enough curiosity to keep his feet on the ground? And will I ever be able to hold my anger inside long enough to make this work?

Abby woke the next morning in Nathaniel's arms. She'd managed a few hours of sleep during the night, between fitful nightmares. But he'd been there the entire time, calming and encouraging, letting her draw from his strength.

As the sunlight drifted through her bedroom window, Nathaniel leaned in to press a soft kiss to her lips. "I'll see you tonight, after your father leaves for work," he promised before standing from the bed. "But you can always call for me at any time."

She sat up on her mattress, looking to his bright eyes. "I know. I love you."

He grinned, lopsided and perfect. "I love you, sweetheart."

Abby stared at the empty floor after Nathaniel disappeared. The gears in her mind shifted almost immediately. She didn't think about Jon's name directly, since she certainly didn't want him appearing in her bedroom. But she knew she would have to see him today. She would have to make sure he still intended to stay here, regardless of how angry and betrayed she felt.

As Abby dressed, she forced images of kittens and puppies into her brain in a sad attempt to calm her temper. She barely looked in the mirror before heading out of her room and marching to the kitchen. Her father was there, standing by the sink. She assured him that she was well, and handed him his pills and watched him swallow them, before exiting through the front door.

Her comfortable little car waited for her in the driveway and she sighed as she sank down in the front seat. She gripped her steering wheel, looking blindly through the windshield, steeling herself for this confrontation.

Dealing with Jon was always easier while she drove, since it made her feel like she was in control of some small part of her world. It also gave her a good excuse to not look in his eyes. Slippery oil or sprinkled chocolate – they each disturbed on different levels.

"Be calm, be cool, don't let your anger get the better of you," Abby chanted. She started the car, listening to the engine hum. She thought about calling him.

Jon appeared beside her. He sat back, lounging in her passenger's seat. The distressing chill of his spirit form filled the innards of her car.

Abby stared straight ahead. "I hadn't called you yet," she grumbled.

"Hello to you, too, Abigail. Sorry if I jumped the gun on my arrival, but it's been two whole days since we last spoke. I think I've been quite patient."

She huffed. "Patient. Sure."

"It's good to see you, by the way. Especially since you're still alive."

Abby made herself look at him. Jon's boiling black eyes and self-satisfied smile blasted her flimsy control to bits. "No thanks to *you*," she spit out.

He had the nerve to look confused. "What on earth do you mean?"

"I mean you *knew*, didn't you? You knew Jason and Randy were going to do that, didn't you? I saw you! I saw you walk into the woods with them lots of times! I can't believe you knew and you didn't do anything to help anyone!"

Jon glared at her, his eyes burning like the depths of hell. He held his breath before it hissed out between his clenched teeth. "First of all," he began, looking irritated enough to choke her, "I knew Randy and Jason were planning something, but I didn't know the specifics. I only found out Sunday morning that it would be at the mall, because that's when they made their final decision. Second, I did try to help someone – *you*. You're the reason I came to the apartment that day, to see if you planned take your normal Sunday trip. When I found out that Nathaniel was going to be with you, I figured you were safe. But I still kept tabs on your mind, just in case. And I was obviously right to do so. Look where you'd be if I hadn't stepped in."

Abby raised her chin. "Forget about me, Jon. What about everyone else? The mothers, the fathers, the kids, the friends? All the people who could have been hurt?"

"What about them?"

"Good God. I just don't understand you. Why would you spend so much time finding out what those two evil boys were planning, if you never intended to do anything about it?"

Jon folded his hands together in his lap. "That's an excellent question. Suffice it to say that I consider myself a student of human nature. All of these *evil* people, to use your overly judgmental terminology, are my independent study. I investigate how their minds work. I explore every wretched thought, every deviant notion. I look deeper into this world than you can fathom, so that I can understand it all."

She shook her head, knowing no amount of study would ever help her to understand *him.*

"Think of it as my hobby," he continued. "Nate enjoys throwing himself in front of people; I enjoy figuring them out. Believe me – I've been places, seen things, and discovered powers you can't even imagine."

Abby chewed on her lip. Jon's words were too purposeful. They scratched at her brain as she put her car in reverse and backed out of the driveway, desperately in need of distraction. "I still don't get it," she persisted while her home disappeared from the rearview mirror, "if you had the ability to save those innocent people, why didn't you?"

Jon shrugged. "Is that really my place? Who am I to change the course of history? I'm no deity. Perhaps Nate sticks his nose in where it doesn't belong."

Abby glanced over. "But you did stick your nose in, Jon. For me."

He met her probing gaze before he chose to turn solid. Jon shifted toward her, his broad shoulders filling out his black leather jacket with sinful ease. His delectable chocolate eyes pinned her pale blues. "Yes, well. The world would be a duller place without you in it. We can't have that, can we?"

She tore her eyes away from him.

"So, Abigail. Is that why you called me here today? To thank me?"

"Thank you? For what?"

"For saving your life."

Abby's head spun fully around. "Uh, what now? You don't really think...I mean, you don't actually believe..." her words left her as her thoughts reeled.

When she finally found her voice, it hit a decibel so high that only dogs could hear. "Holy hell, Jon! Are you actually going to take *credit* for saving my life? For standing there and doing *nothing*? For calling Nathaniel in to get *shot*? For watching him appear in front of me to take a *bullet*?"

Jon grinned at her indignation. "I'm just saying that a thank you would be polite. Whatever way you look at it, I am the reason you're still here."

Abby stared at him in sheer astonishment. She'd never met anyone so wildly irritating...or so unfathomably captivating. She wanted to scream and fight and surrender, all at the same time.

She pressed her lips shut for several grueling seconds before she managed to wrench them back open. "Okay, then. *Thank you*, Jonathan."

He winked at her. "Anytime, ladybug."

Forget surrender. Abby only wanted to scream and fight. "Damn it! What is it with the ladybug thing? Does it mean that you're examining me? Am I just an experiment to you?"

"Well, I believe I also mentioned that ladybugs are considered good luck."

"So, now I'm a good luck charm?" she barked, imagining a tiny pewter version of herself dangling on a chain around his neck. She hoped pewter-Abby would itch and make his skin turn green.

Jon smiled with her thoughts – a ridiculously gorgeous, simply rotten smile. "Perhaps you are a good luck charm for me. Perhaps not. All I know for sure is that you're different. You are the first new thing in...well, in forever. And that makes you important."

"I'm not, Jon. Don't waste your time on me. I'm not important at all."

"Oh, yes, you are. All these years, all this time I've spent wandering around and watching the world grow older, and nothing ever changes. Every city, every high school – always the same people and the same old stories – until this one. Now, everything has finally changed."

"Because of Jason and Randy and what they did?"

"No. I've seen that kind of violence before. I've read those simple minds. They think they're unique, when all they are is pathetic and cowardly. Nothing about them makes any difference to me."

Abby glared at the road ahead with her heart in her throat. "Then what you're saying is that *I'm* the difference?"

Jon's fiery gaze bored into the side of her face. "Yes. Absolutely. You must sense it by now. There's something truly unusual about you..."

"Well, I think it's pretty obvious, don't you? It's because I can see you. It just makes me different in a freakish sort of way. That's all it is."

"Perhaps. The point being that I don't know yet. But I'm perfectly willing to take the time to figure it out."

Time. More time for Abby to flail around beneath his scrutiny. But also, more time to have Nathaniel in her life.

"I guess this means you're still sticking around?" she asked, pulling her car into the parking spot farthest from school, even though she was early enough to get much closer to the entrance. She didn't want the scattered students to see Jonathan in her car. Hell, she didn't even want to see him in her car.

Abby took her key from the ignition and turned to him. "So? You are staying in Charlottesville, right?"

Jon's brow furrowed. "Why are we back to this again? I thought we'd already settled it."

"We did. But I just want to make sure."

"Why?"

"For Nathaniel, of course. So he can stay here with me, where he belongs, instead of following you to God-knows-where."

"Yeah, sure," Jon replied with a haughty laugh. "Just keep on telling yourself that. It's impressive, really, to see how deluded you can be."

Abby stared at him in utter confusion. "What other reason would I have?"

Jon leaned closer to her in the small confines of her front seat. "You're saying the right words, Abigail – the words you think you're supposed to say. But there are other things you want, besides Thor. There are other things you need. Aren't there?"

She tried telling herself that she had no idea what Jon was talking about. But his words were too fresh. *I've been places, seen things, and discovered powers you can't even imagine.*

Why did he tell her that? What was his purpose?

The vision of her mother's sweet face popped into her mind. Abby couldn't keep that image hidden. And she couldn't prevent the barrage of questions now filling her gut with dread.

A slow, insidious smile crept across Jon's lips. His voice came again, deep and tempting. "That's right. You've got it. What is it you really want?"

Abby tried desperately to clear her mind of any and all thoughts.

It didn't stop him. "You want to find out about your mother, don't you? Could Daddy have done that? Could he kill her with his bare hands and still sleep in the same house with you? Thinking about it is enough to drive anyone insane. I don't know how you keep going."

She felt her tears well, fully aware that Jon struck every nerve he could.

"It's okay to want something, ladybug. Desire is a part of human nature. You will always be wanting. Always." He edged closer, the heat of his solid form slithering across her skin. "I can give you the answers, you know. I am capable of that, and so much more. All you have to do is ask. All you have to do is want it badly enough."

Jon reached out. His fingers stroked the side of her face. He watched the movement closely, with a perpetually devilish grin.

An instant later, he disappeared from her car. But Abby swore she could still see him. The feel of his burning flesh against her cheek had branded her skin forever.

CHAPTER

SIXTEEN

Abby should be used to the effect Jon had on her. She should be used to walking away from their encounters with wobbling legs and a sunken heart. But this was different.

She moved sloth-like through the parking lot. She'd last been at school four days ago, but it felt like years. Conversations swirled around her as she stepped past the other students. She caught random remarks on who was at the mall Sunday and who knew someone who'd been there and what they said had happened. Abby wasn't interested in the gossip. Living it was torture and she certainly didn't need to relive it. She just needed to sit down.

She found her way to an iron bench near the school's entrance. Plopping down on the cool metal, she let her backpack fall on the browning grass. She put her hands on her thighs, staring hard at them as Jon's words took on a life of their own inside her brain.

Desire is a part of human nature. You will always be wanting.

I can give you the answers. All you have to do is want it badly enough.

Did she? Did she want it badly enough? Enough to allow him inside? Enough to give him access to all of her – willingly?

Abby clenched her fingers. It was one thing for Jon to pick thoughts out of her head, but it would be another thing entirely to allow him in. She would have to give herself over to his self-proclaimed powers. She would have to give him her trust. And that would be *her* fault, not his.

Of course, Jon knew this. Every argument she would inevitably have with her own conscience was predesigned in his mind. He wanted her to be tempted. He wanted her to need him against her will. He wanted her to have a choice between right and wrong - to be certain of the difference - and still not be able to stop herself from choosing the wrong path.

And that's what this was. It was the wrong path. Jon was the wrong path.

But did that mean she couldn't go down it? Was there a way for her to make this journey with him and come away unscathed? Probably not. But what was the alternative? Abby already knew that answer. She lived it every day. Helplessness. Fear. Despair.

Nathaniel's presence over these past months had distracted her from it all. His practical advice – that knowing what happened to her mother wouldn't improve anything – made perfect sense. If Mom committed suicide, that was horrible. If Dad killed her, that was horrible. Therefore, the truth shouldn't make a difference.

But it did. That desire – that absolute need to know what happened – had driven Abby over the edge before. It had driven her into a psychic parlor, into a cushion-stuffed room with a makeshift oracle offering false promises. Now, that desire had driven her here, into the tempting arms of a makeshift friend offering sinful, fruitful, knowledge.

Would this forbidden knowledge be its own reward? Would it bring her peace, or shatter her in unimaginable ways? Was she an idiot to consider turning her back on the bliss of ignorance?

Abby exhaled purposefully, heaving the air from her lungs as she worked to uncurl her fists. She desperately needed a distraction from her own thoughts. They were driving her insane.

"Hey, Abby. You mind if I sit with you?"

She glanced up to find Eric Nichols standing beside her.

"I don't mind," she answered him.

"Thanks." Eric flopped down on the bench. He wrung his hands. "Look, I just wanted to tell you that I didn't know. I didn't know what Jason and Randy were planning. They talked a lot of crap, but I never imagined they would do anything like that. I don't want you to think I'd ever be involved in something so awful."

Abby observed Eric, unsure of why he was so concerned. She hadn't really considered him at all in this whole mess, even though she'd seen him with Jason and Randy numerous times. Also, she could easily understand why Eric hadn't known what they'd been planning. Hell, Jon didn't figure it out until Sunday morning, and he could read minds.

"I believe you," she said, watching the pained look in Eric's eyes ease.

"Thanks. That means a lot, especially now."

A sophomore girl walked by their bench then, looking straight at Eric as her face scrunched up in disgust. Abby's eyes darted up, catching the glares of several students who shuffled past their bench and into school. Eric's head dropped, but Abby glared right back at them.

This is odd. She was used to being the one on the outside. She remembered the not-so-subtle whispers and strange stares after her mother died. She felt fairly immune to it all now, but watching someone else deal with this ostracism brought out her maternal lioness.

Abby looked up at the blackened clouds centered over the school. There would be no picnic bench reprieve for her today. "Eric, would you be interested in a new lunch table?"

He pushed away the long black bangs falling across his face. "Yeah?"

"Sure." She'd never noticed the vibrant green of his eyes. "I eat with Sondra and Brett, but they won't mind."

Eric grinned. "Um, yeah. That'd be cool."

Abby grabbed her backpack and stood. "Okay, then. See you later."

"Thanks, Abby. For the lunch table. And for believing me."

She matched his smile while she turned away, ambling up the stairs and through the front doors. She expected to walk into the same old building as always. But today, everything was warped beyond recognition.

An uneasy hum filled her ears – the murmur of hushed voices. No one shouted. No one laughed. Abby could think of many words to describe high school hallways, but *somber* was never one of them.

What was this? No one from school was harmed at the mall Sunday, so why was everyone so affected? Could it be the thought of those two boys walking these halls for so long, without anyone knowing what truly went on in their minds?

Abby wanted to reassure everyone, especially Eric. After all, if Jon and Nathaniel hadn't been able to see it coming, no one could have. She shook her head, still not quite believing any of it, as she reached her locker.

Sondra walked up beside her. "Hey, Abby, how's it going?"

"Um, okay, I guess. It's weird in here today, huh?"

"It is. But you should have been here yesterday. I swear you could have heard a pin drop. Where were you, by the way?"

"I took the day off. My dad was pretty shaken up about the mall thing."

"Yeah. My parents, too. Although they still made me come to school."

Abby nodded in sympathy. She liked pretending to be a normal teenager responding to a tragic event that didn't directly involve her. "Hey, I hope you don't mind, but I invited someone to eat lunch with us."

"Really? Who?"

"Eric Nichols?"

Sondra's eyes widened. "Oh. Wow."

"He didn't know about Jason and Randy," Abby assured, watching her friend grimace when she mentioned the boys' names. "People are treating Eric like he's diseased or something, just because he used to hang around with them. I don't think it's fair, so I offered."

Sondra straightened. "Okay. I actually asked someone else to lunch, too."

"Yeah? Who?"

"Holly?"

Abby's brow arched. "Holly? How did that happen?"

"Well, she came to apologize to me yesterday. Everything was so weird after the mall thing and it made me think that life is short, you know? She was a good friend once, and I feel like I should give her another chance. After all, Brett gave me a second chance, and I'm so glad he did."

"You're right," Abby agreed as she pulled her books from her locker. "I think second chances can be really good."

ABBY BARELY MADE it through her morning classes without bursting at the seams. Jon's offer had her mind so bent and twisted that she was only half-aware of the odd quiet in the lunchroom when she finally found her way to Sondra and Brett. Holly already sat at the table with them. "Hey," Abby said, easing into the chair beside Sondra.

"Abby, this is Holly," Sondra introduced.

Abby smiled and Holly returned it. The girl looked far better now than when she'd been cowering under Chuck's fist with her back plastered to a tree. Abby attempted nonchalance, reminding herself that she wasn't supposed to know what happened in the woods on Halloween. "How's it going?"

"Good, thanks," Holly replied before her eyes darted up to Eric. He pulled out the chair next to Abby's and sat, looking to her for guidance.

Abby patted him on the shoulder. "Eric, this is Sondra, Brett, and Holly. Everybody, this is Eric."

"Hey, everybody," he said. "Holly, I think you're in my math class."

A twitchy smile shifted Holly's lips and Eric fidgeted with his lunch tray.

Abby paid no attention to the students at other tables who sneered at him. She figured they would find something else to dwell on sooner or later.

Holly cleared her throat. "So, were any of you at the mall on Sunday?"

Sondra and Brett shook their heads. Eric soundly stated, "No."

Abby remained silent.

Holly glanced at Eric. "Did you...did you know Jason and Randy well?"

Abby looked to the boy sitting beside her, sorry for his uncomfortable spotlight, but figuring it best to get this out of the way. Besides, she was a little curious herself.

"Apparently not," Eric replied. "It's wild to think I could hang out with people I thought were my friends, people I thought were okay, and have them turn out to be so totally different."

Holly stared down at her food. "Yeah. I understand that," she said, her eyes rising slowly back to his. "What were Jason and Randy like? Why do you think they did what they did? I mean, if you don't mind talking about it."

Eric shrugged. "I don't know if I'll ever be able to figure out why they did it," he began. Sondra, Brett, and Holly leaned into his words. "They had plenty going for them. I mean, Jason's family is really well-off..."

Eric kept talking, but Abby fixated on one thought. Eric didn't understand why Jason could be so vile when his family was wealthy, but she knew money did funny things to people. Her father fixated on money whenever he got sick, whether he was manic and letting it run through his fingers, or depressed and convinced that their family would starve to death. Meanwhile, Nathaniel didn't care about money at all; he didn't even want what he had. And Jonathan? If she had to guess, she would say he was the epitome of the spoiled rich kid: cocky, self-satisfied, unconcerned about any life but his own. He used people and then tossed them aside like garbage.

Abby figured Jon would toss her aside one day, too...after he'd finished with her. She imagined her body lying beside a dumpster in a back alley, bruised and dirtied. But even as that corrosive image accosted her brain, she considered a different possibility.

If people are expendable to Jon, then why can't he be expendable to me? If he wants to use me, then why can't I use him, too? What's to stop me from getting the answers I need?

She crossed her arms over her chest, attempting to physically hold herself together. She didn't know if she was capable of using another person like that, even if it was Jon. And she definitely couldn't afford to think about it now, here in the middle of the cafeteria.

Abby forced herself to refocus on the conversations around her. Eric had finished talking about Jason and Randy, and the discussion had somehow turned to teachers' wardrobes, for which everyone had an opinion. Holly laughed at Sondra's astute dissection of Ms. Pennington's state birds scarf collection, while Brett and Eric nodded their agreement. Abby found herself laughing along with the people at her table. Maybe they were all just a gaggle of misfits. But in a room full of aliens, she'd at least discovered some from her own planet.

ABBY EXPECTED to see Jon in her classes that afternoon. She expected him to wait for her in the parking lot, or lounge in the passenger seat as she drove home. But he never returned, and the odd calm set her nerves on edge.

She spent several hours with her father after school, trying to convince him that her day was fine and she was going to be safe at home alone tonight. He left begrudgingly for work while she displayed her most reassuring, toothy smile. As soon as Mark was gone, her angel appeared.

Nathaniel brought with him an instant sense of calm. All Abby had to do was look in his brilliant eyes, and feel his strong arms come around her, and she was soaked in happiness. He was bubble bath for the soul.

They ordered pizza before snuggling up on the couch to watch a movie. Abby insisted that they watch the original *Highlander*, because it was about an immortal who became mortal right around the time he fell in love, and that sounded like the perfect case scenario. Nathaniel agreed to watch it, even though it was made in the '80s. He seemed to understand her purpose enough to look past the awful clothing and hair. For an entire evening, she forgot about the mall and about school and even about Jonathan.

When night fell, Nathaniel secured her in bed beside him and treated her to a lullaby in his self-proclaimed awful singing voice. Abby didn't think it was quite that bad. Although she wasn't able to sleep until he stopped.

He was still beside her when her sleepy eyes opened in the morning. She giggled with the scratchiness of his cheek stubble while he pressed soft, tiny kisses all over her face. Nathaniel remained curled up with her in bed for as long as he could, until Abby had no choice but to leave for school.

She sighed when he disappeared, aware that he wouldn't show up in any of her classes today. He'd spent the past few days at the hospital, standing guard over the two victims from the shooting. Abby didn't think he could really do much for them now, but she knew he felt guilty. At least, those two people would be okay. She wasn't sure how he would ever cope if they weren't.

After dragging off her pajamas, Abby threw on a shirt and jeans. She dwelled on thoughts of her angel, knowing he would do anything for her. But there were some things she just couldn't ask him for.

If she did ask Nathaniel to find out about her mother's death, he would try to give her that, and it would kill him to do it. He would suffer if he had to give her bad news, and he would suffer watching her mother die as he'd watched his own, and she couldn't ask him to do either. But Jon? He wouldn't suffer at all. Jonathan Fitzhugh wouldn't give a rat's butt about what happened between her parents, or what effect it had on her.

Abby considered Jon's offer for the millionth time while she pulled a brush through her tangled hair. She kept considering it on her way to the kitchen, and as she met her father for breakfast, and as she handed him his morning pills and watched him swallow them. She still considered it even as she left her house, got into her car, and started the engine.

Her jaw clenched while she drove to school. Just yesterday, in this very car, Jon had planted this insidious idea inside her. Now, she couldn't let it go.

Abby wanted to know so much more about the process. How would Jon actually find out what happened that night? Could he somehow pick the answer out of her brain? She didn't see how that was possible, since she wasn't there when her mom died. Why did Jon believe he could reach into her mother's past? Exactly what powers did he have?

Those questions were both terrifying and intriguing. Abby felt like she had every right to know the answers, since this was an important decision and she needed to have all the facts. Once Jon gave her the answers, she could take time to mull it all over and make the best decision – the *right* decision.

Abby felt pretty good about that reasoning when she finally pulled into the student parking lot. She walked with confidence into school, through the halls, and to her class. She still felt a sense of calm when she stepped into her second class of the morning. She smiled with the understanding that she would talk to Jon on the way home today, gain the knowledge she needed, and begin her informed decision making process.

She could do this. Everything was going to be okay.

Abby walked past Ms. Pennington's desk and down the aisle. The moment she slid into her seat, Eric and Sondra both turned to her. "Hey, guys."

"Hey, Abby," they replied in unison, leaning toward her from either side of her desk. "Did you see the car this morning?"

She looked from one of them to the other. "What car?"

"I can't believe you didn't see it!" Sondra squealed.

"In the parking lot?" Eric asked, his eyebrows arched to his hairline. "The brand-new black Jaguar? The one that must have cost a small fortune?"

Abby shook her head. She'd been in her own little world this morning, as usual. "No, I didn't see it. Maybe one of the teachers got a raise?"

"Hell, they'd have to win the lottery," Eric said, making Sondra laugh as the bell rang.

The rest of the students settled into their seats. Abby reached into her backpack and pulled out her English book. She flopped the large volume onto her desk before she looked up.

Jonathan walked in through the open classroom door, causing Abby to jump in her seat. He wore his black T-shirt, jeans, and leather jacket. His sunglasses were perfectly in place, his hair just so, his smile as devious as ever.

Abby knew she shouldn't be happy that he'd come to see her. However, she did have a lot of questions in need of answers. She just couldn't ask them here, in the middle of class.

I can't talk right now, Jon, she scolded him. *Can we do this after school?*

He came to a stop near Ms. Pennington's desk. His smile widened.

Abby wondered why he wasn't answering her. She was the only reason he would show up in her class, after all. And their mind-to-mind connection was quite strong, as Jon often liked to tell her.

She stared at him in silence for another few seconds before realizing that the entire class was silent. Abby glanced around, noting that every student was now focused intently on the front of the room. She'd never known any of them to care that much about what Ms. Pennington had to say, especially since their teacher hadn't even started talking yet. Abby looked back to Ms. Pennington, whose eyes shifted toward the empty space where Jon stood.

Ms. Pennington adjusted her Cardinal-on-a-Dogwood scarf. "Oh, yes," she chirped, fumbling for a book on her desk. "Class, we have a new student. This is Jonathan Fitzhugh. Here's your text, Mr. Fitzhugh. Please find a seat."

Abby's jaw nearly hit her desk.

Sondra turned toward her and mouthed the words, *"Holy crap."*

Abby shook her head at her friend before looking back to Jon, certain this couldn't be happening. She watched him move down the aisle with everyone staring. When he slid into the empty seat behind Eric, everyone else tried to look casual. Most of the students' eyes managed to turn back toward the teacher. Abby's did not. She gawked directly at him with her jaw unhinged.

Jon eased his sunglasses off, the chocolate sprinkles glinting in delight. *Turn around and look at the teacher, Abigail. You're making a spectacle of yourself.*

A spectacle? Are you kidding me? Who exactly is making a spectacle here?

You, actually. You're staring rather hard. If you don't stop, everyone will think you just can't tear your eyes off of me.

Abby threw herself forward in her seat. She pinned her eyes on Ms. Pennington, trying without words to warn her teacher of the danger now seated in their room. Couldn't this woman see that a hot grenade had just settled into their class, twirling its pin around its finger?

Sondra glanced nervously at Abby, and then at Jonathan, before looking down at her desk. Abby's heart sank into her stomach, knowing her friend was already drawn to the dark presence in the room. Good Lord, what on earth was Jon doing? Why was he here, in the flesh? What unholy game was this?

I'm just here to learn, Jon answered. *Isn't that what high school students do? I'm really interested in - what class is this?* He glanced at the textbook. *Oh, yes. English. I'm really going to love this English.*

Abby shook her head. *There's something terribly wrong with you, Jon.*

His deep chuckle echoed in her mind. *You have no idea, ladybug.*

Abby bit into her lip. He was obviously trying to throw her off kilter, and she wasn't about to let him. She picked up her pen, set the point on her notebook, and wrote down every word out of their teacher's mouth. She could hear Jon's laughter resonating through her head until the very end of class.

ABBY TORE out of English class the instant the bell rang. She didn't wait for Sondra or Eric to walk with her to lunch. She had to get the hell out.

Jon's arrogant smile burned inside Abby's brain as she dashed to the cafeteria and into the food line. She attempted to lose herself in the swarms of students, never so happy to be swimming in this pond with all the other fish. Especially now, when there was a crazed, flesh-eating shark on the loose.

"You got here fast," Sondra noted when she sat down with Abby at their table several minutes later. "You looked like you were running away from us."

"Sorry," Abby offered. "I guess I'm just really hungry today."

"Okay, then," Sondra relented as she set her tray down. "We have more important things to discuss, anyway. Like what do you think of Mr. Black?"

"Mr. Who?"

"You know. Black shirt, black jacket, black sunglasses..."

Abby pressed her lips shut, not daring to add to that list out loud.

Chocolate eyes, devilish smile, damned soul...

"Thank goodness I'm with Brett," Sondra continued. "If I wasn't, I'd be all over that. And I know for sure that I'd be in trouble."

"Brett is good," Abby managed to squeak out before Eric, Holly, and Brett joined them.

"Wow," Holly said while she sat down and took a drink of soda. "I thought our school would never recover from the mall incident, and already everything is all about the new kid. Have any of you seen him?"

"He's in our English class," Eric piped in, taking a bite of his pizza. "Name's Jon-something."

"Jonathan," Sondra corrected. She glanced at Brett and then down at her food, obviously regretting saying the name aloud.

"Is that him?" Holly asked.

Every head turned. Not just at their table, but at every table. Hundreds of eyes watched Jon stroll in through the cafeteria doors, leisurely holding his books in one hand, nodding to the flustered girls who barely cleared a path for him to walk.

Abby stared down at the plastic tray in front of her. There were fifteen raisins in her salad. Ten croutons. *Can he see me?* Eight chunks of chicken. *Am I camouflaged well enough behind Eric?* A few too many carrot shreds to count, but she could try. Anything to clear her mind. Anything to keep Jon from knowing how disturbed she was on so many levels.

"He's headed this way," Brett mentioned.

"No, no, no," Abby mumbled.

Everyone at their table looked up in unison – everyone but her.

"Hey," the deeply familiar voice came from just over her shoulder. "Aren't you guys in my English class?"

Eric nodded.

Don't just nod like that! Abby mentally chastised the boy.

"Mind if I sit down?" Jon asked as he moved to the chair between Eric and Holly, directly across from Abby. His question was apparently rhetorical. He sat. "I'm Jonathan, by the way."

Abby's eyes rose slowly to his as she listened to the table roll call.

"Eric."

"Sondra."

"Brett."

"Holly."

It was Abby's turn. Jon stared at her expectantly, with the most inviting smile playing against his sculpted lips. Did anyone else realize how conniving that grin was? Or did they all think it was normal? Or even *cute*?

"Abby," she grumbled.

Jon leaned across the table toward her. "I'm sorry. I didn't catch that."

She shook her head. How he loved his petty torments. "Abby!" she yelled over the lunchroom din. Multiple people stared.

He chuckled. "I got it that time."

She refocused on her salad, attempting to count individual lettuce leaves.

"So, is that your Jaguar in the parking lot?" Eric asked.

"Yeah, what do you think?"

"Awesome."

"Thanks."

"How does it drive?" Brett chimed in.

The boys kept talking, but Abby zoned out as she scanned the rest of the lunchroom. The level of curiosity Jon generated was astounding. Every student, guy or girl, took time to glance his way. Some peered sneakily over their shoulders while others craned their necks. In short, the entire school was now very aware of their little band of misfits.

Abby's eyes came back to the people closest to her. Sondra forced herself to look at Brett, or at her plate. Abby knew Sondra didn't want to screw up her second chance with her new boyfriend. Yet here was temptation incarnate, settling into a seat at their table.

In contrast, Holly scooted in the opposite direction. She inched herself closer to Sondra and farther from Jon. She didn't even look at him, except in fleeting bursts that she seemed to regret. Holly probably saw a thousand Chucks crammed inside Jon's tantalizing body.

Abby picked up her fork and stabbed it into her salad. Jon wasn't actually planning to keep up this charade, was he? He wasn't planning to go through the rest of high school as a student with her, was he?

When their lunchbreak was nearly over, Abby risked glancing at him. Jon's eyes met hers instantly. *Yes, ladybug. I plan to stay right here with you.*

The food in her stomach knocked against her esophagus, asking to come back out. Abby reached for her water and drained it. When the bell rang, she stood so fast that the empty bottle clanked to the floor.

Eric picked it up. "I'll get your tray, Abby," he offered with a smile.

"Thanks," she said, mumbling goodbyes as she darted from the table.

She'd never been so happy to find her way into Mr. Puryear's history class. That is, until Jon walked in along with everyone else. *Damn it, I thought I was safe here. I thought I'd have some reprieve.*

Jon sat directly behind her, beside Eric. The boys chatted until the bell rang to start the class. Abby tried hard to care about Mr. Puryear's droning lecture, but she could feel Jon's eyes boring into her back. She worked hard to drum up her Viking fantasy again, but even the image of Nathaniel's hoard-worthy face couldn't calm her frazzled nerves.

At the end of the day, Abby wobbled out of the building on legs that felt like permanent Jell-O. School had never lasted that long or felt that disturbing. She stumbled through the parking lot toward her car, desperate for solace. But when she heard footsteps approach from behind her, she realized the torture wouldn't cease anytime soon.

Jon's long strides caught up to her with ease. "Hey. It's Abby, right?"

"Oh, don't give me that crap. No one's listening," she barked, determined not to look at him while making a beeline to her car.

"Actually, I think everyone wants to hear what I have to say. Or haven't you noticed?"

"Yeah, Jon. I've noticed."

"Then I'm just trying to keep up pretenses, here. I mean, I should try to blend in, right?"

Abby saw several students clamoring around his shiny black Jag. They scurried away when they saw him coming. "Blending in. Sure, you are," she huffed, ogling the dark, sleek, ostentatious vehicle. It was exactly like its owner. She stopped in her tracks, steeling herself to look him in the eye. "Well, this car of yours makes it blatantly obvious. You come from money, don't you?"

Jon grinned. "Are you fishing for a ride, Miss Impossibly Slow Driver?"

"Um, *no*." Abby forced her legs to move again while various groups of people gawked at them. Her determined footsteps led her and Jon farther away from the crowds, toward the very last parking space, which should be marked with her name. "And that's not what I mean about the money, either. It seems like you're used to having it. You have that air about you."

"Are you calling me a snob now?"

Abby reached her car and started opening the lock, but he leaned against the door, preventing her entry. She fisted her keys and glared up at him. "If the shoe fits, Jonathan."

"You still don't know anything about my shoes, Abigail."

"Oh, I've been in your mind. I know enough. And you're dodging the question. Do you have money or not?"

"Yes, I have it."

"When did you make it – back in the '80s?"

He hummed, as if recalling a pleasant memory. "Well, it certainly grew in the '80s. They were good years. But I had plenty before then."

Abby stared down at the key-shaped impressions in her palm. She decided she didn't want to know where his money came from. Nathaniel didn't rob banks, but she wouldn't put it past Jon. Who knew what he'd done in his past? Who knew how long he'd been wandering through the world as a spirit? She figured it had to be much longer than Nathaniel, especially since Jon could do so many more things. Nathaniel seemed like a youthful, exuberant ghost compared to Jon's ancient, crotchety one.

His eyes widened. "You actually think I'm crotchety? Seriously? Have you seen any of the looks I've gotten from these girls today?"

Abby sighed. Of course, she'd seen the girls salivating over him. She'd half-expected them to break out into a bra-and-panties musical number right in front of his eyes. But this was what he did best – he wooed women. It was the only reason he ever become solid. Nathaniel became solid to defend the lives of others; Jon became solid to get in girls' pants. It was a basic difference.

The only thing Abby didn't know was who his intended victim was here. Sondra? She was taken. Holly? He scared her stiff. And he would definitely know better than to come after her. Abby belonged to Nathaniel, and Jon knew it. So, what was his purpose?

With a sharp inhale, she looked up at his perfectly carved face. "Why, Jon? Why did you decide to be a part of my school? Why now?"

"I didn't decide to be part of your school. I decided to be part of your life."

"Yes, I'm aware. But why now?"

"To reassure you. You were worried I would leave Charlottesville, and now you don't have to. I'm going to be right by your side."

"And that's supposed to reassure me?"

"Yes, it is. I know you want me to stay. For several reasons."

"Just one reason."

He shrugged his shoulders, devil-may-care, beneath his clinging jacket. "Whatever. I'm still reassuring you. That's what friends do, right? They tell each other everything's going to be okay, and other such nonsense?"

"Really, Jon? You're serious about this friend thing? You're going to sit in my school, day after day, pretending you're a teenage boy, and be my friend in front of all these people?"

"That's exactly what I'm going to do."

Abby huffed. "Okay, then. What are your ulterior motives?"

"Why do you think I have ulterior motives?"

"Because you're you."

He smiled, all blinding white teeth and adorable puckered dimple. "You know, if I didn't want to be your friend, I wouldn't have offered to help you with your little problem."

She froze in place. With those insidious words, Jon derailed her thoughts, erasing every other concern. It didn't matter that he was a student at her school. She couldn't care about Sondra's or Holly's discomfort at the lunch table, or which of the girls currently ogling him in the parking lot might be his next woo-ee. All Abby wanted to know was if he could actually give her this.

"H-how would you go about helping me, exactly?"

Jon cocked one eyebrow. "Are you saying you want my help?"

"No!" she yelped, completely unprepared for that commitment. "I'm just wondering if you really can help." *Especially when Nathaniel doesn't know how.*

"Like I told you before, Nate hasn't tried to discover the possibilities of our world. I have utilized my time wisely. I can do all sorts of things."

"So, then? I'm listening. Exactly what would be involved in this?"

Jon's eyes held hers as he slowly shook his head. "Oh, no. Not so fast. I want your assurance first."

"What am I supposed to assure you of?"

"Well, I know how much you want this information. I know how much you *need* it. And I must admit, it won't be easy to get it for you. Even with all my experience, I'll need your full cooperation – one hundred percent."

Abby folded her arms across her chest and glared her foulest glare.

Jon gave her a sly grin. "All I'm asking is for you to commit to the process, ladybug. I need to know that no matter what this involves, you'll do exactly as I say. Can you give me that promise?"

"Do exactly as you say?" she echoed, staring at him in bewilderment. How could she possibly agree to such a thing? If he wanted her promise before telling her the specifics, then the process itself must be pretty bad. And being Jon's puppet was a state of mind she couldn't fathom.

Abby's body sagged against her car. Once again, Jon was trying to bend her to his will. Once again, she was at his mercy. If only that wasn't the case. If only she had his powers. If only her mind was as strong or as devious. If only *she* could extract information from *him*.

An idea struck her then – so simple, but so tempting. She straightened in front of him, stiffening her spine as she stared into his decadently chocolate eyes. She'd been in his mind before, watching the forest scene with Chuck and Holly. Could she do it again? Now that she understood what Jon's mind was like, and knew the exact patterns his thought-waves painted, could she find them on her own? Even when he hadn't invited her in?

Abby focused all of her energy on him, drawing herself toward the cold, harsh place she remembered. She sought out his crisp, clear patterns – the precise inner workings of his complex brain. She leaned toward him, concentrating at peak intensity, her entire being tuned fully to his.

An image flashed in front of her eyes then. It was an image of her own face. Abby realized she was seeing herself, right here and now, as Jon saw her.

She looked unnervingly beautiful. Not in a soft and serene, purple-hued way, as she was in Nathaniel's mind. Jon saw her in a stark, vibrant light, with every detail distinct and defined. She stood out from everything else, singularly highlighted, the crisp world around her blurred in comparison. She looked like a child and a woman at the same time – her eyes wide and innocent, her body lush and tempting.

Abby watched through Jon's mind as she moistened her own dry lips.

The birthday candles fired to life in his eyes. "What are you doing, Abby?"

She blinked several times, severing the connection between them. "I'm... I'm not doing anything. Nothing at all."

Jon rested his arm against the door beside her head, drifting closer. "Oh, I wouldn't call that nothing. Sweet little Abigail Forrest, trying to take someone else's thoughts against their will? My, my. What a little power can do."

She took a step backwards, away from the fire. "You're one to talk."

"Yes, but that's me. We've already established that I have some – well, let's just say I have some *spiritual* issues. But you? You're a good girl. You're *Nathaniel's* good girl." Jon inched even closer. The smile on his lips grew darker. "Or do you have a little of me in you, as well?"

Abby's head shook, back and forth, over and over.

The invasive heat of Jon's body crawled across her skin, yet his breath was sweet against her face. "I'd remind you to think about my offer to help you with your little problem, but I already know you will. Just tell me when you're ready to commit, and I'll fill you in on exactly what it will entail. You know where to find me."

When he turned to leave, Abby nearly collapsed against her car. She steadied her arm on the door and gasped in air. The instant he looked back, she quieted.

"You know, I really thought you'd be more pleased that I've decided to be solid for you. I know you don't like my eyes when I'm not. But now, you can rest assured that you'll always see me like this."

Right at the moment, Abby didn't know which was worse: the hideous black oil, or these delicious chocolate offerings.

Jon laughed, the delighted sound making her flinch. She silently damned him for listening to every errant thought that tumbled through her mind. Somehow, someday, that would have to stop.

"No time soon," he told her. "I promise."

His laughter trailed behind him as he slid inside his Jag and drove away.

———

ABBY SAT on the couch in her living room, staring at Nathaniel's rigidly tight muscles. His shoulders remained squared and his fists balled. He asked the same question for the third time.

"Jon did *what*?"

"Showed up as a student at school," she repeated, only softer this time.

Nathaniel muttered an impressive stream of curse words that almost made her blush. When he finally stopped, the muscle in his jaw twitched furiously. "I can't believe he actually did that. I could wring his goddamn neck."

Abby remained silent, sitting close beside her angel, as she watched him run a hand roughly through his hair. She'd purposefully waited to tell him about her day's adventures until late at night – after he'd gotten a belly full of food and she'd gotten plenty of cuddle time – because she knew it would alter the atmosphere between them. Jon always did.

Frustration oozed from Nathaniel's bones. "My God. All these years, and Jon hasn't changed one single bit. Doesn't he know he's supposed to change?"

"Apparently not," Abby answered with a lighthearted laugh, hoping Nathaniel would join her. Being here with him now gave her the ability to ignore the menacing spirit in her life. At this moment, she truly didn't care about Jon. She wasn't concerned about his effect on the girls at school, or about the origins of his abundant money. She didn't even care about what he thought he would accomplish by becoming a permanent part of her world. At this moment, Abby was with her angel, and she was blissfully happy. She just wished he didn't have a livid scowl etched on his heavenly face.

Nathaniel exhaled. "That does it. I'm coming to school with you from now on. Every day, without fail."

"Please don't feel like you have to do that. I know you need to watch over the people at the hospital. Besides, I'm off tomorrow for Thanksgiving, and then there's a long holiday weekend. By Monday, I'm sure Jon will have tired of this – whatever it is."

"But I have to be where I'm needed most, Abby. As of now, that's with you. The two people in the hospital are being released tomorrow and will be home for Thanksgiving, so that's not an issue. What is an issue is Jon. He'll toy with you and every other person at your school. This cannot end well."

She fought back a shiver. "Jon can't affect me if I don't let him."

Nathaniel looked to her with earnest concern. "I appreciate your bravery, sweetheart. But I'm still watching over you."

"Will that make you happy?"

"Yes. It will."

"Okay, then. Come to school with me. You know I always love having you around. And I'm sure Jon will hate it, so it should work out well on all fronts."

Abby smiled, elated by the prospect of having Nathaniel with her around the clock. If she never had any time alone with Jon, then she couldn't choose the bad option. And she knew it had to be bad, because he wouldn't even tell her what finding out about her mom's death would entail. Informed consent was definitely a thing, yet Jon refused to let her have it.

Her smile fell, since she knew she shouldn't even entertain the possibility of accepting Jon's help. But she could see how her worst emotions – her fears and anxieties – might drive her to do something reckless and rash. She dreaded sinking low enough to give in to the temptation.

She wouldn't do that, though. As long as Nathaniel stayed beside her, she could resist. Her angel would watch over her, keeping her emotions blissfully sound. Abby could settle herself with the idea that she wasn't supposed to know what happened to her mother – she was supposed to go on faith. She would put her faith in Nathaniel.

Abby looked to her angel now, to his tense jaw and bunched muscles. She scooted toward him across the cushions, sliding her body up onto the side of his, doing her best to mold to his shape. She snuggled closer and nestled her face into his neck, yet Nathaniel remained stiff as a board. It was like trying to cuddle with the statue of Honest Abe at the Lincoln Memorial.

Her fingers fiddled with the collar of his shirt. "You know, school is still days away," she reminded him. "How about we forget Jon until then?"

"How about I go wring his neck and be back in just a minute or two?"

"Do you really think it would take that long?"

"If I did it correctly."

Abby giggled, but Nathaniel's hardened expression didn't change at all. She turned to face him, drawing up on her knees and circling her arms around his shoulders. She shimmied forward to place tiny kisses on his cheeks and nose before nibbling against his rigid jaw. She waited patiently for some response from him, but nothing helped.

Settling back on her heels, Abby gazed into his big blue eyes. They brimmed over with anger, pain, and fear. No one but Jon could ever put Nathaniel in this foul a mood, and she couldn't just sit by and do nothing.

"Hey," she said, resting her hand on his heart. "I have a secret to tell you."

"A secret?" he echoed, his body still stationary on the couch cushions.

"It's something I've never told anyone. Never, ever."

"Never, ever? What is it?"

"Well, you know how you are a master impressionist?"

"Yes. I am."

"I know. And I'm a master at something, too."

"Really?"

"Really. I'm a master of...of dance."

His brow rose. "You're a master of dance?"

"Oh, sure. Lord of the dance, even. Or Princess or Queen, maybe."

"Well, now. This is something I have to see."

"You most certainly do," she announced, backing herself off of the couch to stand in the middle of the living room floor.

Having barely ever danced a day in her life, Abby tried to recall some of the things she'd seen in movies. What came out, she was sad to say, was a pitiful combination of *Dirty Dancing* and the most recent cheerleading flick she'd seen. She looked like a fledgling pole dancer who would occasionally try to spell out letters with her arms.

She watched him from the corner of her eye as she gyrated to her internal music. She tried to spell out NATHANIEL, but couldn't make it past the N. She didn't know how those cheerleaders did it.

Abby finished her treacherous performance with a lopsided somersault and an Olympic-style arms-in-the-air victory move. Then she stared at him, eager to hear his laughter. Nathaniel didn't even crack a smile.

"Oh, come on. You have to laugh," she insisted, fisting her hands on her hips. "I dance like an inbred chicken."

"Does an inbred chicken dance worse than a regular chicken?"

"Of course. Why wouldn't they?"

Nathaniel still sat and stared at her, entirely immobile.

"Okay, then. You asked for it," she warned. "I am now going to spell out the rest of your name with my body, in a feat of dexterity so stunning that it will leave you speechless."

She thought she saw a hint of a grin on his lips, but he hid it well. "I can't wait," Nathaniel stated.

Abby nodded firmly, even while her mind grappled with how to actually accomplish this. She contorted herself to make the N again – fairly well, even – which managed to pull an actual smile out of him. When she got to the A, with her hands clasped together above her head and her legs spread wide, he began to chuckle. After she did the T, cocking her arms side to side, Nathaniel broke into a full laugh.

"Good Lord. How am I supposed to make the H?" she wondered aloud, twisting her body in bizarre ways in order to achieve her goal. He watched her like a hawk, his eyes pinned to her every peculiar move. Abby did the best she could, writhing wildly in front of him, until he finally broke.

Nathaniel tackled her. His arms wrapped around her waist with lightning speed, yanking her forward and spinning her around until she lay flat on her back against the couch. His solid body hovered over hers for a split second before pressing her fully into the cushions.

He stared into her eyes. "Holy hell, Abby. I love you so damn much."

She whimpered just before his mouth landed on hers. Then, she allowed herself to enjoy the perfection. Nathaniel's lips were actual magic. They smoothed over her jaw and up to her earlobe, sending a thousand shivers skittering across her skin. Her hands drew to the hem of his shirt and tugged it upward. She prepared herself for a wrestling battle in order to remove the offending material, but instead, he arched up, yanked it over his head, and threw it on the ground. His chest settled back against hers before his skin even had the chance to cool.

Abby closed her eyes and absorbed every sensation: their bodies pressed together, his teeth grazing her neck, his hand slipping over her shoulder and roaming down her side until he reached her waist. He balled the hem of her shirt in his fist, moving his fingers beneath the fabric to trace her bare stomach. His touch was soft and smooth as he eased his hand up to the lower edge of her ribcage, releasing a rabid pack of wolf-butterflies inside her belly.

She barely managed to control them before Nathaniel's mouth found hers again, tempting her with his tongue, tracing the full lines of her lips. He moved his hand back to her face but left her shirt drawn up several inches. The heated flesh of his stomach shifted over hers in the most mesmerizing way.

Abby had never experienced the feel of his skin on hers like this before, since he'd never allowed the removal of any of her clothing. Nathaniel's body molded so perfectly to her own. She wanted to scream about how unfair it was that she couldn't have him this instant, but thought better of it. Even in her hormone-drugged state, she knew the uproar would make him stop, and she definitely wanted to savor every reckless moment.

Her clawed fingers pulled against his spine, dragging his body down harder onto hers. Her leg hitched up around his waist, urging him closer still. Her tongue slid over his, tasting and teasing, as his groans filled her ears. When she arched her back, he wrapped his arms beneath her and pinned her in place, as if she would ever dream of being anywhere else but here.

Nathaniel lowered his mouth to her collarbone and nipped her skin, causing her heart to surge erratically against her ribcage. Abby wondered how long she could sustain this tenuous state. She had to figure out a way, or else live off of his body indefinitely. She could do that, of course – if only she had a more comfortable surface to do it on.

"Nathaniel, can we, um...can we move this to my bed?"

His answer came out as a rough rasp. "No. God, no. Too dangerous."

"But it would certainly be more comfortable."

He smiled against her neck. "Trust me, Abby. The impracticality of this couch is the only thing giving me the slightest amount of control right now."

She exhaled. "Darn couch."

Nathaniel chuckled, causing the bare flesh of his stomach to shift across hers once again. "Mmm," she hummed. "I like that."

"What do you like?"

"The way your skin feels on mine. Could I possibly have a little less clothing on?"

He drew back to meet her eyes. "Are you actively trying to torture me?"

"Oh, I think you're the one trying to torture me."

"Should I stop?"

Abby pressed her hands flat against his back. "Don't you dare."

"Okay. I'll happily continue, if you promise not to tempt me any further."

"Does that mean no bed? No soft, comfy mattress, with lots of room to..."

"Do not finish that sentence, temptress."

She grinned at him. "Then what am I allowed to have, Mr. Willpower?"

"Willpower. Sure," he huffed. "Unfortunately, you can only have kisses."

"But maybe one day you'll rethink that?"

"One day?"

"You know...if you get to be alive permanently?"

All of the air whooshed out of Nathaniel's lungs. "Damn, sweetheart. If that ever happens, you may never get the chance to leave the bed again."

"Promise?"

"Promise."

Her face lit like sunshine. "Then kisses it is. For now."

"For now," he echoed, returning his lips to hers.

Abby cooked all day Thursday. She'd never attempted an entire Thanksgiving dinner by herself before and was astounded by the amount of work involved. The men did offer to help, but her mother could have done it by herself, so Abby wanted to try.

She was glad she'd slept well, even though she would have been content to wake up on the couch this morning with a cramped neck and sore muscles, if it meant she could have stayed in Nathaniel's arms. Instead, he'd left late last night, having refused to either enter her bedroom or allow her to sleep with him on the couch. She'd grumbled about it at the time, but now she was grateful she'd rested. Cooking was hard work. Being with Nathaniel wasn't.

Abby smiled as she stood in the kitchen, putting the final touches on their meal. Even with the horrifying incident at the mall this week, and Jon's unexpected entry into her school just yesterday, she felt peaceful. Her angel planned to be with her every day from now on, both at school and at home, and she knew she could rely on his strength and be happy.

Nathaniel had arrived early today and watched football with Mark for most of the afternoon, except when Abby got him to lug the turkey out of the oven. She loved how her father and boyfriend sat together and chatted. She loved that Nathaniel blended so seamlessly into her life. And she loved setting the dining table for three again, even though the unoccupied fourth seat still left an ache in her heart.

"Food's ready," Abby called while bringing the last serving plate into the dining room. The men followed her like lemmings over a cliff, their eyes wide as they soaked in the monstrous spectacle. Turkey, stuffing, gravy, mashed potatoes, corn, green beans, cranberry sauce, rolls with butter, and both pumpkin and apple pie all fought for room on the red linen tablecloth.

"Honey, this is amazing," Mark said while he sat at the head of the table.

"Absolutely incredible," Nathaniel seconded, settling in across from her.

She grinned with their praise. "I'm glad you like it. I wanted to make it special, like Mom would have." Abby regretted her words immediately, not wanting to make her father sad on such a good day. But Mark looked to her with bright, clear eyes.

"Your mom would be proud. She *is* proud," he assured.

Abby sighed as she looked over the feast. "Should we just start eating?"

Mark shook his head. "No. I think we should give thanks, like always."

"Yeah. That sounds nice."

He turned to their guest. "This is a family tradition of ours, Nathaniel. Before eating, we each say what we're most thankful for. In the past, my wife always used to start, but..." Mark refocused on Abby. "I think you should start this year, honey."

"Really?"

"Definitely. She would want that."

Abby reached her arms out to her two men. Mark took her right hand and Nathaniel her left. She gripped onto each of them. "I'm thankful for the two of you. Through everything this year has brought, I feel so blessed and grateful to be sitting here with you now. I love you both so much."

Nathaniel smiled and squeezed her hand. Her father smiled, too, not looking at all surprised by Abby's declaration. She figured he already knew how she felt about Nathaniel, and she just needed to say it out loud. After all, Mom always encouraged honesty – never more so than during this tradition.

Mark cleared his throat. "I'm thankful for my wife, Crystal. She gave me the best of everything. The best home, best daughter, best care. She'll always be with me. With us."

Abby nodded profusely. Her father squeezed her other hand. Her tears welled as she looked to Nathaniel. "It's your turn."

"Okay," he said, meeting her eyes across the table. "I am thankful for this – all of this. The company, the meal, the home. I'm thankful to know what it's like to have a family again."

Abby held fast to the two people who meant the most in her life. "Eat," she instructed, trying to keep from sobbing at the dinner table, when she finally released their hands. She grabbed the platter of turkey to begin the customary passing of the trays, watching as her men piled their plates high and devoured their meals with intent, childlike fervor. She'd never had so much fun watching people eat, except for every other time Nathaniel had ever attacked something in front of him.

When they finished their meal, Mark and Nathaniel tore into the pies. Abby couldn't believe Nathaniel managed to consume four entire slices after the meal he'd had. She swore men had unending pits where their stomachs should be.

The two of them insisted that Abby relax as they cleared the table and did the dishes. She was more than happy to oblige. It was delightfully cute to watch Nathaniel and her dad working side by side like Christmas elves. All they were missing were little green hats and pointy shoes.

Once the men finished with the dishes, they all moved into the living room to slump down on the couch and chairs.

"Are you two in the mood for a little *Risk*?" Mark asked.

"You're up for world domination on such a full stomach?" Abby asked.

"Absolutely. What about you, Nathaniel?"

"I'm sorry, sir. I'm not familiar with *Risk*."

"Really? What is it with kids today – no board games? And it's just Mark."

"Mark," Nathaniel amended.

"*Risk* is a game of war strategy," Abby explained. "You battle to try to take over each other's countries. Whoever gets them all wins."

"Come on," Mark goaded.

Nathaniel nodded. "I'm willing."

"All right," Abby agreed. "Let's do this."

The game was truly pitiful. Mark took complete control of the world in record time. Probably because Abby was inherently un-ruthless. And because all Nathaniel wanted to do was attack France.

Nathaniel finally made his exit late that night. He tried to shake Mark's hand, but wound up hugging him in an awkward-but-sweet kind of way. "Thank you again for inviting me. I can't tell you what it meant."

Mark patted him on the back. "I was serious about what I said earlier this week. Consider yourself part of the family."

Nathaniel grinned as he walked out onto the front porch. "I'll see you soon, Abby," he promised before hopping into his Jeep. Her pulse skipped while she closed the door behind him.

When she turned back toward the living room, Mark stood watching her. "What?" she asked, unable to wipe the silly grin off of her lips.

"Oh, I was just thinking about you and Nathaniel. You two are pretty much permanent at this point, aren't you?"

Abby wished that were true. "Yeah, Dad. We pretty much are."

Mark glanced to the floor before meeting her eyes. "You know, your mother was seventeen when we met. Sometimes, you're lucky enough to find the right person when you're young. Nathaniel's a good guy. You chose well."

"Thanks," she said, still wanting her father's approval as if she were a child presenting him with a hand-drawn picture. "It's been a really long day of cooking. I think I'm going to head to bed, if that's all right."

"Sure. You did a great job with dinner, just like your mom always did."

"Thanks, Dad. I love you."

"Love you, too, honey."

Abby followed him into the hallway. She stood and watched while he walked into his bedroom and closed the door, hoping he would fall into a turkey-induced, coma-like sleep very soon. It would be best if he didn't hear any sounds coming from her room, since she wouldn't be sleeping anytime soon, if she had her way.

Turning to her right, she skipped to her bedroom and slid inside. Abby closed the door behind her and flipped the lock. Nathaniel already sat on the edge of her bed, barely visible in the darkness.

She brought her forefinger to her lips, encouraging him to remain silent, as she walked to her stereo. She turned the knob until soft music filtered through the air. The moment Abby felt certain that the background noise would mask their voices, she tiptoed to the bed.

Nathaniel started to stand, but she put her hand on his shoulder to hold him in place. He didn't move as she climbed onto his lap, straddling his legs and seating herself on his thighs. She leaned in to ease her mouth over his.

He responded instantly. His arms cocooned. His tongue tasted. His hands wound down to her hips, grabbed hold, and pulled her closer.

Abby's heart flared. She reached into his hair, combing her fingers through the longer length. After stretched, sinful minutes, she eased back to meet his eyes. "Mmm. Your hair is quite a bit longer than when we met, you know."

"Yeah. I did notice that."

"Spending so many nights solid with me has made you change."

"It has, a little. Although, I still don't look nearly my age."

Abby laughed, wondering how the universe would carry on if every octogenarian looked this hot. "I do like your hair longer. But does it bother you to change? And to spend so much time away from the spirit world?"

Nathaniel shrugged. "I don't mind the changes, honestly. I was getting tired of always looking the same. And spending time with you is perfection, so I'm incapable of regretting it."

"Well, that's good. But what about being away from the spirit world?"

His hand traced over her spine. "I won't say it isn't difficult to be away. I guess I'm like a toddler with separation anxiety. But I'm growing into it, and the emotions are always waiting for me when I return."

"Do you worry that one day you won't be able to feel them anymore?"

"No. I know they'll always be there. I'm more worried I'll miss someone in need of help. I still feel the need to help people. I suppose I always will."

Abby glanced down to his collar, hedging around her next question. "Nathaniel, do you think it's possible that your work here is done now? Do you think you're supposed to leave this town and go somewhere else, to help other people?"

He took her face in one hand, drawing her eyes back to his. "Is that what you want?"

"No!" she shouted, so loud that she cowered from the echo. "No, no, no. Absolutely not. I want you to stay. For as long as you can. Forever."

Nathaniel brushed his thumb across her lip. "You know, I wouldn't blame you if you felt differently. I probably should leave. I would, in a heartbeat, if you asked me. You deserve a man who can give you everything. You can't live your life with someone who isn't real."

Abby rested her hands on his warm, solid chest. "You're sitting here with me. I can see you. I can hear you. I can touch you. You're as real as anything in this world. And I need you to stay."

He nodded slowly. "If that's what you want, then every moment I have is yours. But only if you're absolutely sure."

"Yes, I'm absolutely sure. How can I not be? If being completely head-over-heels in love with you isn't enough, there is that whole thing with you saving my life. I mean, you took a bullet for me."

"Of course, I did. I would die for you."

Abby tensed in his arms. She knew those words. People said them in movies and sang them in songs. But nobody actually meant them – not like he did. He'd already almost died for her once. She didn't know if she could live through another close encounter, let alone the real thing.

"Nathaniel, please don't say that. I don't want you to die for me."

He tightened his hold on her. "But I want to."

"What? Why? Why would you even think that?"

"Sorry. I guess I'm not being very clear. I want to die for you...of old age."

"Of old age?"

"Yes."

Abby's head tilted. "So, if you were given two doors to choose from – the first one leading to the pearly gates with the bright, pure light and everything in your dreams; and the second one leading to a dull, normal life with me – you'd still walk through my door?"

Nathaniel leaned forward, grazing his lips over hers. "First of all, I can't imagine my life with you ever being dull. You're far too intelligent, silly, and beautiful for that. Second, all my dreams have you in them. And third, I don't think normal gets enough credit. I'd be blissfully happy with normal. Hell, I've watched people finish high school, go to college, get a job, get married, buy a home, and have kids – and the next thing you know, they're miserable. I've never been able to understand that. Those things wouldn't make me miserable. Those things sound like sheer bliss. After the past sixty years in limbo, all I want is a normal life. I would never take it for granted. Not for one second."

Abby pressed closer, trying not to think about all the madness, fear, and pain her family had been through these past years. "God, Nathaniel. I would never take it for granted, either. A normal life with you would be everything."

"Can you imagine?" he asked, eyes bright with hope. "Damn, if we had the chance to really be together, there are so many things I would do for you."

"Yeah? Like what?"

"Well, let's see," he hemmed. "I would pick my dirty socks up off the floor and put them in the hamper like you told me to. I would be irritated with my boss but still work my butt off to pay the mortgage. I would take the kids to the park to give you the day off. I would still date you after forty years of marriage. And I'd try to figure out what happened to my knee caps and my lower back when I'm finally able to retire."

Abby giggled, wriggling on his lap. "And when we're retired? What then?"

Nathaniel hesitated, apparently content to gaze longingly into her eyes. But then he grabbed her by the waist and pushed her off of his lap. She groaned in protest, not wanting to lose contact for a single second, until he scooped her up in his arms like a bride being carried over the threshold.

"Ooh, are you proposing a demonstration of our married life?" she asked as he laid her down on the bed. "Because I'm all for that."

"No, wicked temptress," Nathaniel answered while resting her head on her pillow. "I need to turn back into a spirit now."

"No! Please don't!"

"It's okay," he soothed, running his hand over her hair. "It'll only be for a few minutes. Just long enough for me to give you an image."

Abby sighed, allowing her shoulders to sink into the mattress. "Very well, if you must. But then you'll turn right back to solid?"

"I promise."

Nathaniel crawled onto the bed and laid down beside her. He looked to her face as he shifted into spirit form. Abby rolled on her side and propped her head in her hand, watching his eyes illuminate to create a constant light in the darkened room. His cool swirl of air chilled her skin, adding goosebumps to her already flustered body.

She closed her eyes, eagerly waiting for the vision he wanted to share. His thoughts linked with hers, slowly and gently, allowing a scene to emerge in her mind's eye. A two-story white house with a full, surrounding front porch came into view. Two rocking chairs sat side by side near the front door, each one occupied. On the left sat an older gentleman, and on the right sat an older woman, both with gray hair and abundant wrinkles. The vision appeared bright and clear in her mind, except for the purple hues that bathed the two seniors from their silver heads all the way down to their practical shoes.

Abby was used to witnessing the color of desire when sharing Nathaniel's fantasies, but it wasn't usually associated with the geriatric population. She crinkled her nose, confused but intrigued, while she concentrated on the porch couple. The image advanced, closing in on their aged, worn bodies. When she could see them fully, she gasped.

"Holy crap. Is that supposed to be you and me?" she questioned, noting that their eyes were exactly the same, even inside their weathered faces.

"Yeah, it is. You're the gorgeous one on the right."

"Gorgeous? I'm old. Really old. And yet, amazingly, still purple. How can you have me be purple?"

"Are you kidding? You're going to be the hottest grandma ever."

Abby laughed hysterically, shifting the bed beneath her. "Sure, I am. But what are you going to do about it? You look like you can hardly move."

"Oh, I'll chase you around that porch. Although, I'll probably be pretty slow, so I don't know if I'll catch you."

"Don't worry. I won't run that fast. I think I'll enjoy being caught," she assured, giddily watching as his vision unfolded. She saw old-Nathaniel rocking in his creaky chair, staring at old-Abby. He reached out to her, taking her crinkly hand in his, slipping his thumb slowly across her fingers.

Abby stared at the scene in aching wonder, amazed by how exasperated she felt with this image he gave her. She just wanted old-Nathaniel to do more. Even in this aged fantasy, she craved him in every way.

Frustration built inside her bones as the timid handholding scene played out before her. Abby thought back to the first fantasy she'd ever shared with Nathaniel – of all the decades he'd envisioned for then – just before he kissed her for the very first time. The only thing that would have made those images perfect was if she could have participated. At the time, she hadn't even thought to try. But now, the possibility teased her brain. Jon had scolded her for sneaking into his thoughts, but would Nathaniel even care?

Abby took a fortifying breath. She concentrated on the feeling of Nathaniel's mind at this moment, when it was bound fully to hers. She focused on the pattern of his thoughts and emotions, and on the image of her powerless geriatric self. She zeroed in on the weathered old gal and on the body that should, by all rights, be under her control. She urged Granny Abby to get up off of her butt and do something.

She nearly bit through her tongue as she concentrated with all her might. When nothing happened, she entertained the thought of giving up. But eventually, the image changed. Old-Abby finally jumped up from her rocking chair and plopped down on old-Nathaniel's lap.

"Oh, my God," Nathaniel gasped. "What did you just do?"

A smile crept onto her lips. "Sorry. I just needed a little more action, and I couldn't resist. Do you think that rocking chair is going to hold both of us?"

He leaned toward her, his cool air chilling her heated skin. "Forget the rocking chair, Abby. This is *my* fantasy. How on earth did you get involved?"

"Oh, you know," she sighed. "I wanted it, so I made it happen."

Nathaniel stared at her with intent, glowing eyes. He remained speechless for several seconds. "Wow," he finally managed to say. "You really are amazing. Do you know that?"

She kept smiling, listening to the pained creaking of the chair rails as she encouraged old-Abby to fully grope old-Nathaniel. She would have felt guilty about her aggressive elderly self, except that old-Nathaniel was certainly holding his own. She was impressed that she could still feel his lips on hers through a world of fantasy - and through her weathered, wrinkled skin.

"I don't know how amazing I am," she answered. "You've got mad kissing skills in this fantasy. For a geezer, I mean."

Nathaniel huffed out a laugh. "I'll show you mad kissing skills."

The image disappeared from her mind the instant he transformed. Abby would have missed watching old-them kiss, if not for the fact that Nathaniel pounced on her, right here and now. He flattened her onto her mattress, gathered her into his solid arms, and planted his mouth against hers.

Abby melted into a purple goo beneath him, blissfully happy that they weren't ninety years old yet. She was just learning to appreciate the fiery emotions brought on by her uncontrolled teenage hormones. She wasn't ready to give that up yet, especially not when he could take her breath away, and change the rhythm of her heart, and turn her bones into mini marshmallows.

Time flew by until Nathaniel stopped them. He grumbled in frustration even as he tucked her securely into the crook of his arm, ensuring that neither of them could get carried away. Honestly, the concept of getting carried away felt ridiculous to her at this point. As far as she was concerned, they were already Geezer Nathaniel and Granny Abby – just with a few years left to go. She was already his for the rest of their lives.

Right this minute, it didn't matter how long that would be. Being able to rest her head against his chest, and hear his heartbeat beside her ear, and breathe in his scent, meant that she was already in heaven. Maybe he was, too. Maybe they both already had their reward.

Abby smiled, and sighed, and fell asleep...safe in her angel's arms.

Tina is the author of multiple books and the owner of the publishing company Day and Knight Romance Publications. Writing as Day for her young adult novels and Knight for her adult novels, she offers a wide variety of journeys to satisfy your appetite for romance, love, and passion. Tina enjoys couch surfing, movie theaters, steamy reads, and bonding with fellow obsessive romantics who 'ship all the 'ships there are. Fortunate enough to have stumbled onto her soulmate back in the 1990s, she has been married for over a quarter century to a man who still tells her she's beautiful, no matter how many wrinkles she grows or cupcakes she eats. They live in Virginia with their two children, multiple fish, a fuzzy kitten, and a silly puppy, who are all frankly just too darn cute.

Visit Tina Online:
    Facebook.com/TinaDay3W
    Instagram.com/TinaDay3W
    Twitter @TinaDay3W